The Light Thrower

When Violet Got Bored

by allison keli

The Light Thrower|When Violet Got Bored

First Edition (with second ISBN)

Copyright © 2022 allison keli

Published in the United States.

This is a work of fiction. The characters are fictitious. Any resemblance to actual events is purely coincidental, with the exception of verified historical events and/or personal events. All incidents, descriptions, dialogue and opinions expressed are the products of the author's imagination, and are not be be construed as real.

Please enjoy reading about Violet! ☺

ISBN: 979-8-218-20850-9
Book & Cover Design by allison keli.

AUTHOR'S NOTE & DEDICATIONS

October 21, 2022ce

What a process this has been! This book began as personal therapy in 2018. My son was in preschool, and I had a few hours to myself again. It spewed out of my heart and soul, helping me heal some things from my past. Fast forward to the Fall of 2019, and I was trying to find a new work-life balance since the kid was in Kindergarten. Well, we all know what happened after that: Covid-19, and as my son was so young, I decided to homeschool him for the next two years. I didn't look much at my book until late 2021, when the passing of my friend lit a fire under my butt to pay attention to it again. It was then that I realized not only did I have an actual novel, I had a couple of others, too! I moved the original ending into the second book, and was ready to self-publish it, buuuuut my step-bro, who is also an author, **Andrew Stevens** (plug-plug-plug), suggested I query my novel.

I didn't know anything about any of that, so this is how I spent the first part of 2022. In the meantime, I also decided I was going to finally publish the children's book I had created (even before Violet's story!). That came out this past summer.

So now, here we are, four years after it started, and I am finally, finally, FINALLY releasing Violet's story into the Universe! The story has morphed quite a bit in the past couple of years—Violet is a much more capable individual than she started. World building and herstories continue to unfold and unfurl; you can expect more exploration of that in the future novels. Turns out it's quite complicated! Just like life, right?

But for now, let's celebrate this first book, *When Violet Got Bored*. Yay! So I'd like to dedicate this book to **anyone who might actually be reading it**. Thank you so much for letting me word vomit all over you. This book really was therapeutic in so many ways for me, and I hope Violet's boredom brings you at least a small moment of realization about your own magic, and power, in your life.

Mom: Thanks for reading this genre you don't give a crud about. To that, I raise my wand!

Zach: Remember that rune-inscribed charm bracelet you found around the time Grandpa died? Translated as best as I could, it said to 'give luck'. It also inadvertently gave foundation for Violet's story!

Georgia Reiki Crew *(you know who you are)*: Thank you for helping bring magic back into my life all those years ago! It's been a long time since I've seen most of you, and I miss you! A lot of the magic in this story belongs to you guys!

Mike: Reiki on, brother. From this life, to what lies next.

Lastly, I'd be foolish not to <u>dedicate this to **my own inexplicable connection** and **creation**</u>. Boys, I don't know how or why, but the magic is real! Love you to the moon and beyond! Ehwaz!

PART I: INITIATION

1

An epiphany struck me during my ritualistic, Friday night, candlelit yoga class. It came on suddenly and unexpectedly, like I had been skipping on a hiking trail covered in Autumn leaves, enjoying myself, until I suddenly and rather violently tripped and landed on my stomach, all air being pushed out of me. Since this epiphany *was* so strong and sudden, the fact that I was in a compromising position in a crowded room full of people meant it would not go unnoticed as I stumbled out of the pose.

Graceful, I know. And not at all embarrassing, right?

Picture this: pretzeled arms (*eagle arms*) while in an unflattering-from-behind wide-legged squat (*goddess pose*). I started sweating uncontrollably as the epiphany struck—the damn thing came on like a peri-menopausal hot flash. Sweat was sticking my hair to my forehead like an unwelcome spiderweb adorning my face, hairs flying every which way.

I had intended to get my legs to straighten up at the same time my arms were releasing their bind, but I found myself wobbling a little bit to the left, and then a little bit to the right. Because of this, I about plowed into the floor, snapping several important bones. However, I was lucky enough to catch myself from complete annihilation, but unluckily, the good-looking yogi gentleman to my left had seen the whole debacle.

He indicated concern for my welfare, and while I wanted to develop large claws to rip open the floor so I could fall into said hole, I felt I needed to respond to him. I smiled a giant, idiotic smile as I brushed myself off, and settled into a self-directed *child's pose*, trying not to panic.

I felt a giggle rise up in my chest as I reached back to my heels.

Our lovely spiritual leader continued to guide the class as I stayed tuned into myself like a snail. The class had moved into flowing poses and there I was, still tucked into myself, silently giggling and mentally unzipping, brains leaking out into a gooey mess on the floor. I felt the teacher's presence come up behind me, and I sheepishly glanced up at her.

Her eyebrows knitted together in a slight huff when she realized I was fine, but perhaps having a mental breakdown.

She, of course, being my very best friend, had little patience for my antics, especially since I was attending one of her newer classes at this particular studio. *So much for being Zen*, I sighed to myself, quickly regaining composure and rejoining my fellow yogis in the rest of the *vinyasa*. Finally, it was the end of class and I could flop onto my back into, in my humble opinion, the most amazing pose that exists—*corpse*.

Elizabeth led us into a brief meditation at the end of the class, spritzing us all with her *self-mixed lavender and citrus oil blend*. The smell was quite lovely; the fact that she seemed to dump half a bottle on me in frustration was not so lovely. She told us to go out and spread peace into the world as she headed towards the exit of the studio, leaving us to our thoughts, or lack of thoughts, as we sank into the floor. I heard a gentle click letting me know she was gone.

I slowly let out my breath, opened my eyes and stared up at the dimly lit ceiling. The other people in the class started to file out of the room, closing the door quietly behind them. When I finally sat up, only one other person remained and it was the same man who had earlier questioned my welfare.

"Hi," he proffered a hand and helped me stand up.

"Hi," I returned, caught off guard by his introduction.

It wasn't common to speak to someone you didn't know inside sacred space like that. All the chitchat happened in the hallways; I tended to keep to myself and not socialize too much, but others lived for it. Where we lived was notorious for having fickle yogis—people had their favorite studios, their favorite teachers, and some skipped around from one place to the next, stirring up gossip and drama wherever they could. The feel-good, do-good crowd didn't always uphold its name.

Unfortunately, as I was thinking all of these random thoughts in my head—remember, I was having a mental breakdown—the man continued to stare at me. I felt a slight blush creep up on my cheeks when I began to register his rather good-looking face again.

"Are you okay?" he asked in a slight accent I couldn't place. It wasn't quite an American accent, and as I looked a little more closely at his green eyes and dark hair, my best guess was European of some sort.

"Oh, I'm fine, thank you for asking. It's been a long week, and I find myself having a mental breakdown." I paused, rolling up my light brown mat. "I'm not always this dramatic, I promise."

I wanly smiled, and he laughed in return, rolling up his own mat before opening the door for me. Elizabeth was on her way back into the studio, thinking only I had remained. "Oh, goodness, I'm so sorry!" she exclaimed as she about mowed us over. From the expression on her face, I had a feeling she was about to yell at me. I recoiled in the type of fear that only a best friend could create within you.

Ha! Just kidding. I wasn't about to be bullied by my bestie. When the man wasn't looking, I stuck my tongue out at her.

While Liz had only been practicing at this studio for a few months, she had been a yoga instructor for years. I still wasn't exactly sure what had happened at the previous location, but I knew she was motivated to make the new place work. My internal self-explosions on the mat probably weren't supposed to play a role in her achieving those gains…

The three of us stood awkwardly in the doorway, my lack of being present making the situation worse until the man cleared his throat and stuck a hand out to greet her. "I'm Nathan, I'm visiting the area for a short while and am happy I came across your class. It was wonderful."

Elizabeth took her sweaty, long blond hair and tucked it behind one of her ears. Her beautiful, oval face broke out into a genuine smile as her blue eyes brought out the freckles across her nose. "Oh, thank you so much! I just started teaching at this studio and it means a lot to hear that people are enjoying the class. I'm Elizabeth."

"Do you teach any classes during the evenings?"

I stepped around them, walking down the narrow hallway, tossing my mat into the cubby hole that lined the same wall the studio door was on. I impatiently searched for my cover-up, hoping I could avoid talking with Elizabeth. After my epiphany, I didn't really feel like talking to anyone.

Elizabeth was taken with this man, I could tell, but her curiosity about what I was doing was distracting her. Others were still in the hallway with us, and I was trying to use that to my advantage to hide what I was doing.

"Oh, yes, yes, that is, yes, I teach Wednesday nights as well, and some day classes. I—" she broke her speech as I silently tried to sneak around the corner with my mat.

Nathan turned his green eyes my way, and as I looked up realizing I had been caught, his lips turned upwards into a slight smile, as if he knew what I had been doing.

"Violet!" Liz admonished.

I half-laughed, threw my arms up into the air and said, "You caught me, what can I say?" I forlornly looked after the rest of the people disappearing around the corner.

Nathan tossed his green yoga mat into a rental return basket and grabbed a light jacket that had been hung up on the wall opposite the studio door. Elizabeth turned back to Nathan and said, "I'm so sorry for my rudeness. Thank you so much for coming. I hope to see you again while you're still in town." He waved goodbye to her and began to walk towards me as I pressed myself into the cubbies, slowly inching myself back towards Elizabeth.

I guiltily looked up at him as he walked by, and our mysterious Nathan smiled in return and said, "I look forward to seeing you again, *Violet*. Maybe next time you can tell me about your mental breakdown." With a look that one could only describe as fascination and delight etched into his face, Nathan turned the corner. Moments later, we heard a chime as the door locked behind him.

"Mental breakdown? Mental breakdown! You're going to cause *me* to have a mental breakdown if you behave like that again! Come on, don't leave, help me clean up."

I sighed, placing my things back into the cubbyhole, begrudgingly helping Liz clean up.

2

The next day as I meditated in bed…okay, let's be honest. I wasn't meditating. I was *thinking* about meditating, because my cat's rear end was in my face and my dog kept scratching herself. I thought maybe I should do some Reiki instead, that maybe that would help me focus, but then my dog farted.

I removed the cat from my chest, glared at my dog, threw back my covers, and slid into my slippers.

It was well before 9 AM, a time I most certainly did not enjoy seeing on a Saturday, *especially* since I'd recently surrendered working my Saturday massages so I could take weekends off. I put the tea kettle on my stove and turned the heat up to high. I rummaged through my tea bags, trying to figure out which option would suit me best for the day set before me. My tea decision-making was interrupted by the chirp of my cell phone.

I chose to ignore it.

It was early, I had no caffeine in my body, and I didn't want to talk to anybody.

Now, or ever, really.

My epiphany from the previous night weighed heavily on my heart and mind.

The phone chirped again.

Why the *hell* had I thought it funny to add a bird sound to my text messages?

I fed my cat and scratched my dog's behind, hoping she wouldn't emit another foul odor my way. I opened the back door to my balcony and the dog bounded outside to smell the fresh air. As the tea kettle screeched, I took it off the burner and poured water into my cup.

My epiphany, while nothing too earth shattering, was that I was *bored*. Bored out of my damn mind. Here I was, in my mid-thirties with quite frankly nothing to look forward to. I enjoyed my personal life—all sorts of meditation classes, yoga classes, exploration of metaphysical studies, hanging out with friends and their families… but… I was *bored*.

Work was great—I enjoyed helping people, doing bodywork and teaching classes. Believe it or not, I was also a yoga instructor, but I mostly just did one-on-one sessions.

I had been living on the south-side of Atlanta for about fifteen years now, five of those years post-breakup from my ex. I still worked part-time for his father's consulting business doing bookkeeping. Post-breakup I had gotten my license in massage therapy and completed my 200 hours in yoga-training. I taught Reiki classes, volunteered at a local hospital… I was pretty close to doing the bodywork full-time and was leaning towards finally quitting my ex-father-in-law's business. He had been close to retirement age for years now, and I was pretty sure he was ready to call it quits for good and enjoy his later years by *not* working so much.

I got along much better with my ex-father-in-law than his son. His son was a jerk.

I had considered moving back to the mid-Atlantic after completing my massage studies. My family was more or less from there, so there was a "somewhere" I could return. I missed the ever ubiquitous waterways and historical nature of the area… but something had kept me in Atlanta.

I wasn't sure what it was yet.

But as I realized I was bored and felt stagnancy in my life, I found I was contemplating moving back home again, just for a change.

My phone actually began to ring as I sipped myself deep into reverie. I realized I couldn't avoid the phone any longer. I wasn't sure if it was a family call or a friendly call, I just knew it was insistent.

"Hey, Liz. What's up?"

"Violet! You never answer your damn phone!" So came the anxious voice through the crackling service.

Damn Verizon.

"Liz, I can't hear you. Let me call you back."

I hung up, wondering what it could *possibly* be about at this hour on a Saturday.

"Calm down, E! I can't make out what you're saying."

She finally calmed down enough and told me to check Facebook. "Alyssa's been murdered."

"Huh? What the hell are you talking about?!"

Alyssa was the owner of Liz's previous studio. Talk about frenemies. Actually, everyone was an enemy of Alyssa. She had been in the yoga/healing business for twenty years or more, and her competition was becoming steep. I had a feeling this is why Liz had been fired from the studio, but I couldn't be sure.

Elizabeth was beautiful, funny and graceful. She could sometimes be extremely full of herself, alarmingly devious, but overall, was about as genuine as they came. Due to her near-perfect external form, you would probably expect her to be more of an asshole, but I think her naiveté kept her pure. I mean, if that's not reason enough to fire someone from your studio...

I wrung my blue-highlighted hair around my finger again and again as she explained about Alyssa.

"Her body was found early this morning outside of her studio. Her wife reported her missing last night after the studio closed, and even looked for her *at* the studio and found nothing. This is crazy! This is just crazy!"

It sounded like Elizabeth was about to hyperventilate. Even though I had taken my yoga training from Alyssa years prior, I had not been as close to Alyssa as Liz had been.

I just didn't get as close to people as Elizabeth. Or reliant upon.

"Meet me at the studio in half an hour so we can check it out."

I put my cup of tea into the sink and looked at my pug, Phang. She looked up at me expectantly and snorted. I reached down and patted her head. "Ready to go for a ride?" Her black muzzle and sharp white teeth pointed at me in response.

She really did look like a baby vampire, you know. Assuming Dracula's child was actually a pug.

***

About thirty minutes later I was standing in a cordoned off parking lot with fellow yogis and the general, curious public. A breakfast nook was tucked into the corner of the building that the yoga studio was located, and a long line of people were outside pretending to be interested in their breakfast biscuits.

Phang was wrapping herself around and around her orange leash as I impatiently waited for Elizabeth. I recognized a few people from several of the local studios, but most were strangers. In this tiny little community of gossipers and golf cars (in town there were over one hundred miles of interconnecting recreation paths that some chose to drive golf cars on to get around), word had gotten out quickly.

I finally saw a blond head bobbing through the crowd. As she was making her way towards me, a passerby's Weiner dog sniffed Phang's butt. I then scooped Phang up and held her in the crook of my arm. She snorted at me.

"Where have you been?" I crankily asked in greeting.

"Sorry, Jenny about chewed my head off at the car." She threw her purse over her shoulder, looking magnificent in her black yoga capris and purple, flowing tank top that read *'let it flow'*. I was wearing dirty jeans and a rumpled rose v-neck I'd pulled out of the hamper... Sunday was laundry day.

"Why would she chew your head off?"

Jenny was the best friend of Alyssa's wife.

Elizabeth's mouth was opening, but then closed when, lo and behold, the dude from Liz's yoga class appeared.

"Ohhh, heyyy," purred Liz as she greeted him with a sexy smile.

"Hello again, Elizabeth. Violet." He then directed a nod at me.

"Contemplating returning from whence you came, I bet."

"Yeah—this is pretty intense."

"You're telling us. *Nothing* ever happens here, this town is usually boring and extremely predictable."

At that precise moment, Phang decided to jump out of my arms and into Nathan's. I was mortified. "Oh my God, I'm so sorry! I don't know what's gotten into her!" She began to snuggle into his arms with a couple of sloppy licks on his wrist and snorts at his face.

"She seems to like me," he said, curiously looking at Phang's unique puggy face.

I reached back out for her, and she nibbled on my fingers. I sighed. "Dammit, Phang. I can't take you anywhere."

"Fang?" Nathan asked, his mouth curving into a full-blown smile. There was no mistaking it now. This man found me amusing.

"Well—P-h-a-n-g. She's fancy."

Just then a police officer with a megaphone chose to speak

into the crowd. The people down the way in line didn't even pretend to be waiting anymore. They closed in on the rest of us as we formed a half-circle at the front of the studio (as best as we could anyhow, what with the crime scene tape all around).

"You all need to go home. You are impeding our investigation. We will release details in a couple of hours at our press release to the major local stations and newspapers; you can await word then. *Unless* you have information you'd like to share with us, please return home back to your regularly scheduled Saturdays." He smiled.

This guy.

A huge groan emitted through the crowd as people began to return to their cars, their golf cars, or back in line at the breakfast nook. Only a few yogis remained in tight-knit little groups gossiping when a commotion broke out near the front of the studio.

"Well, if Sergeant Sexy isn't being a buzz-kill." I looked over at the officer, and realized it was one of Elizabeth's many ex-cohorts. This particular relationship had only lasted about a month, though. I wasn't quite sure what had happened, but I gathered Sergeant Sexy wasn't really interested in Elizabeth to begin with. Nor did she seem interested in him.

"I *have* to get in there," a female's voice began to nervously rise as Sergeant Sexy—I mean, Officer Dunham—tried to turn her away.

Liz and I began to inch closer to the store-front with Nathan trailing behind. She looked at him apologetically and I just shrugged my shoulders. I felt no shame in being overtly curious about what was going on.

Once we got closer, we recognized the female. She was someone I had massaged many times, and someone who had been in Elizabeth's former classes at the now crime-scene studio. I glanced at Liz with a questioning look. "That's

Rebecca!" I whispered.

Phang began to cut off my circulation, so I put her on the ground where she promptly plopped her fat butt onto Nathan's perfectly manicured toenails. Who *was* this guy? I distractedly smiled at him and turned back to the show unfolding before us.

"You don't understand! I left my purse in there yesterday and inside of it is…" she hesitated.

"Yes?"

"Never mind," she mumbled and began to stomp away back to her car. This behavior was totally uncharacteristic of her. She turned back with a raised voice, sounding like tears were in her eyes. "When will I be able to get back inside to get my things?"

Officer Dunham stated he didn't know for sure, and then Jenny appeared out of nowhere, angling her golf car through the rest of the remaining crowd. The line-people at the breakfast nook had begun to trickle back over to us, and the mid-day cupcake place in the middle of the building had its owner paused at the door with her key half-way to the doorknob.

We stepped out of the way.

"Get out of here! You have no right to be here!" Jenny screamed at the tear-stained Rebecca. Rebecca wiped her face with the back of her hands and quickly got into her car and peeled out.

The officer went up to Jenny's golf car to explain that that behavior wouldn't be tolerated, and Jenny apologized and quickly drove off to the recreation path behind the studio.

I reached back down to pick up Phang. I smiled at Nathan and said, "I really have no idea what to say to you. I'm just, uh…"

Elizabeth chimed in, "…at a total loss about what the hell just happened here?"

I looked at my phone as the frantic chirps began to come in. *Christ.* My father had somehow caught wind of what was happening in my little town. He must have been reading the headlines of my local paper again. I sighed, "I'm sorry guys, but I really need to return home. Phang isn't going to last much longer and..." I trailed off, not wanting to share intimate details about myself with the mysterious stranger.

Elizabeth turned on her charm and reached for Nathan's elbow. "Are you free? I'd like to convince you that you aren't visiting a crazy town. I'll buy you a coffee, if you'd like," and she gestured to the breakfast nook whose line had dwindled considerably as things were finally quieting down in the parking lot.

The cupcake shop's lights turned to *Open.*

"I'll have to take a raincheck... I've got some consulting I need to tend to for the day. I just happened to ride by and see *you*, Violet, so I thought I'd say hi."

I was taken aback. "Oh... yeah... sure thing," I said feebly. It almost seemed like he was brushing off Elizabeth for *me.* Not that I wasn't single or anything... But Liz was always the one who was addressed when it was just the two of us. However, she was currently unattached, too. Of course, this guy wouldn't have known that about either of us.

"If I may be so bold, can I give you my number for you to text or call at your leisure? As it turns out, my father's dog recently passed so I have some items I need to help him part ways with, and I'd love to give them to Miss Phang."

I shook my head briefly to stop being so stunned about this man's attention. "Oh... sure... Um, your dad?"

As he texted my phone to give me his number, he responded, "Yes, I'm staying at my Dad's place right now." I let Nathan know I had received the text and he started to walk away with his long, lean legs. He hopped onto a bike to take him to the path. I hadn't even noticed the bike until he walked over to it. He took the green khaki satchel that was hanging off of the bike and tossed it over his body, pedaling away after putting very sporty looking sunglasses over the bridge of his nose.

"How about that, Vi. I think that guy has a thing for you." Liz seemed a little miffed.

Trying *not* to enjoy the view, my eyes burned a hole in his back until he disappeared out of sight. I needed to get my mind out of the gutter. I then noticed an out-of-place piece of ripped, aged parchment as it got caught in a wind tunnel of debris, floating towards Phang's open mouth. I grabbed it as she snorted at me. "Curious," I said, as I flipped it from one side to the next.

It had beautiful blue writing on it, almost hieroglyphic in nature. It felt warm to the touch. For some reason unbeknownst to me, I pocketed the parchment before Elizabeth could question me about it.

"We still on for tonight?"

"Of course. I'll be at your house at 7. See you then."

"Tell your dad hi."

"I will." I took Phang to my car and got in as Elizabeth walked away to her own vehicle.

3

It had taken me hours to calm down my father. He desperately wanted me to move back home, and this murder had given him new volume to his voice. He was sickly and in the type of care facility where residents live mostly normal lives, but had access to nurses at all times. He even had his own little kitchen, but I think he usually ate whatever excess his neighbors had.

"Dad, I'm fine. How did you find out about it anyway?"

"I was on that internet, reading your local paper's website. You should really read that paper. It's kind of interesting."

The publisher of that 'interesting' paper and I didn't see eye to eye. He was in his forties, stubborn as hell, and walking around with a stick up his ass. He was a womanizer, and a complete jerk whose father had given him the paper when he retired. In a previous life, I had written some articles for the paper, but quickly stopped when I realized my views weren't appreciated.

I may have dated the asshole for awhile, too, before the paper had become *his* paper. My own father had a touch of dementia and had clearly forgotten my history.

By the time my dad had calmed down, it was time to hurry up and change for my night out with the girls. We'd all learned yoga together through Alyssa's yoga school, and although we had done different things with our training hours, we still hung out together as often as possible. There was a tiny amphitheater in town, and since it was a warm, early October evening, it was going to be a wonderful night out with the girls enjoying some live music.

Except someone we all knew had been murdered.

***

Samantha, with her dark, reddish hair piled up on top of her head, had her light brown eyes flashing at Elizabeth's blue eyes as they hooted and hollered to the music, cheap beers in hand. Layla, short black hair tucked behind her ears, slightly slanted deep brown eyes, was rolling in laughter at the drunkenness of the other two. She was hanging out with me in camper chairs, tapping her foot along to the music. The other two were at the bottom of a hill dancing, the lights from the show reflecting off of them. Layla flicked her cigarette to the ground and let out a huge whoop when the current song ended. I shook my head at her cigarette and she just smiled. There was a designated smoking area. She never seemed to find herself in said area, though.

"I'm going to grab another beer—want one?"

I indicated no, but that I would walk up anyway to the upper part of the amphitheater. The top tier was where all the food and drinks were sold. Once we made it up to the top of the stairs, I blinked into the garish light. I looked down the hill on the left side, seeing all the wealthier business men and their families sitting at picnic tables, candles flickering gently in the light breeze. I could see my ex and his family at their table, and unfortunately for me, it appeared he was making his way to use the restroom.

"Oh shit," I muttered. Layla looked the way I was looking and groaned.

There was no way to avoid the collision course we were

on. We were stepping out of the beer line the very second he would be passing us to use the restroom. He was such a jerk, he never said *anything* nice to me.

"Oh, Violet. How shocking to see you here with a member of the freak squad."

It was especially annoying hearing this from him, considering when I'd attuned *him* to Reiki, he'd had many tearful breakthroughs and claimed he was becoming a new man, one less angry and more enlightened.

Layla looked ready to sock him in the jaw, but was rescued by someone clearing his throat behind her.

I couldn't believe his impeccable timing. The always-appearing Nathan from the yoga studio was before us.

Layla, of course, had heard all about him over dinner, so she knew exactly who he was before he even opened his mouth. A giant smile broke out onto her narrow face, growing larger with pleasure as each second passed that Damien awkwardly stood silent.

After a beat, he curtly nodded a goodbye at us.

I didn't even know I was holding my breath until I let it out.

I responded to Nathan's raised eyebrows and said, "My ex."

"Ah."

Layla broke out with a very loud, overzealous, "EEE! Vi, my favorite song!" and she ran off back to our chairs, singing along with the music.

Abandoner.

"Well, I tried to warn you. Mental breakdown and all. See, I'm a crazy person, and I'm a member of something lovingly referred to as the freak squad." I smacked my forehead.

He reached out to touch me on my arm with an amused grin. "I find you very intriguing, Violet." I felt a slight flush heat up my cheeks and wasn't exactly sure how to follow that comment.

Luckily for me, Damien was exiting the bathroom at that precise moment. This allowed me opportunity to *not* respond to what Nathan had said.

Now, Damien was still good looking in the face, but it was quite obvious his stature was several inches below Nathan's. It was also apparent his married life had made him quite rotund compared to the lean, fitter body of the dark haired man standing at my side.

He opened his mouth to say something snotty, but perhaps saw the same steely glint in Nathan's eyes that I did. Nathan's eyes were disconcerting. Whatever the case, Damien marched on his way without saying anything at all, and to my pleasure I saw him glance back at us one more time before descending the stairs to his over-priced picnic table.

"Thanks for that. I don't think I could stand to hear another obnoxious thing out of his mouth." I sighed. "Sorry. You really must think I *am* crazy. If I were you, I would stay away from me."

He laughed, and gave my hand a solid squeeze.

"On the contrary. I do hope you'll meet me sometime this week for dinner."

"Oh... Uh," I awkwardly stammered, wondering how I had stepped into this twilight zone. This man was not only good looking, he seemed well-mannered, well-spoken, and genuinely interested in me.

It's not that I had low self-esteem, it's just that... Oh, fine. Maybe my esteem could use a little boost.

At that moment, Elizabeth and Sam sprinted up the steps to grab themselves another beer. Liz clearly had had bitten off more than she could chew, because she reached out and forcefully pumped Nathan's hand. "Sam! This is the new yogi in town that I was telling you guys about. Nathan, from.."

I curiously looked over at him, wondering if he was going to enlighten us with where that accent stemmed from. "Hello, Elizabeth. Sam?" She nodded yes. "I was born in the U.S., but spent a large portion of my life throughout...various cities in Europe."

Ahhhh, I thought. I was terrible at placing accents, but this at least explained why I thought he was European, even though apparently he may actually be American. "He is a consultant, rides bicycles to and from work, and practices yoga at least weekly, am I correct?" Liz ticked off the facts she had at her disposal, counting on her fingers as she did so.

He smiled, but I noticed it didn't quite reach his eyes. Liz's forwardness was apparently bothering him. She, of course, had no clue. Sam, though, must have picked up a vibe between him and her, and she directed Liz towards the restroom...

Hm. Looks like they won't be getting another beer.

A huge popping sound came from the stage. I turned, looking down in the darkness. People were whooping and hollering and the singer came on the mic and apologized for a speaker blowing out. In spite of the loss of sound, he began jamming on the guitar.

I looked back at Nathan who was expectantly looking at me.

I took a deep breath in, and said, "Sure, why the hell not? The way things are going, we'll all be spontaneously combusting by week's end anyway."

He looked pleased at my response, again squeezed my hand, told me he would contact me early in the week, and bid adieu. As he walked away down the stairs to find his seat somewhere in the middle aisle, another speaker popped on stage. The crowd groaned but the band kept playing.

At that moment, the girls walked out of the restroom and grabbed my hands, pulling me down to our seats. They wanted to hear every detail about what had just transpired.

25

4

My fat, tabby cat was once again on my chest with his rear end in my face. Phang was at my feet, this time snorting in her sleep rather than farting. I heard my phone chirp and I growled at it. The clock on the wall said 8 AM. It was *Sunday morning*, for Pete's sake!

I turned onto my stomach after hurling the cat onto the floor and tried to suffocate the life essence out of my body by use of a pillow.

No no no no no!

That's it. From now on, I was turning my phone off before bed.

I rubbed my eyes, stopped pouting and rolled up supine. I picked up my phone.

Ugh. That figured. It was a blank message from an unknown number. What dumb luck.

I tried to fall back asleep but couldn't.

I decided that the best way to burn off my anxious energy was to go for a jog. My apartment complex backed up to the recreation paths; there was a nice three mile jog I could take around a small lake with docks. Seeing as it was still early, there was some creepy fog rolling along the path. Seeing as there was a murderer on the loose, potentially aimed at energy workers, I was a little nervous.

I put on some running tights and a short-sleeved shirt, grabbed my inhaler, my phone and my ear buds. I told my furbabies I'd see them later. My stretching consisted of walking to the path. Once I got on the path, I felt a huge weight lift off of my chest, even as my breathing instantly labored.

I refused to take my inhaler.

I'd gone about a mile into my run when I came across some walkers with their dogs. I grunted hello. Up ahead as I ran alongside one side of the lake, the fog eerily draped across the path. I ran up a particularly torturous hill, being thrown into a neighborhood at its crest. I turned the music up a bit to get me up yet another hill. I saw some people in their golf cars, and a couple of runners up ahead.

Descending back down the other side of the path, I felt an extra pep to my step until I about tripped over a root. When I looked up into one of the path-lining trees, I caught a hawk watching me. It was unnerving, and it was definitely watching me.

"Crap," I muttered, rubbing my ankle as I paused against the tree with the hawk and its beady eyes. Up ahead, I could see a couple of people slowly walking. I shook my ankle out, and started to huff and puff in their direction.

There were two of them. From a distance, they didn't look like normal fitness-walkers in town. Most people walked quickly, with purpose, wearing designer clothes and perfectly maintained hairstyles trying to top the other people they were walking with. These people looked slightly unkempt, carrying an odd air about them. One was a woman with grey streaks in her hair and a flannel; the other was a younger man with an untrimmed beard that seemed to have arms reaching out from it. It was less their physical appearance, though, and more about the flat look in their eyes and set to their mouths that made me uncomfortable as I came up on them.

I grunted at them as I passed, feeling like they watched me too closely. The man seemed to want to say something, but the woman put her hand on his arm and shook her head. I picked up my pace to try and get away from them.

Once I crossed the street and passed another golf car, I felt more at ease. I wasn't being followed, and perhaps my imagination was getting the better of me because of the murder, or hell, because Halloween was right around the corner. Rather than continuing on the route I had originally planned on, I chose to head towards the docks and take a short break.

Recently fallen leaves crunched underneath my feet. I was happy to see that I wasn't the only one in the parking lot. There were fishermen, and a small group of people looking like they were about to go for a jog together. A mother walked alongside her son learning how to ride a bicycle.

I looked back across the street and saw nothing. I turned to walk towards a dock when I, yet again, ran into the one and only Nathan.

He didn't bother to hide his smile as he reached out to steady me. His hands lingered a little longer on my shoulders than I was comfortable with, though, and I squeaked, "Oh my God! I'm so sorry!"

He nodded at my attire. "You're a runner?"

I caught my breath and wiped some sweat off of my brow with the back of my hand. "If you can call it that. I need one of those turtle stickers on my car that says 'I *am* running'." I glanced at what he was wearing, and inquired if he was also going for a jog.

"No… My bike's over there." It was propped up against a tree next to the lake.

Just then, a police cruiser slowly pulled into the parking lot. I squinted to see what number was on it… yes… it belonged to Sergeant Sexy. I sighed. It looked like I wasn't going to be able to finish my jog anytime soon because he was creeping directly towards Nathan and me.

The window of the driver's seat rolled down, and I said, "Hi, Jason." I motioned towards Nathan, introducing the two of them.

As Jason got out of his car, he raised an eyebrow and said, "Yes. I've met Mr. Murphy."

I was startled to say the least, but hoped I quickly was able to regain facial composure. Nathan said nothing. I found his behavior curious.

"Look—we've had complaints of two folks of interest lurking about. You know how it is around here—anybody who doesn't fit into the local jello mold is cause for concern for the rest of the folks who live here. I don't suppose either of you have seen—"

I interrupted him. "Oh my God! Yes! I thought they were two people practicing to be zombies or something... They realllllly were a bit off." I felt a little embarrassed at my admission of judgment of these poor people, and I glanced at Nathan to make sure he wasn't offended by what I had just said. To be fair, a pretty famous zombie television show was being filmed in the area. How did I know if these people weren't training for a future on TV?

However, when I turned to face him, I was shocked to see that he had that steely glint back in his eyes, the same look that he had had when speaking with Damien the previous night.

"Excuse me, Officer Dunham, Violet. I have a prior engagement that I must hurry back to." He tilted his head in my direction. "Be careful, Violet. I hope to see you soon," he said, almost softly. Too softly. I shivered a bit as he half-jogged to his bike and took off in the direction of the Zombies.

Jason couldn't contain himself, and lost the professional persona immediately. "What the hell was *that* about, Vi?"

Jason and I weren't necessarily friends, but he and I had spent a fair amount of time together before and during his tryst with Elizabeth. I certainly considered him slightly-more-than-an-acquaintance.

I murmured, "I'm not sure," as I looked after the back of Nathan Murphy.

"Hey—are you okay? I know you were friendly with Alyssa and all."

"Oh… well… I think it's still sinking in. I can't quite believe it. A murder in this town—and someone I actually know? I just hope we aren't being targeted or anything."

"What makes you say that?" He asked quickly.

"Ha, paranoia?" I laughed. "It just seems rather odd that a yoga studio owner would be randomly targeted, that's all. And in spite of how this crowd always promotes love and healing, well, I've met some rotten apples before."

He nodded his head, glancing back towards where Nathan had headed. It was almost as if I had lost his attention.

"Well—be careful who you associate with, Violet. Mr. Murphy may be intriguing to you, but…" he broke off.

"What?" I impatiently tapped my foot.

How exactly *did* he know Nathan? Jason didn't frequent the energy group circles, at all. In fact, I felt inclined to believe that his view of yoga was that people stood in silly Twister-like poses while self-inducing hyperventilation.

"Not my place to say, Vi." He sighed. "I guess I need to question others about those two… Zombies that you saw. Did you feel threatened by them?"

I didn't appreciate the change in conversation, but I answered him. "No, but I didn't get the warm fuzzies, either, if you know what I mean. Look, I better get back to it, Jas." I gestured back in the direction my run was supposed to be taking.

He put his hand on me. I looked down at his hand on my bare skin, and looked up into his light blue eyes, surprised. He had shown no prior interest into my wellbeing, so when he earnestly told me to be careful, I ran off not knowing *what* to think.

***

I was certainly happy to be home, showered and lounging on my couch. What a crazy morning; from another run in with the ever-ubiquitous Nathan, the warnings from Jason and, well, these *Zombies*.

I was so stuck inside my thoughts, that when my door was knocked on, I jumped about a foot into the air.

I stood on my tippy toes to look through the peephole to see Liz and Layla.

I opened the door, glad I didn't have some sort of zit cream smeared across my face. It wasn't normal to have visitors without at least a cursory text of one's arrival.

I stood at the kitchen counter as they sat on the stools. I offered them something to drink, but neither of them wanted anything. I took a sip of water and inquired as to where Sam was.

"We're not sure," said Layla with a glance to Elizabeth.

"What do you mean you don't know where Samantha is?"

"Well, after we got home last night, Sam wanted to go back out to get some food. I told her I was too wasted to go out, that I just needed a hot shower and sleep... I didn't even notice she wasn't home until a few hours ago." Elizabeth's lip began to wobble.

"What? You mean she's missing?"

My heart sank. First Alyssa... now Sam? Sam was one of *us*.

"It's probably nothing. She probably just ended up meeting someone and went home with him..."

Sam may be into free love and all that, but she wouldn't typically just go home and have a one-night stand with a stranger.

"She hasn't answered her phone?" I asked in a small voice.

"No."

"Did you tell Jason?"

"No! He hasn't spoken to me in weeks."

"Dammit," I swore. "What are we going to do? Can you ping her phone?"

Layla spoke. "Well… we were able to do that through her iPad. And that's why we're here. It pinged close to your apartment."

"Well, what the hell, guys! Let's go!" I stood up, grabbing a jacket then turning back around to the two who hadn't moved. "Why—aren't—you—moving?" I asked slowly, trying to figure out what I was missing.

My cat, Barnaby, chose that exact moment to jump onto the kitchen counter and rub his tail into Layla's face. I couldn't understand what she was saying because of it. "What?"

She picked Barnaby up and placed him on the floor.

"Her phone is pinging from… Rebecca's."

My brow furrowed in complete confusion.

"Rebecca? I didn't even know that her and Sam hung out."

Elizabeth glanced to Layla. "We should just tell her, Lay."

"Tell me *what*?" I growled, stomping back over to the counter.

Layla spread open her arms towards Elizabeth, indicating the floor was hers.

Without any pretense, Liz spoke. "Rebecca is—I mean, *was* —having an affair with Alyssa. Alyssa's wife found out about it and was furious. When I got to the crime scene yesterday," she choked, "Jenny accosted me because apparently she knew that *I* knew about Rebecca and hadn't said anything."

"Wait… Alyssa was having an affair with Rebecca, and you

knew about it?"

Liz's peach colored skin turned white. "Yes," she whispered. "I caught them one afternoon. I had forgotten my things after closing up, and I saw them in a entangled position in the studio… it's sort of why Alyssa asked me to leave the studio."

My mouth dropped open. "And you didn't feel compelled to tell me this?!"

"You were having problems with your father. I didn't want to add to your stress."

I closed my mouth and nodded curtly at her. "Okay, well, how does Sam play into all of this?"

"We don't know." Layla shrugged as she looked at Elizabeth.

Elizabeth sighed and spread out her fingers onto my counter and looked up at me guiltily. "Damien knew, too, and was going to publish this information in the paper, but I got Jason to threaten him for slander as there was no proof."

"How the hell did Damien find out?! He doesn't even *do* yoga!"

"No, but his wife *Amanda* does." My mouth formed into a perfectly shaped O.

"She was there that day?"

"No… she saw them another time. They were getting messy about it. I think Rebecca wanted Alyssa to leave her wife for her."

"So… why is Alyssa dead, and why is Sam missing?"

"I think I'll take the shot of liquor now, Vi," grunted Layla.

After a round of what-the-hell-do-we-do, I made an executive decision to call Jason. I told them how I had run into him earlier that day, anyway, so he wouldn't be totally shocked to hear from me. They nodded in agreement.

5

Jason stopped by about an hour later. The girls were still hanging out at my place, drinking and panicking by not hearing from Sam.

When we told Jason what had happened, he glared at us, "Why didn't you just call the police station?" He glanced around and saw my almost empty bottle of vodka, some olives strewn about and grumbled to himself.

Layla let out a burp. "Don't they usually say you gotta wait twenty-four hours before you can file a missing person's report?"

Jason barked, "This isn't a goddamn TV program, Layla."

I pushed my vodka bottle towards him and gave him a crooked grin. He raised an eyebrow and shook his head. "Can I talk to you, alone?" he asked Elizabeth. She stood up, did a pirouette, and followed him outside of my apartment.

I frowned. "We've got to curtail her drinking, Lay. That's two days in a row she's gotten sloppy."

"Maybe now that everyone's going to learn about Rebecca, she won't feel compelled to drink so much."

"I can't believe she didn't tell me."

"Your dad's visions... They were happening so frequently at that point."

I sighed, wanting to steer the conversation far away from my vision-having father.

Layla wasn't fooled, and asked, "Do you believe in magic, Vi?"

I scoffed. "Look, Layla. I know some of the shit we've seen or done doesn't have a rational explanation… but—"

She snorted. She was the least woo-woo of the four of us, but she'd heard the rest of us babble about things we had seen or felt. She never meditated, and while she had taken her 200 hours of yoga training, it had more been about physical strength for her than anything else.

"I'd say that."

"But you're the last person I would expect to ask about anything woo-woo."

"Yes, but—"

She was interrupted by a sober-looking Elizabeth and a flustered looking Jason. He ran his fingers through his wavy, dirty blond hair, and placed his hand under his chin as if in thought.

"If you guys don't hear form her by tomorrow morning, go down to the station. Violet, I'm about to break procedure here, but I feel compelled to tell you that Nathan Murphy is related to Alyssa."

My mouth dropped open to form yet another perfectly formed 'O'.

"We already knew about the affairs… I can't say that we necessarily have a suspect, but there are persons of interest. We've already taken Liz's… Elizabeth's statement… If we need to speak to either of you, I'll let you know. This latest development of Sam… I don't know. I don't know. I'm sorry. Keep your fingers crossed she turns up soon."

As my mouth was still hanging open, Jason grimly closed it for me.

I blinked. That's twice in the same day he had touched me.

Layla cleared her throat and Elizabeth said, "Wait... You said affairs. As in, more than one?"

It was time for Jason to clear *his* throat. He tipped his hat and helped himself out of my apartment.

All of a sudden we all spoke at once.

"That's it—I'm going to Rebecca's."

"Affairs? Who else was having an affair?"

"Nathan is related to... Alyssa?"

My door creaked back open and Jason stepped back in. "No no no—*You* three are staying put. You are *not* going to investigate the ping of Sam's phone. No. Way. You are *not* becoming the Scooby-gang."

I half-laughed, but then quickly felt sick at the thought that the rest of us could be in danger as well. Elizabeth turned on her charm; it was odd, it's like you could see the switch in her aura. She sidled up to Jason and batted her long eyelashes at him.

"No freaking way am I taking you guys to Rebecca's. No. Way," he repeated.

Liz began to purr at him. "Pretty please?"

Jason's eyes cleared when I broke the spell by asking the next question. "What about the Zombies? Do they play a role in all of this?"

Layla tore her eyes from them to me and smirked. "No magic, huh, Vi?"

Things were getting out of control.

Jason brought Liz back to the counter just as Barnaby jumped back up and put his tail in Jason's face. At that exact moment, not only did my phone chirp, but Phang chose to let out the cutest little fart as well.

Things were *completely* out of control.

Before we could all speak over one another again, Jason held up his hands. Before he spoke, though, he handed Barnaby to me, who I promptly placed at Phang's drooling face. Barnaby glared at me, but I ignored him and turned my attention back to Jason.

"I will go to Rebecca's right now and then call you. Okay?"

We all demurely nodded. He shook his head, muttering to himself as he left, no doubt wondering how he'd been suckered into going to Rebecca's.

***

Jason had been gone for about twenty minutes or so and Layla declared she was ordering a pizza to sober us up. While she placed her order, I remembered to glance at my phone. Interesting, I thought to myself. Nathan had texted.

Liz looked over my shoulder and raised an eyebrow. "Please call me? It's important?"

I shrugged and plopped down on my couch.

Layla finished ordering the pizza and sat next to me, propping her feet up on my coffee table.

"I want to go after him."

"To quote Sergeant Sexy, 'No. Way.'" Liz nervously giggled.

I groaned. "We've got to stop calling him that. I swear I'm going to slip up one day and say that to his face." A part of me wondered if Jason would like catching me with that slip-up. I shook my head; no way was I going after Liz's leftovers. No. Way.

Sigh.

"Call that guy."

"I don't know."

"He probably wants to tell you about Alyssa before you find out somewhere else."

"That may be, but I don't even know the guy. Why does it matter to me that he's related to Alyssa?"

"Ummm, because he just blew into town and she turned up dead! He could be the suspect!"

Elizabeth was chewing on her fingernails. "I seriously

doubt anyone that hot could be a murderer."

"Not to mention, but what possible reason could he have for killing her?"

We all jumped at a knock on the door. Layla looked at her phone. "Can't be the pizza. Too soon."

"Wouldn't Jason have just called me?" Elizabeth looked at her blank phone.

"Aw, crap. He called *me*," I said, opening up the door without looking through the peephole.

Probably not a smart move, as a tear-stained Rebecca helped herself into my apartment with Sergeant Sexy nowhere to be found. "Rebecca," I squeaked out, looking at her backside as she walked towards the other two. I didn't feel threatened at all, but I was embarrassed, and also irritated. "Sure, come on in."

My phone annoyingly buzzed at me; I could see it was Jason but I was not going to miss whatever it was about to come out of Rebecca's mouth.

"You guys," She interrupted herself with a hiccup. "You guys sent the cops after me? Seriously??" Hiccup, hiccup, snot smearing across her face. Not the put-together Rebecca that I knew. "I'm grieving here!"

Layla grabbed Rebecca by the shoulders and put her on my couch. Elizabeth looked ready to jump out of her skin. I was still just pissed that she had walked into my apartment without invitation. Another knock. Not having learned my lesson, I opened the door without looking. I half expected to see Nathan waltz in, but, no, it was Amanda, Damien's wife.

Amanda?!

Okay, Grand Central Station was *closing*.

"Get the hell out of my house!" I shrieked upon realizing who had walked in. I didn't have any particular beef with Amanda, other than when she had gotten together with Damien (years after he and I had separated), she had gone psycho on me and tried to intimidate me. Frankly, though, I didn't care one bit about her. Or him. I was more than a little surprised that she even knew where I lived, let alone had helped herself into my apartment.

She scoffed, looked me up and down and reached her hand out to Rebecca. "Rebecca, come here. It's okay; we're both victims here."

Rebecca stifled a sob and said, "But Alyssa's dead! Who killed her? Who would kill her?"

Layla stood up and walked over to me. "Please. You know she was no angel and had pissed off God knows *how* many people. I can see where several people wanted to off her."

A hush came over the room.

Just then, yet another knock on my door.

If it weren't for Barnaby and Phang, I would have just left the damn thing open. All I knew, though, was that when Damien himself was strolling into my apartment, it was time for me to use my voice.

It was a one bedroom for Christ's sake!

I started shaking. Layla held my arms at my side.

"Out. *Get. Out. All of you!* Unless you know where the hell Sam is."

Damien glared at me and started to plead with Amanda. She bit her lip and shook her head; Rebecca however had stopped crying and was watching with great interest. After all, this was the man who had wanted to smear Alyssa's name in the mud in the paper.

"You. How *dare* you come in here!" Rebecca growled.

"Please. It's not like it's your residence." Damien glanced at me. "Nobody of any caliber would live in *this* dump."

At that precise moment, Amanda chose to look me in the eye. She straightened herself up and said, "I'm sorry how I've treated you over the past few years. Damien, is in fact, a piece of toffee colored shit. Damien; I want a divorce. You can stay at your parents tonight. Rebecca—you're with me."

They flounced out of my apartment, leaving me, Layla and Elizabeth stunned and standing around my door. Damien was trying to regain composure by my coffee table.

My door magically opened by itself this time.

It was Jason, and Sam. I threw my arms over Sam's shoulders and cried out. Liz and Layla joined me. I met Jason's eyes over Sam's head and he smiled until he noticed Damien by my coffee table, and both his eyebrows jumped out of his head. I stepped behind Jason and pushed him and the girls forward into my place; I held the door open for Damien.

"Get the hell out." Barnaby swiped at him as he passed; Phang farted again.

"Fracking freak squad," is all he said as he walked past me. "Better watch out, Jason, you don't want to be stung by this bi—", and I slammed the door on him, still shaking in anger.

I looked at the back of the door.

The girls were now on my couch, heads all touching, deep in quiet conversation. I took a deep breath in.

I turned to look at Jason. "I obviously don't know what happened, but thank you for finding her."

"Sure... And I can't say I'm not happy that I missed whatever just transpired *here*. I'm *extremely* happy I missed it."

I smiled, and, out of character, gave Jason a big hug. He was startled, but I then felt his warm body lean into mine. A slight blush came across his cheeks as he pulled away. "No problem, Violet." Before he could say anything else, the door was knocked on again. He excused himself as the pizza guy came in with our order.

After he left, Elizabeth looked up with some emotion in her eyes that I couldn't quite read. I didn't have any energy to try and figure it out, so I let it go.

Over pizza, Sam told us her story, and by the time they all left, it was about 9 PM. Much too late to call Nathan back, so I just sent a quick text.

I'm so sorry—it's been a crazy evening. LMK a good time to call you tomorrow.

About five minutes passed, and he wrote back:

So you're not avoiding me? :)

Ah. He was teasing.

Not at all. I look forward to talking with you tomorrow.

*How about *seeing* me tomorrow instead? Can you do a quick lunch somewhere, around 11 or 12?*

Sure. Do you know where Beans and Grapes is?

Yes. I will see you at 11?

Yeah—see you at 11 at B&G.

Good night, Violet.

ZZZZZZZZZ.

Here's hoping I wasn't going to have lunch with a murderer.

6

My dreams that night were fitful. There was red-colored fog that followed me and zombies scraping along on the recreation path. One of the zombies grabbed me and looked into my eyes with his beautiful, green eyes, flecked with gold. When I realized it was Nathan, I screamed, but he put his hand over my mouth and shook his head, as if to hide me in the fog.

A bright light shone, and Jason strolled up, gun cocked at his hip. Out of nowhere, a foul odor hit me…

The sun was peaking through my curtains, and I realized Phang had farted in my face. She didn't usually sleep at my head, but I imagine my tossing and turning all night had given her cause for concern to be closer to me.

Or, she just wanted to be at my head and fart.

My alarm wasn't set to go off for another twenty minutes. I sighed, turning onto my side and looking out the window. Barnaby jumped up and put his paw on my nose with Phang trying to park her butt up against my chest. As they fought for space, my phone chirped.

That's it. I'm changing my damn text tone.

I didn't even take the time to see who had texted before changing the tone to something beautiful and melodious sounding. No more would I be aggravated by annoying birds.

Phang growled in her sleep.

I rolled onto my back, and looked at my phone.

Oddly enough, it was Damien saying he wanted to talk to me when I got to work. Today was my eight hour day at his dad's office, which, coincidentally, was near my massage office. Any time I needed to leave one place for the other, it was perfectly easy to do so. It was also in the same shopping center as the restaurant Nathan and I were meeting at for lunch.

I was lazy like that.

I wasn't sure why Damien wanted to talk to me, let alone be at his dad's office. The paper's office was in a nearby city, not even located where we all lived. He should have theoretically been at work by the time I pulled into his dad's place.

I flopped onto my other side, thinking about what Sam had told us the night before.

I called bullshit on her story, but I couldn't, for the life of me, figure out what she wanted to hide, or why. I figured I'd just let it go, drop it all, and try to get back to normal life. That meant work and keeping mostly to myself.

Thank God I had Phang to claim needing me so I could avoid, well, living a life.

***

Damien was already in the office when I stepped inside. I had seen his car, so I knew he was there. The lights were still off.

"You could have at least turned the damn lights on."

"Shush. I'm not here for a fight. I'm here to find out what Sam told Amanda."

I closed and locked the door behind me, switching on the lights. I walked over to my desk and flopped my bags onto the never-sat-in sofa chair. It faced out into the parking lot; I didn't often have visitors, but sometimes I had to receive payments for his father. I pulled my hair out of my mouth, frowning. The blue highlights were starting to look like dead mermaid scales.

"Earth to Violet, earth to Violet," Damien impatiently said. I walked around, turning on the printer, and popped a pod of coffee into the Keurig that his father had demanded to purchase for the office. I pulled one of my bags off of the sofa chair and placed it next to me as I sat down into my desk chair. I turned on my computer, casually tapping my fingers on the desk.

"You know," he said snottily, "My father is too afraid to tell you, but he plans on closing his business once and for all by the end of the year."

I sighed. "I'd already figured that out for myself."

"What will you do? You can't possibly survive with your little freak sideshow business."

I ignored him. He wasn't entirely wrong; I could survive, sure, but the pay cut would make a huge dent in my lifestyle. Either I needed a roommate, to pick up another part-time job, or to do more massages and potentially hurt my body by doing them. Or, of course, just be broke all the time.

None seemed particularly appealing.

"God dammit, Vi! What the hell did Sam tell her?"

I cleared my throat and typed my login information into the computer prompt. "I have no idea. Sam told us she had run into Rebecca the night before, and after hanging out at a bar, they went back to her place and passed out. She said she didn't even know anyone was looking for her until she looked at her phone in the evening."

"And that's it."

I looked him squarely in the face.

"That's it."

"If I find out you're lying—"

"What?" I smirked. "You'll murder me like Alyssa was murdered?"

He sputtered and called me a damn fool before storming out.

It appeared that all of my friends had been hiding things from me. Was I really too weak, too emotional, too sidetracked by my own personal crap that they didn't think they could come to me for anything anymore?

I had to clear my mind, so I opened up a new spreadsheet to sort out the facts.

- *Friday/Saturday: Alyssa murdered.*
- *Possible suspects: ?*
- *Incidental: Blue inked paper can dance.*
- *Rebecca and Alyssa were having an affair.*
- *Elizabeth knew about it (and probably told Sam and Layla).*
- *Alyssa told E to take a hike.*
- *Jenny pissed about affair, but also pissed E knew.*
- *Amanda caught Alyssa and Rebecca, too.*
- *Amanda and Rebecca are victims?*
    - *Because of the slander?*
- *Amanda wants a divorce from Damien.*
- *Damien's a douche.*
- *Sam disappeared the other night.*
- *There are Zombies walking around.*
- *Sergeant Sexy is investigating.*
- *Nathan is related to Alyssa. He's too pretty to be a killer.*

Ugh. I wasn't getting anywhere.

I switched off the screen and started to do some work.

***

My phone rang an unwelcome ring a little after 10:30. It was good that it rang, though, because I'd been totally engrossed in my work and hadn't been paying close enough

45

attention to the time. It was just about time to meet Nathan.

I answered the phone.

"Hey, Dad, what's up?"

He sounded anxious. "Are you busy?"

"I'm just about getting ready to close up shop here and meet someone for lunch."

"Is it… is it the fellow I dreamed about?"

"Jesus, dad," I spit out, turning my monitor off. "I told you that that dream you had months ago was nonsense. I honestly can't believe you even remember it." I bit the inside of my cheek. *Damn.* Parts of his stupid dream seemed to be coming true, and *I* had totally forgotten about it. *Do you believe in magic?* Tsk.

"It's him, isn't it… he's not what he seems, Violet… you can't trust him."

"Dad, nobody is after me, I'm not going to have my soul sucked out," he sputtered after I said that, "and it's just lunch with a guy I met at a yoga studio. That's *all*." And he's related to the woman who was just murdered. And there's lifeless looking people wandering around the town. And my friends are hiding shit from me.

"Be careful. If you notice any weird electrical things happening around this man… Just…"

"Dad—gotta go. I will call you back sometime this week. Tell Mina hi."

"I love you. You're very special."

"Love you too, dad—bye."

Mina was *his* pug. Mina and Phang were sisters. Cute, right?

I stood up and turned the lights off, stepped outside and locked the door behind me. I slid my sunglasses up the bridge of my nose, took a huge whiff of the fall air into my body, did a quick little stretch and started walking on the sidewalk towards the restaurant at the opposite end of the parking lot. It would take me a couple of minutes to get there.

I smoothed out my dark navy skirt, and looked at my heavily worn flip flops. Oh well. At least my long sleeved black blouse was clean... Oh damn... I started to lick a bit of toothpaste off of the collar. *Oh, stop it,* continued my inner dialogue. You have no interest in him, nor he you. He's probably a murderer!

I decided I was going to sit outside on a bench and wait for him to show up. I was in the process of texting a client about a massage opening the following day when a tiny little red smart car pulled into the parking lot. I laughed to myself. It wasn't exactly the car I thought Nathan would be driving. I heard a noise from across the parking lot, put my hand up to block the sun. I wasn't certain, but it looked like Damien, for whatever reason, had just pulled back into his dad's office.

God dammit.

As Nathan walked up, Damien fell far from my mind. Nathan smiled at me a little nervously, or so it seemed. He had on dark jeans and a black short sleeved t-shirt that was rolled up to reveal his obviously maintained biceps. There was a hint of a blue inked tattoo peeking out of his left sleeve, but I couldn't tell what it was, and I certainly didn't want to stare. His dark hair curled around his ears, almost as if it was still slightly damp from a shower. His eyes were that perfect shade of green mixed with golden flecks. Eerily spot on from my dream.

His overall, amazing appearance made me stammer.

"Hello, Violet," he spoke, grabbing my hands into his own and briefly squeezing. Yowza. I about melted on spot.

"Shall we?" he asked as he held the door open for me. He was being a gentleman totally without pretense. It was merely just how he was. Once inside, the dim lighting made it easier to see. The people who worked there were used to seeing me about once a week—usually alone—so it was embarrassing when they greeted me in obvious interest because of who I was dining with.

I raised my lips upwards in a slight hiss to one of the girls who served there. She was openly admiring Nathan behind his back. I wasn't sure if he had seen my growl at the girl, but I quickly turned my attention back to him as we got situated.

"What have you been up to this morning?" I asked, genuinely curious about why this man had found himself in our town.

"I did a little bit of work early on, but then went for a bike ride and showered... thus why my hair is still wet. Sorry about that."

"Are you apologizing for having damp hair?" I asked incredulously.

"I... I suppose I am," he sheepishly smiled.

He seemed like a totally different person than the one I had previously met. I was a little surprised at his, well, humanness. Before he had seemed perfectly cued, timed, composed. Now he seemed a little shy.

"Tell me about your morning," he then said, turning the conversation around to me.

"Oh, you know, went to work," I gestured towards the office across the parking lot, "got accosted by my ex, spoke to my demented father." *Shit.* I looked down at my hands, and then spread my arms out in apology. "I'm telling you... I'm slightly crazy."

"I don't think so in the slightest. Crazy people don't go around trying to convince people they're crazy. They try to convince you that they're sane."

Our water had arrived, so I lifted my glass and said, "Cheers to that." He smiled.

We continued to have small chitchat until we ordered our food. At that point, it was becoming obvious that we were beating around the bush to the topic at hand. Before I could open my mouth to make myself look further-the-ass by forcing him into submission, he made eye contact with me, let out some air, and then looked off in the distance.

"I suppose you're wondering why I asked you to call me yesterday."

"Of course."

"I... I wanted to speak to you before you heard rumors. I've been here a little over a week and I'm starting to get the feeling that everyone knows everyone's business."

"To say the least."

"Yes, well," he took a sip of his water. "Well, and you may already know this by now, but I'm related to Alyssa Murphy. She's my half-sister."

I couldn't hide my surprise. "Half-sister! But she's so much older—"

"Yes," he murmured. "She is—was—at least ten years my senior. We have the same father. I'm actually staying with my father right now, did I tell you that? I obviously wasn't planning on Alyssa dying. She and I were not close and I'd only met her a handful of times. I never got the impression that she liked me very much."

"Oh, that's just Alyssa. She thought everyone was out to get her." I gulped, realizing that someone *had* been out to get her. "What I mean is... don't take that to heart," I said feebly.

"Noted."

"Why didn't you mention something when you saw me and Elizabeth outside of the studio on Saturday? Or anytime after that?"

Just then our food arrived. He tilted his head, closed his eyes and murmured some words. It almost sounded like it was in a foreign language. I was taken aback; not that I had never been around people who blessed their food, but it was certainly unusual for someone of his caliber. In public. With me.

He opened his eyes, indicating I should start eating and continued. "I really have no answers for you. I guess I just didn't feel it was ever appropriate."

"How is your father doing? Alyssa's mother? They must be devastated."

"My father has Alzheimer's so he really doesn't know it happened. Her mother is dead."

"Oh... Gosh... I'm so sorry about everything. This has got to be extremely difficult."

"Yes. It has definitely added some stress to my travels."

I played with my fork, spinning it over my salad. "So... You're definitely not staying. I vaguely remember you saying you were here temporarily, but then I couldn't figure out if I had made that up or not."

"Yes, well. The consulting work I do brought me here, and it was convenient, as I have family here and it never hurts to see your father, right?" *Ugh.* Right in the gut. "But now that Alyssa has been.. murdered.. I just don't know what to do. I suppose I'm at the police's mercy for the time being."

My fork clanked against the plate. "You can't be serious. You're a suspect?"

"A 'person of interest', I think is what they call it." He wiped the corners of his mouth in between bites of his sandwich, looking amused.

"But—but—," I sputtered.

"My family has had its issues, unfortunately, which doesn't make me look good. But I've been doing some investigating of my own—and people are more than willing to talk, so I don't think the police should have a hard time figuring it out. Unless..." He drifted off.

I was hanging on every word. I had to clear my throat to get him back on track.

"Sorry. I just mean that it appears Alyssa may have made some enemies with her competitors. Not to mention, she was having that affair."

"So you know about that, too?! I just found out yesterday. It's like I've been living in a cave." I grumbled, he, of course, not really knowing what I was talking about. "Never mind," I said.

He finished up his sandwich and I mused things over. The female wait staff was ridiculously attentive today.

"Nathan."

"Yes?"

"Yesterday, you took off after Jason—I mean Officer Dunham—after we were talking about those odd people down by the lake. They don't have anything to do with any of this, do they?"

"Ah. You are pretty astute." He half-laughed, seemingly without mirth.

I raised an eyebrow. "That doesn't answer my question."

"I was merely concerned for your welfare as you more or less said they made you feel uncomfortable." His head tilted just a bit.

"Well, the man was starting to reach for me, but—concerned for my welfare?" I became flustered after what he said began to sink in.

He toyed with his napkin.

Just then the light above our table popped out. The electricity had gone out.

"That's weird," I said, looking outside and seeing nothing but blue skies for miles. The staff came up and manually charged us for our food, and the conversation had been dropped for good.

I didn't feel like questioning him further. I felt like I needed to keep my distance from him. Not that I was afraid of him or he was a danger like my father had implied (*ha! ha!*), but, well, he had plans to leave. There wasn't a reason to get too close to someone who was going to leave soon.

Like me, wasn't I planning on leaving?

My life had gone from boring and predictable to being a geyser of confusion. It was my fault, really. I had begged for it and the Universe had listened too closely.

Outside of the restaurant, Nathan scuffed his shoe at the curb. I gestured I was going to head back over to my office. He took me by the arm, alerting me to the fact that he planned on walking me back. I was shocked at his touch. It felt too energized, like an electrical current was wrapping around our arms extending out beyond our bodies. It was kind of like being lightly, but steadily shocked over and over again. I let out a long, wobbly exhalation to regain composure, but I could still feel a steady hum as we walked. There was no indication that he felt the same thing.

I gave him a quick tour of the office, then walked a few doors down to my massage studio. "Now, this place is my true home. The energy always calms me down when I'm in here... even though I'm the one doing the work," I laughed. "I do bodywork here a few times a week, teach yoga at the local Cancer Wellness Center once or twice a month, and if anyone wants a private lesson, well," I gestured to the area we were standing in.

Nathan gave a devious smile when I suggested a private lesson and I felt a blush creep over my checks. "I didn't mean it that way." I mumbled.

"I'm merely teasing. Although, I wouldn't mind a private lesson."

Yikes.

"Pardon me for my forwardness," he quietly laughed. "I'm just teasing, like I said."

I awkwardly punched him on the shoulder to let him know everything was fine, and held the front door open to escort him back out into the fading fall light. We walked back over to my ex-father-in-law's office. "Well, this is where you can drop me off."

"Violet. Thank you for allowing me to explain myself today. I appreciate it."

"I enjoyed myself. Thanks for inviting me. I hope you get cleared soon, though, so you can go about your business without delay."

I think he understood my double meaning with my comment, and he cleared his throat. "I still have those dog toys I'd like to give you for Phang. Are you available tomorrow at all?"

"Nope. I've got massages all day and then I'm teaching yoga at the hospital. I might be available Wednesday or Thursday afternoons, but it just depends on how my schedule pans out."

"I'll be in touch, then." He waved goodbye.

I stepped inside and locked the door, realizing I had stopped breathing as I watched him walk back to his car. My heart flip flopped in confusion, and that had nothing to do about the mystery surrounding Alyssa's murder. I had hoped that I wouldn't have to run into this guy again after this lunch, but it didn't seem like he was going to let it go.

After I turned the computer back on and saw my spreadsheet of my notes regarding Alyssa, I became less confused and swore. *Dammit.* I had forgotten Damien had come back. And he clearly had read my spreadsheet.

What was it to him?

7

I laid low the next couple of days. I was busy with work and over the drama   concerning Alyssa's murder. Elizabeth commented privately about my lack of comments on our group text, and I just told her I was feeling under the weather. I hadn't even told her about my lunch with Nathan.

It was mid-day Wednesday and I was at the office sending emails before I heard anything else from him. He mentioned he had caught wind of a free meditation class Thursday evening at one of the local studios, and wondered if I wanted to join him.

I wasn't sure if I did.

There was a knock on the door, and I looked up. It was Jason, fully decked out in his navy police uniform He didn't typically make house calls, so I figured this was going to be good.

I put my phone down and stood up, opening the door and gesturing him to come inside. I looked at him warily.

"Yeah?"

He took his cap off as he stepped over the threshold and raised an eyebrow.

"Grr. Sorry. I'm grumpy. Have a seat," I plopped down, motioning for him to sit opposite me in the sofa chair.

"I'm here on official business, just so you know."

"Okay… ?"

He cleared his throat. "I wanted to let you know that all of the local yoga studios—studios who also have massage therapists—have been broken into. Well, all the cities in our county anyway. This hasn't extended beyond here, up into Atlanta or anything."

I leaned forward, extremely interested. "How about *simply* massage studios?"

"Not yet."

"Phew," I said, leaning back. "I mean, it's not like I store much in there anyway, but—"

"You only take appointments on recommendation, right?"

"Yeah, of course."

He rubbed his forehead in frustration.

"You aren't any closer to learning about Alyssa?"

"No. It's getting more complicated. And the further we get away from the actual event, well, they don't call that show *The First 48* for nothing."

"Any idea why they're searching the studios?"

"Well, I was hoping you could shed some light on that."

"Me? I don't even work in a yoga studio."

"Yeah, but you teach yoga—"

"On occasion."

"And you know the inner workings of all this woo-woo voodoo crap."

I stifled a laugh. "Is that what police officers call it?" My laughter no longer became stifled. He pressed his lips together, then joined me in actual noise-making.

"I'm sorry, Vi, you know how I feel about this stuff. I'm one of those I-have-to-see it to believe it guys"

"But are you atheistic?"

"No? But I was raised under the assumption that 'God' was everything, and everywhere. I can't argue that."

I pushed my chair back to stretch out my legs. "This really is no different than that, Jason. And why me? Why not just ask Elizabeth?"

He chewed his lower lip. "Well, she's not a massage therapist, for one."

"For two?"

"She drives me crazy."

"In a good way?" I smirked.

He returned the smirk and shook his head. "No, not in a good way. There's a reason why we didn't last long."

I was honestly surprised. For all of Elizabeth's quirks that could drive a person crazy, I still wasn't sure why she didn't stay in a relationship long. Other than, maybe she simply just didn't want to be in a relationship. I could relate to that. But I was usually alone. She was usually attached.

"Alright, then. Ask away. I'll try to help you out as best as I can."

He unfolded a copy of a print out of what looked like odd lines going in jagged directions. He then handed it to me, and I furrowed my brow. The odd lines were indeed going in jagged directions, but it was apparent it was some sort of secret code. The writing was in the same brilliant blue as the piece of paper I had found outside of Alyssa's studio the day her body had been found. Apparently the Sheriff's office could spring for excellent copies.

"Uuuummmm," I reached into my purse, into my Harry Potter wallet, and pulled out the folded parchment paper I had found. I really hadn't given it much thought. As I took it out, I noticed a slight warmth to the writing. I traced one of the lines with my fingers before handing it over to Jason.

"So you recognize this print then?" He took the paper from me, and turned it over. "What is it?"

"I have no idea."

Jason looked up.

"I found this outside of Alyssa's the day her body was discovered."

"You found this and didn't share it with the police?" He was slightly incredulous at my lack of foresight.

"Look, I wasn't anywhere *close* to her studio, you guys wouldn't let us anywhere near it! I was in the parking lot and it caught my eye. It danced in the wind, I just happened to grab it. I have no idea what it means."

"Is it Sanskrit?"

"Doesn't look like it, but I'm no expert in any language other than English. And I'm not an expert in that, either." I looked at the copy he had handed me. "It looks more hieroglyphic-y, I think."

"Yeah, we've sent a copy of this up to several colleges in Atlanta, to see if those scholarly people know what it is."

"Scholarly?"

He smiled.

"Well, alright, thanks for your input." He stood up, placing his baseball cap back on, looking like he was about to pocket my parchment.

"Ummm, I want that back."

"This? It's evidence."

"Evidence of *what*?"

"Evidence that this written language is important to the studios being broken into."

"Oh my God, Jason, that seems kind of far-fetched. Talk about woo-woo."

"Is it? What if this is some sort of secret language you people use, and it's going to bring about the end of the world?"

I laughed out loud. "Been watching Netflix?"

"Fine. Make a copy of this for me. If I need the original, though, I'm going to ask for it."

"Deal."

I made a copy and fingered the original again. "I'm not going to lie... the original is definitely carrying an energy about it that the copies don't. And look at this ink... It almost seems alive, it's sort of iridescent."

"Now who's the one who sounds crazy?"

"Hey, *you* came to *me* for the woo-woo nonsense."

"True."

I walked him over to the door and held it open for him. "Thanks for, uh, warning me, I guess, and confusing me more."

"That's what we do, ma'am," he tipped his baseball cap at me and grinned.

"See ya, Jason."

He was several feet away from my door when he abruptly turned around, looking earnest. "Please be careful, Violet. There's something weird going on, and I'd be upset if anything happened to you."

My heart did a little somersault. "Sure, Jason," I said softly.

It had become apparent that Nathan wasn't telling me everything, so I was definitely going to join him at meditation the next night.

So much for laying low.

And I sure wish that Jason would stop flirting with me out of nowhere.

8

It was unusually windy the next evening as I waited in the parking lot for Nathan. This particular studio was actually in the next city, but only by a sneeze's length. I stared at the bright lights of a Starbucks' sign, watching people enter the studio across the parking lot. I was deep in thought about the strange written language on the paper tucked into my sling bag. I wasn't sure how I was going to approach him about it, but I *was* sure I was going to approach him.

Something about Nathan didn't measure up. His timing, his timing was always perfectly choreographed. Maybe he had nothing to do with Alyssa's death, but his showing up here was no coincidence. Whatever "business" he was tending to was somehow related. Whether or not he wanted to share that with me, or was able to, was another thing altogether.

The Starbucks sign did one of those horror-movies-blinking-off-and-back-on thing. I could almost hear the buzzing as it flickered. Just then, Nathan pulled up. I got out of my car and wrapped myself tightly in my knee-length cardigan, tucking the hieroglyphs a little bit deeper into my bag. I ran over to Nathan's car, re-wrapping my light brown hair into a pony-tail.

"Crazy wind tonight!"

He got out of his car, and I let his body assemble before me. Some sort of lightweight almost harem-y pants in black with a little design at the waistband adorned his legs; he must have had a short sleeved shirt on underneath his black pullover fleece jacket. He was also wearing flip-flops, which made me inwardly smile. I had on Chucks. My feet were freezing.

"Hi," he said, giving me an awkward half-hug as he walked me to the entrance. "Have you been here before? I just came across it yesterday during my work."

Hm.

"Yeah, I come here every so often. The yogis around here have a tendency of not staying in one place for long, so if you like a teacher, you'll follow him or her to a new spot. And then there're the instructors who are hired to teach whatever kitschy thing is popular at the moment... they'll go anywhere."

I took a short breath and continued. "Is it like this where *you* live?" Damn straight I was trying to catch him off guard so I could get an honest answer about *anything*. He opened his mouth to respond to me, but I cut him off by pointing to a new discovery. (I definitely stepped on my own toes here.)

Since there was no massage therapy at this studio, I didn't think it would have been one that was broken into. But I saw a brand new sign on the door as we walked up to it:

New! Healing Touch Therapy! Inquire inside for more details.

Ah. I wonder if this place *had* been targeted after all. "Wait, look at this," I said to Nathan. "That's new."

There was an unusual hush over the group as we meandered into the room where people were sitting on zabutons, getting cozy for the meditation. It was mostly the usual suspects; people who had done *A Course in Miracles* study group at one location, or learned about essential oils somewhere else. One was one of my Reiki clients; she waved at me when I walked in.

Nathan's appearance seemed to be the only thing that was distracting everyone from their murmuring, and it quickly dissipated once the owner of the studio walked inside the room.

One of the men sitting on a purple cushion immediately addressed her.

The room got super quiet.

"Was this studio one of the places that got broken into?"

Nathan looked at me inquisitively, and I nodded my head indicating I would talk to him after the meditation. Nobody dared breathe until she gave an answer.

She paused dramatically. "No… but around the times that the other places had been broken into, my husband and I were actually here. It would seem that we thwarted the criminal by our mere appearance!"

Inner eye roll. These people could be so dramatic sometimes.

The audience drank it in like Kool-aid, though. I glanced at Nathan and saw his mouth and eyebrows twitch in response. I had to bite my tongue to keep from laughing aloud.

"However," she continued, "as we have new people with us tonight, I'd rather not discuss such negative topics, to avoid bringing more dust into our light."

I looked around. There were a few new faces indeed. Everyone must be coming out because of what was going on. Safety in numbers, or just sheer curiosity.

"I would like to share with you, though, that there will be a vigil for Alyssa this Saturday outside of her studio led by *this* studio, as well as a few others. It's at 7 PM, we will provide candles."

My gut was telling me it was a good marketing stunt.

"Now. Everyone take a deep breath in, the deepest breath

you've taken all day. Feel the cold air as it tickles the inside of your nose; feel the warmth as you breathe it out…"

***

When she had finished the meditation, people slowly started to get up, dropped their "love" donation into a basket, and either gossiped some more by the entrance, or quickly headed to their cars to go home for the night.

After she had spritzed us (it seems everyone was spritzing these days, and hey, who didn't love a good spritz?), I flopped myself down into corpse pose rather than staying seated.

After most of the people had gotten up, I was still lying down. Nathan cleared his throat and leaned back on his elbows, and then looked up at the ceiling. "Gaining some insight from up there that I'm not?" He glanced back at me.

I sat up. "We need to talk. Is there anywhere you need to be right now?"

"Well, yeah," he said, pushing his cushion up against a wall. "With you." Crooked smile.

We walked out, dropping our love donations. I wanted to avoid any chatter with anyone else, and seeing as nothing else would be open at that hour other than a Starbucks, I quickly motioned in the direction across the parking lot.

Once we were inside, Nathan wouldn't take no for an answer and bought me my herbal tea. He reminded me that he had planned on taking me out to lunch, but that when the power popped, everyone was so distracted he wasn't able to do it.

One other couple from the meditation was there; two sisters. They nodded at us as we found our own seats near a fireplace.

I sipped my tea and burned my tongue. Dammit. I started talking with a fat tongue, and Nathan laughed. I liked making him laugh.

I was annoyed with that realization.

"I suppose you hadn't heard about the break-ins?" I sighed. Time to get to work.

"Well, yes, I heard about a couple, I didn't know there were more than that. What do you know about it?"

"Jason—I mean Officer Dunham—stopped by my office the other day to warn me about it. They weren't sure if therapists were being targeted, or just yoga studios. As of now, it's only studios who *have* therapists that have been broken into, and only in our immediate area. He didn't offer any more information than that." I paused, hesitated, and then quickly blurted, "And then he showed me this." Before I could pull out Jason's copy of the writing, though, Nathan spoke.

"Jason is important to you."

My hand paused halfway in my purse. "I suppose so? I mean, he dated Elizabeth a few months back, that's really when I got to know him—why? What difference does that make?" I was flustered.

His gaze looked distant, and he wouldn't quite meet my eyes. "Just an observation." For a beat neither of us said anything, until he finally returned his eyes to mine, his own expression clear and focused. "I digress. Please continue."

"Oh. Okay." I looked down at my bag, and then pulled the paper out, handing it quickly to him in case anyone was watching.

Wow. I was really getting paranoid.

Nathan remained expressionless, and barely glanced at it. "And Jason brought this to you. Why would he do that?"

This wasn't exactly the direction of the conversation I had planned on heading, so it took me a moment to collect my thoughts. "Well—the cops already sent it to Atlanta to be translated, but I guess he wanted to know if I recognized it."

"Why would *you* be someone who recognizes it?"

I didn't want to answer the question. One reason why was I didn't really *have* an answer. The second reason why was because I wanted Nathan to admit *he* knew about this secret glyph.

"Look, cut the crap and just tell me what it says!" Pretense be damned. I demanded an answer. I was suddenly very angry that I was in this predicament of potential danger mixed with half-truths and misdirection.

Nathan made no indication that I had ruffled his feathers in any way. He calmly replied, "What makes you think that I know anything about this?"

"For lack of a better way to say this, I know you're here because of... of whatever's going on." I grasped at the air. "Whether or not it was always going to involve Alyssa really doesn't matter, because it was already happening without her."

I had no idea where these words were coming from; they were pouring out of my mouth like liquor into a drunk's mouth; a nice, flowing stream of words with purpose. A part of my brain was left observing this uncontrollable diatribe. I was hostile, I was forward and I was throwing a temper tantrum because of my frustration. But the more I spoke, the more I felt like it was no mistake that I was somehow involved. Or Nathan.

Nathan broke my inner dialogue.

"Violet."

I swallowed. "Yes."

He seemed to carefully choose his next words. "I can't tell you all that you need, or want, to know. But part of what you're guessing is accurate, even though you don't have any details. Which is further proof that I shouldn't, nor will I, share everything with you"

"Excuse me?"

"What I'm saying is, *yes*, I know about this written

language. It's a special variation of the elder futhark, ever heard of it? Runes. Runestaves. And, yes, you, or someone you love, may be in danger." He audibly sighed. "You are correct in assuming that this is why I am here. I am just not sure who I am protecting yet."

I sat back in my chair, a lifetime's worth of air being pushed out of me. This couldn't be real. I had fallen asleep after hitting my head on something.

Do you believe in magic? Yes, of course… the parchment script was written in runestaves. I had seen runes before, in metaphysical bookstores. I had seen the jewelry. But I had committed very little to working memory about who had written them, or why. Other than perhaps ancient Celtic people used them in spellcasting or something. Ancient. Old. Out of use.

"Magic. Woo-woo. Psychics. I know enough, to know enough, but—" I cut myself off with a thought, and without meaning to, I cried out, "My father. My father has visions."

Nathan looked around, suddenly realizing we were in a public place. He seemed spooked.

"We shouldn't be here. You've got to let me come to your place, or you have to… No, we need to go to your place."

I tucked my hands into themselves and chewed my bottom lip. "How do I know you're being honorable? That this isn't some ruse to… harm me?"

For the first time since I had met him, he looked deflated. He groaned into his hands, pushing them back through his thick hair before looking up at me. "You don't."

"Fuuuck!" I made a horsey sound with my lips.

He gestured to a back corner of the Starbucks, where two people were quietly sitting. One was on his phone, the other was "reading" a book. After closer inspection, I realized they were the same people who had been on the recreation path. The same people I had referred to as Zombies. They still had the same dark look in their eyes.

"What the—? Who *are* they?"

"Scouts."

"Scouts for what?"

"I can't say."

"Okay, so we are at an impasse. Yet again." I paused. "Who the hell are *you*?"

Without a beat, he monologued, in a rather stream-of-consciousness, "I am Nathan Murphy, my parents divorced when I was young, my father ended up in Atlanta and my mother mostly lives on a tiny European island. I grew up here and there—anytime I stayed somewhere for long, it was when I was with my father. Alyssa was my only sibling. After university I moved to Boston, secured a job, and stayed there for awhile until I was approached for my current work, and now I've lived here and there again. There is nothing more to tell."

I pushed myself back in my chair, throwing my hands up in defeat. "Okay!"

He put his hands in his lap, crunching his knuckles.

"We really should leave."

"Okay."

"They're watching us. They know who I am."

"Do they know who *I* am?"

"*I* don't know who you are."

I glanced over at them. They knew we had spotted them, so they weren't even trying to hide their stares. I wanted to hand over the original copy of the writing that I had, but I imagined it was a bad idea. There was no other choice. Either he had to come with me, or I'd continue being in the dark.

9

Our plan was to go to Sam and Elizabeth's rented condo, unless they didn't answer their phones. In which case, Nathan and I would talk in the parking lot for my safety. It was getting late, and I really didn't want to disturb them. I was on the fence about calling them as we pulled into the parking lot.

I exited my car and walked over to Nathan's tiny vehicle, wondering why I had agreed to do this. He got out, and leaned up against it. He looked like a giant standing there, next to a toy car. I joined him, looking him squarely in the face.

"I didn't call them."

"Oh."

Without any flourish, I pulled the parchment out of my bag.

Nathan swallowed. Hard. He took it, then looked at me, searched my eyes and asked tersely, "Where did you get this?"

"It's warm." I defiantly answered.

He swallowed again. "Please. Answer me."

"It was twirling outside of Alyssa's the day her body was discovered... what does it say?"

He carefully chose his words, yet again. "It's complicated. But what it means is more important than what it says…"

His pauses in speech were driving me crazy. My heart started to pound outside of my body, and the longer he took to say anything just made it worse. I had no idea what was going on, or *what* he was going to say, but I somehow knew in my gut that *this* was the beginning of something I'd never be able to walk away from. I felt that this moment would quite possibly be *the* defining moment of my life; when my lifelong search for *something* would finally end. Whether or not I wanted to believe his next words, whether or not I wanted to engage with his next words, didn't matter so much as in this *one* moment, my life would just make sense. I could surrender and allow myself to exist within his words.

"You are… special. Of great import. Fate… Destiny… You are, in fact, the person I am supposed to protect. To train." The last part he said to himself, as if in wonder. He began to fold the parchment.

I closed my eyes, letting his words fill my body and reverberate around the walls of my human existence.

And then I got belligerent. "Protect from? Train to be? Again, I ask, *who* are you?" I spit out.

"Some of it you'll have to discover for yourself. However, *my* job is to help you understand the path that has been chosen for you. I am here to guide you, train you, protect you during your apprenticeship. You are my new apprentice." He slid the parchment into his back pocket and faced me like a Colonel; he was no longer casually leaning up against his car.

"My… apprenticeship?"

Do you believe in magic?

"We have to begin training immediately. You need to study the runes and their historical significance; you need to learn self-defense; how to uncover your talents to protect others. Darkness is rising."

Train. Protect Others. Darkness.

He rattled on and on. The longer he went on, the more numb I became to the cold weather, to his words. I couldn't digest anything else he was saying other than the fact that I was supposed to *train* to *protect* others from... *Darkness?*

I began to uncontrollably shake. This guy was nuts, and I was standing in the dark, alone, with him. Nobody knew where I was, and I felt the terror leaking into my veins. My eyes glazed over, and at some point he must have realized I had shut down because he stopped talking.

He gently grabbed my shoulders. "I'm taking you home, now. Where do you live?"

"What the hell are you talking about?" I trembled some more.

He steadied me with both hands. "I'm so sorry, Violet," and he genuinely seemed sorry. "Your whole world is about to change. Everything you've ever seen before, or witnessed... It's just been scraping the surface." He looked grim.

This man is crazy. This man is crazy.

Somehow, I found myself strapped into his car as I continued to shake. He sat down next to me and flattened his lips, waiting for me to tell him where to go. Moments stretched into minutes as the silence swallowed us, as the darkness blanketed us. If he was going to torture me, or kill me, why wasn't he doing it?

"Violet... if you don't answer me, I'm calling Elizabeth." He turned to me, a desperate look accosting those very handsome features. His green eyes pleaded with my hollow blue eyes.

I felt a spark of energy shoot from him to me, and while it was unsettling, and I caught a flinch in his eyes, it woke me up. I started to channel anger again. "You don't have the code to my phone," I aggressively challenged him.

"I don't need it." He snapped back, trying to regain control of the situation.

I crossed my arms over my chest, not budging. Feeling was coming back to my limbs and regardless of what was going on, this man was *not* going to tell me what to do. I unflinchingly met his pleading stare.

"Phang."

Dammit. He had me on that one. She needed to be walked one more time for the night. I broke the stare, looking out the window.

"Take a left at the exit," I muttered, pointing to the exit of the neighborhood. He hesitantly nodded and turned on his car.

***

My alarm woke me up that Friday. I had had some wild dreams the night before, and I felt exhausted. Phang farted, Barnaby swatted at my mouth.

The world was normal and I was okay with that.

I stood up, wrapped my robe around myself, fighting with the robe strap. I stifled a yawn and stepped into the hallway, looking at the thermostat. It was a cold morning, so I cranked it up a degree just to get the heat going. I went into the restroom, washed my hands, and wandered into the kitchen.

Barnaby almost tripped me as I turned on the tea kettle. Phang bounded out of my bedroom and into the living room towards the man sitting on my couch, who was quietly typing on a computer. Wait, what? The man scratched Phang's ears, placed her back on the floor, and cautiously looked up at me.

"Good morning."

I slammed back into my refrigerator, like in a nightmare. My heart began to pound as the night before came rushing back. I had tunnel vision staring at this man sitting on my couch.

After we had gotten home, Nathan had been nothing but a gentleman. He didn't say much as we walked the dog, but he stayed very close to me to keep me from bolting. He had somehow produced a toothbrush and bedtime clothes and prepared the couch for himself to fall asleep. I locked myself in my bedroom as soon as I was able to do so, and convinced myself I had made it all up.

But here he was, in the morning, still alive, well, and fully dressed for the day. My blankets were folded neatly on the back of my couch.

"We have a lot to accomplish today."

His demeanor was serious. He no longer seemed like this good-looking, slightly-flirtatious, mysterious guy who was withholding information. No, he was now this brisk, businesslike, yet also cautious *dictator* who was unforgiving to my plight. His mission was more important than my coping. And I was not coping at all. I didn't believe a word of what he'd told me last night in the parking lot.

"Nathan. You're still here. How wonderful." I spoke in a monotonous voice, glancing at the door to escape. I felt trapped, but also feisty.

He challenged my tone. "You can't run from this, Miss Moore."

"Miss Moore?" In spite of everything else going on, that took me aback.

He smiled, rather sadly. "I have no choice. It's dictated in the rules that we are to be formal. It's the only way to keep us safe."

"Ha!" I couldn't help myself, my ego raged. "I am *not* calling you Mr. Murphy. You're just a dude from a yoga studio who has somehow infiltrated my house, and thinks he can tell me what to do." I waved my arms around like a madman.

I poured my tea, grunting to see if he wanted any. He did. I didn't feel threatened, per se, but I also knew that if I attempted to leave, he would follow. So for the time being, I just planned to go along with everything he was saying.

"I know this situation is less than ideal because we met before you were chosen, but I'm going to be formal with you whether you like it or not. To keep the boundaries clean, to keep us safe. You can fight me all you want, but this is happening, this is real."

He turned to his computer as I placed his tea cup in front of him. I sat next to him wondering how he expected me to behave, so I could act the way he wanted, and potentially get him to leave me alone. I'd lock him out as soon as I could! Then I'd call Jason for help. *Mr. Murphy* was delusional!

"Sure thing. So what do you have on the agenda for today?"

"Miss Moore," he sighed, tapping the middle of my forehead, "I can tell you aren't on board with all of this just yet," he swept his arms out sideways. "Be warned, though, you are no match for me. My only purpose right now is to serve you, keep you safe, train you. I will succeed, or we *both* fail." He emphasized the last part before looking back down to his computer.

"I have appointments today," I muttered.

"Reschedule them."

"*You* reschedule them."

"Fine, show me how and I'll do it for you."

"Do I have to pay you?"

"No."

"Who pays you?"

"That's not pertinent information."

"Do I get paid?"

"Yes."

"By you?"

"No."

"But you're the one… training me?" The words felt funny on my lips.

"Unless I truly can't handle you. Then someone else would step in."

Hm. He seemed to have answers without actually giving answers.

"So what am I? Like a vampire slayer? Do I get to avenge Alyssa's death? This has to do with her, right? Do I go to the upside down now?" I was *definitely* feeling feisty.

"Stop watching Netflix." What a poignant phrase for everyone to use regarding, well, everything.

I sipped my tea and sighed. "Okay, so you reschedule my appointments for the day and we do what exactly?"

"Go over what is to be expected of you. Explain to you how all of this works. Paperwork. History. Prove to you that I am not the enemy, but that I am here to support you as you learn what you're about to learn."

"Even if I *did* believe you, Nathan, which I don't, this is too esoteric. If there's nothing tangible to train me for, how will I even know if I'm learning something? Last night you mentioned that 'Darkness' is rising. What does that even mean?"

I couldn't help myself. The longer I sat with him, the more at ease I felt and the conversations we were having turned genuine. My thoughts and words were directly in response to what he was saying. My curiosity was getting the better of me. I wondered if he was doing something to pacify my doubt, my fears. Logically, I still thought he was as crazy as a loon. Due to my comfort level increasing with the nonsense he was spewing my way, I was starting to think that I was *also* a lunatic.

This in turn made me angry. My dad was crazy. I didn't want to go bananas, too.

I sighed, pushed up off of the couch, and my phone rang.

"Am I allowed to answer that?" It was Elizabeth.

"Yes. Just don't tell her about me until I know she can be trusted."

"Elizabeth? Seriously? My car is there, she probably saw it. She's no fool."

"Everyone has secrets, Miss Moore. And your car is *here*."

I blinked in surprise, and then stomped to the bathroom.

Elizabeth was wondering what I had been up to all week since she hadn't heard much from me. I wasn't the best at lying, or rather, omitting things, but I did tell her Jason had come by to warn me about the possibility of my place being broken into. Her studio was on the safe list—there were no practicing healers there.

After I told her about Jason, though, she wasn't listening as closely anymore to what I was saying. "You're important to Jason."

"Good God, would people stop saying that?"

"Well, it's obvious he has a thing for you," she said huffily.

"What difference does that make if it's true? You aren't seeing him anymore."

"Do you like him?" she asked in a small voice.

"Seriously? You guys dated for about half an hour, why do you even care?"

She didn't say anything.

My bad mood was returning. Plus, I knew Nathan was listening to every word I was saying, fully capable of putting together who we were talking about. This pissed me off so much that the tips of my ears started to burn. I didn't want to take the time to figure out what in God's name that could possibly mean, but my mind wouldn't stop connecting the dots to the real plausibility that I was physically attracted to the crazy man in my living room.

"Wow, Violet, that was shitty." Oh yeah, we were talking about Jason.

"Look, I don't care if he's interested in me or not. I'm not going to date him, or anyone else," I muttered, thinking about how my future consisted of late nights studying runic languages and slaying the beast. Come to think of it, Nathan still hadn't really told me what he was training me to do or be. Good God. I was living in a dreamworld, a farce of reality.

Her mood instantly changed. "Good. I mean, not good, but I was thinking of asking him out again."

Wow. Frenemy indeed. Of course, I knew he wasn't interested in her, so I snippily said, "Good luck with that."

"Geez, Violet, what the hell has gotten into you?"

Just then Nathan knocked on the door, opened it without warning, and saw me pathetically sitting on my toilet, squeezing some toothpaste onto my toothbrush, only missing the toothbrush. I watched it plop onto my pajama pants, leaving a glob of gooey goodness.

I met Nathan's unreadable eyes. Elizabeth wasn't speaking, I wasn't speaking, and Nathan just stood there, watching me. Then he tapped his watch.

"Hey, E, I don't think I'll be at yoga tonight." Nathan and I still held eyes.

"What? You always come! Besides, don't you want to see that hot guy Nathan anymore?"

Nathan's hearing was apparently very good, and he looked quite pleased with himself. I'm not sure what compelled me, but I threw a Kleenex box at his head. He ducked and smiled, tapping on his watch again before leaving me in the bathroom. The door was still open. I gritted my teeth.

"What is that noise?"

I stifled a laugh. Well. Maybe the crazy guy and I could have some fun while he pretended to train me to be a superhero.

"I've got to go. I'll see you at the vigil tomorrow."

"How'd you find out about that?"

"It's a long story that I'd love to share with you, just so long as you fare well in a background check." Nathan grinned just outside of the door.

"Violet, go get some sleep. Drink a whiskey or something."

10

My first day training for ..whatever.. was spent mostly indoors, although Nathan let me clear my head a bit and take Phang for a walk. I'm surprised he let me leave by myself, I half expected him to turn into a bat and fly above my head to keep an eye on me. All Snape-like.

No such luck. Apparently shape-shifting wasn't something he or I could do. And if that was a real thing, I sure didn't want to know about it.

When I got back to my place, Nathan had actually left. There was a note on my coffee table that said he'd be back soon. I was afraid that meant he had gone back to his dad's house to retrieve some more things so he could move in with me.

Shudder. I liked living alone, it was a one bedroom and I didn't need some warlock-magician-telekinetic-psychopathic-whatever-the-hell-he-was cramping my style.

Not that I had style.

I checked the time; it was 2 o'clock. I wondered what he had in store for me the rest of the day. The majority of the morning was spent going over the known history of runes, and then some of the runes themselves. He hadn't yet told me *why* it was important. He had emphasized that learning to recognize the symbols and their various vibrations was what should matter to me.

It was all just so surreal. I didn't understand why I was entertaining this whole concept, yet there I was, doing just that.

Nathan could be ingratiating on my nerves. When he got too irritating, I would refer to him as my Watcher, as Dumbledore. He did not find me amusing at all.

He had started off my morning with a lecture.

"Magic doesn't exist as it is represented across pop culture. The truth is taken and stretched, morphed for base enjoyment. What do all of these TV shows and books have in common, though? A semblance of truth. Even Jesus performed magic, if you will, was he not a healer? How about Mother Theresa? Was she not magical? Or Ghandi, or Martin Luther King, Jr.? All of these people carried their own type of magic. Being magical merely means you are in tune with your own power. It does not save you from death, or pain, but rather it connects you to the collective all-is. Understand?"

My eyebrows were about five feet past my head at that point. He had sighed and decided the best course of action for me was to do something tangible. Study the ol' runes some more, physically touching some stones that had markings on them.

Apparently runic script had been around for at least two thousand years and was used as a way to worship Odin, or Thor, or some other archaic God like that. They were magical, divining, and a plethora of other things I didn't understand. If these runes weren't going to open up a chasm into a world where I would be riding a dragon, well, why should I care?

I decided I was hungry, and I started rifling through my food pantry and refrigerator for food. I had nothing to eat. I guess I needed to go to the store. As I was pondering what I was allowed or not allowed to do on my own anymore, my phone rang.

Crud. It was my dad.

With Nathan still gone, I figured it was best to take the call then.

"Hi, honey! How are you?"

Ah. This dad was the clouds-are-fluffy-and-taste-like-marshmallows dad. Easier to talk to, but equally annoying.

Nathan must have duplicated my key, because just as I was about to get off the phone with my father, he slipped in. I didn't even flinch as I saw the door knob move. I'm pretty sure I *was* having a mental breakdown.

Sure enough, a duffle bag was attached to Nathan. I was hoping it was full of wooden stakes, but I had a feeling it was loaded with clothes and toothpaste.

He dropped the bag onto my coffee table and walked back to my door to lock it. I helped myself to his bag, still saying yes every so often to my father. Nathan walked back over to the sliding glass doors to my balcony, with his arms crossed, watching me.

I sighed. Yup. Clothes.

I pulled out a pair of men's briefs, and twirled it around on my fingers before hurling it towards the TV. One side of Nathan's lips turned up, and he made his way to my bedroom with an equally devilish glint to his eyes.

Noooooo.

"Yeah, dad, that sounds great. Mmmhmmm." I followed Nathan and whispered threateningly, "Don't you dare!" He started opening my drawers.

When he found the *right* drawer, I thought I was going to die from embarrassment as he pulled out... Look, they weren't *exactly* hole-y granny panties, but the comfortable underwear I typically wore were definitely bikini-on-the-extra, with some ripped elastic showing.

I was furious.

"Dad, I'm sorry but I really have to go. Work and all."

My dad's voice suddenly changed as his demented mind began to take over. "This isn't about that young fellow, is it? He's been here before, you know. Don't trust him, Violet, please. He isn't who he seems."

Nathan picked up a pair of my black underwear, taunting me. *I'm not embarrassed. I'm not embarrassed.*

"Dad, no, he's not here, no, he's not here twirling my underwear around on his fingers, searching my drawers for a bra…" I clenched my jaw.

That caught my dad off guard and he pretty much went deep inside his mind somewhere. I turned away from Nathan. "Goodbye, Daddy," I whispered. I felt guilty. He grunted goodbye and I heard the phone go graveyard dead.

I rapidly turned back towards Nathan, and tackled him. Believe it or not, I surprised him, so when I knocked him onto my bed, he was tangled in my unmentionables and was having a hard time getting *un*tangled.

I took the opportunity and grabbed his arms, pinning them to his side. At this point, I knew he could overpower me pretty easily, but he let me keep him pinned anyway. My chest was heaving from having rushed him, and every part of my body that was touching his body was tingling with electricity that I shoved into the deepest recesses of my mind to forget.

I gritted my teeth. "Why is your shit in my living room?"

He calmly looked at me, his hair tumbling on my pillows, green eyes meeting mine without question. "Right now I need to be close to you."

"As in, *live* with me?"

"Yes."

"For how long?"

A shrug. "I train you, and then you're on your own."

I pushed off of him and flopped onto my back next to him.

I rubbed my eyes and started up at the ceiling. "Why is this happening to me? This can't be real. I mean, what if I didn't have a couch? You'd have nowhere to sleep." I'm not sure why logic was a part of my rambling.

Nathan sat up and began to untangle my underwear. He murmured, "I'm so sorry I took the bait. That was ridiculously unprofessional of me."

Unfortunately, this response tickled enough of my soul to make me feel a bit badly for the guy. I couldn't comprehend most of anything at the moment, but if the guy wasn't 'allowed' to ensnare himself in women's panties, then what was the point? The meaning of his weird-as-hell life?

"You're just lucky I threw away my old skivvies last week." I tried to smile, but fell just short of being authentic.

He closed the drawers and walked over to the side of the bed, reaching out for my hands. For a brief second I thought worry had crossed his features, but I may have been mistaken, for all he said was, "Truce."

I let him pull me up and responded with a 'truce' of my own. The electricity from previous touching was gone, and I felt anger pulsating between us.

I was going to have to let that go.

I followed him back into the living room and pulled his underwear off of my TV stand. I put it back into his bag as he watched me. I zipped it back up and brought it into my bedroom, calling over my shoulder, "You may as well store this in my bedroom, I have an extra drawer and some closet space if you want."

When I came back into the living room, I felt like I was handling the ludicrousness of the current situation rather well. Nathan was at my countertop in the kitchen with a late lunch. I had somehow missed him bringing in takeout as I was so taken with the duffle bag. I could have sworn that look of unease passed over his face again, but as soon as it was there, it was gone.

"I never have to buy my own food again?"

He laughed as he opened it up. "You wish... And I hope you like Greek food."

All this learning made me hungry. I lunged into the food, trying to mentally prepare myself for more runic study.

***

He handed me handbook after handbook, even a W4 form which he assured me would have to be promptly destroyed upon reaching my employer. "Who *is* my employer, there, Yoda?"

"Complete the mission and you'll find out."

I tossed the paperwork onto the table. "And if I don't? Complete the 'mission'?"

I leaned back, itching for a jog. I was tired of being cooped up. I realized Nathan hadn't answered me and Phang plopped herself down at my feet for a belly rub. Barnaby was on the back of the couch sleeping with one eye opened. I didn't think he was thrilled about my new live-in.

"You will."

I could tell there was no pressing for more information, so I stood up, tripped over the dog, and wandered into my bedroom for running clothes. "I'm going for a jog!" I shouted behind me.

Nathan had apparently followed me and I had my t-shirt half way off of my head already. I rapidly pulled it back down and his inflamed cheeks matched mine. "I'm sorry," he murmured. "But it's not safe for you to go alone. I have to join you."

"I already went for a walk by myself today!"

"With Phang."

"*Phang* is going to protect me?"

His skin was returning to normal color. "It's not that... It's that I knew you couldn't get too far from home." He grinned.

"I'm used to doing things alone."

"I know. I'm sorry." His grin disappeared.

"Stop saying that." I sighed. "I'm a slow runner. What's your pace?"

"I'll match whatever you choose to run."

I turned around and lifted my shirt up again, throwing it onto my bed and reaching for my sports bra while simultaneously unhooking my regular bra. "Get out of my room." I felt him leave rather than heard him, and when I turned back around in my running shirt, I felt depressed.

11

The jog went pretty well. Nathan didn't cause me any problems, he matched my pace, slowed down when I did, and sprinted when I did. I knew *he* knew I was working out my frustration, let alone mystification, with everything. He had so many answers and I had so many questions and yet I felt like I wasn't allowed to know anything of worth.

I had no idea *why* I was learning to read runes, what it had to do with meditation, or why all of my massage appointments had been moved to the following week. I had no idea why he handed me a mental and physical work-out schedule to immediately start. I had no job title, no employer. I had nobody I could tell what was going on, I couldn't trust Nathan, yet I had to do everything he said, and take the rest at face value.

And of course, creepy 'Scouts' were lurking around town, acquaintances of mine were being murdered, and yoga studios with massage therapists were being broken into. And somehow here *I* was, chosen to protect others from Darkness. To wit, I could only assume it had something to do with the Scouts, Alyssa, and studios.

I really had to figure out a way to walk out of this nightmare I found myself in. Or rather, *run* as fast as I could to get away from it.

We ended up at another set of docks quite far from my apartment. Several lakes existed in town, and this one was usually the busiest. For a Friday night which was a little warmer than usual, this was exactly the case. I ran up onto the dock and crouched, hands on my knees as I panted.

Nathan was also out of breath as I heard him behind me making it to the dock. When I had taken off at the fastest sprint of my life, letting out a huge guttural growl, he had deliberately given me space and kept his distance.

I got on my knees, placing my hands next to me, looking up at the sunset across the water. Nathan squatted next to me, and put a comforting hand on my back. "It'll be okay," he huffed.

As sweat poured off my face, I said. "I can't figure you out. One second you're my best friend, the next second a drill sergeant."

He laughed sardonically. "That just means I'm not good at my job. Thanks for that."

I stretched out, taking a swig of water, wiping the sweat off my brow. I handed him my water and he hesitated before he took it. "Not a germaphobe, are you?"

"Boundaries, Miss Moore. I find myself having a hard time keeping them with you." He looked away to the sunset himself as he also stretched out his long legs, his feet hanging off the end of the dock as he drank some water.

I lifted my shirt to wipe some more sweat off of my face. "And that's a problem?"

He didn't answer, but my gaze lingered on him. I tried to assess him objectively, but it was just too damn hard. I stared back at the sunset and we sat quietly side by side for several minutes. His body heat was keeping me warm.

"I'm gonna take a short-cut back, I'm zapped. I'm probably going to walk most of the way back as long as I don't get too cold. Are we doing anything else tonight? Or can I just go home, shower and eat?"

Shit. This guy was living with me now! I had to share my shower with him! I didn't even know if my shower was clean! *Stop thinking.*

"I just want to go over your schedule for the next week. Today was more of an introductory day."

"How much is this going to interfere with my regular life?"

"Lots of early and late hours. We don't want to take away your life, or your regular lifestyle. You're undercover and all. At least for now."

"Are you ready to tell me what exactly it is I'm supposed to be doing?"

"No… but look into the parking lot and tell me what you see. Or feel."

I stood up and headed back to the path. I closed my eyes. I could feel Nathan behind me. "I feel you… Your heat. I feel a pulse in my head."

"Do you see anything? Just focus on your third eye and describe what is there as best as you can."

"Alrighty then… the color is purple, it's opening up like a flower. Ha… It kind of looks like Dart." I sighed. "I sense something 'red' in the direction of the parking lot. I'm not seeing it, but that's how the color feels… Your warmth isn't there anymore. But I sense…"

My heart all of a sudden rushed into my throat and I opened my eyes. Nathan stood before me, expectantly. I had started to panic, and tears were pressing at my eyes. I was having a hard time catching my breath as my heart continued to violently thud.

"Hey, are you okay?" No formality there, he reached out to steady me.

"What *was* that?" I could still feel the electricity, and it was the same as before—like I was being shocked a million times.

"Don't you feel it?" I whispered.

His eyebrows came together and he said, "No, I don't."

I was afraid I was going to hyperventilate as I choked out, "This happened when you linked arms with me after lunch the other day. I felt like I was being shocked over and over again." I was sweating profusely, eyes dilated. I tried to slow down my breathing.

"Violet, look out me. Steady… Steady" I looked into his eyes as he grabbed me by my chin. "You're okay. Be present, focus on me, put your hands on my arms. *Feel* me. Feel my touch." He paused for a moment, his eyes searching mine as he spoke to me, trying to lull me into a calm space.

I wiggled my toes and I held onto his arms, pressing with a death grip as I stared at his face. I could feel the world starting to come back into focus, Nathan's touch tethering me to the Earthly plane. Still clutching him, I gazed over at the lake feeling the sun's fading rays on my skin again.

"Do you know EFT?"

"Not well enough to use, but it's okay… The electricity's gone. I'm feeling better." I started to breathe evenly and met his eyes again with my own slightly wet ones. I licked my lips and gave a wan smile.

"Alright, Violet, experiment over. Let's go home." He spoke firmly as he steered me onto the path back towards the direction of my apartment, arm over my shoulder, holding me near.

"Okay," I said weakly. Once I focused on the sound of my feet crunching dead leaves, I felt even better. We walked about a quarter of a mile with his arm around my waist, keeping me upright, slowly and without saying anything to one another. At some point we must have changed position, because after another quarter mile, I realized I had slid my arm around his, holding onto him. I felt foolish and embarrassed. He sensed the change and put distance between our bodies—the level of comfort and ease that we had had during the silent walk was officially gone.

In addition to being mortified, I realized I was cold because he was no longer touching me, so I decided to take off running again at a 'sailing' speed—an easy, yet decent pace. Once we got back to my apartment complex, we walked up the hill, cooling off before making it to my door.

I paused at the door before unlocking it. "Thanks."

"It's my job," he goofily smiled.

"Literally." I abruptly stopped once I put my hand on the doorknob.

"Whoa. It's hot. What does that mean?" I asked, surprised.

Nathan put his hand over it and chanted something, eyes closed. I watched him, trying to appreciate what he was doing rather than scoffing at him and calling him a giant weirdo. "Well?"

His eyes popped open and his green eyes went from hazy to perfectly clear. "They're gone."

"Who?"

"They know it's you," he calmly said.

"*Who?*"

"Scouts… They're probably the ones breaking into the studios, and now they've tried to break into your apartment," he groaned. "This is how they tracked us to the lake. Come on, get inside." He opened the door for me, gesturing for me to go inside.

I didn't want to become that girl, you know, the one who was several octaves above a dog whistle, but it was happening. "What are you talking about, Nathan?"

Just inside the door was Phang, and she barked as I picked her up; Barnaby crawled out from underneath my couch. I reached up into my cabinet while holding the dog and said, "That's it. I can't take it anymore. All this crap is just too nutty, I've had a mental breakdown and I'm trapped in the multiverse. Captain Morgan is going to get me the hell out."

I slammed down a shot. After feeling a nice, spreading warmth from my throat down to my stomach, I turned to face Nathan who was looking slightly amused. "This is no laughing matter!"

"You're funny. Yes it is." He tapped me on my third eye with a smile.

I pushed the bottle to him. "Shot?" He shook his head no. "Wimp."

He raised an eyebrow, walked back to the door to make sure it was locked, and took Phang from me. He was standing so close I could feel his heat again.

"Remember the 'red' you felt in the parking lot?"

"Yeah?"

"That was them. Scouts. You need to keep working on identifying that particular type of energy."

"Oooookay. Sheesh. Don't be so serious all the time." I found myself irritated again as I stepped around him, unraveling my wet ponytail and wrapping the hair tie onto its doorknob dwelling.

"You just got mad at me for laughing!"

"Oh yeah." My mind was a mess.

How annoying. I was assessing his full form, and damn if it didn't look good being all sweaty and hot, holding an adoring Phang in the crook of his arm. He opened the fridge and grabbed a water, looking as if he belonged in that spot, as he had always belonged.

"When did I get those?" I asked warily.

He swallowed and ignored my question. "Go shower, and I'll tell you why the Scouts are after you, and why it's important you recognize them."

"Who are they Scouts *for*? Why weren't they able to get into my apartment? Why are they looking for me?"

He placed Phang down and pushed me into the bathroom.

"Take. A. Shower. I'll order dinner."

I opened my mouth, and he closed the door on my face. I stood staring at the door, placing my hands on it, and counted to three. "You're a big bully!"

It was apparent he hadn't gone far, because he responded, "I love you too, Violet."

Yikes.

12

The day had come and gone, and it was after dinner and Nathan and I were standing awkwardly in my kitchen after having cleaned up. He slid around to the kitchen counter and sat down on a stool, looking at Phang, and then looking at me. She was sitting on his foot. Barnaby was nowhere to be found.

I pressed myself up against my fridge and held my arms across my chest. "So now, what? You're really... staying?"

He reached down to grab Phang and place her in his lap. "Yes." She happily snorted.

"And you're going to constantly watch me? I have zero freedom, zero privacy?" I sighed, stepping around the counter to sit next to him on my own stool. He turned to face me.

"Miss... Violet..." I reached forward to pet Phang on the head. Barnaby appeared out of nowhere and jumped up on the counter, sitting down closest to me, with one eye on Nathan.

"If I were to walk out right now, and call the police, what would you do?"

He placed Phang on the floor, and reached for Barnaby, who strangely enough, let Nathan pet him underneath his chin. "You won't do that, Violet."

I slid my arms onto the counter, and rested my head in them, pushing Barnaby out of the way. "Why am I starting to believe you that this is real?"

"Because it is." He took my hands in his, and we both felt a zing of electricity pass between the two of us. I flinched; he blinked. He turned one of my palms facing up, tracing one of the lines on my palm. I tried to remain stoic, but it was hard. He wouldn't meet my eyes as he did this. He clamped his hand down onto my hand, and my heart began to race. I wasn't sure what he was doing. He whispered something to himself, and as my panic began to rise, he slid his hands away from mine, turning to face the cat again and not me.

"Nathan?" I asked.

He glanced at me, half-smiled, then stood up. "It's late, you should get some rest. We need to wake up very early tomorrow."

"Nathan," I reached out and gently placed my hand on the back of his elbow as he had turned to walk toward my bathroom. He paused, but didn't turn my way.

I let him go.

The next morning when my alarm went off, I didn't want to get out of bed. I knew what was expected of me before I was to do anything else, and that was the meditation. You know, something I used to attempt, off and on for, oh, I don't know, ten or more years, but now it was being demanded of me.

My alarm kept buzzing.

I threw on my robe and stumbled out into the darkness into the bathroom to relieve myself and brush my teeth. It was 5 AM. Who in their right mind would want to be up at 5 AM?

Exiting the bathroom, I heard a smooth voice come at me from the dark living room. "Discipline, young Padawan."

I smothered a yawn with my hand and didn't respond. He had at least set up my living room to make it look more appealing for this ridiculous, now daily, exercise. The coffee table was out of the way and an interesting piece of black fabric with bright, blue glowing runes practically jumping off of said tapestry was draped across the floor. Lovely, plush zabutons were there for us to sit on. Even though I was grouchy, the set-up was calling to me.

"Where did you get all of this stuff from?"

"My car is bigger than it looks."

"Ah."

"Can you make out some of these symbols?" he asked, gesturing to the tapestry. The dim light coming from the kitchen was enough for me to see.

I didn't answer, but gently brushed my fingers over the fabric. "I can feel the heat... does that only happen with certain ink?" It was beautiful.

"Yes and no. There is a certain type of ink that has been secretly used throughout the generations, and it does have its own essence. Usually it won't be warm, though, unless a Rune Master uses it."

"Who wrote this one?"

Small smile. "I did."

"Ah. What is the ink made out of?" I asked, fingering the fabric.

"A special type of blue crystal only found in Germany, mixed with regular inks. More or less." He gestured back to what he had written. "Even so, not everyone can feel the heat."

I continued to trace the runes, feeling that certain tingle I was coming to expect from the ink. "That's eihwaz... elhaz... algiz..."

"The simplest translation is 'so in life, is death'. It's a mantra, I suppose, to remind you of your karma. Words to live by." He paused, then snorted, almost to himself. "I was particularly moody when I made it." He indicated I should sit on one of the zabutons, and continued, "At any rate, it's a good mantra to remember to always do the right thing in our field. Even if it's not the easiest choice."

"This field of…"

"Spreading light."

"Ah, bummer. So I'm not a battle warrior, like a Valkyrie? Or a dragon queen, like Daenerys?"

He ignored my quip and again indicated I should sit down. He began to chant almost immediately, and I could feel it vibrate inside my body, starting at the tips of my fingertips, moving up into my chest then spreading to my feet and head. It made me feel more alive than anything else ever had in my life. I could almost see the little blue runes dancing through my body.

If this had been a cliché scene in a movie, a wave of light would have been seen shooting up through the top of my head, my hair blowing around something terrible. The glow would surround my features, and make me appear beautiful. At least, that's how I felt.

Of course, I had no idea what he was saying, but it was lovely, and it did make the time pass. At some point he had asked me to join him, and I did so without hesitation. I was shocked to find it was over an hour later, and that the sun was starting to rise, peeking through the blinds in my living room.

When I opened my eyes he had already moved into the kitchen. I watched him in the dark, completely calm, energized and at peace. I almost felt like I could float away. He didn't make much noise as he grabbed a coffee pot and filled it with some already-ground coffee that was sitting in a container next to my sink.

The smell of brewing coffee began to waft towards my

nostrils as the water percolated. I didn't want to break this peaceful silence, it was the most wonderful feeling I had ever felt.

He brought a cup of coffee to me after it was finished brewing; neither of us had said anything. He opened up my blinds to allow the sun rising to take place before us. He sat next to me, almost touching me, but still not speaking. Phang and Barnaby walked over to the door, scratching to get onto the porch. I stood up and let them out, and turned back to Nathan.

He was sitting cross-legged with his eyes closed. He looked deep in thought, or maybe in more meditation, I wasn't sure. He was barely moving, save an even rise of his chest with each breath. He reached for his coffee without opening his eyes, and took a sip. His hair danced around his ears, streaked with gold from the rising sun, his peach skin having a rosiness wherever the sun rays hit. He looked otherworldly.

I felt the energy start rising again, and rather than panicking this time, I chose to be at ease with it. My breath caught; and instead of repeatedly being shocked, I felt a unique, indescribable type of warmth spread into my very bloodstream. It was as intoxicating as a first kiss, but somehow even more elevated than that—this seemed inter-dimensional.

As I watched him, I realized I felt like I was in love with him. I cocked my head to the side in such wonder. How unusual to have such strong feelings for a stranger. I had read about such things, of course; love at first sight, twin flames, soul mates.

There was no other way I could define it.

I had somehow known this man before. And whether or not I had ever really believed a before had taken place, didn't matter; the feeling of familiarity was *so* strong.

I was surprised he couldn't feel it, too.

As I continued to stare at Nathan, I realized he had been chanting under his breath. He let out a slow exhale. I sat back down, this time blocking the sun and facing him.

I reached out my hands towards his hands, which were facing upwards. I had no idea why I felt compelled to do this, but even so, there I was with my hands hovering above his, simply feeling the energy. I felt almost lifetimes of communication through these waves between us; it was like we were trees connected by an underground root system. It didn't even matter which tree we were separately; what mattered more was that we were together. United.

These crazy thoughts flooded my mind.

He opened his eyes and his breathing changed.

I wondered if that meant he *did* feel it. Perhaps he was trying *not* to feel it, because I was his current assignment and it was forbidden. Perhaps it had nothing to do with this paranormal secret ops thing we had going on, and maybe, just as a human, he didn't want to connect.

He looked down at our hands, unable to move. From deep within me, I heard the runic chants about life and death. It was so damn loud, it was as if the angels themselves were shouting at me. Once it quieted down, the hum remained.

He opened his mouth as if to say my name, but no sound came out.

I dropped my hands into his with curiosity more than anything; I wasn't worried about what any of it really meant, or if it really made a difference. The steady reverberation of dancing fireflies filled my body. I could almost see the light inside us connecting. I tried to remain objective and sensible, but it was hard. His eyes met mine.

And then…

And then, the spell broke. I'm not sure if my mind strayed half a second to something else, or if it was him, but the moment ended. He removed his hands from mine and placed them back into his own lap.

Still, neither of us spoke.

I lied down on the floor next to him, resting my head on one of the cushions, facing the ceiling.

Still, neither of us spoke.

Phang came back inside, snorting happily. She sat in Nathan's lap. I rolled onto my side, and Barnaby came in, looking Nathan over with his one eye.

I let out a long sigh, and then our silence was broken, too.

Nathan reached over to the coffee table, grabbed his computer, a second computer I had never seen before, and a folder full of paperwork.

In the quiet of the new morning, I softy said, "Reporting to duty, Sir."

***

Each day was to begin at 5 AM with meditation. Nathan's belief was that a weak mind made for a weak body. After meditation, I was supposed to have breakfast if I was hungry. At 7 AM, I was to physically train at a local dojo his *employer* had rented out. (Whomever that was.) Nathan would teach me mixed martial arts, and by 9 AM I was allowed to work my regular job.

During any breaks during the day, I was to study runic theory; learn to translate them, how to speak them, how to write them.

After dinner, I was supposed to study any other matter of transpersonal psychology, metaphysical studies, etc. I was allowed to work out in addition to the MMA in the morning; I could still take my yoga classes, or run, or become a gym rat if I wanted. It was nice to know I had options.

Oh, so not true. I felt totally trapped.

This was the general order of how my life was supposed to work. Apparently nobody expected it to unfold a hundred percent smoothly, as there were so many unaccounted factors that could exist within this time-consuming schedule; namely, having a life outside of this fantasy world that was being created for me.

Nathan was to accompany me until my first mission was complete. After that, he would move on to his next apprentice while I would be assigned a liaison. From there, I would be given two to three missions a year, usually local to my area. If needed, another person of my caliber would join me, or I him/her for a mission. Regardless if I had another Jedi with me, I would be assigned *Mission Support*. A therapist was also assigned to me, one who was in the know. That way, when I talked about all this crazy shit, she or he wouldn't throw away the key to my straight jacket.

Many times I asked Nathan why that parchment paper with the written runes had alerted him to the fact that *I* was supposedly the person he was supposed to train, but he ignored the question every time I brought it up. I thought an explanation would be freeing, but he wouldn't budge. I had to assume that this was one of many things that I would never get an answer about.

I couldn't believe how well-refined this whole thing was, or how far reaching it seemed. It spanned across the globe. It either had to be government-sponsored, or some sort of rogue-black-ops-anti-government group. It was anxiety inducing to think that some places may refer to us as terrorists—even my own country for all I knew.

Why was I so quick to let this happen, to surrender my life for this cause I knew so little about? I wondered this.

Often.

I didn't think I was working for the 'bad' guy because my only job was to 'spread light', as Nathan had said. If light was more or less unconditional love, then there was no way it could be perceived as negative or harmful.

I hoped so anyway.

It was all so very fantastical, and I couldn't wait to meet with my therapist as soon as possible. I found it also probable, though, that this therapist was hired to further brainwash me, which I knew I'd have no problem accusing him or her of such. What really unnerved me, though, was the fact that I couldn't meet with any of these people I was hearing about until the first mission was complete.

Once a close friend or family member was cleared in his/her background check, I was allowed to tell them whatever I felt comfortable with, while leaving major details out.

Apparently the police department knew who Nathan *really* was, or mostly who he really was, because once they had cleared his name in Alyssa's murder, he began to work with them to find out her murderer. Only a few people in the department had clearance about the inner details. Some knew absolutely nothing. Jason's knowledge was only that Nathan was a good guy, so I wondered what he would think when he realized I was working with him. It made me feel a little bit bitter.

I was going to tell Elizabeth, Sam, and Layla, of course. And Jason. Other than that, I figured nobody else needed to know, and I would just have to figure out how to cover it up on an as-needed basis.

Nathan warned me more Scouts would be appearing as my abilities grew. He told me that this was my mission; once the Scouts had grown in big enough numbers, it was up to me to eradicate them.

He did not tell me how. He did not tell me what Scouts did, or who they were, or why they existed.

Sundays were supposed to be my "off" days, and Saturdays were the day for the largest *physical* exertion. I felt like I was training for a marathon. Beyond the MMA, I was to cardio myself into a coma. Nathan was to be with me at all times to protect me, until I could protect myself. This happened to be either when he deemed it so, or when the mission was complete.

Whichever came first.

Assuming I didn't fail.

By getting us both killed.

13

After a late breakfast, Nathan brought me to the dojo. There was a small, glass enclosed room inside of the dojo that housed regular work-out equipment. Nathan told me I could use it at my leisure. He also informed me he would be purchasing me a wetsuit so I could swim in one of the lakes. I could not swim at all. He told me he would teach me.

I did not understand why he was training me to become the Incredible Hulk.

"While you can be nothing without mental strength, you need a strong body to *grow* your mind."

I was tired of his psychobabble.

"Are we fighting today or not, Obi-Wan?" I tiredly asked.

He raised an eyebrow. "Anxious to start?"

Hm. Nathan didn't really seem ready to train me. I guess for him that was supposed to begin on Monday. He was a man who followed the rules, that was for sure.

"We can do some light training today, I suppose, if you really want. Do you know how to dance at all?"

I took my bag off of my shoulders and placed it on a chair that was lining the wall of the dojo. "Dance? No. I've never thought of myself as having grace or rhythm, to be honest. Aren't those things needed to dance?"

He kicked off his shoes and nodded I should do the same. Barefoot on the mat after bowing to one another, in the quiet and darkness of the dojo, he reached out his hands and gently grabbed my wrists. He kept my arms in the air as he instructed me to move my feet forwards and backwards without looking.

I found this incredibly frustrating and didn't see what this simple movement had to do with karate chops. Plus, with him that close to me...

He tried to diffuse the tension with some teasing, but it didn't help.

"I'm sorry, Violet, I haven't prepared our weekly sessions yet, so I'm ill equipped to properly train you today."

I took my hands back from him and placed them on my hips. "Shameful." He opened his mouth to respond, then realized I was joking. "Nathan, it's not your fault I have no coordination or balance. And don't even remind me I'm a yogi—I get it. I'm a conundrum. Grace is nowhere found in my name, trust me."

"And if you believe that, you'll always struggle," he said quietly.

"Touché." I reached back to give him my hands, feeling hopeful. "Maybe you could let me look at my feet at least?"

He shook his head. "Doesn't work that way. Don't worry. I'll come up with something that will work for you." I dropped my hands back to my sides.

"Or else we fail."

"Or else we fail." He smiled.

We put our shoes on and headed towards the entrance. My phone rang; it was Elizabeth. Nathan nodded that it was fine to take the call.

"Sooooo… you literally didn't make it to yoga last night."

I stood with my back to the dojo entrance as Nathan stepped out onto the walkway. "No," I sighed. "I told you I wasn't going to make it."

"Hmmm," said Elizabeth. "Guess who also wasn't there." She started to sound smug. "That guy Nathan, remember him? He seemed to be popping up all over the place and then, POOF—he disappeared last week, kind of like you."

Oh, shit. I realized that she was on to me, and I had a sneaking suspicion she was somewhere nearby watching me stand in front of the dojo with Nathan. I started scanning the parking lot to see if I could find her car.

I motioned for Nathan to come closer to me. He walked over with a curious expression on his face. I covered the mouthpiece and whispered, "Elizabeth knows we've been together! I think she sees us now! What the hell do I do?"

Nathan had a look of irritation cross his face as he pulled his hands out of his pockets. He swore under his breath.

"What's that, Vi?" asked Elizabeth sweetly. "It's like you're covering the mouthpiece and I can't hear you."

"Oh, no, I was just blocking a sneeze."

Dammit. She knew I was lying.

Nathan drew a line across his neck; I took that to mean to get off the phone.

"E, it's not really a good time for me to talk. Can I call you back this afternoon to get tonight sorted?"

She didn't even try to hide her discontent. "Ugh. Fine, Violet. Call me later so we know when we all can meet with— *you*—okay?"

I swallowed. "Okay," was all I could muster.

When I slid my phone back into my bag, Nathan came up next to me and held my hand. "What are you doing?" I hissed.

"Violet," he started, not letting go of my hand, "I don't think there is any other way around this. Clearing your friends isn't really a priority of Headquarters, so I think the easiest solution is to..."

My eyes became rounded and full; I was no longer fighting his hand-holding, but rather limply resting my hand in his. "Is to what?"

He sharply breathed in, held his breath for a moment, and then rushed out, "Is to pretend we're dating. Just for a few days until you can tell them the truth, that is, whatever truth you want to tell them."

And there it was. Now I was pretend-dating this guy, this stranger I'd spent every waking hour with during the past week, this man who I loved on some cellular level that I couldn't even begin to understand, this man who I was undeniably attracted to on the most basic level, this man who infuriated me because he was basically controlling my every move, this man who was taking up my closet space… Yeet, it was complicated.

"Are we being watched?"

"I believe so. I detect her energy behind us."

"So now that you're my boyfriend, you really aren't going to leave me alone, are you?" I snorted. "You've just weaseled your way into every damn thing I do."

"Violet, you're forgetting a few things. One, it's my job. Two, you actually like me and don't mind spending time with me."

His face reminded me of Toothless the dragon attempting a smile for Hiccup the Horrendous. It was quirky and cute and I wanted to behead him for it. He tilted my face up to look at his, but he had also taken another step back to protect himself, sensing my animosity. I grated my teeth. "Stop being cocky. I think it's the other way around. You can't seem to get enough of *me*."

I moved to head towards the car, and he fell in step with me in an easy gait, gently placing an arm over my shoulders. "The fairer sex does cause problems, you know."

"Man's inability to deal with that thing in their pants?

Definitely not *my* fault because I'm a woman."

Laughter continued to erupt from him.

"I hadn't intended that to be so funny," I said stiffly. I couldn't believe he was actually laughing at all of this. It was most definitely not funny in any way, shape or form.

We were at his car, and he stood next to my door, blocking me. "You know, I really do wish..." He trailed off, and opened the car door for me.

I refused to get into the car without him finishing his thought. "You wish *what*?"

He clenched his jaw, but said with a smile, "I wish you weren't so obstinate."

"That's not what you were going to say."

"Like now."

"Another impasse."

"Not at all." He swooped in and gave me a quick kiss on my forehead. I looked daggers at him, especially because my breath had caught at the suddenness of it. Because, you know, he was hot as hell.

"God dammit, Nathan," I swore. I was pretty sure he knew that I was just one small misstep away from being completely enamored by him. If it wasn't for my obstinacy and raging temper, I wouldn't be able to fend off my attraction to him. The worst part of it was well, let's be honest. There were too many to count at that point.

He wasn't laughing anymore as he gently shoved me into the car.

Once inside, I wouldn't look at him.

"Miss Moore, if I overstepped my boundaries, please let me know," he said from his side of the car before placing the car into gear.

I looked out the window as he drove off. "It's Miss Moore again, is it?"

He let out a loud sigh and muttered something under his

breath.

"Where are we going?" I asked, ignoring whatever he had said.

"I thought maybe you'd want to go home and eat something. I'll make us lunch."

"When did you have all this time to buy us food?" I couldn't help myself. I swear to God he was always with me, yet somehow my fridge was stocked and I was well-fed.

"While you sleep," he said softly.

"Jeez. Are you a freaking vampire?"

"No. I usually just need about six hours of sleep to function. Sometimes just five," he cheerfully chirped as he put on his blinker.

I finally looked at him. "You're crazy as hell, you know that, right?"

He ignored me, and after a few minutes said, "We're being followed."

"By whom? Friends or Scouts?"

"Neither. Well, I guess friend. It's Dunham."

"Jason?" I sat up straighter and was about to look back when Nathan stopped me.

"Don't look back. I'm not sure if he's watching us because of your friends, or if he needs to speak with me."

"I hope he didn't see you kiss me."

"Ha! Why is that?" He glanced at me, half-amused, half-annoyed.

I looked back out the window. I didn't answer and simply closed my eyes.

He cleared his throat. "I'm still pulling into your complex but be prepared for whatever. I'm not sure which route I'm going to need to go yet. Just follow my lead."

"Fine. My life doesn't matter anymore. Whatever you want," I said without emotion.

"Violet... It won't always be this hard."

"Don't call me Violet."

He again started muttering under his breath. He pulled into the parking lot and got out before me, leaving me in the car to wait. Jason got out of his patrol car, and took Nathan aside to speak with him.

I watched Jason's face to try and discern what they were talking about. It was serious, whatever it was. At one point he glanced at me with raised eyebrows, and I could tell they were arguing. Jason put his hand on his belt, which didn't go unnoticed by Nathan. I figured it was probably a natural defense mechanism, even though nobody was in danger.

Well, except the both of them.

I'd had enough.

I got out of the car. "Look—I know you guys are talking about me, and I don't appreciate it. Nathan, *you don't speak for me.* Jason, you can ask me any damn thing you want, and Nathan's just going to have to deal with the repercussions." I was furious, I had my arms wrapped so tightly around myself I was leaving behind red marks on my skin.

"If you have something to say, either of you, do it now. Because otherwise I'd like to go inside and eat something."

I saw Jason's adam's apple move, Nathan's lips pressed together into a flat line. His eyes were flashing.

"You're working with him?" Jason finally asked.

"Yes. Anything else?"

"You were… drafted?" Jason continued, trying to come up with the right words to describe what was going on.

"Yes."

"Does anyone else know?"

"Not yet," interrupted Nathan. "I'm waiting for things to clear from the office. Which, because of this, we're putting on a show for her closest friends. Liz—"

"Yeah, Elizabeth is suspicious and I'm pretty sure saw us outside of the dojo Nathan's *employer* is renting so he can teach me martial arts and—"

"Martial Arts! Is she in the field then?!" Jason interrupted, growling in Nathan's direction.

I opened my mouth to continue, startled at the ferocity of Jason's demeanor.

Nathan spoke again, "Yes, she's in the field, but she will be fully trained—"

"Look, Nathan, no more deaths! No injuries! *Nothing* can happen to Violet—"

"Don't you think I know that?" he hissed. "It was *my* sister, after all, who was victim to this Darkness—"

"Darkness!," Jason scoffed. "I don't care what nonsense you call it, I'm in the real world, buddy, and it was murder by a bludgeoning to the head! You can call that all the woo-woo you want, but—"

"Wait, what? Alyssa was *bludgeoned* to death?! Is my life in real danger here?"

"Yes."

"No."

The men glared at one another and I just stood there, like a naive and helpless child.

"Nathan," I managed to get out, turning his direction.

He wouldn't look at me.

"Nothing is going to happen to Violet. I will protect her."

"Like you protected Alyssa?"

"It wasn't my job to protect her, that wasn't my assignment, and—"

"Everything was fine until you showed up," growled Jason.

"That's not true," Nathan responded stubbornly. "I've been called because things were *not* fine. How not fine, you ask? That's why it's trickling into *your* damn jurisdiction. If this area weren't so prone to—prone to negativity—none of this would be happening."

"There is nothing wrong with the people of this town."

I had to stifle a laugh at that one. I had plenty to say about the people of this town. Their priorities usually were a little skewed, but who was I to judge? I certainly wouldn't defend their objects of desire, though.

Jason turned to me, as if remembering I was there. "Violet —I know you feel you have no say, but I bet there's a way I could get you out of this. You don't have to do this."

"That's not how this works, Jason," Nathan bitterly muttered.

For the first time, I was starting to feel good about my position. I was scared shitless, absolutely clueless, but, always one to err on the side of humor, I gave Jason a wicked grin. "Nah, it's alright. He's training me to be a Jedi or some shit."

All I had to do was find a way to reclaim my power with my new skillset. Just Skywalker my way to the end. I could do that.

I saw a hint of a smile touch Nathan's lips as he looked away. Jason rolled his eyes and he took a step closer to me. "Alright, Vi. I'll support you. But know this—both of you—I may be able to help you in ways that Nathan can't. So if you ever need me and what I can offer over *him*… you know how to find me."

I could sense a change in Nathan's stance. I supposed what Jason was saying was true, and Nathan wasn't okay with that.

Interesting.

Not to mention, Jason had the local law and police help on his side. I still wasn't sure who my employer was. It must be legitimate though, I thought, since Jason wasn't questioning this whole secretive rubbish.

Jason hesitatingly put his hands on my shoulders and I looked up at him, stubbornness etched into the cracks of my face. Nathan stiffened beside me, but still wouldn't turn towards us. "What?" I asked defiantly.

He took a step back and shook his head, some sort of thoughts infiltrating his mind. "I guess I'll see you tonight."

Nathan finally looked back towards Jason, and glanced at me. "Right now we're pretending to be a couple." Nathan put his arm around me, almost challenging Jason.

Jason outwardly groaned, but didn't take the bait. "Fine. I'll see you tonight," he repeated, then walked back to his car, backed up, and left the parking lot.

Nathan still had his arm around me as we looked in the direction of Jason's receding car. "You can remove your arm."

"I don't want to."

Nathan could be stubborn, too.

14

Vigil Time.

I was nervous as hell. I wasn't sure how I was going to behave around my friends with Nathan at my side. I didn't know how to answer their probing eyes, with these lies wrapped tightly around my body like that. I didn't know how to respond to Jason in the crowd, either.

Apparently before I stepped out of the car Jason told Nathan that they had a suspect in custody. The suspect was a supposed "homeless" person who had asked Alyssa for help when she was outside of her studio. When the homeless man was denied, he purportedly hit Alyssa over the head, panicked and hid her body in the woods behind the studio.

At least, this is what the police were probably going to tell the news outlets.

On the inside, we knew that wasn't exactly the case. Nathan suspected it was a Scout looking for confirmation of who the next apprentice was. Alyssa was simply in the wrong place at the wrong time, and for whatever reason, the exchange had turned deadly.

In a way, I was responsible for Nathan's sister's death.
Great.
I also knew the energy community wasn't going to accept

that as an answer, and I warned Nathan about that. I planned on telling Jason, too, that they were going to have trouble believing the official story.

I had no idea what Alyssa's wife would think, or Rebecca. But I'm sure they were both happy to be cleared for murder.

It had been a crazy week in our little town.

And now I had to walk into this crowd of people, where a fair chunk knew me, or at least recognized me, and walk into it with Nathan's hand. Yup. I was going to have another mental breakdown.

"Vi!" yelled Layla from a light pole that was in the middle of the parking lot. "Nathan," she said, with a knowing look in her eye and sound in her voice as she slapped him a 'hi' on his back.

He went oof, looked at me, and smiled at Lay. "Hi... Layla, is it?"

"Yeah! And hey, so you know, Sam and I don't care about being in the dark about y'all. It's just E who's bitter about it."

I looked at Nathan again with a slight smile. I knew he wasn't used to speaking in such a relaxed manner with people he didn't know very well. However, he looked delighted. What an oddball.

"Speak of the devil," said Layla, as Sam and Elizabeth walked up.

When they got there, I cleared my throat, "I know everybody already knows everybody, but let's get the formalities out of the way. Sam, E, Nathan. He and I are dating now and there's nothing more to say. Okay? Okay."

He casually put his arm over my shoulder, said hi to them and whispered in my ear, "You're fine, Violet. Breathe."

I exhaled, but Elizabeth was carefully watching me. Her eyes slightly narrowed, as if something wasn't adding up quite right. Layla was the chillest person I knew—she didn't care if you were smoking her or not; it wasn't her problem.

Sam was sort of oblivious and ditzy and took everything at face value. Elizabeth was smart and calculating. I knew there'd be hell to pay once she found out the truth.

I shrugged at her.

"Alright, guys, the vigil candles are near the front of the studio. Friday morning I spoke with Lady Light from *Soul's Breath* and she told me she was supplying them for everyone."

Elizabeth smirked when I shot an uneasy glance at her. Nathan just tightened his hold on me, because, after all, it had been his idea to go to the meditation there on Thursday night. Obviously Lady Light had mentioned how I had brought a gentleman friend to her studio. I hadn't introduced him as my anything there, we'd just sat down and done the class.

And the next day we were an item?

He leaned in again, saying just as softly, "Breathe." My tense body loosened a bit.

I warily let Elizabeth lead us in the direction of the tables, hoping I wouldn't actually be getting one from Lady Light herself. Luckily, Layla did a quick headcount of everyone, and shouted (as it was starting to get loud—I guess nobody had anything to do on a Saturday evening), "I'll get everyone's lights!"

Elizabeth blatantly bit the inside of her cheek. She had wanted to catch me! I narrowed my eyes at her; she feigned innocence. I weaseled my out of Nathan's grip leaving him with Sam. I grabbed Elizabeth's hand and pulled her to the sidelines of the crowd up a level on the curb.

"Alright, let's have it out."

"*Why* didn't you tell me you were seeing this guy?!"

I saw Nathan's head in the crowd, pretending to listen to Sam but obviously worried about me. "It's complicated."

"Complicated?" She glared at me. "'Hey, E, remember that guy we met at the yoga studio? Yeah, well he and I have spent all week together. We even went to a meditation together'. You know I would have wanted to go to that meditation." She sounded a bit hurt.

Just then, Jason started to head over to us. Oh, God, what a nightmare. She followed my line of vision. "And, not only that! What is up with Sergeant Sexy being up your ass, too? It's like you're all in cahoots!"

Wow. Elizabeth was good. I smiled crookedly at her.

Luckily for me, Jason was called to attention by someone else before he could make it all the way to us. An obvious, huge sigh of relief escaped my lips. I didn't even pretend to hide it.

She gave me this crazed look, pursed her lips and threw her hands up in the air. "Alright, Violet, whatever, you can have them both and freeze me out. I've got my eyes on some new candy, anyway." I followed *her* line of vision, and met with.. *Damien?* No way… She gave me a look that read 'as if', so I kept looking into the crowd. A guy had just walked up to Sam, Layla and Nathan.

He was about as tall as Nathan, and slightly more built, and equally good looking from a distance. His eyes seemed a lot darker than Nathan's, though. I got a slightly 'eh' vibe from him from across the way. "That guy?"

"That guy. His name is Jared. He just moved here because his job relocated near the airport. He wanted to be closer to work and he'd heard good things about the community."

Hmm... I twirled my mermaid puke hair strand in my fingers. I wasn't buying it. Nathan was giving off some subtle vibes, too, that he was uncomfortable. I wonder if he knew this guy, if they had crossed paths before.

Elizabeth reached her hands in the air to say hi to him and jumped back onto the ground. Over everyone's heads, he made eye contact with me. It was like a rolling fire flashed in his eyes; it scared the hell out of me. As I slightly stumbled forwards due to the intensity of the gaze, Nathan saw my response. Obviously concerned, he started to make his way to me, but Jason showed up at my side first.

"Hey—are you okay?"

I swallowed hard as he caught me and pulled me back onto the sidewalk. He still had his hands on me as Nathan found himself at the curb. Nathan was slightly shorter than me from this perspective. He reached out to take me from Jason as if it was the most natural thing in the world, and Jason visibly hesitated. I saw, literally saw the energetic tension between them and I took another step backwards. "Guys," I said, with my palms facing outwards at them, waving a giant white flag their way.

Nathan stepped up to join us, hands clenched at his sides. Jason's were at his waist. I cleared my throat so they would stop this glare-off battle. Nathan turned first.

"Yes. I see you recognized right away that Jared is trouble."

Jason looked out to my group and saw the man standing there talking to an animated Elizabeth. It was evident, though, that he was watching *us* out of the corner of us eye.

"That guy?"

Nathan looked back at him, then towards me and Jason. "Yeah, that guy. He's not a bad guy, per se, but he's not really a good guy, either."

Jason joked, "Anything I can arrest him for?"

"No."

"Is he going to make y'all's job harder?"

"Possibly."

Just then Lady Light and Tricia Tanaka from another bodywork studio started to speak through a loud speaker to get the vigil started. Nathan handed me my candle, and their business names were beautifully adorning the paper that the candles were perched on. I *knew* it.

I rolled my eyes at Nathan and he smiled.

"Gotta go," Jason quickly disappeared into the crowd to get back into rank with the rest of the police officers minding the area. There were several TV stations present as well.

"Miss Moore," Nathan extended his arm.

"Mr. Murphy," I responded as I took it.

We stepped back into the crowd.

***

Somehow the vigil had turned into a major marketing scheme, indeed. I hadn't noticed it when we'd first shown up, but by the edge of one side of the parking lot, tents were set up. *Soul's Breath* and some of the other studios and healers were offering services right there, while other businesses were hawking their goods. I couldn't believe it.

There was a soap maker in one tent, some jewelry in another.

It was pretty chilly, so there was even a preplanned fire pit.

Lady Light had handed the microphone over to the Police Chief who was currently making a statement before the vigil. As planned, he told everyone, as well as the local news, what the official story was, and that the perpetrator was arrested. You could see Lady Light and Tricia pass a knowing look between them, like they knew better than to eat the crap that was being spoon-fed to them. Some, however, cheered in the crowd, happy the murderer had been caught.

Once the chief stepped down, Lady Light led everyone in a quick prayer for Alyssa's studio, as well as her life. The crowd buzzed in somber prayer, Alyssa's studio's interior still eerily lit in the fading light of the day. Tricia started to sing some sappy song with a ukulele player next to her.

Jared was cordial to me when I stepped up to the group, but I certainly never wanted to be alone with the guy. Elizabeth had her hand on his arm the whole time, and every now and then, I could sense him looking in my direction. I never caught him, though. It seemed like he had a second, invisible head constantly focused on me.

Sam, forever the party girl, started to get the crowd to sway and dance with the ukulele, and somehow or another, it was turning into a dance party for the spiritual sect. I couldn't wait to get out of there.

The groups were starting to split up; some still dancing, some visiting the tents, others just chatting. The impromptu dance floor was nearest to the studio. Nathan leaned into me, "Want to dance?"

"Ha!" I exclaimed, looking up at him in surprise. He blew out our candles and stuffed them into his pocket after they'd gone out. He didn't respond to me, but started to pull me out onto the dance area. I started to feel a wave of anxiety begin to plague me. What the hell was he doing? Hadn't we already failed at this?

The ukulele—and now keyboard—where did that come from?—sang a sweet, sad tune, drifting over the parking lot. He pulled me close, and I could feel his breath on my ear. I had no idea why we were dancing. I wasn't sure he did either. Everything around us turned dark, and I could only hear the music in the distance. I could smell a slightly earthy scent mixed with ginger overtones, and could feel the rough texture of his shirt against my neck. And then I felt the vibration between us again, feeling myself calmed by the ebb and flow this time rather than shocked by it. I knew he was feeling it too by the change of his breathing.

He wasn't going to deny me this time.

I pulled back and made him look at me, totally mystified by the whole thing. "What the hell *is* this?"

He looked down at me, eyes full of sadness and confusion, as if he didn't quite understand what was between us, either. I understood the confusion, but the sadness made zero sense to me. What could he possibly be sad about?

The next thing I knew, his hands were in my hair, brushing

my hair out along my shoulders.

A small, shake of his head was all I needed to know. About everything.

"Violet," he breathed softly.

And the spell was broken, yet again. The song had ended, and the ukulele was now playing something upbeat. "It's fine," I said, shaking the remaining energy tendrils off, mustering strength from within. "It's fine. Whatever. Come on, I think you've done enough convincing tonight. I'm ready to go home and lose myself in *Nightmare Before Christmas*."

"Violet," he started, but I disappeared into the crowd.

I pulled my full-length sweater tightly around my body. I didn't turn to see if Nathan was following me or not. I bumped into a few people as I kept walking to his car; Layla and Sam being two of them.

Layla asked if I was alright, Sam leaning in, "He really is a good-looking guy, yeah?"

"Yeah," I murmured to Sam, and I nodded at Layla. Elizabeth was nowhere to be seen.

"I think I'm—we're—headed home now." Sam raised an eyebrow and Layla furrowed her brows.

Layla mortified, asked, "He's not *living* with you, is he?" at the same time Sam inquired if hot apple cider would make us stay longer.

I laughed in response to both of them.

"I'll see you guys later."

They nodded at me, and I continued on, still not looking for Nathan. I was afraid I was going to run into Jason—I didn't want to see him, either.

Naturally, I tripped over Jared.

Elizabeth was still nowhere to be seen. And seeing as I didn't have Jared's entire story, I was extremely uncomfortable.

"Enjoying yourself?" he asked in a deep tenor, widening

his smile at my discomfort.

"Yes, it was lovely," I quietly intoned, hoping I could just brush past him. He didn't move.

"It was nice meeting you, Miss Moore."

I looked up quickly, searching his eyes. "Miss... Miss Moore? You're a—"

"Yes, of course I'll be good to your Elizabeth."

She had appeared out of nowhere. I got lost in Jared's teeth; they were perfectly white and perfectly even. They stood out in contrast to his deeply tanned, leathery looking-skin. Wherever he had just come from, it had to have been somewhere warm and full of sunshine.

"Oh, hey, Vi, you leaving already?" Elizabeth asked sweetly.

I cleared my throat. "Actually, I've just decided to stay."

Jared's smile deepened.

Nathan appeared at my side, and I could feel, more than anything, that his eyes must have been that steel color again, slicing at Jared's smile like a sword's blade. Jared didn't flinch.

"Your girl was just saying how she changed her mind about leaving. Just so she could keep hanging out with us."

This was not lost on Elizabeth although she feigned ignorance. She caught my eye, and I tried to gesture that I would explain later.

"Actually, I just realized how tired I am after all," I purred at Nathan, grabbing his hand and placing my other hand on his stomach to indicate closeness. His muscles tightened at the unexpected touch. "Let's go home."

"Later," Elizabeth called, slightly miffed. Jared was so arrogant he couldn't tell that she was on to him.

***

We hadn't spoken much on the way home. I could tell he wanted to say something, or reach out to me, but I made it clear that I didn't want to be bothered.

Once we got inside, even though it was fairly early, I said, "I think I'm just going to turn in for the night and see you tomorrow for meditation and training. Is there anything you need?" I asked, hanging my jacket up on the wall and unraveling my scarf around my neck.

He stood on the inside of my door, looking lost. And young. Painfully young. "I think I'm going to go back out... And... And remember, you can take tomorrow off."

I blinked. "What? You're not going to look for Jared, are you? Or more Scouts?"

He ran his hand through his hair, messing up the curls around his ears. I was starting to get concerned.

"No, Vi... Miss Moo-... Violet. I'm not going to look for trouble, I promise."

"I'll go with you, then," I started to wrap my scarf back around my neck. It wasn't that I didn't trust him; I was more afraid for him. I didn't recognize this mood and I didn't like it. It was distracted and seemed a little careless.

"No, I need you to stay here. It's safe here."

"But—"

"It's okay. I promise."

"When will you be back?"

He didn't answer me but said, "Call me if you need me."

"Nathan, I don't understand. Don't leave, or let me come with you."

He looked at me almost pleadingly.

"I... Alright, just, whatever you're doing, please be careful, okay?"

I awkwardly reached out and placed my hand on his shoulder. He nodded distractedly, then turned around and walked out.

15

It was around midnight when he came home. I hadn't been able to rest while he was gone, and now that he was home, I just listened. About fifteen minutes or so after I'd heard the door close, the only remaining sound I could hear was a light snore coming from the living room.

I crept out of my room, leaving Phang asleep on her back, snorting. Barnaby awakened with his watchful eye as I disappeared from his view. The cat was starting to look like a Pirate; I supposed I should get him a patch.

I peeked around the corner and saw that Nathan was, in fact, asleep. He was making noises, too, but I couldn't quite make out what he was saying. I had a tank top on and flannel PJ bottoms; he was wearing his harem pants and no shirt. He hadn't closed the blinds all the way and the moonlight lit up his chest and tousled hair in his face. His lips were slightly parted.

My chest and throat tightened; he looked so peaceful. A small groan emitted from his mouth, and there was no mistaking it—he said my name.

With goosebumps spread across my flesh, I crept closer, only a few feet away from him. Since it wasn't covered, I noticed the rest of his tattoo for the first time. I realized it was crudely done in the same blue ink that the runes were written in. The tattoo seemed to include the adage he seemed so obsessed with—*so in life, is death.*

I also noticed platinum-colored ring around his neck that appeared to have the same transcription, along with what I recognized as a triskelion symbol. I wasn't sure why he didn't wear it on one of his fingers.

Just then, his eyes burst open and he took a deep breath in.

Crap. I stood there before him, like a ghost, and he appeared startled. But his eyes re-closed and he fell back asleep, so I didn't think he had seen me. Just then Barnaby chose to walk into the room with a mew. I walked over to him, grabbed him, shushed him and put him back onto my bed.

I did not set my alarm for meditation after all.

***

It was around 10 AM when I finally wandered out of my bedroom. I had stayed in bed, reading and dozing off and on. I couldn't ignore Phang anymore, so I scooped her up after brushing my teeth, adorned my feet with slippers, and shuffled into the hallway, heading to the door to let her go outside to use the restroom.

I opened the door and a huge burst of wind came in. Realizing it was actually quite cold, I turned back inside the house to grab a jacket. Nathan was nowhere to be seen.

I covered up, opened the door again, and headed down the stairs. I took Phang off to the left of the building into the woods for her to do her business, and Nathan pulled up with his bicycle. He attached it back to his car before heading over to me with two coffees in his hands.

"Good morning," he said, handing me one of the coffees.

"Thank you."

We both then spoke at the same time. "I'm sorry I left last night, I shouldn't have done that. But I was completely thrown from seeing Jared. And then of course, there's the matter of us."

I said, "Let's just forget about everything that happened yesterday and just move forward with training. That's what this is all about anyway, right?"

"Violet... You may want to ignore it, but I don't think that's a good idea."

"Well, why not?" I asked, thrusting out my chin. He took the coffee back so I could reach down to pick up Phang's poop. We walked over to the trash bin to throw the poop bag away, and then he gave the coffee back to me. I sipped it, looking at him expectantly.

"I contacted some people last night when I was out, trying to get some answers about this energy between us."

I took the bait. "And?"

We walked up my stairs, and he held the door open for me.

"The general consensus was that we shouldn't ignore it. But nobody had anything worthwhile to say about it, either. Everything is mostly hearsay. Even in these circles, it's pretty rare."

I put my coffee on the counter.

"So what are we supposed to do with that?"

"I don't know. It doesn't really change anything, as far as I know. I mean... you're my new apprentice. I train you, and then..."

"You leave." I sighed. "I know."

I started to get excited, though. If I could just push the attraction down, and look at the energy only, without judgment, then maybe we could power through it. "Last night after you came home, and I was watching you—oh yeah, you'll have to tell me about the tattoo—and anyway, the feeling that kind of washed over me was like how a mother might feel for her child... Maybe I was your mother in a past life?"

Yup. Totally grasping at straws here.

He sipped his coffee. "Do you believe in past lives?"

"I don't know. I mean, I know there are people who *do* believe in them, and these feelings we have are sort of inexplicable. And confusing. And I think if we just leave them as what they are, probably something in some past timeline or something... then we don't have to worry about it now, right?" My argument came up weak. "I guess what I mean to say is, there's no reason to think we need to explore it 'now', just because it exists."

Even as I said it, I could feel the acute ache start in my chest. If that part was true, I apparently didn't believe it. But, logically, I tried to tell myself that that could be because I was physically attracted to him. But so was every woman who met him!

He searched my face, trying to figure out if I believed what I was saying. He dragged his hands through his hair, sighed and said, "Well okay. I think we need to keep an open dialogue about all this, so we don't accidentally blur the lines. We keep it strictly professional, because..."

"Because that's what we're supposed to do."

"And when I'm done training you, and the mission is complete, I move on."

"In the interim, though, I don't see any harm in doing more research about it? It's pretty wild, right?" I asked tentatively, trying to hold a steady face so he couldn't see past my farce.

Just then my phone beeped. Nathan looked down at it, putting on what I believed was an equally brave face. It didn't appear he was totally buying into what we were rallying, either.

At least I knew we were on the same page, though. It didn't matter what it was, because, at least this go around, we wouldn't be together. Our lives wouldn't allow it. And that was fine. Maybe every life we just needed to fulfill a relationship of some sort, and this time it was this. If different lives existed. If they mattered, though, because we were here, now, and man did I really feel—.

Nathan handed me my phone. "It's Jason."

He turned and walked into the other room.

"He wants to meet me for lunch. Is that okay?"

"Yeah, of course. You're supposed to have Sundays off anyway, remember? And you'll be safe enough with him." He gave a tight smile, in spite of himself.

"Well… okay… I mean, I don't mind doing work when I'm home, though."

"Go out. Have some fun."

"What about you? Don't you deserve some fun? Your life can't possibly just be about work."

"I'll be fine. I'm not new to this, you know. I'm used to being alone. The apprentice still has to live her or his life. People can even be married with kids, although that usually isn't the case." He paused, almost like he'd said something he should not have said.

Something about that peaked my interest, but it slid off my radar almost immediately.

Jason and I agreed to meet at one, which meant I had some time to study with Nathan, although he basically went over the schedule again and all of the different things I was going to have to learn to be able to eradicate the Scouts in the area.

He told me about Jared, too. He was a private company 'Scout Seeker'. Whatever company he worked for did it differently; once you were trained, you were always in the field, by yourself. According to what Nathan said, he also had different means of doing his work, and didn't really have to answer for the crimes he committed to achieve his goals.

Therefore, they were rivals working, sort of, to the same ends. Nathan said he didn't believe Jared's end game was a brighter, happier, safer world. He believed Jared enjoyed the power it gave him to seek the Scouts out, essentially destroy them, then dismantle whomever's lives got uprooted as the result. Jared's methods could be underhanded and dirty.

He was definitely using Elizabeth to get closer to me. For why, though?

Nathan said he had an extra bad feeling about this go around, and he wasn't sure what it was. He had only run into Jared himself twice, although he had seen some others from private companies over the years. Jared, though, had made quite a name for himself.

It was close to time for me to meet Jason, and I felt terrible about leaving Nathan alone, on so many different levels. "Nathan, just come with me."

"Ha!" snorted Nathan. "That would be an ugly surprise for Jason, now, wouldn't it?"

"This is a friendly visit."

"Is it?" Nathan asked dryly, walking around my counter into the tiny kitchen. He reached into one of my cabinets and pulled out some brandy, and poured himself a glass. I didn't even know I had brandy.

I walked into the tiny kitchen myself, blocking his exit by standing next to my fridge. "Yes, it is."

He sipped some and didn't say anything, but looked out to my animals sitting on the couch. "Don't worry, I'll take care of the children while you play."

He was teasing now.

"Nathan."

He vehemently spoke, "Of course I don't like it! But you're a free agent, Violet, you can do whatever you want. Like I said, you'll be safe enough with him."

I took a step closer.

"And..."

"And don't be so naive. I imagine he's a good guy. I

suppose you could do worse."

I snorted with laughter, my mood uplifted. "Gee, thanks for your blessing. I guess now you're trying to marry me off. Alright, if you don't want to come, I guess I'll get going. What*ever* will you do without me?" I walked to the door, grabbing my jacket.

<h1 style="text-align:center">16</h1>

As it turns out, Nathan and I were both right. Jason and I ate lunch together alone, but he had plans to follow that lunch meeting up with Elizabeth. Jason and Nathan were like day and night; one was light, one was dark. Jason was just shy of Nathan's stature, although, strength-wise, they would probably be a good match.

Jason was wearing regular clothes today—just jeans and a t-shirt. It was nice to see him in something other than police clothes.

"Violet. Thanks for meeting me on such short notice," he said, opening the door for me to the quiet restaurant he had chosen. It was one of my favorites—Mediterranean food.

It was also a seat-yourself place, so he left it up to me. I chose a table by the window so I could see the comings and goings of people. "No problem. I apparently have Sundays off." I smiled and shrugged at the same time.

We ordered our food making idle chitchat, and then the conversation turned serious. "Is he treating you well?" he asked tightly, abruptly changing the conversation.

I played with the stirrer in my tea. "Yes, Jason. I'm fine."

He reached out and stopped my hand from moving by placing his over mine. "That's not what I asked."

I looked up at him, surprised. "Mr. Miyagi's mostly harmless."

"Mostly?" He removed his hand, and rolled his eyes.

I decided to change the direction of the conversation. "You said we were meeting up with Elizabeth after this? What is that for?"

He pulled at his perfectly manicured goatee; I noticed that a few grey hairs were mixed in with the blond. "She introduced me to that fellow Jared after you and Nathan left. I made all sorts of conclusions about him upon that meeting. He eventually left Elizabeth and the others, and she approached me. She said she knew something else was going on and she was optimistic I would tell her."

"Uggggh. Damn her," I swore. "So what do you expect me to do? You know I'm limited in what I can say. She hasn't been cleared."

"Violet, you and I both know she'll be cleared. So just tell her everything."

"She probably won't even believe me. And I don't think I can go against Nathan *or* my employer like that. If you're looking to spill secrets, why don't *you* tell me who's employing me?" I leaned forward, overly eager with a telling grin smeared across my face.

Bread and hummus came out. He dipped some of the hummus on the bread and carefully chose his words, "If Nathan hasn't told you that, I'm sure there's a reason for it. And Liz's a part of your woo-woo group, so why wouldn't she believe it? You almost have *me* believing it," he said wryly.

I laughed. "Jason. Hell, even I don't believe it!"

He smiled in return. "I like when you laugh," he said quietly, a blush cresting his cheeks and I felt my face heat up in response. We both focused on the food, and bumped fingers in the hummus.

Nervous laughter. My heart began to pound.

I didn't know what to do. I liked the attention from Jason—I was willing to admit that. But I also didn't want to lead him on. One, the timing was terrible with what was going on in my life. But two, it didn't feel right to lead him on with Nathan sleeping in my living room and sharing my toilet, even *if* nothing could ever happen between Nathan and me.

But I spoke anyway. "Jason..."

He looked up, then back down at his hands. "I know you like that guy, Vi. It's obvious he's got at thing for you, too. Don't worry. I didn't think of this as a date. I know you're not interested in me that way."

I reached out for his hands and wouldn't speak until he looked at me. "It's more complicated than that." I said softly.

"Elizabeth?" He looked surprised. I really don't think it would affect her much, trust me."

"Yeah, that too," I sighed, bringing my hands back to me. "But I meant between me and Nathan." I hesitated and continued, "It's more of that woo-woo stuff that even *he* doesn't understand. And honestly, I don't think we're meant to." I put my hands up in the air in surrender.

The food was brought to us. "So you and Nathan are like soulmates or something?" He shoved some food into his mouth, eyes inquisitive.

I shrugged. "I don't know. I mean, I think there can be *many* soulmates for a person. But there are other things called twin flames that are supposed to be the other half of your soul incarnated."

"Y'all are all crazy," he laughed. "How about this?" He had a renewed sense of confidence. "I like you, Violet Moore. I would love to get to know you better. I realized that when I stopped hanging around Elizabeth and her crew, it was really you I missed." He looked at me endearingly, with his stupid blue eyes trying to suck me in.

My breath caught. My breath seemed to be catching a lot lately. My heart tugged at me, too. "Jason. Timing right now is just not good..."

"Look, you don't need to answer me right now. I'm a patient man; I can wait. Once this all blows over, and Nathan's gone... Well, maybe then you'll be willing to explore something with me? I think we'd be a good fit." He wasn't being cocky at all—that was the nice, refreshing thing about Jason. He was pretty genuine.

I lifted my mouth in a half-smile. "Deal." We shook on it, and laughed. And once all that had been settled, he and I fell into a natural conversation about all sorts of things that had nothing to do about soulmates, Elizabeth, or the crazy Darkness trying to swallow our town whole.

It was nice.

***

Jason refused to let me pay for my own lunch, so while he was standing up at the counter, I had walked back towards the door and all of a sudden felt a sharp pull outside. I looked up and saw Jared getting out of a car.

I swore under my breath as Jason walked up next to me. "Great," he said, following my eyes. He put his arm around me in a protective way and said, "Let's just face it head on, shall we?"

I took a deep breath. I hated this guy. He was a damn thorn in my spine and a threat to Nathan. I didn't take that lightly. I could almost visibly see dark tendrils of smoke emanating off of his smug looking face.

"Follow my lead, Vi," Jason whispered right as we walked up to him.

Jason must have sensed from my tense body that I was ready to charge the man like a damn rhino.

"Ah, Officer Dunham. Miss Moore. How nice and unexpected to run into you two." Those teeth, those damn teeth glinted off the sun as he smiled his oily grin at us. He somehow knew damn well that we were going to be there.

"Mr. Tenebris. You have chosen wisely for a place to eat; the food is very enjoyable here."

It was funny—you could tell Jason wasn't being sincere, but his voice and body language were otherwise so convincing. It was apparent that Jared was having a hard time reading him.

I wanted to cut the bullshit, though, so as I opened my my mouth to speak, Jason squeezed me tightly to keep me from doing so. I chose to smile a big fake smile instead.

"Do enjoy yourself."

Jared's mouth upturned even more as my discomfort continued to grow. Jason tried to steer me away from him, towards our cars, but Jared reached out to touch me as we walked by. It made me visibly shudder.

"Oh, I already have. Please tell Mr. Murphy that we ran into one another. Actually, I'm surprised he isn't with you right now, Miss Moore, especially since you are on the arm of another man. I find it intriguing indeed."

I froze, so Jason wasn't able to move forward. It was as if time stood still, and the only thing that had any sort of movement in the moment was Jared's eyes connecting with my eyes. I blinked myself out of the reverie and pulled Jason a little more forward.

I had no response for him, nor did Jason, so we just continued on. I got in my car and followed Jason as he pulled out of the parking lot. I could feel Jared's eyes on me as I followed Jason.

I was angrily shaking as I dialed Nathan.

"Please answer. Please answer. Please—"

"Hey, what's wrong?" came the anxious voice from the other end of the line. He had sensed something was wrong with me. I could barely talk I was so furious.

After I told him what had happened, he said, "Don't worry about it, I've got Jared covered. As far as Elizabeth, go ahead and tell her what you want. The documentation actually arrived early—your friends are all, of course, cleared."

He had calmed me down quite a bit by the time I pulled into Elizabeth and Sam's parking lot. "Are you sure you don't want to come over? I'm sure they'll have a lot of questions for you, Mr. Spock."

He laughed. "Have fun, Violet. I'll see you later."

"All work and no play makes Jack a dull boy!"

"Goodbye, Violet."

"Ugh. Alright. Bye."

17

It was as I thought. Elizabeth nor Sam, who was also present, believed me. They thought Jason and I were playing a joke on them. And not a very funny one at that.

"Why would we make this up?!" I exclaimed, looking at the two of them on their couch with their arms crossed.

"And why would I help her?" laughed Jason. "You guys know how I am about all of this stuff."

Elizabeth blew her hair off her face and semi-pouted. "Okay; fine. Let's say I believe you. This essentially means you're *The Chosen One* and we're, oh I don't know, Ginny and Hermione?"

I vigorously nodded, "And Nathan's Dumbledore."

There was a pause, and the three of us started to laugh our asses off. I could tell Jason was starting to see a shift in the atmosphere and began to realize his presence was no longer needed… We were turning silly.

Layla arrived shortly thereafter, having been requested to stop by with refreshments. She showed up, no questions asked. She brought some wine and chocolate and we popped it open as soon as she got there. Jason started to inch away to leave us, and I jumped up before he could escape.

I was barefoot and without my long sleeved sweater when

I followed him out the door. He waved goodbye to the others who had just turned on some music.

"Leaving so soon?"

"Ha—yeah. I was beginning to feel all that estrogen in there. Makes me nervous."

I grinned wildly. "I can't believe they're so willing to believe what we've told them!"

He looked off in the distance towards the parking lot and then back at me. "Yeah, me neither, honestly." He laughed.

"Especially since neither you nor I believe it." I started to laugh with him. "I guess we play pretend until it becomes real?"

He turned towards me and saw the state of undress I was in. "Violet! You don't even have any shoes on! It's freezing out here."

Laughter bubbled in my chest. I was feeling carefree for the first time in what felt like weeks, maybe even months. The past week had been chaotic and stressful, but it had given my life new meaning and direction that I hadn't had in so long. It was hard to believe that a short while ago I had considered myself stagnant. Every thing in my life was new, challenging, unbelievable.

He responded to my laughter by taking a step closer to me. We were standing just on the other side of the girls' door. "Keep in touch, okay? I want to know how training is going and help in any way I can. But above all, I want to make sure that you are safe." He put his hands on my shoulders and smiled shyly. "I had a good time today, save for the run-in with Jared. But other than that..."

I narrowed my eyes. "Me, too."

He smiled, gave me a quick squeeze and started to walk away. "Remember, Violet, I have all the patience in the world. I'll be seeing you..."

"Hey!" I exclaimed, running up behind him. I turned him

him around, shocked him with a quick, perfunctory kiss on the lips, gave him a devilish grin, and ran back towards the door. Before I opened it, I said, "Thanks for having patience."

His mouth had half-way dropped open in disbelief. I raised an eyebrow at him and slid back inside the door, not waiting to see his response.

***

It was about an hour later and Nathan texted me, asking if I was going to need a ride home. He must have sensed that it was turning into an impromptu drinking fest. I wasn't intoxicated by any means, but I had definitely gotten to the point that it probably wasn't safe for me to be behind the wheel for another hour or so.

Elizabeth is the one who saw my phone light up and she had started to text back Nathan before I could get to the phone.

"Your honey's on the way."

"What!" I grabbed my phone. Sure enough, she had told him that I needed a ride. "Thanks a lot!"

Sam put her phone down as Layla exited the bathroom and a hush came over the room. Sam asked, "So we're going to be able to ask The Watcher anything we want?"

"If you guys want to ask him questions, I'm sure he will be more than willing to answer whatever he's able to answer."

"So this is real?" asked Layla quietly.

I shrugged. "I guess so."

One for action, she inquired, "Is there a way that we can help? To support these missions?"

"I don't know."

"It seems like a waste for us to just be on the sidelines doing nothing," she pressed.

"You'll have to ask Nathan. I'm just glad you all passed clearance so I could tell you what's going on! Tomorrow I have to be up at 5 wretched AM for meditation. Then I have to go do martial arts training, find time to eat something before heading into work! Meanwhile, these Scouts keep accumulating, and we just hope that by the time they're about to overpower this area, I can stop them."

"How do you do that?" questioned a breathy Sam. I looked at her hair wrapped up in a disarrayed bun, her hands pressed firmly against her lap. Something was definitely off, and I couldn't figure out what it was.

"I don't know." I shrugged. They were getting frustrated, and certainly I could relate.

Knock Knock. Nathan was there. Elizabeth let him inside and walked him through the foyer, down the long, dark hallway into the living room. He reached out and placed his hands on my knees as I sat on the couch, painfully aware that all eyes were on us.

"Are you ready to go home?" he asked quietly. I could tell he was thinking I was far more intoxicated than I was.

I sighed and stood up, brushing imaginary dirt off of my knees. "I'm not drunk, Nathan, Liz just wanted an excuse to get you over here so they could interrogate you." I picked up a kleenex box off of the table and threw it at Elizabeth's head. I seemed to be doing that a lot lately.

"Missed me," she stuck out her tongue.

"Ah," he said, smiling and standing up next to me. He spread out his hands. "Well, I'm here, ask away. All of you. Including you, Violet."

The girls sat expectantly on the couch as I took my place next to Nathan. Elizabeth had brought out chairs for us to sit on and face them.

I looked over at him and wickedly proclaimed, "I just want to know when I get my magic wand. I'm ready for it!"

Nathan groaned.

Everyone spoke at once.

"Can we get an owl?"

"What's her patronus?"

"How about a dragon?"

"I'd like a phoenix feather."

"Can you shape-shift?"

"Do you know Thor?"

"Do you know *aliens*?"

I looked at Nathan and grinned. "I think they're all onboard. Everything's really going to be okay. I clearly have my Hermione, Ron and Ginny."

Layla stood with her hands on her hips. "Does that make me Ron?" she scoffed.

Nathan smiled.

"It's like we're living in a children's fantasy novel."

"Except it's real."

"Except it's real."

The kleenex went flying again. We turned to face the firing squad to answer their questions.

18

I wasn't sure he had assuaged their fears or answered questions well, but he did what he could. That night, when I was at home in bed, I summoned him to my room. I had my blankets piled up on me, as well as Phang and Barnaby. I could barely move as I sat up.

Upon entering my room, he snorted with laughter at the sight of me. He looked amazing as usual, another pair of dark, harem pants, lightweight t-shirt barely covering his tattoo. Sigh.

It wasn't that late, yet, only about 8:30, but I knew he was going to wake me up bright and early. As soon as we had gotten home—me driving my own car, of course—I showered and got into bed.

"I can't sleep."

"You've barely tried."

I patted my bed next to me. He sat opposite me, one long leg tucked underneath the other leg, with one foot supporting him on the floor.

"I kissed Jason today."

"Oh?" He looked down at his hands, awkward. "Why are you telling me this?"

"I don't know. I don't know," I murmured, looking at the

closed glass doors in my room. The blinds were still cracked open, and a little bit of moonlight was streaming in.

"I've already told you, I approve."

It was my time to laugh and he reluctantly met my eyes. "You approve, you who hasn't known me but just over a week, yet quite possibly know me better than anyone will *ever* know me, you approve. That's good to know." I shook my head.

He leaned in, and I felt the warmth of his breath as he spoke.

"You know I don't *really* approve, but what can I do?" He sat back, lifting his shoulders in a shrug.

"Nathan?"

"Yeah?"

"Tell me something about yourself that nobody else knows."

***

We ended up talking for hours, alternating positions and rooms. It was nice that he was willing to share with me as much as he did. Although I knew he would still keep things from me, I felt it only fair that I should get to know the guy training me to save the world.

5 AM came much too soon, and as I groggily got out of bed, stumbling into the living room for meditation, I knew it was going to be a long day.

"Good morning," Nathan's low voice lulled me into instant hypnosis as he handed me some hot tea.

I sat in a perfect lotus position to start, knowing full well that I wouldn't keep the position for long. Almost instantly, Nathan led me through a full-body recognition awareness meditation. By the time he was getting to my knees, I began to doze off.

I had an amazing, aesthetically astounding short-lived dream. We're talking Wonderland colors, here. Nathan and I were standing in the middle of a clearing, and it was dark. Fireflies were dancing around us as we stood there, hand in hand, looking at their dance. The earth below began to hum along with the fireflies, and along the edge of the trees I could see will-o-the-wisps pop up, beckoning us to follow. Nathan took my hand and began to lead me to the forest to follow the wisps. I became frightened and stood back at the edge.

"Violet," said an insistent voice from beyond the trees. Nathan's mouth wasn't moving, but it was his voice.

"Violet," he said again. I felt him touch my shoulder.

Oh. "You fell asleep," he said gently. "We start again."

I nodded.

On the way to the dojo, I told him about my dream. "I'm sure it's just symbolic about the journey we're on. Your apprehension about believing and trusting me," he said wryly.

"Well, to be fair, it *is* hard to believe. I'm doing all of this because, well, I guess because I have nothing else to do at the moment." I maniacally laughed.

***

The next few weeks became a blur of physical activities: running, learning how to swim, practicing martial arts, drinking some delicious matcha tea. (Nathan was hard-wired and set in his ways—he loved a good tea ceremony.) It was also mental: chanting, meditating, educating. I learned about the Vikings, Celts, Germanic peoples; I learned about the elder futhark, Yggdrasil, Odin. Nathan touched on an even older magic than the original elder futhark, but deliberately seemed to keep those stories aloft.

I began to see and feel things I never thought possible. I could feel my mind changing, my body changing, and all so quickly. It was so very fascinating, and draining on all levels —physically, mentally *and* emotionally. I was exhausted, and I started to get frustrated.

It seemed I wasn't able to absorb any more information—I had hit a plateau. My mind began mixing facts about leprechauns and dragons, magical inks and poetry penetrating the great divide between man and God herself, all while I danced in a sea of *Lucky Charms*.

Again, I was exhausted.

Nathan was a natural born teacher and leader. He was able to detach from the emotional drama with me—most of the time—and encourage me when need be, offer no leniency when need be, listen as a friend when need be, and offer advice when I was at a loss for how to proceed.

He brought me into the field when Scouts gathered, and taught me how to focus my internal energy, pushing *out* lightness and goodness *at* them. It was incredibly difficult to do, and incredibly incredible sounding.

He taught me how to find grace within.

My life had gone from boring with tinges of magic here and there, to fantastical and outrageous at every turn. All in the blink of an eye.

One time we were outside of the dojo and it was dark. There were Scouts watching me from somewhere in the parking lot, but I could only sense them instead of see them. Nathan gave direction for how to focus the healing energy and push it out at the apex of its power. I could *feel* it take leave of my body towards them. It was like I had suddenly turned into a storm releasing its torrent of, in this case, positive, protective, kinetic energy.

That was the first time.

The second time I started to panic over the feeling of power I was channeling. Nathan had to push the Scouts out on his own—which I later learned wasn't his strong suit— and usher me back inside the dojo to calm me down. The energy was so intense, the power was inexplicable. After an initial catatonic response, I was rendered terrified and in tears. Nathan was able to soothe me back into a pacified state.

Then he forced me to do it again.

The third time there were a handful of Scouts—and apparently, if a 'good' enough job wasn't done, the Scouts were likely to reform and come back at you. It's not like Scouts weren't fully functioning humans—they were. They lived regular lives, worked, had relationships like the rest of us. They just had lost their connection to the light; they were so embedded with negative emotions there was no longer a way for them to break out of the dark and heal themselves. They needed someone to help break them out of the mental jail they found themselves stuck in.

They needed a *Light Thrower*. (Nathan had yet to give me a better title. He seemed to find what I'd come up with as humorous, so he kept using it.)

It's like I was hurling lightning bolts of cleansing energy into their hearts to help them change their minds. If they changed their minds, they could spread joy and kindness again rather than their general eye-for-an-eye bullshit.

Negativity bred more negativity, and that's why Scouts gathered in groups. They fed on one another's hatred and discord, and once they organized enough, they were able to spread their ways across an area like a darkened blanket. Somehow or another, some of these groups were *extremely* organized and aware of people like me. Nathan didn't tell me who was in charge of these particular groups—he alluded I would learn more about all of that as time went on. But for now, my job was to take them out before they took me out. But if I wasn't able to overpower *them*, they could advance on *me*, and ultimately, if there were enough of them, overtake me.

Luckily, I probably wouldn't die, and I certainly wouldn't be turned into a Smoke Monster or anything, but I could become such a psychological mess I'd find a new home in an insane asylum. Joy.

It was pretty scary to think about becoming trapped inside my own mind, but obviously I had had bouts of that already with anxious, or depressive, thoughts. Everyone had. And that's the start of the negativity taking hold.

It was so esoteric, yet exoteric, intangible and completely tangible.

It was hard to believe that there was a job title for this line of work—that employers and employees existed—but Nathan tried to convince me otherwise. He spoke of psychotherapists, and soldiers, Captains and Lieutenants. He spoke of nurses, and doctors, EMTs. He spoke of steel workers and warehouse workers and everything in between. It was a yin yang effect that one couldn't exist without the other—this group needed me to overpower, and I needed them to fix.

Nathan wanted to make sure he was there with me when *The Big Moment* happened, but he also needed to make sure I was able to stand on my own without him.

I hadn't had a lot of time to see any of my friends, or speak with my father. Damien's dad had finally come into the office one day I was there and informed me he planned on closing down the business before the end of the year. He hoped that my massage business would be able to compensate any loss of funds from what he was paying me; I assured him everything was fine.

Damien naturally sent a smart ass text soon after his dad had spoken to me. Elizabeth left me a message detailing what was going on between Amanda and him.

Jason and I had spoken a few times on the phone, and grabbed a quick coffee here or there, but he had only just asked me out on an official date for the upcoming weekend. I told him yes, although I was still hesitant, not just because of my mixed feelings for Nathan, but because I hadn't had time to process anything that was going on, inside or outside of my training.

After a particularly hard week of training my mind and body, I wasn't feeling up to *any* company. I really just wanted some quiet time to myself.

I think Nathan sensed that, so he told me to go to Elizabeth's Friday yoga class without him. He told me to be careful, and to avoid Jared if he was lurking around. We hadn't caught wind of Jared's movements in over a week, but Nathan was still on edge about him being in town, especially since Jared seemed to be taking a special interest in me.

I asked Nathan what he was going to do, and he said he was going to a yoga class at another studio. "Are you sure?" I asked, hesitating at the door before leaving.

"It's fine, Violet. It's not a big deal. I know you need some time without me."

"It's not that. I mean, it *is* that. But it's not because of you being you."

"I know." He grabbed his yoga mat and gently pushed me through the door.

"Don't worry about rushing home after class or anything." He tensed up a bit before continuing. "I know the past few weeks have been rough, and you probably feel like I own you or something. You're definitely due for a break. I want you to relax this weekend, okay?" He kindly smiled. "I'll make sure to spend time with my dad at his house this weekend to give you some much deserved privacy. But, know that the tension continues to build. The little skirmishes we've had are nothing compared to when the Scouts will really try to overpower you. We aren't running out of time per se, but you may be forced to perform before you really *want* to perform."

We walked down the stairs of my complex.

At the bottom of the steps, a brisk wind caught my hair and I shivered. "Have a good class." He turned to face me, and without thinking, tucked my hair into my jacket.

I shivered again, but this time not from the cold.

We had not been very good when we were just Nathan and Violet, standing in a parking lot, going our separate ways. We had been great as Teacher and Student. We had plenty of moments of forgetting we were actually Teacher and Student over the past few weeks, and he was usually much faster than I was at correcting the behavior.

We stood awkwardly face to face, neither of us really knowing which way to go. Why had he touched my hair like that? It was too personal, too familiar. We both started to speak at the same time and twittered with some nervous laughter.

Nathan finally caved by groaning, "Ugh, I really thought I was getting better at this."

I moved closer to him, the wind whipping around us, leaves making a scraping sound near our feet. "Me, too." I licked my lips and swallowed. I could feel the heat from his body even though we were not touching.

"Violet," he whispered. "Stop." He searched my eyes, the gold flecks in his green eyes illuminated by the fading sun.

I felt the first inkling of his body actually touching mine as one, or both of us, naturally began leaning forward into the other. As I continued to look up into his eyes, his eyes became pleading. "Please... We'll be late for class."

I'm not sure why I felt so bold, or bratty as it were, but I did not back down.

"What are you so afraid of, Nate?" I breathed, questioning him. He was definitely afraid of something, and I felt like it was beyond falling for his apprentice, even as forbidden as that probably was.

What didn't I know?

My arms were pressed against his chest, and I could feel his arms reluctantly wrap around me. His forehead touched my forehead and the wind picked up speed—it filled my ears almost as much as my heartbeat did. He lifted his head up just a bit, resting his lips on my forehead, just holding me. My mouth was gently pressed against his neck, and I could almost taste him. He smelled like a pumpkin spice latte and decaying leaves and it was all I could do to hold still. We held that position for what felt like eternity; time definitely slowed down.

Before he could answer my question, a car pulled up into the parking lot. Nathan slowly backed away from me as the person turned their car off, followed by their lights. The person wasn't going into my building, but it was enough to give Nathan the strength, I suppose, to not answer me.

He continued to walk away from me, looking just past me and not making eye contact. "Go to class. I'll see you later." He turned and walked away, his hair brushing the collar of his jacket, shoulders slightly hunched. This haunting image burned a spot in my memory and would never go away, I just knew it. He unlocked his car door and slid his body into his ridiculous car before driving off.

Eventually I followed suit once I realized I was standing in the parking lot, alone, and freezing. I cranked the heat on overdrive once I got into my own vehicle, and sped off to my yoga class.

I was almost late by the time I got there, and Elizabeth was not amused.

19

After class I helped Elizabeth mop up. We discussed plans for the weekend since it appeared I was going to finally have downtime. She hadn't heard from Sam all day so she wasn't sure what she was doing that evening. Friday nights Layla usually went up to the city to meet up with some friends who lived up that way.

After the last person left, Liz and I were standing at the check-in desk at the front of the studio. I propped myself up on the desk, feet dangling above the floor. Elizabeth grabbed one of my bare feet.

"So. What's up with you and Nathan this week?"

"Ugh. Anything but that." I leaned over and put my head in my hands.

Elizabeth jumped up next to me and pushed me a little bit.

"How about Jason?"

"Ugh. Not that either."

She laughed. "Have you spoken to him this week? I know you've been busy so busy with your training."

"Just once, but... I never told you. I kissed him that day at your house."

"What?!"

She jumped back down and forced me to look at her in the

face.

"Why didn't you tell me this?"

"I didn't think it was a big deal. I mean... I hope not. But he's told me repeatedly he will wait for me, and he seems so sure that I will give in. I also agreed to go on a date with him tomorrow."

"Buuuut..."

"Buuuut... Nathan."

"Ah. And you spend all waking hours with Nathan."

"Yeah, but it's usually not like that. We're typically very good at our roles. But before I came here..."

"Yeah...?"

"Let's just say, we weren't really good at our roles." I slapped my knees and jumped off the counter. "We had a moment. *Another* moment. I'm so tired of these meaningless moments! I wish he'd just act on it, or at least tell me why he won't."

"Oh, Vi. I'm so sorry." Elizabeth walked up to me and gave me a brief hug.

"Alright, I'm done whining. Let's go see a movie tonight. Or drive up to Atlanta and hunt down Layla. Find a band playing? Just anything that doesn't involve any boys or any thinking about boys!"

"Ummm.. Are you *allowed* to leave the city?"

I groaned. "I don't really know. Nathan may have to come."

It was her turn. "Ugh. I miss when it was just the two of us. It's been a long month, Vi, you have no idea."

"Has it really only been a month or so?" I asked bleakly. "Did I tell you that I'm out of a desk job by the end of the year?"

Elizabeth pulled a shirt over her leotard. "No, but I know you thought that that was in the process of happening. We might be hiring, you know, but you'd probably have to quit the massage thing altogether. We don't do part-time."

"I know. And thanks. But I think I'll be fine, since I started…"

"Being a vampire slayer? Yeah, I know."

She locked the door behind us. It was extremely cold outside the studio, seeing as it was completely dark now. The wind had died down, but from the lack of heat from the yoga class made it seem even colder for us.

My phone beeped. I pulled it out of my jacket pocket and frowned. "It's Sam. She sent her location and wrote 'hurry'." I checked to see where her location was. It looked like it was off of one of the trails down by the creek. "Why would she do that?"

"That's really weird, but I wouldn't go over there at night. That's way too creepy."

I looked at Elizabeth. "But Sam could be in danger."

My phone beeped again and Sam wrote: *In trouble. Need help.*

I showed the text to Elizabeth and she groaned. "Alright, fine, let's go. I'll drive, but you should text Nathan or Jason about what we're doing. You've got me so freaked out about everything these days—who knows—it could be a damn trap. It may not even be Sam!"

I rolled my eyes and said, "I'm sure she's fine. She probably just tripped or something."

"Vi—it's essentially dark now. There's no way she was still hiking at this hour."

I looked at Elizabeth as she drove, and sighed. "Fine. I'll text Nathan what we're doing, and ask Jason if anything's going on down there. Deal?"

She nodded and drove towards the trails in silence. We were stopped at a stoplight when I sent Jason and Nathan a message on the same thread, and when I looked up, I noticed there was a car that was really close to us. It made me nervous, but I wasn't about to alert Elizabeth and make her more paranoid.

We finally made a left into the parking lot for the trails, with only one way out in and one way out. The car followed us in.

"Shit," I said nervously, looking behind us.

"*Nobody's answered you?*" Elizabeth asked a bit shrilly, inquiring again about my fruitless texts. It had only been about ten minutes from the studio to the trails, but no. Nobody had answered me.

"It's so dark…"

There was no lighting in the tiny parking lot we were approaching, and the bumpy road was even trickier to navigate during the night. I could see lights from houses off in the distance, but they certainly weren't close enough to help us if we needed it. We saw that another car was there, and it did appear to be Sam's.

"What do we do?"

"I don't know."

We were almost at the point where we were going to have to park, or try to dodge past the car that had followed us. Elizabeth looked like she was ready to flee, when someone stepped around the parked car with her hands up.

We simultaneously shouted, "Sam!"

She wasn't alone, though. There were several, masked Scouts with her. Cowards, hiding their identities.

"Oh my God," I shrieked, causing Elizabeth to slam on her breaks.

She yelled, "Who the hell are they?" Sam and the others blocked us.

I *knew* she had been acting weird. Had something happened? Was she going through something terrible, and I had been an awful friend and neglected to see the Darkness take hold of her?

"They're Scouts," I said quietly. "You have to listen to me very carefully and do exactly as I say, Elizabeth."

She looked scared.

A slew of other Scouts got out of the car that had followed us in, blocking our exit.

"Don't unlock the door whatever you do. The second you get a chance to pull out of here—gun it. I'm going to get into a trance and try to push them away from us, okay?

"I don't know what that means!" she exclaimed.

I started to get anxious as the Scouts circled our car, chanting God knows what, but I calmly continued, "And while I do my thing, please try Nate or Jason again, okay?"

"Okay," she grabbed my phone and shakily took it from me. The Scouts physically began to rock her car, clearly trying to get us to exit the vehicle. I could hear her frantically texting them while I turned inward and tried to follow my training as best as I could.

There were only about fifteen Scouts total—it would be easy enough to drive away from them given the opportunity. I knew Elizabeth would probably be able to do it without hurting anyone, even though we were completely blocked at the moment.

But, for Sam's sake, and because of my guilt, I had to at least try to remedy the situation even though I didn't feel strong enough in my skills, even though I hadn't had access to any of the pre-elder futhark inscriptions. I was going to try anyway, I was going to do my best.

Hamarr undir Helga ve theta ok hald vordh!
Hammar yfir Helga ve theta ok hald vordh!
Um mik ok I mer Asgardh ok Midgardh!

A warmth began to fill my body with each verse I chanted. It felt like the molecules of my body were speeding up so quickly that I began to disappear.

Now sparks of fire
  With speed spew forth;
  Lend thy quickness and life.

I couldn't see or hear anything anymore; it was like I simply *became* the chanted verses. I *felt* more than saw the red and orange vibrating lights around and through my body. The hum was loud, overpowering and overwhelming. I started to shout basic runes, desperately trying to muster anything at my disposal to regain control of the madness.

Uruz! Thurisaz! Kenaz!

Suddenly, a force greater than myself pushed outward with a giant shockwave; it made a whooshing noise and I fell backwards onto the car seat with such a force that the car itself moved.

After I was thrown back into the carseat, reality came rushing back into focus. Elizabeth was screaming, my heart was pounding out of control and sweat was streaming down my face. The Scouts had all been rendered momentarily useless; they were scattered around the car like little doll bodies.

I wasn't sure what was supposed to happen after the force field exploded out of me like that, so over the dull roar that remained outside of the car, I yelled to Elizabeth, "Get out of here!" Tendrils of darkness seemed to be receding from the Scouts, slithering back into the treeline.

She jerked the car into gear and hightailed it out of there. She turned so quickly off of the dirt road and onto the main road that the car violently careened. It abruptly skidded to a halt about six hundred yards from the entrance to the hiking trails. We screamed simultaneously as the power pole and ditch rapidly approached us; I looked over at her as her airbag began to deploy, feeling my body shift sideways at an angle as it moved forward due to the lack of me being buckled.

The last thing I visibly remembered seeing before I blacked out was Liz being pushed backwards as I crashed through the windshield flying forwards, my airbag exploding and my body hurtling sideways in space before landing onto the hard pavement with a bone-cracking thud.

20

I was in and out of consciousness; time was a novel concept without merit. I heard my mother's voice as I watched my body be pulled from the wreckage by firefighters. She stood next to me, holding my hand. I felt calm, a little confused, but safe under my mother's touch. When I realized I was *feeling* the touch of my dead mother's hand, I panicked, made eye contact with her, and slammed back into my body.

Nathan's face blearily came into focus as he crouched beside me. I saw him hovering his hands over me as he chanted something under his breath. I remembered seeing a purple and green wavelength of light emit from his hands and it being magnetically pulled into my body. My own light was devoid of color until Nathan's purple began to change my coloring into hues of golds, greens, and whites. With each shockwave of color, my body convulsed, until I felt cold air searing into my lungs.

I heard Jason's panicked voice shouting orders at everyone around us; from a distance I saw Liz being pulled from the car and placed onto a gurney. There were other times she was right next to me.

I remembered the pain, the loud vibration of the chaos unfolding at the scene. It felt like I couldn't move or see with my eyes. Instead, I seemed to visibly sense things with my mind.

I felt the Darkness dissipate, and heard Sam's anxious whispers on the wind.

Nathan's arguing with one of the medics swam into focus, but then for a brief moment I thought Nathan had *become* one of the medics. I saw Jason pull Nathan away as he desperately tried to stay with me as I was placed onto my own gurney.

Bright lights faded in the distance, and in the darkness a soothing voice consoled me as hands poked and prodded my body. Finally, the ambulance itself quieted save the bumps in the road, and a warm hand placed itself on my arm for comfort. I heard soft murmurs from the medic, and steady, hazel eyes lulled me to rest.

White lights of the hospital came into focus, waking me up in a panic. I floated above as my body was surgically cut open below me. My mother sat next to me as we waited to see if I would live. She never spoke, just held my hand and smiled. I wasn't afraid of her touch this time. I heard loud bells, beeping of machines and choirs of angelic voices, all simultaneously.

I heard the astonishment of the doctors as my cells seemed to magically repair themselves right before their eyes. *Miraculous* came the whispers.

Even so, the pain of being slammed back into my body for the last time was incredibly intense and I screamed as it happened. Although I was loaded with painkillers and the magic of Nathan's healing touch, I felt like I had been run over by an 18-wheeler, multiple times.

With eyes half-opened, I saw my arm was in a cast, and I could feel some crusted blood forming on my face. I felt detached from the whimpers I was hearing, and it wasn't until Nathan's face swarmed through my tears that I realized the whimpers were mine.

"Violet," he murmured, his face contorted with too many emotions to read.

My throat felt incredibly dry and sore; I tried to speak and still could only whimper. I tried to sit up, but found that I was also unable to do so. Was I paralyzed?

Nathan must have hit a button to call a nurse, because a man suddenly appeared and the lights turned on. I realized I was hooked up to a bunch of machines by the sounds chirping and beeping alongside me. That's why I couldn't move—there were too many wires hooked up to me. I saw that I was receiving fluids, and this accounted for why I was so damn cold.

Nathan gave me a weak smile as I began to get my bearings straight. He sat next to me and still held my hand. The nurse spoke to me in calm tones, saying he would wait for the doctor to come and give me the full rundown about what had happened, but my recovery time wasn't looking like it was going to be a long, daunting process at all. You could hear the mystification in his voice.

He said while I had many abrasions and cuts, the only broken thing on me was my arm and I only had a minor concussion.

I finally croaked out what I had needed to; Nathan squeezed my hand. "Elizabeth?"

The nurse incredulously answered me, "Also fine, although doing better than you because she was buckled in. What *were* you two running from?"

The nurse walked out of the room and I began to get drowsy. "Nathan," I mumbled.

He leaned his head next to mine, trying to get a read on what I was saying.

"Samantha."

"She's okay. We can talk later about it when you're out of

the hospital. Don't think about anything right now other than recovery. And resting. Lots of rest."

"Nate..." I mumbled again, this time whimpering into a sleep.

"I know," he whispered, and I felt hot wetness on my face before blacking out.

I was in a canoe, and the sky was black and full of twinkling stars. There were tall grasses on either side of me as I floated alongside a narrow waterway. I was alone, but not afraid. I slowly drifted towards a small island, and I walked on the water to get to it. Nathan was waiting for me, and stood up next to a small table with a flickering candle on it. The table was wooden and had two chairs next to it, and he pulled a chair out for me.

After sitting down, he reached his hands out to me and opened his mouth.

Rather than words coming out, the air from his breath blew the candle out.

It was dark, and I was not scared. I could still feel Nathan holding my hands. I looked up at the stars, and could see the milky way before me. I breathed in the cool air as a glowing, white light drifted from the heavens towards us.

It was my mother again.

She was smiling, and nodding encouragingly at Nathan and me. The light was enough so I could see Nathan perfectly well. He started to shudder and the image faded back into blackness, and I realized I was back in my body again. The beeping wasn't as loud this time, and I could hear someone snoring softly next to me.

Another nurse was in the room, an older woman, checking the monitor next to me. She smiled and nodded at Nathan. "You've been here for two days now and he's barely left your side. Stubborn, that one. He's very devoted to you."

I half-nodded, and saw a new silhouette fill the doorway.

"I'll leave you alone with your visitor." She walked out, nodding at the policeman was was standing there, holding his hat in his hands at his waistline.

He cleared his throat. "Can I come in?" He glanced nervously at the sleeping Nathan, although I figured by his current lack of snores he was probably awake.

I nodded.

Jason sat on the opposite side, and took the hand from my non-broken arm. He chewed on his lower lip and said in a soft voice, "I thought I was going to lose you."

I finally spoke. "I don't remember a lot. How long ago?"

"It's Tuesday evening."

"Can I have some water?"

He handed me some water and it cooled my throat, making it easier to speak.

"Thanks."

He nodded towards Nathan and gruffly said, "He won't leave your side. We've tried to move him," he laughed without any mirth.

"I'm sure he feels responsible."

"Well..."

"He's not, Jason." I croaked.

He shrugged.

"Elizabeth?"

"Home with a few bruises. She's been here every day so far to visit you. Your release is supposed to be tomorrow, and Nathan said your debriefing would probably be at the start of next week. They're going to let me be present in spite of my ranking. Just because I'm close to you." He said the last part to himself.

"Did Liz tell you what happened at the trails? With Sam?"

"Yeah." He looked uncomfortable.

"Is Sam okay?"

"She'll be fine. I guess your employer is going to get her

therapy or something."

"Therapy?" I raised an eyebrow.

"All a part of the debriefing."

"Any tickets for Elizabeth?"

"It's being handled."

I started to cry big, wet tears. "It was terrifying. All of it." It was an ugly cry for sure.

Jason leaned into me, trying to cradle me as much as possible given the restraints. I continued to blubber as he spoke, "You did amazing, Vi. You weren't fully trained and what you did was… amazing. The accident was just that; an accident. But what you did…" He looked at me in awe, releasing my body, and gently swept across my broken arm.

"I'm so sorry for your injuries, though. But, I mean, you'll be okay. Whatever he did to you guys after the wreck," he jerked his head at Nathan, and said in awe, "You guys walked."

His voice cracked. "And I'm so glad you did, Violet. I was more scared than I've ever been in my life. I know we don't know one another all that well, but, that is… I really care for you." He trailed off, a little lost and unsure as he looked at Nathan.

I gulped, and looked down.

I didn't know what to think.

But I needed to talk to Nathan. About everything.

21

Jason stayed for a little bit longer until I got sleepy. He smiled when he realized I was drifting away. He leaned forward and kissed me on my forehead.

"I'll see you tomorrow, Violet."

The dream picked up where it had left off. My mother was encouraging Nathan and me, but Nathan was resisting. He shook his head, showing his helplessness in the situation.

My mother frowned, and opened her mouth, rune after rune after rune floating from it, creating verses of our past, present and future. Nathan shook his head.

I was confused. I didn't understand *his* confusion. All I knew was, I had to try and remember the runes my mother was writing in the air so I could tell Nathan once I woke up.

Once I woke up. That meant I was asleep. I reached out for my mother as the dream tore itself away. She smiled at me, and nodded as I faded.

I bolted upright, sweating. Nathan was in the doorway, talking to someone I couldn't see. His clothes were finally changed. That was a good sign. He was holding something in his arms, and he turned towards me as I gasped awake.

I shook my head to clear the cobwebs. "Phang!"

She started barking like crazy when she saw me. Nathan

brought her and placed her gently on me. She walked on my broken arm (ouch!) and started licking my face with zeal.

I laughed, and looked up at Nathan's beautiful, tired face. His smile matched mine, but I noticed the dark circles under his eyes and the stubble on his chin.

I noticed someone had followed him inside, and it was Elizabeth with a yellowing eye, split lip, but otherwise, perfect as always.

"E!" I shrieked.

She crumbled on top of me like a sand castle being stepped on by a little kid. She started sobbing all over me and Phang. Phang turned to her and started to lick *her* face. I held onto her as tightly as she held onto me; pain in my arm be damned.

We clutched one another what seemed like hours, until Nathan cleared his throat. He was standing awkwardly at the foot of the bed, arms crossed, looking down at the floor.

"This guy!" Elizabeth said, wiping her nose and eyes on the back of her hand—graceful Elizabeth, of all people! She walked to Nathan and gave him a hug.

"He's been wonderful. He's barely left your side. His magic saved our lives, Violet. You weren't awake to witness it, but I saw the whole thing." She quieted down. "It was amazing."

Nathan had placed his hands behind his back and nodded in embarrassment.

It was my time to clear *my* throat. "You're not just a trainer, are you?"

He shook his head, having a hard time meeting my eyes.

"Do I get to know?"

"You have a debriefing next week. I'm not sure what exactly you'll get to know."

"Is… is that why… is that why we can't be together?" I had a hard time putting the words together to make sense.

"It's complicated," he said softly.

Elizabeth took a step back, and laughter bubbled up inside of her. She walked over to me and squeezed my hand.

"Violet, Violet, Violet. What ever is it like to be so loved?" My eyes flickered over to her, and she gave a big, wry smile my way. I raised my eyebrow. "Oh, hush, Vi. I think I'm a little in love with you, too!"

I was sort of shocked at her seriousness. She, however, looked a hundred pounds lighter than I had ever seen her in, well, a very long time.

"Don't worry, Vi—it's not going to change anything. But I finally feel free. After I saw them wheel you away into the ambulance. I realized, I realized that what I felt for you was more than just friendly, if you will."

My mouth dropped open, and she let out a slight giggle. "Trust me. This is a *good* thing."

She straightened herself up, tossed her hair a bit, gave Phang a quick hug, a squeeze on my good shoulder and said, "I'll be by tomorrow. Everyone at the studio is worried sick about you. Love you, girl."

She strode out, leaving me and Nathan in a sort shocked humor.

One side of his mouth was still turned up as he sat down next to me, running his fingers through his hair. "Well. Wasn't expecting that. But it makes sense, I guess."

"Ummm… yeah… She seems so happy, though. It *is* a good thing, maybe she'll stop being so grouchy." I laughed.

Phang started to paw her way towards Nathan and leapt off of me to get into his arms. "She's been really needy. Actually, Barnaby has been, too. They both miss you horribly." He looked at me soberly, then barely audibly said, "Me, too."

I felt so tired, and so confused, so grim, so sad. And in so much pain. I tried to sit up a little more comfortably and

Nathan leaned forward to help me. "Do you want another pillow?"

"I don't know what I want. I want answers, I guess, but I'm too tired at the moment to care." I stifled a yawn.

He put Phang back on me and patted my hand. "I know. But you still need to rest. Most everything will be answered when you're ready to get out of the hospital. Anything I can help you with now?"

I stifled another yawn and said, "I keep dreaming about my mom. In fact, I think I saw her at the accident, when I was pulled out of the wreckage. I saw all sorts of things as I watched them give me CPR... As I watched you chant over me and Elizabeth... But I've been dreaming about her since then."

Nathan leaned in with great interest and rubbed Phang's belly. "She was singing in this lovely language, and you were resistant to what she was saying and I wanted to remember it so I could tell you what she was saying... It's like she was trying to tell us we needed to be together. There were stars... And a candle... And a boat..." I yawned again.

Much like Jason had, Nathan leaned in to kiss the top of my head. I couldn't handle all this affection from these people anymore, it was starting to drive me crazy. I didn't know if I was in love with all of them, or none of them. It made me angry. But again, I was actually too tired to care. Anytime I started to feel a big emotion, sleepiness would overcome me.

I started to wonder if Nathan was causing it.

"Not fair," I whined as my eyes began to close.

"Dream now. We will talk later."

I felt him sit back in the chair next to me and let out a huge sigh as I drifted off to sleep.

This time the dream was different. My mother was solid, and it was daytime. We were still on the same island, though.

"Mom?" I asked.

I hadn't seen her in this solid form in a good ten years or more.

A beautiful melody erupted from her mouth, one I couldn't understand, but could rather feel the sensation inside my body. She squeezed my hand and then smiled, the melody wafting through the air outside of her. Nathan walked up, and she grabbed his hand, he in turn looking at her in shock.

She pushed his hand to mine and made sure our hands continued to stay touching while she sang some sort of sweet lullaby, or so it seemed. I could feel the energy start to pick up and flow throughout our bodies as she kept singing. I looked from her to Nathan, then at our hands entwined with my mother's hands now hovering above us.

His green eyes turned almost entirely gold as he stared at me, lips pursed in wonder. Perhaps he was really seeing me for the first time, recognizing who I was. He was no longer hiding himself from either of us. My mother began to walk away, and the enchantment broke.

I continued to hold onto Nathan, but as she walked away this time, I knew she would be gone for a long while. I looked after her with sorrow in my heart as she began to disappear, and I saw her mouth the words 'I love you'.

I woke up with hot tears on my face. Nathan was not awake, sitting on my right side this time, hunched over me and slightly snoring. It looked uncomfortable. Phang was at my feet, and I looked at the clock. Almost another entire day had passed, and every time I woke up I was getting more and more anxious about leaving.

I hesitated, and reached out to touch his head with my good hand. I shifted my weight enough to be able to do it without waking him up. He let out a slight groan as I ran my hands through his hair, brushing it softly away from his face, the texture feeling coarse between my fingers. He began to wake up from the feel of it, with the words, "I remember," on his lips. He looked at me and blinked when he woke up, half-asleep still and mumbling, "It took longer this time."

I cocked my head to one side and he shook his head. "Sorry, I must have been dreaming. Are you okay?"

I leaned back into the bed.

"I'm ready to go home."

22

It was incredibly cold the next day as Nathan wheeled me out in a wheelchair to the front of the hospital. I was finally being released, and he was going to take me home. He left me in the foyer as he walked into the parking lot to get his car. While I waited for him, shivering, Jason walked up.

He had texted me earlier in the day and I told him I was finally going home.

I was happy to see him, but also nauseated. I was torn between him and Nathan like you wouldn't believe. It was an awful feeling.

"Hi," he said, hesitating. I was covered in a jacket, a stuffed animal of Phang that Sam had brought me, balloons, a bag full of candies and my cell phone. There were multiple messages that I needed to call my father STAT, but Nathan himself had ferried a few responses to my dad.

He picked up the Phang toy and laughed. "Looks like you've been in the hospital for a month, not just a few days with all this stuff you've managed to collect."

"I know, right?" I smiled.

Jason nodded towards the parking lot. "I take it he is getting the car?"

"Yeah," I murmured.

Jason squatted next to me in the chair, rather kindly tucking in my jacket. He turned me to face him. "I know you have feelings for him. But, I also know he's leaving. So after he's gone, I really hope you will humor me and let me cook dinner for you one night." He smiled a lopsided grin, and then continued, "I wish I was the one taking you home with me. Not you going home with him." He said it quietly and quickly, as if he didn't want to lose his resolve to say it.

My heart began to thud.

Before I could answer, Nathan pulled up. He stiffly got out of his car and walked into the foyer to greet us. A huge tension filled the air as they more or less glared at one another. It was dreadful, and I couldn't believe I had somehow sandwiched myself between them.

I had to make a grunting noise to get their attention away from one another; it was as if they had even forgotten that I existed.

Jason finally broke the awkward silence. "I guess I'll be seeing you in Atlanta on Monday?"

"Yes. I'll drive her up there to meet everyone."

"And I'll take Sam and Elizabeth."

"What are you guys talking about?"

Neither looked at me, both said, "The debriefing."

"Oh." I began to shiver from the cold. That snapped Nathan out of his testosterone-driven nonsense, and he opened up his car door. An orderly came out to retrieve the wheelchair from us after Nathan had me in his car with all of my stuff.

Jason had kissed my hand goodbye much to the irritation of Nathan.

It was Friday afternoon, which meant I had a few wonderful nights to do nothing before this big debriefing. Whatever the hell that meant.

Nathan was a good nurse-maid. He had bought a bunch of

my favorite foods and stocked my fridge. He immediately made me hot tea once we got home and he propped me up on my couch.

I told him I wanted to go for a walk, but he shook his head no. "Maybe tomorrow. I don't think you should overdo it."

I glared at him.

"Some stretching at least?"

He sighed. "So long as you don't hurt your broken arm."

I yawned, and growled, "I don't know how you keep making me fall asleep, but stop it."

He half-laughed. "You give me too much credit, Violet."

He grabbed some DVDs and asked which one I wanted to watch. "*Twilight.*"

"Really?" His jaw twitched, trying to hide an incredulous smile.

"Yeah. It's something I can relate to. Werewolf, or vampire?"

He rolled his eyes. "Alright, alright."

He popped the movie in and I quickly drifted off to sleep. When I woke back up, my phone was ringing. It was my dad, and since Nathan and already told me what my dad was privy to knowing, I figured talking to him would be okay.

Turns out, for once I was right. My dad was lucid, upset I had been in a car wreck, and was hoping I would come home soon to visit him. I promised I would.

After I hung up, Nathan served me soup with toast on the coffee table.

After dinner, he popped in the next *Twilight* movie and excused himself to go for a run. I was jealous as hell. I texted Elizabeth and Layla and began to get tired again. I felt a little chilly, and was about to get up to go to my room to grab a sweatshirt, I looked at the floor and froze.

I felt tears press at my eyes. Nathan's bag was neatly placed on the side of the couch. I hadn't seen it when we had walked inside, but it was completely packed. It was unzipped, and the top row of things was messy, but underneath that everything was perfectly organized.

Oh my God. He was really going to leave.

I pulled out the long-sleeved shirt that was haphazardly folded on top. I unfolded it and pulled it over my head. It smelled like Nathan, spicy and warm. I made sure my hands were covered with the sleeves and held it close to me as I began to cry, yet again, for the millionth time in the past week.

I was exhausted from the tears. I wasn't even sure what I was crying about anymore.

When I woke up the next time, Nathan was home and had taken his running shirt off with sweat glistening on his chest. His hair fell across his forehead as he drank coconut water in the kitchen. It appeared he had thrown the running shirt on top of the washing machine situated at the end of the narrow kitchen. He didn't know I was watching him.

The TV had turned to fuzz because the movie had ended at some point while Nathan was gone. I stood up and wobbled my way over to the opposite side of the counter. Nathan took in the fact that I was wearing his shirt and his face reflected that of someone who had been caught.

He looked guiltily away.

"When?"

I took a breath, holding it for what felt like millennia. "After the debriefing."

"Where?"

"DC for about a month, then from there, I'll get my new assignment."

"An apprentice?"

"Possibly. They may also want to shift my duties elsewhere." He used a towel to wipe his face.

"Which reminds me," he continued, thumbing through

mail on the countertop.

He pulled out an envelope and handed it to me.

With my good arm, I flipped it over. It was marked *US GOVERNMENT* as the return address, and nothing else. I raised an eyebrow and started to open it one-handedly but of course, was having all the problems you could imagine doing so. Nathan smiled and took it from me, opening it for me.

It was a paycheck for $30,000.

I raised both eyebrows.

"Explain."

"You assumed you work for the government, right? Well, you do. At the debriefing, they'll go over your pay and health insurance, too."

I cleared my throat. "This is almost more than what I make in a *year*."

"Yup."

"So I basically don't find out about any of this stuff till after I do my first job, because if I'm dead, it doesn't matter, is that it?"

He spread out his hands with a grim smile. "More or less. They would have paid for your funeral if you had died." He motioned at the check. "Hazard pay is included with this particular paycheck. Because you got injured. But your health insurance is free, and you're covered for life. You don't even have to go through regular channels to get government sponsored healthcare, because you're sort of dark ops, not on the radar at all. Think deeper than Roswell, yeah? If you noticed, the envelope said a very base 'US GOVERNMENT' on it. Your check, though…"

"…has nothing on it."

"Right."

"Too confusing!" I groaned, not looking forward to the whole meeting on Monday, but overzealous with the fact that I had more than enough money to get me through so many months.

"You'll probably have to file some sort of claim because of the massage thing, but I have a feeling that broken arm is going to heal rather quickly."

"Because of what you did."

He looked away. "Because of what I did."

"*Who* or *what* are you?"

He smiled and took a sip of his water. "I'm like you, Violet, only I've been in the game longer."

"I don't believe that for a second. I'm just human. You seem sort of superhuman." I looked at him with wide, innocent eyes.

He stepped around the kitchen counter to, what I'm assuming, take a shower, but I blocked him. I didn't really care about the banter we were having—I'd have to deal with all of that later. What I needed to deal with, now, was that he was leaving. "If only I held an ounce of the beauty and strength you embody, Violet." His eyes met mine, and I blushed. "I'm no superhuman," he said faintly, and pushed to get past me.

"My *mother* has indicated we are supposed to be together. *My dead mother.* What do you make of that, Nathan?" My voice went up an octave, and I was testy as hell.

He looked over the top of my head, seeing God only knows what.

"It's complicated. You're going to learn things next week, and you probably won't quite feel the same way anymore."

He looked down at me, eyes briefly meeting mine before he looked down at the floor, defeated. I pressured him to look at me. "I doubt that. There're no words to even describe what's between us, words don't even give it *justice.* You know that as much as I do. And—"

"Violet," he murmured, looking up and cupping the sides of my face. "Stop it. I just… can't." I felt his breath on my face and saw a faraway look in his eyes. His hands felt cold and soft. He dropped his hands and hedged past me.

"Jason is a good choice for you."

I turned to face his back. "Stop saying that." His shoulders hunched over as he walked to the bathroom and closed the door.

Just then, a knock on my door caught my attention, and I heard the shower start. I swore under my breath. I was tempted to follow him in there and force him to tell me what the hell he meant, or, you know, get in the shower with him and see him naked.

I happily opened the door to my friends, even an extremely quiet Sam. I knew at some point I was going to have to have some alone time with her. She needed to know that I did not consider her the enemy, but rather, a victim.

23

The next couple of days flew by, me mostly hanging out on the couch healing my arm and spirits as people came and went. In the evening Nathan and I were alone, and it sucked. He was too stubborn to stay at his dad's house because he wanted to help care for the animals while I healed, but he also made sure to keep a safe distance from me—if he would so much as touch me, he would awkwardly skirt away. I was miserable; he was miserable. However, anytime we dozed on the couch, we would always wake up essentially wrapped in one another's arms. Apparently the magnetism between us worked better when we weren't fighting it! Nathan would get flushed, apologize, and leave the house for awhile.

Did I mention how awful it was?

He drove me up to Atlanta in silence. It was understood I would be riding back with Jason's crew. However, as he drove me, he held my hand, or rather, he desperately clutched it. It's like we were both gripping onto the present with an insane, non-reality binding us together. That morning he had stopped refusing to touch me—he had placed his arms on my shoulders, hands at the small of my back, he'd even brushed my hair from around my face. I let him do whatever he wanted—I was afraid of spooking him by speaking about it.

I knew that he would not discuss anything about 'us' anymore, and I wasn't even sure I would get to say goodbye to him in private before we parted ways at the debriefing. I was beyond devastated—I was completely numb, I felt disconnected from my body, disconnected from myself.

Considering how many people were about to be stuffed inside of it, the conference room was shockingly small. I realized quite quickly, though, that people were going to be coming and going all day depending on their clearance. I was sitting at one end of a long table, with Nathan sitting on my right. A couple of men and women I had never seen before sat opposite of us, wearing business clothes. Nathan also looked rather formal, but I had a simple shift on. My friends, who I'm sure were going to dress up in jeans, were not slated to arrive until noon.

A friendly, mid-50s woman spoke first. "I am Dr. Brenda Angevin. I have been assigned as your psychotherapist, as well as your friend Samantha's counselor. I have specialities with the supernatural, as well as some of the common terms we use to describe these conditions. Not everything can be explained through science, though, but we try our best." She smiled.

"I'd like to introduce you to everyone else present. This here is Miss Nicole Barton, she is your new liaison and will be your point of contact concerning all assignments. Later on today you two will have a private meeting. To my left, these are Misters Michael Perez and Robert Cox. Mr. Perez and Mr. Cox oversee the department in this region."

I nodded hello.

"For everyone present, I ask you to state your name, your position within this company, and as many details about the past month as you can. This will be used to gauge your mental status, but also so we can sort out facts from fiction for you. Please do not leave any details out, nor what you made of these events, if anything."

I looked over at Nathan with a question in my eyes. He said softly, "You can tell them about us, too."

So for the next hour, I spoke to my new therapist in front of a bunch of other people. It was awkward and extremely difficult. The doctor asked many questions to prompt me when I found myself in a corner I didn't know my way out of, and it included *everything* from my father to the hallucinations I had about my mother. Dr. Angevin did not clear up whether or not she thought they were real, but she did refer to them as hallucinations. Nathan interjected when he felt appropriate, or when I got confused, and he was very professional throughout it all.

When it came to the inexplicable connection between him and I, I found myself incredibly self-conscious and embarrassed. Nathan, however, knew all of this was coming so any flush that crept over his cheeks was quickly able to muted.

Luckily, though, the doctor did not force me to talk about it too much, although I could tell that she was incredibly interested in it. Another man and woman in the room were, too, but the second and third man could care less. I supposed they were the more practical people in this whole charade.

After I told my part and was offered water, someone knocked on the door and wouldn't you know it, Jared Tenebris walked in. I couldn't believe it. I looked at Nathan in alarm, but he just curtly nodded his head at Jared and ignored my probe.

"I don't understand. What is he doing here?"

Mr. Perez spoke, "Mr. Tenebris works for an independent contractor, and is often called in when we need his expertise."

He had a smug look on his face. Nathan looked irritated. "Turns out we didn't need it this time." Nathan's face became smug, and Jared just cleared his throat and spoke to Mr. Cox.

"I was told to show up at 11 for the debriefing, so here I am."

Mr. Cox waved him to sit down, and he chose to sit on the other side of me, cockily propping his legs up on the wooden table. I caught Nathan's eye and rolled my own.

Dr. Angevin sat back and listened as Mr. Cox explained, very dryly, the events that had recently taken place. Scouts were already gathering in the area, and with Nathan's arrival, they knew a new apprentice was being minted. They weren't happy about this, so they had orders, if you will, to seek out the apprentice and destroy him/her before Nathan could find her/him. No one mentioned who was in charge of this particular group of Scouts.

They assumed this is why Alyssa was murdered—the Scout had been looking for me and Alyssa got in the way. I can't even begin to describe how deeply it affected me, knowing that Alyssa had essentially been murdered because of me. I could tell Nathan was carrying some of the burden for her death, too.

Nathan had sought out an apprentice as soon as he got into town, learning about various people in the area, who worked where, who did what, etc. For some reason not explained to me, it had crossed his mind that *I* was in fact the new apprentice, and so he stayed close to me. Once the parchment made its way into my hands, though, only then was it confirmed to Nathan who I was.

It reminded me of how the wand chooses the wizard. No one explained how it was written, why I was chosen, or if that was usually the thway apprentices are picked, so either it wasn't important, or it was deliberately left as a mystery. I had a feeling it was the latter, and I would continue being left in the dark about certain topics.

Once I was chosen, Nathan began to train me. Jared was

called in because the Scouts were not following a typical pattern of formation. I suppose Jared had more expertise than Nathan outside of what was 'normal' because Nathan played by the rulebook. The group wasn't behaving according to this unspoken rulebook because they had Sam in their ranks. She had inadvertently become a Scout, and when the others realized she knew the apprentice, they sought to defeat me that night.

They were as underprepared as me, which is partially why I was able to push forth the light energy as easily as I did. I could tell, however, that Nathan, and even Jared for that matter, thought it was more than that—perhaps I was preternaturally gifted above and beyond what a regular apprentice might be.

Mr. Cox did not share that sentiment, but he also didn't indicate he didn't think so the other way, either.

They asked if I had any questions, and I was so overloaded after the past few hours that I did not. They had had lunch delivered to the office, so we broke for some food around the same time that the others arrived.

Jason showed up in uniform, and seemed very official as he shook their hands. Sam stood back, awkward, and Elizabeth made a beeline for me as soon as she saw me.

"You look terrible," she said in a throaty voice.

"Thanks," I wryly returned. "I'm already exhausted and we are nowhere near done. They've got to talk to you, I've got to talk to my new liaison, and then maybe it's over."

"Until you have to do it again."

"Until I have to do it again."

"Well—at least this spread is good." She nodded towards the food, changing the subject. I laughed as she anxiously grabbed a bagel. I really wasn't that hungry, but I did pick up an apple to munch on. Nathan and Jared were tersely talking, but then Jared slapped him on the back, shook hands with the others and slid out like a snake.

He did not glance my way again, nor did he acknowledge Elizabeth. "Ugh. What a slimeball."

Elizabeth made herself scarce when Jason walked up. "Hey," he said, "How are you holding up?" He gave me a squeeze.

"As well as you can imagine."

"How's the arm doing?"

"It still hurts, but I suspect the cast will be cut off sooner rather than later."

"And then back to it?"

"And then back to it."

The break came and went, and I found myself face to face with the new liaison while all the others went back into the bigger room. She held a thick file that read *The Moore Family.* My heart began to race as I looked from the file to her face.

"I'm going to try to make this as painless as possible, but you can ask questions at any time and of course, you can take as much time as you want from here on learning about your past, as well as that of your family's. Nathan is a professional so I know he didn't tell you about your family, but in short: Your bloodline comes from a long line of light bearers. Your father's side. I don't have clearance about your mother's side, but I believe there was some supernatural power, if you will, there as well. Nathan's family is a mix, but he personally was assigned to your father years ago."

"My… father?"

"Yes. And unfortunately one event was too much for your father to bear. Nathan was his liaison when his mind broke, and then was reassigned once we placed your father in the care facility he currently is in. After that, Nathan went to another assignment, but then he became an apprentice trainer and eventually was assigned to find *you.*"

I tuned her out after she relayed this information to me.

My mind started traveling to my late childhood, all the things that had happened, or things that hadn't made much sense. My mom's death, my father going into the nursing home, his rantings. His rantings about, well, *Nathan.*

Oh. My. God.

Nathan. I started to wrack my brains—had I come across him as a child? He was older than me, I wasn't sure how much, but he easily could have been in his mid-20s when I was a teenager..

Could this explain some of the emptiness I had felt as a child? Or was it just the loss of my mother, as my previous therapist had said? I turned back to Nicole and realized she had been patiently sitting there while I tuned her out.

"It's a lot to take in, I know. And you have all the time you need to process it with Dr. Angevin. I don't mean to be unkind here; it's just I have a different job with you than she does. My job is to make sure you are trained and fit, both mentally, physically and psychically for whatever challenges you and I face. I expect you and I to become very close, as my other light bearers are. In fact, here," she said, handing me an invitation on parchment.

I opened up the envelope and pulled it out, reading:

Welcome the new light bearer!
November 20 7 PM, Location TBD.
Dinner will be provided.

"Me?"

"You. I've got four other clients, two women, one man, one transgender who is FTM. We form one team in the Atlanta area. I'm sure you'll meet the other teams at some point, but our team is what will be most important to you in terms of fighting the good fight in this area."

I nodded and stretched out my legs in frustration.

She leaned forward and patted me on my knees. "It gets easier, I promise. Once you integrate with the others you'll have so many of your questions answered, and it will become more clear what your actual path is. The good thing for you, is, you're older than some new recruits. It's usually easier for older people to accept their roles than the younger ones."

I looked more closely at Nicole and realized, despite her lack of visible wrinkles other than at her eyes, she was easily in her mid-40s.

"How long have you been doing this?"

"Fifteen years."

"Were you always in this position?"

"Nope. I started out like you, but quickly realized field work wasn't really for me."

"So I can change my role, as long as I continue to 'fight the good fight'?" I echoed in question.

"Of course. There are always options. You can always opt completely out, too, and return to civilian hood, but we'd have to wipe your memory." She smiled a quirky smile, slapping her folder shut.

I had no idea if she was joking or not.

24

It was mid-afternoon and the day was getting long. I couldn't believe the debriefing was taking all day—even though Nathan had warned me it would be a lengthy process. We were having a coffee break, and were all going to momentarily convene together. Well, except Sam. She was going to meet with Dr. Angevin.

She looked scared from the tips of red hair to the roots on her head. I smiled empathetically at her as she was walked into the room I had recently sat in myself.

Nathan and I had more or less been separated all day—there was just too much going on to have a private word. I knew this was the last meeting, the one that included almost all of us and how to proceed from here. I knew that after this was over, Nathan was driving his car to Washington D.C. For all I knew, that's where he actually lived most of the year, maybe he even had an apartment there.

Stupid me had never thought to ask about where he lived when he wasn't on assignment. I had been too wrapped up in my drama to inquire. Although, he probably wouldn't have told me anyway.

Everyone was in the conference room but him and me. I could hear the chairs scraping as people began to settle down for the last long haul. Nathan blocked me from entering the door, looking defeated. "Did she tell you?"

I nodded, looking down at the floor. He tilted my face upwards to force me to look at him, and, looking pained, continued, "I'm so sorry for my part in so much of your pain. When I came here and realized you were located in this town, I had a bad feeling you were going to be the next apprentice. When I found you at the yoga studio, I was hoping you weren't."

I had looked away as he held me in place, and he continued. "I felt our connection, right away, you know. I just ignored it." He seemed desperate.

My eyes were probably very round with exhaustion. I had no response to him, and I felt immobile as the gold flecks in his eyes faded and his green dimmed.

"Nathan," called someone from within the room.

He wanted me to respond. I un-tarred myself and began to move towards the doorway. He blocked me again. I lifted my broken arm at him and pushed him as forcefully as I could without hurting myself. He looked shattered as I passed by him.

I wasn't sure what to think, but in that moment, I was angry.

He should have just told me. "Rules" or not.

I'm sure I wouldn't have believed him, though. Not in the beginning. Not until I had experienced our connection firsthand would I have eaten what was served.

Luckily, this meeting didn't last long. They basically just connected our stories, told Elizabeth to support me and Sam since she was in the know, and told Jason that he was going to be their new point-of-contact for the local police department and he was to directly report to his Chief (who was now also present at the meeting).

And that was it. We were dismissed. We trickled out of the

room, me shaking hands with Dr. Angevin and Nicole.

"I guess I'll be seeing you guys relatively soon."

"Pleasure to meet you, Miss Moore," said Dr. Angevin warmly grasping my hand. Nicole gave me a hug.

The girls excused themselves to use the restroom and Jason smiled sadly at me. "You're quite the little powerhouse, aren't you?"

"Ha. I guess so." I shrugged and leaned against the wall that he was standing next to.

"You ready to go home?" he asked, then looked at Nathan who had just walked out of the room. He saw me with Jason and a visibly hurt expression crossed his face.

Jason, being the good guy, gave me a gentle shove. "Go talk to him, Vi. I may not understand what it is between you, but I know two despairing people when I see them."

I looked up at Jason and sighed. "Alright."

"We will be waiting for you. To bring you home." He said pointedly, and loudly enough so it wasn't lost on Nathan across the room.

I slowly walked over to Nathan. I glanced back at Jason who now stood with Elizabeth and Sam. Jason quickly turned away, Elizabeth had a grim expression and Sam looked at the floor. We walked to a quiet corner where nobody could see us.

I spoke first. "I'm sorry for my attitude earlier. It was unfounded."

"No, it wasn't."

An impasse. For a moment, neither of us spoke. But then he found his voice. "Violet, I want you to take this." He took the necklace of his beloved runic inscribed ring off his neck.

I looked at him, shocked.

"But—"

"It was a gift from my mother, yes."

"I can't."

He put it around my neck.

"I won't."

He clasped it.

"It's not right." I started to panic.

"Hush. It's yours. My mother would want you to have it. So in life," he started.

"Is Death" I whispered, a lump forming in my throat.

He quietly responded, "I will miss you, Violet." He placed his hand over the ring on my neck. I felt a jolt of electricity engulf me, this time obviously coming from the ring. With my naked eye, I saw white light pouring from it, engulfing us in an infinity sign. It disappeared as quickly as it came on.

My breath caught. "Did you see that?"

Without warning, he reached down and kissed me. Hesitantly at first, but when I responded, it became passionate, with an incredible amount of warmth and, well, *love*. The stubble on his chin rudely scratched my face and one of his hands placed itself on my lower back, while the other one was on my upper back. My good arm was wrapped around his neck, gripping him for dear life. The embrace was intense, safe, warm. Although I didn't want the magic to ever end, I had to break away. As I leaned back ever so slightly, I looked up and met his eyes. They were practically gold.

His lips formed a flat line as his chest heaved, trying to regain his breath. He swallowed, hard, and I blinked, equally as hard.

This embrace was not to be.

"I have to go, now, or I'll never be able to go," I cried out, quickly turning to leave. This final image of him standing in place, not fighting for me, not moving towards me, just surrendering and letting me go took up ridiculous amounts of space inside my brain.

I felt the fire from his eyes bore into my back, him speaking not a sound as I ran away from him. I grabbed Elizabeth and

Sam's hands, clutching them with all of my strength so I would not turn back and look at him. Once in the car, I blandly looked out the window. The girls had put me in the back with Sam. Elizabeth carried the conversation with Jason on the ride home.

I vowed then and there that I would never wonder about Nathan ever again. I would stop moping about what wouldn't be. It was time to have my future as my present, and that meant an existence without Nathan Murphy.

Jason made a point to drop the others off first before taking me home, even though it was out of the way. When we pulled up to my complex, he turned his car off in a parking space. I took a deep breath and faced him. "I don't really want to be alone. I'm not sure what food or anything I have to offer other than what Na… what he stocked before leaving, but…"

Without saying a word, he got out of the car, opened my door, weaved his arm into mine, and together we walked to the staircase that led to my apartment.

PART II: PROPHECY, VISIONS AND BROTHERS, OH MY

25

Christmas-time was finally here, and I was riding up front, driving a rented golf car with Layla sitting next to me. Elizabeth, her new girlfriend, Janette, Samantha, and a guy she was seeing, Thomas, were sitting behind us. Layla was happily single, and I was officially in a relationship with Jason, AKA Officer Dunham, AKA Sergeant Sexy.

Lots of things had changed in just a couple of short months.

My broken arm had magically healed, and how it had healed so quickly was never fully explained to me by anyone, including my psychotherapist, Dr. Angevin, or light throwing liaison, Nicole Barton.

I had recently quit doing bookkeeping for my ex's father, which was a welcome relief as it officially cut off all ties between me and my crazy ass, almost-divorced-from-his-wife-Amanda ex. I would miss his father—and I did hope to see him in town—but to be free of Damien, once and for all, was a huge blessing.

Amanda, however, had somehow started to weasel her way into my extended group of friends and colleagues. So I had to see her sometimes. But it wasn't as awkward anymore, as she had finally realized Damien was a pompous ass and I

188

was actually kind of cool.

Only my inner circle knew about my additional super-spy job, though, and what had really happened to the Mother Hen of the Yoga Sect a few months back. Alyssa had been murdered, sort of inadvertently, by people who were out to get *me* before I knew who *I* was. Our community gossiped about what had happened, about why things had gotten quiet. Everyone found it curious that Elizabeth and I had been involved in a nasty car wreck so soon on the heels of what had happened with Alyssa, and everyone found it even *more* curious that the man I had been attached to had suddenly disappeared without a word—but nobody ever came outright to ask Liz or me about what we knew. We happily kept mum while the rumors raged.

I pulled into the parking lot of our amphitheater, and everyone jumped out, wrapped in parkas, holding coffee mugs full of all sorts of yummy spiked things. Elizabeth linked arms with Layla and me as we walked into the amphitheater.

It was a Saturday night, and a bunch of school choirs were going to be putting on a free Grinch show, followed by some carols. From there, we would get back on the golf car, line up with other golf cars, and drive in a procession on the recreation path to City Hall, where the festivities would be followed up with dancing, Santa, and the lighting of the tree.

It was fun, if not a little silly, for a bunch of childless thirty-somethings to attend.

I had a feeling, though, that Elizabeth's latest relationship would actually turn serious quite soon, with thoughts of adoption on the horizon. And who knew, maybe even wild child Sam would settle down with Thomas. Both seemed rather content at the moment. I was happy for them.

I was also pretty happy; I definitely loved Jason, and could see a future with him. Yet I was held back by my unresolved emotions with the phantom that was Nathan. Jason knew my complicated emotions still existed, and would never pressure me into anything. He was an amazing man.

I suspected he deserved better than me, because I wasn't sure I would ever be able to give him what he needed.

Which, of course, was the white picket fence, a wife, and a kid or two. I'm sure some dogs would be thrown in there, and well, Barnaby, my always-suspicious, treat-wanting tabby cat.

Jason was working that night, keeping the amphitheater safe from hoodlums like us, and hoodlums like the teenagers who were old enough to drive golf cars alone, but not old enough to drink illegally the way we were. They'd probably steal their parents' whiskey before coming out.

My friends walked down an aisle on the right to sit down while I motioned towards Jason. "I'll be back in a sec," I said to nobody in particular—I didn't think anyone was listening to me.

He was standing with his back to one of the walls looming above the stage. He was in the opposite direction of where my gang was sitting, so he had missed us coming in. I had peppermint striped gloves on, a silly santa hat, and a big grin for him when I crowded his space.

"Merry Christmas," I said, pushing my hands into his chest, giving him the type of kiss that would make him remember me until he was off-duty.

"Hey, now!" he exclaimed, laughing. "Egg nog getting to your head?"

"Something like that."

"Cute hat," he smirked.

"How come you're not wearing one, Sergeant Sexy?" I teased. "The department hasn't issued you your elf hats yet?"

Elizabeth had recently come to turns with her bisexuality (and unfortunately for her, feelings for me) and had referred to him as Sergeant Sexy. The name had stuck, and when he'd started showing interest in me, I had had a hard time calling him Jason. Eventually though, after we'd gotten quite cozy, I'd told him his former nickname.

He of course liked it. It fed his ego. The worm.

A man started to speak over the loud speaker to let us know that the show was about to start, so I kissed him again, said, "See ya!" and ran off to rejoin my friends.

I wasn't the type to normally sing out loud, but the egg nog was definitely getting to my head, so I joined in with my friends. The show ended, I waved at Jason (he was going to drive over to City Hall after everyone left the amphitheater) and got back onto the golf car.

"Ugh," I said, looking over at Layla.

"You're drunk, aren't you?" She laughed. "Hand me the keys, I'll drive."

I didn't think I'd had *that* much, but suddenly I didn't feel so hot. In the distance, a loud popping sound came from an indecipherable direction. Layla and I switched seats. Everyone in the area yelped at the sound, and then there was tons of laughter as people pulled into the golf car line.

I raised an eyebrow at Layla and said, "Hm." She did a quick search of the area, and shook her head.

I asked if anyone had water, and Sam let me drink her bottle. She suddenly looked a little nervous, and I wanted to make sure to pull her aside once we got to our next destination.

That popping sound? It had seemed a little supernatural to me. I wasn't currently on any specific assignment, although I was told to always remain vigilant. Initially Elizabeth had been my go-to with all the woo-woo crap, but once she started dating a yoga student of hers, she disappeared. Layla, the one who had taken yoga training with us strictly for the physical component, had really stepped up to help me out.

I think it fulfilled some fantasy of her being a bodyguard.

Cute little Layla, though, was only 5 feet tall and about 100 pounds soaking wet. She *did* know martial arts, though. Of course, at that point, I knew some MMA, too, as part of my training.

As we got into line, I told her I was feeling really dizzy and I didn't think it was from the egg nog. "Well, I didn't see anything out of place. I know I don't feel things like you and Sam, but—

"Hey, watch out!" barked Layla at a golf car that had come barreling at us out of nowhere. Everyone on our golf car screeched with laughter. Layla gave the driver a dirty look and drove onto the connecting cart path.

"Oh jeez. No wonder I feel like crap. That idiot on the golf car was a Scout."

26

We made it to City Hall without any problems in spite of the Scout trying to scare me by practically running our cart off the path. As it turned out, one Scout wasn't really a threat, although, any single human could obviously cause some sort of harm. I pulled Sam aside as soon as we got off of the cart and parked.

"Did you feel that?"

"Yes," she said nervously. "But I promise, I'm fine. I'm scared, but I'm never going to be pulled down that path again. It's too powerful—and in a bad way."

"I know," I said, squeezing her. I let her return to Thomas for some fun. She certainly deserved it.

She had been involved with a group of Scouts a a couple of months earlier. She had been depressed, and fell victim to people who had used her to get to me. I had forgiven her— but she hadn't entirely forgiven herself just yet. I still felt very guilty about not noticing that Sam had been sinking into depression. I had been so wrapped in myself—dad drama, ex-boyfriend drama, sudden new career drama. Although, to be fair, Layla and Elizabeth had missed it, too, so when Sam had literally joined the baddies I was supposed to be fighting, we were all stupefied.

Because I'd gotten into such a bad car wreck when they had tried to overrun me, the group had disappeared into the shadows, waiting to re-form and wreak havoc. Sam, because she'd come to her senses when she saw what they were actually trying to do, had been rehabbed.

I was still trying to understand on the most basic level who or what a Scout was, who they served and why, but the government, naturally, was withholding information. I could only guess at how they gathered and worked. All I knew was, it was currently my job to keep them from hurting more people with their false pretense of setting humanity free.

I closed my eyes for a few moments to gather my wits about me. I still felt little dizzy, and the sound of the Christmas bells and people's voices began to disorient me. Layla and I stepped off to the side near a bunch of trees lining the parking lot while the others gathered around the Christmas tree, waiting for the rest of the golf cars to show up.

"I might toss that egg nog up," I said, hugging a tree.

"Oh stop it. Go chant something and it will go away," she said, semi-mockingly with a grin.

I wished it were that easy. I hesitated, then placed my hand on the ring that was on a necklace around my neck. Jason had never inquired about it, which led me to believe he knew it was from *him*. I hadn't had the courage to take it off. I didn't know if it offered protection, but it always made me feel better to hold it in my hand when I was unsure of—anything.

Sometimes it felt warm and soothing, sometimes it felt electric and hot, shocking. Tonight? It felt electric, hot and shocking. I was trying to figure out if the different feelings each time meant something—other than where my own mental state was at the time.

It wasn't necessarily surprising that it felt that crazy in that moment.

Even so, I held onto it tightly with my eyes closed and centered myself. I envisioned my third eye as the evolving runic writing for peace—*frithuz*—and did a quick breath-holding meditation.

The ring felt like it was on fire, and it took all of my willpower to not drop it. A blue light flashed out of it, and it was so *real* and so *tangible*, that even Layla saw it. "Holy smokes," she said, watching me. "The more I get involved with your Jedi shit, the more in-tune I'm becoming myself!" She laughed. "Of course, I still don't believe in any of it." She winked. "Feeling better?"

"Yes," I murmured, scanning the crowd. "See anything unusual? It's never done that before. I'm wondering—"

"Wondering what?"

"If *he's* here."

Her lips formed an 'O' shape. "Would he really do that, though? Show up and not tell you?"

"I'm under the impression of just that. He's not going to want to disturb me… and nor do I want him to. Come on— let's go join the others. Jason should be by soon and I'm ready to see Santa." Layla cocked her head to one side as if she didn't know whether or not to argue with me, but she shrugged and followed me back into the crowd.

I couldn't shake the feeling that I was being watched, though. And it wasn't by the Scout. I could see him as well as feel him—red energy, standing off to the left of the Christmas tree with some friends. This other energy I felt? I wasn't sure why I couldn't tell if it was *his* or not, but it moved quickly into every color imaginable. I wondered if that was why I couldn't quite pin point it, because of its constant state of flux.

We had joked once upon a time about having superpowers like shape shifting, but I wondered if maybe we could energy shift instead.

Jason came up behind me and held me as an elf started the countdown for the tree. He kissed my ear in greeting, and I felt the energy rapidly retreat on a path, headed in the direction of where *his* father lived.

It almost had to be him.

"5… 4… 3… 2… 1!"

Jingle Bells blared on the loudspeaker as the lights lit up and popped. The Scout was curiously watching me as the popping started and people shrieked with laughter. The lights flickered one more time before staying on. I looked back at the Scout with no fear in my eyes, or heart. I wasn't intimidated. I was irritated he was looking at me that way, though, and I was starting to wonder if he was going to come over and actually talk with me.

I wondered if Scouts ever did that—I'd have to ask some of the other light throwers in my group. After the accident, my professional group of other light bearers had become pretty amazing acquaintances in such a short duration of time. Although most of them had been doing it for almost ten years, and I was the newbie, the camaraderie was instantaneous because nobody else in the world could truly understand our lives. The others were usually able to answer most of my questions, and I was hoping they'd be able to answer this newest question about whether or not Scouts had ever conversationally approached them.

Or I could always task the inquiry to my current trainer, Nicole, but she encouraged us to seek help from the other light throwers since they were also in the field. Nicole was mainly there to school us and whip our asses into full mental and physical shape, to create discipline where I sure didn't want any.

When it seemed like the Scout had made up his mind to approach me, people began to get between us and Jason chose that moment to pick me up and twirl me around.

"Ahhh!" I exclaimed, taken aback.

He placed me back down on the ground and looked down at me. His light blue eyes pierced any barriers I had built up because of the Scout. "Merry Christmas, there, Beautiful," he said, kissing me.

Jason was about as far removed from anything supernatural as you could be; we were kind of an odd pairing in that respect. He believed things he could see with his eyes, things that could be explained only with hard science. When he had a difficult time rectifying the inexplicable, he would choose to laugh it off with a shrug. He knew there was more than what was tangible—on some level anyway—but he wasn't going to let it bother him. He was kind of like Layla.

"Guess what?" he continued.

"What?" I asked, smiling up at him.

"I'm free once this party ends. Got any plans tonight?"

"Just you." He threaded his fingers through my brown hair, yanking on the strands that used to be blue, but were now purple, pulling my head back to look up at him. I puckered my lips for a smooch, but was interrupted.

The crowd was starting to thin out, and Layla groaned. "Oh my God, would you two stop making me want to puke already? Come on, you lovebird, we need to get going. It's past Liz's bed time." I lowered my head down to look at her, laughing.

"I heard that!" shouted Elizabeth, glancing over her shoulder at us.

"And I'm sure Sam has some knitting to do—"

"Hey! How did I get dragged into this?" she asked, furrowing her brow.

Thomas pulled her close and laughed. "You're known as the granny of the group?"

"Ha! Hardly!"

Layla looked from one couple to the next, then crossed her

arms and started tapping her foot. "Well, shit, maybe I should just go home and bury my head under the covers. I just realized you all have someone but me!" Typical Layla.

"Please, Lay. Nobody for *one* moment thinks you actually want to be in a relationship."

Jason started to back up, hands up in defeat. "Good luck, Thomas. The girls are all yours to handle."

The Scout had reappeared and Jason about ran into him.

"Oh, sorry, Officer," the Scout said, semi-maliciously looking my way.

I wasn't having any of it. The others had started to walk back to the golf car, but Layla stood sentinel next to me. "Jas—this guy's a Scout. Just so you know," I said with a hardened voice.

Jason looked shocked, but quickly recovered, took his police stance with his hands at his waist, and asked, "Is there going to be a problem here?" I could almost feel his adrenaline running through *my* veins.

"Of course not. Have a merry Christmas." The Scout joined his friends without looking back at us and walked away.

Jason didn't turn away from the Scout, but asked me, "Is that normal for a light bearer to be approached?"

"I don't know. I'm going to find out, though."

27

It was early. Even though I didn't have to "officially" meditate on Sundays, I was certainly programmed to do so because of the other six mornings a week that I *did* do it for work. I looked over at Jason in my bed. He had one arm above his head, the other outside of the covers at his side. Phang was nestled up against him, and Barnaby at his feet.

Traitors.

He was wearing a tank top, and a strand of dirty blond hair fell across his forehead. He had recently cut his hair to his ears. I didn't know how he was able to wear just a wife beater—I was freezing my tail off in long sleeves and woolen socks.

I crawled out of bed and put a robe on, and turned the heat up a notch, hoping I wouldn't smoke Jason out of bed by accident.

I grabbed a blanket, a cup of tea, and sat on the floor on my purple zabuton. It was starting to get pretty worn; I was thinking of getting a new one for myself for Christmas. I closed my eyes after taking a sip of tea and began to focus on my third eye to get myself nicely centered.

I placed a hand on my heart and one on my stomach, turned my Reiki on, and just followed my breath for a few minutes. Then I began to let my mind wander to various runes, thinking of which saying I wanted to focus on that morning.

Out of nowhere *his* face appeared, and I had to steady myself. *Leave me alone,* I thought to my memories. But try as I might, his face persisted as I fell into the meditation. I decided to stop fighting it and just go with the images that came.

My mother. It was my mother! I hadn't seen her since right after the accident.

She was walking towards me, an otherworldly light glowing around her. She reached out her palms to me, and I looked down into them. She was holding a box of some sort that was etched in runestaves. She looked at me and nodded; the meaning was clear.

I needed to find that box.

There were two other boxes at her feet, both seeming similar. She frowned at them, and because of her expression, a deep sadness welled up within me.

She started to be pulled away from me, and *his* face appeared again, only this time I saw that he was rock climbing the face of a mountain. At the top, though, he was not safe. There was a wild animal there, stalking him. The animal ferociously jumped at him, blocking him from reaching the precipice. I saw his body plummet wildly down, slamming into rock after rock.

I bolted out of the reverie, heart pounding. I placed a hand on the ground and found that Phang was sitting there, happily snorting.

I rarely fell asleep like that during meditation anymore since I was so used to meditating these days. I didn't know much about prophetic dreams, but I figured I had another thing to bring up with the others.

Luckily for me, I was soon meeting with two of them

during an aerial yoga class up in Atlanta.

***

After a very insightful yoga class in the middle of the week, I realized I should never, *ever* do anything like that again. All the twirling and spinning and upside downing made me want to throw up on the studio's perfectly polished floor.

I sat out the last thirty minutes of the class on the sidelines, slowly drinking water and trying to re-swallow the fig bar I'd had on the way to class. The other two light bearers were having *no* problem with the antics of the class, and I wondered why, once again, I had been chosen to be a light bearer. I was barely adept at walking without tripping.

One of the assistant teachers sat down next to me, making sure I was okay. "Oh, I'm fine — just embarrassed I even tried this out. I had a feeling it would not be a good idea." I smiled wistfully.

The girl gave me a squeeze and then rejoined the others.

I started to feel a bit better, and walked over to one of the windows facing the parking lot. The street was full of cars stuck at traffic lights; every now and then you could hear a horn honk. Just then I heard a siren in the distance, and eventually saw a medic trying to barrel its way through the traffic. It was dusk and I could barely make out the setting sun stashed between a couple of tall buildings.

We were in a complex that housed some random stores, with an overpriced grocery store as one of the anchors. However, we were headed to that overpriced store to grab dinner after class and have a pint or two at its in-house bar and grill. I could see people pulling in and out of parking spaces. Nobody was walking by our side of the complex, though — we were at the opposite end of the grocery store.

All of a sudden, my necklace burned so hot and startled me into a loud enough gasp that several of the yoga students looked my way. I smiled I was okay and then carefully pulled the ring off of my neck to look at it. The blue from the runes flashed a quick, blinding blue metronomic pulse and then abruptly stopped.

What did that mean?

I looked back inside at the people playing trapeze artists, and then back out the windows. I couldn't make out anything suspicious. No Scouts, no*body*, like I had said. Well, that wasn't true. I saw a silhouette walking quickly in a diagonal line through the parking lot between cars. Because the sun was shining in my face, I couldn't make out if it was male or female. The figure quickly disappeared amongst the other people returning to their cars, and that was that.

The class ended and the other two light bearers joined me, giant smiles on their faces. We hung out together much more than the other light bearers in the area—one, they lived closer, and two, they were nearer my age. One of the others was a transgender man about fifty, and the other man was young, maybe about twenty-five. He'd only been at this job a few years before I had gotten recruited. The girls? They were both in their thirties like me.

One was about six feet tall, super thin with thick, dirty blond hair pulled back in a pony tail. Janine was about the happiest I had ever seen her. Perhaps she had a future in the circus or something.

"I'm so sorry you didn't enjoy that, Violet!"

"It's alright," I grumbled. "I didn't think it would be up my alley, to be honest. But it was the nausea that made me quit!"

The other light thrower, Tollie, rolled her brown eyes at Janine. She was shaped more like me, if not slightly shorter, and had her black hair pulled back in a pony tail. Her caramel colored skin was shining with some sweat that she wiped off with a towel.

"I think that's a workout for a bean pole, if you ask me."

Janine said, "Hey!"

And we all started to laugh. "Let's go grab a beer!" Tollie smiled.

Soon thereafter, the three of us hung out at the bar with our tofu and organic gluten-free god knows what type of beer. After we ate to our bellies' content, we moved from the bar with our pints to a quieter corner near the window for some privacy.

"So how are things going?" asked Tollie, taking a sip of her drink.

"My arm is completely healed, as you can see. It has been for awhile. Whatever *Nathan* did, he essentially performed a miracle." It was the first time I had actually said his name out loud—or even to myself—in over a month. It felt and tasted awkward on my tongue and lips.

Janine and Tollie had only heard tidbits and pieces about my relationship with Nathan, but I thought Janine could saw through what little I had offered about it. She never pried, though.

"Yeah! Nathan's pretty cool, I've met him a few times. I think he's actually in town right now, I heard that he's being transferred to… *what*?" Tollie grimaced and leaned down to rub her leg.

Janine smiled sweetly at her.

"It's okay, Janine. I don't care."

She raised her eyebrow, and Tollie looked on in confusion. "Would someone please fill me in?" Janine gestured that I had the floor to speak.

"I don't want to talk about it," I mumbled, finding the bottom of my pint.

Janine gestured to the air. "They were sort of a metaphysical supernatural item. But—"

Tollie's face broken out into a grin. "I *knew* there was

something up with you two! He met with Nicole after he first started to train you, Vi, and he was just so *weird* about you. Don't you remember that, J? It was that night I was with Nic and we met halfway between Atlanta and where he was staying. He had all sorts of questions about weird sensations and the implications of 'em." She looked thoughtfully at me. "Nicole didn't have any good information for him, though. She told him to seek counsel with someone of higher clearance."

I looked at her with interest. I remembered that night, it was after one of his nemeses, Jared Tenebris, had infiltrated my group. He had uncharacteristically left me alone for several hours. The following day he had just told me he was inquiring about what he and I were experiencing, and that there were no concrete answers about it.

And that, in even these circles, it was considered rare.

But now I knew our families had a history—and at that, I wasn't sure how far back it went, other than *he* had trained my father at the time of my father's mental collapse. I had been so busy with healing, and working, and getting to know Jason, I hadn't taken the time to really explore my origins. Dr. Angevin and Nicole had both told me that they would give me whatever information they were privy to, anytime I asked.

I just hadn't asked.

And *ugh*, speaking of my dad, I hadn't spoken to him in almost a week. I made a visit to him during the first week after *he* had left, and it turned up fruitless. I didn't get any answers. My father sometimes would hallucinate and delve deep into things that I neither remembered, nor knew what he was referencing. Now that I had some insight into our collective past, I really wanted to see if they were 'hallucinations' or not. But, Dad had been completely lucid when I was there and I wasn't able to figure out any secrets.

"Earth to Vi..." said Janine, looking over at Tollie, slightly worried.

"Sorry. I just lost myself in my thoughts about my father."

They knew a little bit about all of that, too, but not enough to connect the dots. Although, Tollie's face suddenly filled with interest when I mentioned my dad. "Violet—what if your families go back even further than you think? Maybe you came from the original Germanic peoples, right, I mean, these *are* runes we chant, yes? And how about if you and Nathan reproduced, then maybe the—"

"World would implode?"

I started laughing at their wild minds. "Nice one, guys. Refills?"

"Nah—I've got to get home soon," said Tollie, but Janine said she was thirsty for some coffee so she joined me up at the bar.

"Sorry about all the Nathan talk. I know it can't be easy for you, and I know that's not why you wanted to see us today... or is it?"

"No. I mean, I don't think so." I unearthed my ring so she could see it. "Do you know anything about runic powers and maybe platinum? There are no stones on this, it's just embedded with that special ink. I'm assuming it's platinum. I have no idea how old it is, only that Nathan's mom gave it to him, and he gave it to me before he left. Sometimes it gets really hot, or flashes—I mean, I guess I could be making it all up...?"

"Hmmm," she said, fingering it gently. "I'll take a decaf cappuccino, please," she said, directing her attention at the barista. To me, she said, "I'll do some research and get back to you."

I nodded, deep in thought.

"I'll just have a water," I said to the bartender. He looked at us a little too closely, but he wasn't a Scout as far as I could tell.

When we sat back down, I asked Janine about it. "What was up with that guy? He wasn't a Scout, buuuuut, I don't feel like he was 'normal', either?

"Who knows? Our clearance is so low God only knows what else lurks out here. He could be a werewolf." She smiled semi-ironically.

Tollie giggled, a little nervously. "They don't exist, Janine."

I cleared my throat and steamrolled on, "Anyway, I want to ask you guys about Scouts in general. Have any ever approached you to speak with you?" I proceeded to tell them about what happened at the Christmas festival.

My question was met with raised eyebrows. "It's a good thing we're meeting with Nic this weekend."

28

It was Friday night and I was taking my weekly hot yoga class that Elizabeth led. It was hard to swallow that a little over a month ago, though, it had been where she and I had been before being summoned to that hiking trail Sam had bogey-trapped for me.

Being in the studio for only the second time after the accident put me on edge. I know Elizabeth felt it too, because when we were cleaning up afterwards, she was quick to want to go home.

After we locked the door and started heading to our respective cars in our not-warm enough sweaters, I mused, "Why are we always underdressed when we leave class?"

She just gave me a look.

"Alright, Vi, thanks for coming. Any plans this weekend?"

"Training tomorrow in Atlanta with the crew."

"Ohhh, good—you going ask Nicole about the ring's heat?"

"That, and a plethora of other things. I don't suppose... I mean, you haven't seen Nathan around, have you?"

I had stopped at her car and she sharply looked at me. "No. Why do you think that?"

"Just been feeling a little off. I've had some weird dreams

lately and when I saw Tollie and Janine at that aerial class, Tollie let it slip that he was apparently in town. He'd said he was going to be up in D.C. for about a month and then from there he didn't know where he was going. She also said he was being reassigned."

"And you didn't ask what that meant?"

"No. If he wanted to contact me, he knows where I am. He's staying away from me."

"God, Violet. I'm so, so sorry," she looked grim. "I know you like Jason and all but—"

"No buts, Elizabeth. I can't live like that. He chose to leave, and he didn't tell me why. I've moved on. Jason is a good man."

"Yes, I know but—"

"There is no Nathan."

"But if there was—"

"There *isn't*."

"Alright, alright. Go home! It's freezing. Maybe see you Sunday?"

"Night, E."

I walked to my car and felt incredibly stubborn. I gave Jason a call, even though it was not customary for me to call him after class on Fridays. He usually worked Friday nights anyway.

"Hey," he said, sounding slightly concerned when he answered. "What's up?" I had a feeling the not-too-distant past remained on his mind every Friday as well.

I aimed my car at my apartment. "I don't know, I'm just leaving class and feeling grumpy."

"Grumpy? I thought yoga was supposed to make you feel better," he chuckled.

"Yeah, yeah. I wish you weren't working tonight."

"Well, I wish *you* didn't have to go to your Jedi-training tomorrow."

Those jokes never got old. "Yeah, well, I have a lot of questions for Yogurt about the Schwartz, so it's a good thing I *do* have training."

"Yeah—find out about that Scout. I didn't like that at all."

"That doesn't mean you're starting to buy into this stuff, does it?"

"Ha!" He paused. "Of course not."

I smiled as I turned into my complex.

"Good night, Officer Dunham. Stay safe."

"You too, Beautiful. Good night."

***

Oof. I had just been knocked onto my back from a kick to my midriff by Tollie. She reached down to help me up. Janine was sparring with Duane, who was in his mid 40s, black hair, creamy dark skin, brown eyes and a shiny bald head I liked to tease him about. She got so distracted by Tollie knocking me over, that Duane was able to take *her* out.

The fifth person in our group, Victor, was sitting on the sidelines guffawing with his slanted eyes alight with laughter. "What is *with* you guys today?" he shrieked with laughter. He pulled his thick, black hair back into a pony tail and stood up to his full 6 foot frame.

He jumped onto the dojo floor and put himself into horse stance. He looked like a deranged Mulan with a crazed look in his eye.

Luckily, Nicole took to the floor. "Alright you clowns, I can see that nobody today can focus, so let's call this pathetic excuse for training *over.* Why don't you guys clean up and then meet me back here in about fifteen minutes? I'll get some tea and we can talk. I've got some new things I'd like you all to study, and I heard that Violet had some questions about Scouts."

Victor looked sad he wasn't able to spar anymore. We grabbed our bags and pushed one another aggressively to the locker rooms.

Nicole, or rather, the Feds, rented out a huge dojo near Little Five Points in Atlanta once a month. It had showers, locker rooms, and a mini-stove and fridge inside of it. We would meet once a month to make sure the training we did outside of getting together was up to snuff, as well as go over studies, meditations, and whatever else there was to do to keep us mentally and physically sharp.

I supposed at some point we'd be talking about banishing some Scouts, too, but that point hadn't come yet. Maybe there was just too much good cheer around the holidays that kept everyone at bay. *Maybe* I was naive enough to really believe that.

After we cleaned up, we all gathered on the dojo floor on big, round, comfortable zabutons. Duane didn't feel like sitting on one, so he just used it as a pillow for his neck. Nicole frowned at him, but didn't say anything. Janine was using hers to hug as she sprawled out on her belly, and once Nicole saw that, she rolled her eyes.

"My God, this group is such an assortment of misfits. The last *Group of Five*? They were so proper. I've heard that each group is very different! This couldn't be more true." She grinned. "I've got turmeric tea since you all just whupped one another's asses." She sat cross-legged on her cushion, and pushed her thick reddish-brown behind her ear. "Alright, Violet, why don't we start with you today. What questions do you have for us?"

I repeated what I had told Janine and Tollie earlier in the week about the Scout. Nicole furrowed her brow and tapped her fingers on the floor before she spoke. "Well, it's pretty unusual, but I don't think it's anything to worry about. After all, it's not like a Scout is really a supernatural being or anything." Or *us* was left unsaid. "They're regular people, who let the Darkness in too much and thusly make terrible choices. Some of these decisions end them up jailed, in insane asylums, or, dead." She sighed.

That was a sobering thought in lieu of Sam's situation. I mentally made a note to check in with her, and see how her sessions with Dr. Angevin were going.

Nicole continued. "So a Scout has total free will to speak to anyone, *including* a Light Bearer. whose main job is to snuff out his or her Darkness. Was it a male or female?"

"Male."

"Did you feel threatened?"

"No, more irritated than anything. My, um, boyfriend asked him if there was a problem, and the Scout said no."

"Ooooh, boyfriend," chimed in Victor. "Scandal. Does Nathan know?"

"Jeez, Victor," I said. "Is nothing sacred?!" I was semi-amused, semi-appalled.

Nicole sighed and sipped her tea. She stood up and grabbed a plate of scones for us. "I told you these people would become really close to you and know everything minute detail about you"

I nibbled some of the scone and glared at Victor. "Anyway, if it happens again, what should I do?"

Nicole looked thoughtful. "First off, *don't worry*. Unless it starts happening a lot, or by the same Scout, I don't think it's a problem. If that changes, though, let me know, and we'll talk to Cox."

I nodded.

"The other thing is," I hesitated. "Nathan gave me this the last time I saw him. It's been very hot lately, and keeps emitting flashes. It's really disconcerting, not to mention, straight up weird."

Victor sucked in his breath and ogled the ring as I took it off and handed it to Nicole. Duane pushed Victor's cushion out of the way, so that when he sat back, he hit his bottom hard on the floor.

Tollie and Janine started laughing.

"Misfits, the whole lot of you," muttered Nicole as she turned the ring over and over again, examining it. "The thing is, not everyone involved in this field have connections to Germanic peoples. Some people are just drawn to the field because they're decent human beings, or they're psychic. Not so much because of the runes themselves. There are other sets up employees with different gifts, who use different tools, that we don't even know about. *We* only work with the people who have the capability to work with the runes. And how do we choose people to work with the runes, you ask?" She looked up, and smiled. "The runes choose the person, right?" She drily laughed as the rest of us hung onto every word.

She continued, "You know, Nathan's family come from a long line of... Well, we don't really have a word for it that makes a lot of sense, so I liken it to Pure Bloods from Harry Potter."

I swallowed a laugh. "Okay?"

"So his mom, or someone in his immediate family, probably handcrafted this. That's why it's not as smooth as you might see a machine manufactured ring. I'm sure it's heavily infused with magic beyond what the script says. *Eihwaz. Algiz.* Simple, yet profound." She peered at the inside. "The old families had many talents, multiple gifts. Have you seen the inside inscription?"

I shook my head. Stupid me. I had almost been afraid of the ring so I had never looked at its inside.

She read it in the runic language. "Do you know what the translation is?"

I shook my head again.

"It basically says, 'as one soul'. I know this goes without saying, but of course, we don't have an exact translation for any of these inscriptions... Damn language and cultural barriers." She smiled grimly and shrugged. "We do what we can."

I found that I was having a hard time breathing. A huge hush fell over the group, and even Victor was quiet. Janine reached out to look at the inscription.

"So the heat probably has something to do with Nathan?"

Tollie took it from Janine, then offered it to Duane who passed it over to Victor without even looking at it.

Nicole said, "Yes. I'm sure it does. He didn't want me to tell you, but he's in town for a couple of weeks, visiting his father. He'll be returning to post, though, after that. He's no longer going to do apprentice training." She looked slightly uncomfortable sharing this information.

"Oh?" I asked, trying not to sound too interested. Everyone, of course, saw right through me.

Nicole put her hand on my shoulder. "He's being transferred overseas."

And that was that. We spent the next three hours studying and meditating and discussing whether or not anyone felt an impending event building.

Nobody did.

29

It was Christmas morning, and I was depressed. Everyone was visiting their respective families, and then there was me. And, well, Phang's snorting and Barnaby's tail under my nose. "Guys!" I said, moving them to my feet where Phang continued to snort and Barnaby glared at me with one eye.

When I was with my ex, I would alternate Christmases between his family and my family. It had worked out well. When I was single, I had gone home to visit my family every year. Since the death of my mother, my aunts and uncles and their families had begun to separate and move away from one another, so holidays had begun to become choppy and isolated. The last year I had traveled home for Christmas, it had just been my father and me. Since then, his dementia had gotten worse, thus why I didn't go home this current year.

And, well, I was depressed anyway. Going home would have probably just made it worse, and good or bad, my dad probably didn't know it was Christmas. I know. I sounded terrible.

Thinking about my dad made me very guilty, so I reached for the phone to call him. We spoke briefly, and as it turned out, he was aware that it was Christmas and he was sad I wasn't there. I told him that his sister was going to visit him, and that I was too busy with work to get away.

I had somehow turned into a liar on top of it all.

It was 9 AM and the day loomed long before me. I grabbed my little velvet pouch full of crystals that were marked with runestaves on them. No, this wasn't the fairly inexpensive type you could purchase at a bookstore—these were hand carved crystals infused with that magical Germanic ink. *He* had left them with me when he'd moved on to his next assignment.

After I sat down on my living room floor in a cross-legged position, I closed my eyes and tossed them onto the floor before me. I opened my eyes, and found Barnaby was trying to swat at one like it was a toy. "Hey!" I yelped at him, smacking his paw.

Well, that was it. He wasn't going to forgive me after that little outburst. He walked away with his tail high in the air, and jumped onto my couch Lording above me. Phang was sitting at the foot of the couch, rolling onto her back.

I reached out to grab the crystals, and see if I could make any sense of their layout. My intention had been to see how the day would go. I hadn't tossed all of the crystals out, but of the ones I'd used, *Thurisaz* and *Hagalaz* were the prominent ones screaming at me from the floor. There was another rune that was showing up a couple more times, too, but it wasn't one that was a part of the elder futhark writings.

While runes themselves were considered magical inscriptions that had been handed down by God (Odin), *his* family was somehow privy to even older runes, even more magical ones. Some of that script only existed by sound and not by writing—so the stories went, anyhow. And they weren't handed *down* by Odin, Odin himself had come to share them in a visible form. To *his* ancestors.

Oh, boy, I thought. *I'll just put those away.* I decided to gather up my mess, and move on with my day. I didn't need any sort of intuitive guidance after all. I just needed to eat something.

I looked to Phang and Barnaby and proclaimed, "Alright, guys, I refuse to let this day ruin me. Merry Christmas! Let's feast!"

I decided I was going to start the day with a fat bastard, cheesy tater tot casserole and end it with egg nog, bourbon and cookies. I started mixing the roux for the casserole while frantically gathering ingredients for cookies—certainly I could make chocolate chips in a pinch, right?

The casserole was shoved into the oven for forty-five minutes, and my kitchen was a mess. I had absolutely zero chocolate chips. *Darnit.* That meant I'd have to go to a store, *if* one was open. I set my phone timer to thirty minutes—to me that meant if I wasn't on my way home, my house was going to be on fire due to my negligence.

I grabbed a long coat and threw it over my pajama pants, shoved my feet in some fluffy boots, grabbed my keys and told the furbabies I'd be back shortly. I ran down the stairs as I tossed my hair into a ponytail, and skidded to a halt at the bottom of the stairs.

No, it wasn't Nathan, magically reappearing to take me away from my misery by giving answers about the real reason why he'd left; nor was it Jason with a breakfast basket and flowers. Jason was actually supposed to swing by later that night—he was on duty but when he got off work, he was going to spend the night after a pitstop with his parents.

So, no, it turned out to be that damn middle-aged Scout from the parade.

And he wasn't alone.

I was not mentally in a position to throw light at them, although I *was* in a position to kick them in the jaw if I felt like it; they were just the right height so I knock them both out with one kick. As the silence dragged on, I seriously contemplated doing it.

Instead, I finally asked, "What the hell do you want?"

"We would like a word with you if at all possible."

"I'm all ears," I said, raising an eyebrow. "This ought to be good."

The other guy was wearing a hat pulled tightly over his head, but something was oddly familiar about his stance. "Go ahead," the original Scout said softly, with an undercurrent of menace emanating from his tucked-in flannel shirt and greying temples.

My heart rate was elevated, but since I knew I could take them down or even call the police if I needed to, I wasn't worried at all. I crossed my arms across my chest and waited.

"My name is Grayson, this is Jason." Great, I thought—an *evil* Jason. I wish *my* Jason was there to send his ass back to wherever he came from.

"Hi. I'd introduce myself but I'm assuming you already know who I am."

He smirked, "Of course. You're Ms. Violet Moore, Field Operative of the Southeastern Light Bearing Branch of Atlanta. Your superiors are Misters Michael Perez and Robert Cox, and they supposedly answer to the United States Government, Department of...well, nobody quite knows."

"In other words," Jason flashed a wicked grin, "You are a pawn for the ridiculous U.S. Supernatural Black Ops."

Hearing them spell it out in great detail made it *sound* ridiculous. But as I turned to face them, standing even-footed with my hands at my sides, I showed zero craps given and spit out, "Exactly. So I can Wanda Maximoff your asses at *any given time*. Again I ask: Why. Are. You. Here?" A wide smile painted my face.

Grayson looked unsure and glanced back at Jason, who cleared his throat and then snarled at me. But it was Grayson who spoke again, "We know you're training and learning about, among other things, psychic gifts, pre-elder futhark, family lines and histories...," he trailed off. I felt a little shiver move down my spine that unfortunately Jason caught with a half-smile. Any time I heard about family lines and histories, it made me uneasy.

He continued, almost rambling to himself, "We know your lot thinks our group is a bunch of mindless vigilantes for Darkness, but not everyone who works for this 'Darkness' is deplorable, you know. Some are *real* leaders who just see the world work differently than what you've been brainwashed to believe is the right way. The primary goal of 'Vendetta Veritas' is to give the power back to the people."

Where in hell was this little speech going?

"We obviously know how to recruit people quite easily, and generally speaking, while we don't wish harm on others, we *do* believe in taking what we believe is ours. The only reason why *Scouts*, as you call them, choose to seek out the Light Bearers, is because you guys tend to get in the way."

"Ex*cuse* me?! You've got to be kidding. You're essentially spreading Satanism—"

"Ex*cuse* me," said Evil Jason, "Don't confuse religion with pragmatism."

I rolled my eyes. "What are you even here for, other than to criticize me? Look—cut the crap. I ask again. What do you want? I've got things to do. It's Christmas for Thor's sake."

"Thor?" asked Grayson, looking slightly amused. He looked at Jason before returning his eyes to meet mine. "Again, we wish you no harm." The glint in Jason's eyes said otherwise. "We are extending an offer to work with us."

My eyebrows must have jumped off of my face, my jaw lengthening to the ground.

"Because we basically want the same thing..." He trailed off a little uncertain.

I stepped down to their level, Jason looking uncomfortable

for the first time. I'm assuming because he knew I could kick their asses, but perhaps it was something else.

"Let me be clear. Let me speak to you slowly so you understand. We do not want the same things. You seek power to control—"

"But so do you!" exclaimed Grayson as he interrupted me. "We're just trying to get you to change your perspective! It's the *same* thing." His voice changed—he was almost oddly beseeching.

"My job is to clear the crap so people can function better. That is *not* control. That is *helping* others," I scoffed.

"It's the same thing," said Grayson, stubbornly. I was close enough to him now I could see the color of his eyes—hazel, with flecks of green. Something was really familiar about him, and his extremely good looks caught me slightly off guard. "Your 'lightness' is no different than our 'darkness'." He even tossed in some air quotes out as he spoke. "It's just a different word. We want people to move freely about their lives, too."

My phone's alarm went off, and I sighed. Dammit. I didn't have time to go to the store. "I'm going back inside. Just so we are clear, I will never work with you. Unlike you, apparently, I'm in a position to *always* encourage the best of humanity, and frankly, I like that part of my job. So, *Merry Christmas.*"

I turned on them and started to walk back upstairs, hearing Grayson scuffle his shoe against the concrete. "Nathan is in danger, Violet. I have the gift of sight; he and I share a bloodline."

I froze, my heel still lifted above a stair. I immediately reached for the necklace and held the ring in my hand, making sure they couldn't see what I was doing. I felt nothing, but I remembered my dream of the animal which hunted him.

"Ah… that caught your attention, I see. What you call 'Darkness' has started to spread beyond our control—to animals, weather patterns, etc. It's all influenced by these energetic waves of the current consciousness. We consider it a great *Almighty Cleanse* and obviously are in support of what's transpiring." Jason's voice was like ice, no hint of warmth remaining. He continued, "The animals are the danger to Nathan. We're telling you this, out of a kindness, and a sign of faith, so that in the future you'll recognize the importance of returning a favor."

I still hadn't moved, my hand gripping the ring. I heard them start walking back to their car, and I half-turned before continuing up the stairs. Grayson had chosen that moment to turn back towards me, too, and he took his hat off, and muttered, "Merry Christmas, Violet." His eyes met mine for the briefest of moments, his auburn hair looking askew from his hat, his jaw set tersely. It was a peculiar moment between us. There really *was* something strangely familiar about him, but before I could place my finger on it, he turned away again.

I walked back up to the top of my stairs and looked back down the stairs. Their car was already driving away.

I wondered, if I held the ring in a trance, would I be able to contact Nathan?   So, forever practical, I went inside, opened the windows, and turned on all the fans to let the smoke out from my now burning tater tot casserole. I interrupted Nicole's Christmas with a phone call to inquire just that.

30

It was Christmas night, and I was on the couch, wrapped in Jason's arms with Phang at our feet. Barnaby was nowhere to be seen. The fire was crackling in my fireplace, the Christmas tree shone lovely near the balcony doors. I could see the stars twinkling outside through the glass. I smelled remnants of hot cocoa, and saw the messy plates on my bar still sitting there from dinner.

I hadn't heard back from Nicole, or Nathan for that matter. Not that I thought he would contact me—I didn't. I had been quiet when Jason arrived, not quite able to get into the Christmas spirit, so he had forced out of me what had happened. He had sighed heavily when Nathan's name popped up—I started to get the feeling he was afraid he'd never get rid of the guy—and narrowed his eyes when he heard about the Scouts who had visited me. When I had mentioned about my dream, he had remained quiet, and just squeezed my hand.

I took that to mean, in spite of how crazy everything sounded, he would support me in any way that he could.

Jason. Such a good man.

I untangled myself from his arms and left him on the couch, his breathing changing only slightly at my departure. I padded softly to the kitchen, and opened up the refrigerator to look for some cold water. I closed the door quickly, though, when I felt a haze overcome me, forcing me to sit down, and *fast*.

I plopped down onto the kitchen floor sans grace, and tried to right myself. It wasn't that I felt dizzy—I felt weightless. I realized my necklace was burning super hot, and I felt a giant pull from my heart into the ether. I felt like I was racing faster than the speed of light or sound, violently being tugged along some sort of superhighway, and then, without warning, I crashed.

BAM.

I stumbled a bit—inside my mind—but also my physical body felt wobbly on the floor. I was aware that Barnaby had come up beside me, but I couldn't move.

The damn rune toss I had done in the morning was coming back to bite me in the butt. Maybe I should have given it more attention, maybe I should have really pondered about what the runes were trying to show me. As I was having this verbal self-argument inside my head, a hazy entity moved towards me. While it did not take on a complete physical form, I knew it was Nathan.

I immediately laughed to myself thinking I needed to bulk up on fluorite if it was this easy to enter my mind. It was bizarre—I felt him, saw him, sensed him, in my head, but my eyes, my real eyes, could almost make him out in my kitchen as well. I felt like my mind was splitting and that I was going crazy.

The hazy entity stood before me for a beat, and then I could physically *feel* him all around me, his body covering mine as if in an embrace. I felt so safe, and stable, and then horribly confused when I came back to reality and realized what was going on. He stepped back, and imprinted images rapidly into my mind that I tried to convert into words. *He knew about the animals. He wasn't happy his cousin had contacted me.* COUSIN! *He was currently safe—*

I interrupted him with images from my meditation. I could tell it worried him that I had the animal dream/vision before his cousin had contacted me. He seemed almost... angry... and crushed. I threw a question mark his way.

Nathan. It's me. You can tell me anything.

I felt his hesitation, as always. *I will leave the mountain immediately.*

His connection started to falter—I was assuming he was distracted by something in the real world. I suddenly felt the most rage I've ever felt before in my life, and it wasn't coming from me or Nathan—it was an outside source, and I had the sinking feeling the animal stalking him had found him.

Was it through our connection?

Nathan! I screamed. By the barking of Phang, the hissing of Barnaby and slurred-to-fully-awake yells of Jason, I realized I had yelled 'Nathan' out loud. I pushed, pushed, pushed, with all of my might, what I imagined to be a very large, very strong, force field around Nathan. I envisioned him on the mountain, and I saw him, *saw* him look me in the eyes in wonder as his fear dissipated. The animal slinked around him, not being able to reach him, and it growled, growled a deep, guttural sound that pulsed from the depths of Hell.

Nathan carefully made his way to his car, the animal stalking him the entire way. You could sense it saying, *"Next time, then."* The animal was not alone—I felt other red energies near it. As Nathan drove off, the hostile energy lifted from them, and the animals sniffed at his left-behind camp.

I was convulsing at this point, desperately trying to keep the connection open to make sure Nathan was okay, but also curious about the animals at the camp since they now seemed benign, or at least as benign as any wild animal could be. Jason was holding me, and I'm pretty sure he thought I was dying by the sounds he was emitting.

I felt a very faint pulse of gratitude, and then, nothing.

***

I woke up to Jason's pacing in my living room, and the clock blinking 2:35 at me. *Had I made the power go out?* Luckily, my humor was in check, in spite of feeling foggy, confused, and above all, drained. See, Jason looked damn good shirtless as he paced.

I cleared my throat, and he turned to look at me. "Is it my hair?" A thin smile crossed his lips.

"Violet." He kneeled down next to me as I felt the couch cushions around me.

"I'm okay," I mumbled.

"I know. But I called Nicole—"

"Jason! It's two in the morning!"

"—And she told me what she thought happened, and that you would be okay."

"I *am* okay," I growled.

"But, I'm going to find Nathan, and kill him."

I sat up, and threw my face in my hands, shuddering at the memory of Nathan's arm around me. Then I looked up at Jason. "None of this is right."

Jason warily looked at me, taking my face. "I don't care, Violet. I love you." He looked sad.

I wouldn't do it on Christmas. I wasn't that cruel.

But... I knew. I knew that there was nobody else for me, ever. And even if we couldn't be together, there was no reason why I should drag somebody into a relationship with me who would never measure up to the impossibility of the connection that existed between Nathan and me.

I wrapped my arms around Jason, and whispered, "I love you, too."

I was a mess—I was exhausted from what I was losing, everything I wouldn't, couldn't have. I felt drained because of what I didn't understand, which was a lot, as the questions endlessly piled up the deeper I got along into this new life. I begged to wake up before Nathan ever entered my life, back to when things were simple, if not incredibly boring, even if it meant losing Jason.

Jason brought my groggy self back to the bedroom, and as I fell asleep to him watching me with such a sadness. I wondered if maybe I was wrong. Maybe I could belong to two people.

31

It was late February, and Elizabeth had just gotten engaged to Janette and we were celebrating at a local restaurant. They were being ultra-silly, wearing "Future Mrs." headgear. Sam was stag because Thomas was sick; Layla was seeing someone, and I wasn't entirely sure of his name yet. A few other people were there, including Amanda and Rebecca. My ex was lurking around the bar with his dad, I waved hello to them, on the way to the bathroom.

When I emerged, I ran into Jason. Every time I saw him, a huge lump of sadness would rise from the pit of my stomach up into my throat. I was hoping he hadn't accepted Elizabeth's invitation.

He looked good; he always looked good. He also looked sad. He gave me hug, though, as a greeting. It lingered a little longer than it should have. I didn't stop him, but I was the one who walked away first.

I felt Damien's eyes on me, boring into my back as I walked away. I'm sure he took great pleasure in the fact that I was single again. A few weeks after Christmas, I had pulled the plug on the relationship. I couldn't hurt either of us anymore.

Layla slid next to me at the bar, and put her arm around

me. "You seem tired, Vi."

I leaned my head on her shoulder. "I am. E's brutal asking me to come out tonight. Trained up in Atlanta all week, had several massages, met with my shrink. I'm pooped."

Layla pushed her stool back from mine to get a better look at me. "Anything building we need to know about?"

"Actually, yeah. We just don't know where they're going to strike, if it's this spot or," yawn, "Tollie's area. Or hell, both. That wouldn't surprise me. They just wanna render us useless so they can spread twisted," I yawned again, interrupting myself, "crap."

Layla smiled. "Maybe Jason could take you home?"

I followed her eyes and saw him talking to someone I didn't know, a very tall, very physically fit, very pretty blonde. "I can't, Lay. It's not fair to him."

"This crap isn't fair to you, either, Violet. Don't forget the other victim of this whole nonsense is you. If Nathan ever comes back into town, I'm going to—"

I turned to look back at her. "Kill him, I know. Along with everyone else. I will learn my way, Layla. It's okay. I'm okay. I'm fine, I don't care."

"You're not okay. You're in love with a Phantom and yet this guy, Jason, is here, and he's perfect for you."

I followed her line of sight again, and saw the blond touch him. "He seems to be doing just fine," I said drily. "I think I am going to go home, though. Where's Liz?"

I stood up too quickly and had to hold the bar to stabilize myself. And then I felt it—*the Darkness rising*. It felt like terror and fear if those feelings could become solid. It was outside and it felt dense, like nothing could penetrate it (although, I knew otherwise). I wasn't sure how many Scouts there would be, but I was on high alert and grabbed my phone, sending a mass text to the rest of my group.

Tollie and Janine must have still been together, because

they almost immediately responded to let me know they were on their way, and not far out at all.

I grabbed Layla. "Keep everyone inside, and don't let anybody know what's going on, okay? They won't harm anyone in here. They're here for me."

Layla stood up and said, "Does that mean they'll harm people out there?" She raised an eyebrow, indicating she knew what I was thinking.

"Do *not* let Jason come after me."

I slid off my seat and let myself out a side door marked 'emergency'. I knew there was no alarm to the door; I could sense that it wasn't connected. I wasn't sure if *I* had been the one to disconnect it or not, but I wasn't worried about it.

The energy was near the front of the building, and as I had slid out the side, I walked quietly and quickly to my car. I hadn't been detected. I wasn't sure what they were doing, but I didn't like it. I put out feelers to Tollie and Janine so they could energetically find me if they needed to. My phone was on silent. I opened my car door and grabbed my wand.

Okay, so grabbing something that is truly called a wand sounds like I was preparing to wag a stick around a bunch of Dementors while yelling out a patronus. My wand, however, was basically a cross between nunchucks and a walking stick *and* it was self-collapsing. It was just a heavy metal weapon I could use if needed—I wasn't about to approach an unknown number of evildoers without a weapon.

(And of course it was adorned in runes, a funky design and a couple of crystals. Even as a new ninja, pretty still mattered. Nicole had gifted it to me at my welcoming party.)

Taking a deep breath as I felt that hostile pulse grow, I wondered when Tollie and Janine would be there. I looked at my phone and didn't see anything but an empty text on my phone. I sighed. These idiots always affected technology.

I covered myself in protective thoughts, really, thoughts

that somehow translated into light and safety. Who was I to question how it worked? I was no scientist, I just knew the outcome. I could feel the power as surely as I could feel the pavement beneath my feet. I slowly started to walk to the front of the restaurant.

I could see the people inside, safe and having a good time. I could hear some people in the parking lot—as well as the adjoining parking lot of another restaurant. It was dark, but not necessarily quiet. There was enough traffic on the streets. A car pulled from the street into the parking lot, and I paused, hoping it was Tollie and Janine.

It was not.

I continued walking, and took a deep breath in and slowly exhaled as I rounded the corner. Five of them. Not too many. They were standing near a truck that was near the entrance. And a couple of hounds. Okay, so five people, and two dogs. Not bad, right?

I could handle that.

As long as the hounds weren't possessed and demonic.

I started chanting safety chants under my breath as I approached them.

I was not going to get caught off guard like I was the first time I had to throw light at these morons.

Ah, good, I saw a couple of friendly faces in the crowd. My BFFs Grayson and his rhyming buddy, Jason. Fantastic. From what I could tell, they were not touching one another, but a steady hum—be it from chanting or just energetic—was emanating from them. They were clearly trying to draw me out.

It had worked.

I casually walked over, purposefully holding the wand, spinning it like a baton.

"Good evening, boys," I said, breaking their trance. They all looked up, and I realized one was a younger girl in her twenties. "Ah... Apologies." I said.

She smirked, and tightened her hat on her brown-headed self. "How's Sam?"

I paused, and decided to advance no further, also ignoring the girl's question.

"Well, Grayson, you have me. What do you want? Are you going to fight? Try to render me ineffective? Or are you here to chat again so we can become best buddies?"

I had a feeling it was slightly more insidious this time... thus the numbers and the chanting.

"Any Zombies in the mix that I should help set free?" I looked pointedly at the girl, who glared at me in return. No Zombie was she, her look said. I rolled my eyes, and then turned back to Grayson.

"I heard you saved Nathan's life."

How did he know *that*? Did we have an informant? Nicole was the only one who supposedly knew about what had happened. The powers that be decided they didn't want anyone else to know about my new gifts—or that animals were being affected. It wasn't fun keeping my crew in the dark, and it made me wonder, again, what *I* wasn't being told.

"So?"

"So, thank you. After all, he *is* my cousin."

"Okay? Couldn't you have just texted me a thanks? Can't be that hard to figure out my number."

A strange looked crossed Grayson's face, but he continued, "And since I offered you that kindness, I expect one in return."

"How do I know *you* didn't just sic those animals on him?"

He smiled. "You don't." He spread his hands out and shrugged is shoulders. Another car turned in, and Grayson nodded at it. "Ah, the cavalry has arrived, so I'll be quick."

He made a sudden movement towards me, and I spun my

wand around in circles, preparing for a blow. He laughed. Now I could definitely see the family resemblance. He was as good looking as Nathan, albeit in a darker, more sinister way. He seemed slightly taller, too, and maybe a bit thinner, and closer to my age than his *cousin*.

I swallowed hard as he approached me. He didn't seem phased by the wand and I let him get incredibly close to me, trying to show that his intimidation wasn't working.

"I mean you no harm, Violet." He laughed again, and whispered into my ear. "Tell my Saintly cousin that we want the box. Or else those he loves… may suffer the consequences." A chill ran down my spine as he ran his fingers seductively from my ear to my neck. I was frozen in spot; I couldn't believe it.

"Which would be a pity." He smiled, his sinister grin looking alarmingly similar to Nathan's playful smile. His smell wasn't unpleasant, which you would think I would have been repulsed. But he was a mixture of pine and cedar, not unlike Nathan.

"Are you sure you aren't brothers?" I asked, trying to regain composure and movement of my body, choking a bit on my dry throat. The similarities between the two were endless.

A quick flash of a tightly controlled emotion zipped across his face, but it was instantly replaced by a forced, casual smile as he began to walk away backwards from me. Louder, for everyone to hear, including the dogs, who I noticed were starting to growl as Tollie and Janine approached, he said, "Be sure to tell Nathan that what I've seen—cannot be undone. At least that part is destiny. What happens after, well, that probably depends on you, m'dear."

My hand went to the necklace, and Grayson gave a slight glimmer of irritation. He quickly walked back over to me, so fast it took me off guard, pulling the necklace out of my hand.

He met my eyes, and it heated up and flared with a bright blue light that made him drop it. "It's not yours," I growled, "It's mine. Was always mine. *Will always be mine.*"

He searched my eyes for a brief instant—those hazel eyes with a hint of green—and for the life of me, I couldn't figure out why he was interested in the damn thing. Although the girls were flanking me, he reached for my face, holding it firmly in his grip, forcing me to look at him. Janine and Tollie were equally alarmed, now holding horse stances ready to pounce; but I kept my chin level with the ground in spite of the touch, defiantly returning his gaze.

"I bet it could have just as easily been me," he said softly, dropping his eyes back down to the necklace before making eye contact again. He let go of my face after a beat, and then headed back to the truck as the others got in. The barking dogs had begun to attract people from inside the restaurant, and Jason took that moment to step out, hand on his hip as always.

"Don't forget to tell Nathan." He slammed the door and I relaxed my body. Janine was looking back and forth in great mystification between the truck pulling out and me. Tollie had gone over to Jason to tell him and the others that everything was fine; she hadn't actually met him before.

"But is that Violet?" I heard him ask her, as they started to walk towards me.

32

Once everyone caught wind of what was going on with Grayson, Nathan unfortunately had been called in for a meeting. I was to go up to Atlanta the following day for said meeting, and was spending the day beforehand trying not to hyperventilate and have panic attacks. I had decided to go to Target to blow money and do some therapy shopping—anything to take my mind off of seeing Nathan again.

And wouldn't you know it? I was walking towards the shampoo aisle and Grayson was standing at the end of it. He looked up as I approached, and I glanced down the aisle and saw the young, female Zombie in the middle of the aisle checking out hair dye. I raised an eyebrow, made it evident that I had my wand in hand as a greeting and said, "The pet section is a couple of aisles over." We were a few feet apart.

Grayson's hazel eyes turned warm with laughter, and I was slightly taken aback by his response. Warmth, from this yahoo? I was hoping he didn't catch my surprise, which didn't last long, because he quickly turned chilly. "I hear your *boyfriend* is finally coming back to town because of the, hmmm, harassment you've been receiving?"

"Oh, don't worry, Gray—I don't find our visits the least bit bothersome." I reached out to pat him on the shoulder like an old friend, right at the moment Zombie Girl looked up and saw me. He recoiled at my touch, and there was an electrical spark between us. I narrowed my eyes as he visibly blinked—I wasn't trusting of anything when it came to this guy.

Zombie Girl pushed past him to get in my face, and Grayson sighed and pulled her back a bit. "Not now," he said.

"Your girl needs a tighter leash. Again—just a few aisles that way—," I pointed as I walked into the aisle, looking for shampoo.

"Let me have her, Grayson!" she growled at me as I walked by.

I ignored her, and started to look at my shampoo options. I heard her huff and puff, have a tantrum by throwing the hair dye box back in with the others, and bark at Grayson to get out of there. She zoomed past me and back out of the aisle, but Grayson came up behind me. He leaned into my left ear, inhaling, brushing my hair lightly from my ear and said, "I'd get the same coconut shampoo you're currently using." My body turned with his body as he walked away, like a choreographed dance, my eyes open wide in disbelief. *Who was this guy?* He gave me a cocky smile from the end of the aisle before disappearing with a salute and a wink.

The next day, with my hair smelling like coconut, I was at the same office building my debriefing from several months ago had been. Even though it was only March, it was particularly hot and I was wearing a tank top. Right when I stepped inside the building, I realized I had a small tear in the armpit.

Dammit. Not like I cared or anything.

Not like I had horrifying memories from this place battling their way for space at the forefront of my thoughts. Nope. I was a Wall.

I sat down in a chair next to my team, with Tollie and

Duane on one side, and Janine and Victor on the other. I was glad Victor wasn't sitting next to me—I just *knew* he was going to be ridiculous when Nathan and his otherworldly good looks walked into the room. Tollie squeezed my hand under the table. Nicole was talking to Mr. Perez—Mr. Cox was apparently running late. My leg was pumping up and down as if it was running a marathon. A woman I didn't recognize walked inside the room, and then, there *he* was.

I froze. I died.

His hair was shorter than the last time I had seen him—a slightly overgrown buzz cut. He clearly hadn't shaved in quite some time, and his green eyes were heavy-lidded. He probably had come directly to the meeting from his flight from wherever he was stationed at overseas. He looked tired.

Tollie jabbed my side to force me to return to the living, and I immediately found comfort in wrapping my hair around my finger near my mouth.

He had a dark blue v-neck on, and black jeans... And the same damn red chucks that he always had on (unless he was in flip flops). He and I always had joked about those shoes—I told him they were bad luck, and didn't everyone know that?

Nicole said something to Nathan, and he turned to me, his full-on, tired, beautiful green eyes locking in with my ever graceful, hair-chewing face.

His gaze immediately softened, or rather, almost melted, and I saw his adam's apple move as he swallowed. His eyes remained locked with my eyes for the duration of the melt, but then he eyed everyone around me, and I could tell he was humored by how I was obviously being protected by them. "Violet," he finally sighed, and gestured for me to meet with him outside of the room. I felt my body trying to rise against Janine keeping me in place. She stood up, blocking me from Nathan.

"What is the meaning of this? I thought we were all

meeting here to talk about what was going on. Why is he asking to see her—away from us?"

Mr. Perez looked up from his computer. "They're going to speak with Mr. Cox while I talk to the rest of you. When we reconvene, we will all be together. Let's not get caught up in the drama, people. Please just let her talk to him."

I nodded at Janine. "It's fine," I murmured. They let me go, but Victor grabbed me very quickly as I walked by him. He mouthed *damn, girl,* and I smiled.

Usually I felt a giant zap of electricity when I got around Nathan's energy; this time, however, I felt oddly silent and empty. Don't worry, I immediately fixed that by tripping over a slight, incredibly minute fold in the carpet. This propelled me forward directly into the guy. I hit him with such force that he grunted as he steadied me. In horror, my eyes rose to meet Tollie's eyes who were wide-eyed in disbelief. Vic gasped; Janine swatted at him to be quiet, but also quickly looked away from the debacle.

It was fantastic.

The longer we stood there like that, though, the humor in his eyes began to fade and an energetic pulse began to vibrate me as well as him. "Hey!" I yelped, trying to right myself. "Stop that." I was taking action here, I was regaining control of the situation, dammit, as I stepped around him.

"I'm not doing anything," he said, frowning. I peered back through the doorway, and found that nobody was paying attention to us anymore. Nicole was half breaking my view as the rest were still seated. Perez had already started talking and they were happily listening to him. I think they couldn't handle the train wreck that was me anymore. She closed the door.

Nathan was right, though. I closed my eyes and felt his hands on my arms, but I extended beyond him to find the source of the pulsing sensation I felt. It *wasn't* him. It was distinctly feminine. And it was enveloping both of us.

I opened my eyes, trying to make a physical form out of this sensation, and I couldn't. "Violet?" Nathan questioned. I shook my head, and untangled myself from him.

"How do you do that? Turn everything off and on at will? You should have been able to feel that feminine pulsing, too."

He put his hand behind my back and led me to another doorway, the doorway that led us to the room where I had first met Nicole. "Practice. But you said feminine? Interesting."

I realized I was leaning back into his hand, and told myself I needed to put my walls back up, and fast. It was too easy to fall back into a level of comfort.

He left you, Violet. Don't forget that. Abandoner!

"Where's Cox?" I asked.

Nathan had the decency to look sheepish. "He *is* coming. Just not until later. I wanted to talk to you in private first."

Ugh. I plopped down unceremoniously in a chair. "Fine. What do you want?"

He sat down across from me at the conference table, and reached out to take my hands. I tried desperately to block all of the memories that were threatening to come back, and then a very specific one, of him kissing me, right before he abandoned me.

That's right, Violet. He's a jerk.

"How have things been?" He asked casually.

I was taken aback. "Wha-at?" I pulled my hands away and sat back.

"I'm sorry about you and Jason. He should have been a good fit for you."

"Oh my god, not that crap again!" I waved my hands around at Nathan, dismissing his crazy talk.

"By having been away from you, I'm realizing, I can't stop destiny... We have free will, of course, but the Universe course corrects. You and I... "

"Uh—what?" I sat still, annoyed as hell by the very-Nathan-speech-pauses.

He seemed to be off in his own little world. "We were always supposed to be together... And we have to be, because —"

"Um—excuse me?"

That got his attention. His dreamy, glazed over expression came back to reality as his eyes met mine.

"We will *not* be together. You're joking, right? First off—you *abandoned me* and didn't tell me *why*. You had the audacity to *kiss* me like that! And—and then you contact me on Christmas and about drain me from all of my energy—"

"Hey—*you* did that, Violet, I didn't ask you to contact me. You did that on your own," he said firmly.

He leaned back, crossed his arms and looked like he was ready for whatever I had to verbally vomit his way. "You tell me to be with Jason and do everything in your power to *keep* me from being with him by being—being all you—and then you let your cousin—or is it *brother*? You guys look so much alike—you let him *get* to me—I've seen him like three times now, even just yesterday—Did Nic tell you, have you gotten the word, that Grayson said it could have just as easily been *him* and not you? What the hell does that mean? And now this female energy, I mean, what the hell is *that*?" I blew out all of my air, re-crossing my arms at my chest.

Okay, so my little tirade wasn't exactly eloquent and I was stumbling all over my words as I spit it out. And, wouldn't you know it, that same expression I had seen on Grayson regarding the whole brother thing flashed briefly across Nathan's face as well.

And then, his face cleared, and he was smiling again. *Smiling*. Not at *what* I was saying—I knew him well enough to know that what I was saying was having a deep impact on him, as if he fully and finally realizing the consequences of his actions—but he was smiling at my theatrical outbreak.

"Violet."

I sat back in a huff. "Why am I always in the God damn dark?"

"I'm going to tell you what I know." He leaned forward. "Everything. I. Know." He brushed his hand through his non-existent hair, and I couldn't help but think about doing that to him myself.

NO!

"And some things I am merely guessing at. But maybe, with your help, we can figure it out. Together."

He reached forward again, gesturing for my necklace. I dipped my neck down, and he unhooked the clasp. He slid the ring off of the necklace, and placed it on one of my fingers.

"A perfect fit," he mused to himself.

He splayed his fingers out and slid a matching ring off of his ring finger and onto the table. His eyes lifted to mine, and he leaned back.

"So... there are three bloodlines here to consider. My mother's, your father's, and your... your mother's."

I don't know where I was thinking this conversation was going to be headed, but certainly not in this direction. "My... Mom? She was a light bearer—?"

Nathan shook his head. "No. I can't find any record of her working for the government, *or* any other rogue agency. Your dad, of course, was a light bearer for about twenty years or so before the accident."

Yeah—*accident*. Nathan had been my father's liaison during a Scout clearing that had overpowered my father's mind. I still hadn't gotten the details about what had actually happened. I wondered if I ever would.

"His father also had psychic powers, but it was his mother

who was a light bearer before him. From there, it gets even muddier with the record keeping, so I'm not sure what to believe. But I promise to keep looking into it."

Interesting. I'd have to do some research on my own, too.

"Your mother's gifts were varied and great, her parents both having the ability of sight, telepathy and potentially even moving matter. Your grandfather, who was originally from Germany, was enmeshed in the whole Nazi obsession regarding magic, the Holy Grail, etc... but, interestingly enough, he didn't work for the Nazis, he worked for the U.S. Sort of like de Wohl, but without all of the controversy. Adalbert Sealish was essentially a secret weapon during World War II. It appears your grandmother was never formally trained, and only assisted in unofficially helping your grandfather's work. As a result, your mother was very powerful. I have a feeling her death had something to do with her gifts... At this point, I cannot find anything about it, and I suspect that's deliberate." He slid a file full of papers in my direction.

I blinked back unshed tears, flipping listlessly through the paperwork. I couldn't believe that these people knew more about my life than I ever had. Why wasn't I privy to this? I mean, *my own mother*! Why hadn't Dad said anything? Or Oma? Opa and I were never close, but Oma should have—

Nathan interrupted my thoughts. "Violet," he said very softly. "They were trying to protect you. I remember when you were a teenager and—"

So he HAD met me before! Did he know then, who I was?

"—your father was telling me about the things he had seen you do, even though you didn't know you were doing them. He was worried for you. He and your mother had decided they didn't want you to know about that side of them, because they were afraid you'd be too vulnerable."

"Did we meet?"

Silence.

Finally, he had the decency to look down. I heard a clock ticking, over and over again. *Tick. Tock. Tick. Tock.* "Yes," he said quietly, finding the contours of the table extremely interesting.

"Did you know who I was then?"

"No."

I exhaled, not knowing I had been holding my breath.

He continued, looking up and smiling faintly, "I just thought you were a cute, impatient teenager."

"That's creepy, you know."

He snorted. "I'm not that much older than you, Violet."

"You were when I was a teen."

"And I maintain, you were cute. Still are." Damn dimple.

I refused to let the heat rise.

"Did you block my memories of that?"

"I cannot do that. You can," he said raising one side of his mouth, "but I can't."

"Did I?"

He shrugged. "You may have just forgotten. I didn't see you that much. Your dad kept you from me. He probably knew I thought you were cute."

"Ha! Sounds like Dad. He used to joke about locking me in a closet anytime a guy came by the house." I smiled at the memory, feeling a little lighter.

"I never met your mother. She was gone by the time I came into the picture."

"That's a shame. She was wonderful," I said.

"Then you are a carbon copy of her," he responded quickly, taking my hands again. I noticed he had slipped his ring back on.

"*My* mother handcrafted these rings and inscribed them with the runic ink. I think I told you I was a Runologist?" he asked, embarrassed.

"Yes. You made that beautiful tapestry." I remembered when he had lined my floor with it, setting the stage for meditation in the morning.

"My mother's line has the gift of sight, and language, among other things, and she once worked for the U.S. government. Her father, who was Danish, was quite skilled at many things, but never formally worked with his gifts. Mom's mom, my Grandma Catherine, was an American, with her own psychic skillset.

"Are any of your grandparents alive?"

"To my knowledge, no."

I chewed my hair. "Neither are mine," I mused.

Nathan continued, "As an adult, my mother met an outsider who was my father. She was forced to retire early after she married my dad, and then when that didn't work out, she just moved around, trying to find focus in her life. It was hard since she'd been banned by the Feds from doing the work. Sometimes this work is as relevant to our existence as blood is to our bodies," He finished wryly. "She has kept secrets from me. Secrets that I was trying to obtain when I was visiting her recently."

"Oh really? Secrets about?"

"Interestingly enough, my cousin, Grayson. I hadn't seen him in years, and all of a sudden he turned up in Atlanta. Things sort of fell apart between us, and I had kind of forgotten that he was even around, until Alyssa died. And then of course, he started hounding you after the accident. I didn't think it was coincidence. I think someone he works with has given him insight into what's going on with the agency." He paused before continuing. "Mom hasn't given me everything I've asked, but I'm starting to get the feeling—" he seemed really uncomfortable, "—that Grayson may actually be my brother."

"Another half-sibling," I mused. "Was Alyssa gifted, too?" I inquired about his fairly recently deceased half-sister.

"Completely ordinary in terms of our world, but of course, she had natural healing abilities that she used. She wasn't extraordinary, though. Her mother had been a hippy of some sort."

"Grayson is suspecting this, too." I mused. "But I bet he's keeping that from his friends."

"Why do you say that?"

"Just a hunch. And that sort of explains what he said to me. Did your mom choose you over him in regards to something important?"

Nathan looked *really* uncomfortable now. "That's what I'm trying to get her to tell me. I was up in the mountains looking for a box she had buried sometime ago—I have a feeling it has information she has hidden from everyone—but, the mountain lions came, so I abandoned it. At least for now."

I nodded, thinking about the vision I had had. "My mom showed me that box. She alluded it was very important. But wait—there were two other boxes, too. Do you know anything about them?"

He shook his head no.

Knock Knock. Cox was there.

33

I had just finished working, and was outside, locking the door with my back to the newest cupcake place in town. Lulu's had been calling me all day—I was drooling thinking of the sugary delight I was about to destroy inside the confines of my mouth. Spring had sprung, my clients had been fun that day—Nathan was out of town so I felt like I could breathe again—the world was beautiful and full of promise. The fact that this new cupcake place was in the same shopping center as my studio? Clearly God-sent!

I stretched out my arms with exuberance as I turned to make my way to visit *Lulu's Delights*, and quickly lowered them to my sides with a frown forming. It was Grayson. I hadn't seen him in several weeks, even though Nathan had reached out to him. He had refused to answer any of Nathan's calls, though.

Grayson walked up to meet me, hands out as if he meant no harm, "I didn't know you'd be here," he said, as if I would believe him. I gripped my wand, and he looked down at it, smiling ever-so-faintly.

"You didn't know I'd be at my massage studio... Sure," I said sourly, continuing on towards Lulu's, brushing past him.

"Any chance you have room for one more massage

today?" he asked, with a wicked grin stretching across his face. I stopped again in my tracks, glowering at him by his obvious double meaning.

He ran his hands through his hair, not unlike his *brother* might do, and said, "All inappropriate joking aside, let me buy you a cupcake." He strode past me and held open the door to Lulu's. Lulu was behind the counter, viciously scrubbing at some residue icing that had gone haywire, and a big smile erupted on her pale, freckled skin.

Her ginger hair was up in a bun as she said in a southern drawl, "Well, Mr. Grayson and Ms. Violet! How wonderful! I didn't know you two knew one another. Grayson—odd time for you to be stopping by."

He relaxed into that of a normal, functioning member of society as he lazily grinned, "You're astute in your observations. I had training today, so it was only a half day. Not my normal twenty-four."

"Ahhhh," Lulu said, continuing on some more random conversation with him as he leaned up against the counter of her mini-cake delicacies. I zeroed in on Grayson's clothes, and saw that he had on some sort of blue cargo pants, and a blue t-shirt tucked in with the local fire department emblazoned on it. He unfortunately looked good, auburn hair longer on the sides than on the top.

He was a freaking firefighter?

I reached out and touched the crest on his chest in open wonder. Lulu had her back to us, so she wasn't paying any attention. Just rambling on about the specials, and then saying, "But Grayson, I'm sure you want your usual." Grayson had turned his attention back to me, and as my hand rested on his chest, he responded to Lulu nonplussed.

"Make that two, and hot tea, please."

"You two darlings have a seat. I'll bring it out to you when it's ready."

Grayson removed my frozen hand and escorted me to a tiny table next to the window, practically pushing my shocked body into the seat. He twiddled with a daisy that was in a tin coffee container, starting to droop from the length of the day, and reluctantly met my eyes. "Firefighter," I spoke, perplexed.

He tried to harden his gaze, but fell short. "And?"

"And... They help people."

"Okay?"

Our sixty year old Cupcake Fairy Godmother descended upon us, pouring us some tea. "The cupcakes will be iced in one minute flat, dears!" She took back off to the counter.

I tried to regain composure and turned the conversation to what I knew would help my focus: the cupcakes. "What's Grayson's usual?"

His ease returned, and he leaned forward, sipping on his tea. "Bourbon laced cream cheese icing with red velvet cake, of course."

I couldn't help myself. I closed my eyes, mouth watering. What the hell was wrong with me? I reopened my eyes again to find the cupcakes. "Enjoy you two!" Lulu exclaimed, giving me a knowing look, and mouthing the word *'yeeessss'* to me.

I narrowed my eyes at her, then looked back to that which I was about to conquer. I shoved my pointer finger into the icing, licking it in pleasure with eyes squeezed tightly closed. Again—it was like a spell had been cast over me, I didn't know what was wrong with me. I was wondering if Lulu was some sort of cupcake witch and had poisoned her food with desire.

When I reopened my eyes—again—and as the blur removed itself, I found Grayson staring at me, softly swearing, "Jesus, Violet, it's just a damn cupcake."

"Hush," I said, taking a gargantuan bite of the cupcake,

getting a noticeable amount of icing on my nose. I didn't even care—there was the Darkness, there was Grayson, there was the chaos that was my relationship with Nathan, and there were *cupcakes*. "I've been looking forward to this all day—don't ruin it for me."

He reached a hand towards my nose and what he had said replayed in my mind. *Jesus, Violet! It's just a damn cupcake!* He wiped the icing off of my nose, gently laughing, contentedly chewing the remaining piece of his own cupcake.

"I don't even care," I said through a mouthful of red velvet.

Grayson grinned, sipped some more tea, and the energy changed. "Viiiiiiolet."

I narrowed my eyes again, wiping my mouth. "What?" *Please don't bring up Nathan.*

He sighed, running his hand through his hair again. He sat back before speaking. "You know, Nathan knows what's in that box, he is just not willing to tell you."

I chose to ignore his statement and instead replied with a question, "Why aren't you taking Nate's calls?"

He leaned forward and took my hands into his—I tried not to flinch, but he noticed. He also noticed the shock of electricity that ran through us, but didn't comment on it, either. "If you choose to work with us instead of the Feds, you'll never be in the dark again. I'll share with you everything I know about you—me—*all* of us. I won't hide anything from you, in the name of *protecting* you." He snorted. "That type of behavior has Nathan all over it."

I ripped my hands out of his and hissed quietly, "You're just that guy Jason's puppet, you don't think I know that? At least Nathan is honest and only channels the Light rather than your bullshit of channeling the Dark for your own gain!"

Grayson scoffed at first, but then his eyes narrowed, and I swear I saw a hint of fire burning beyond the hazel. "My own gain? What do you think I gain from any of this?" He spit out.

I continued, "I hate to quote a teenage fantasy, but your mood swings are giving me whipla—"

Just then, Lulu came by to see how delicious everything had been for us. We turned back on our smiles, and after she departed I brushed my crumbs into a napkin. "Thank you for the cupcake, Grayson, but I have to be going. Have a great weekend." I stood up, him mirroring my movement, not letting me move past him to the door. The tension was hot, the tension was thick. His lips were at my forehead as he looked down at me, sparks of green shooting from his eyes, my eyes a steely blue.

He leaned forward to my ear, and said, "I'll be seeing you."

I shuddered, said thanks to Lulu, and walked out, leaving him to pay the bill.

***

It was mid-April, and Elizabeth was finally making her debut as a beautiful bride. Her and Jannette had rented a quaint lodge-like place at one of the local lakes. I was standing next to her wearing a spaghetti strap, lace-bodice, simple sea-foam knee length dress, my brown hair lying in waves at my shoulders. I fluffed her veil as she turned to face the attendees. Just then the sun peeked out from behind a cloud, and everyone clapped.

It was nice.

Afterwards was the usual dancing, drinking and stuffing your face extravaganza. The party had extended beyond the indoor sanctum they had rented into an outdoor semi-tented area closer to the lake itself.

Jason was there with his new girlfriend. She was the same pretty blonde he had met at Liz's engagement party. Go figure. She was very friendly to me, there was no flaw I could see about her. I approved, and I had just told him that after taking a shot of whiskey.

Free liquor, you know?

"Thanks, Violet. But..." he hesitated. *Don't say it! Don't say it!* "...I still miss you."

Dang. He said it.

I was regretting not having had *another* shot of whiskey before approaching him. Luckily, his girlfriend came back and twirled him away to dance to some stupid song the DJ was playing. I rolled my eyes as Layla sidled up next to me.

"That should be you on his arm."

"Please," I said, narrowing my eyes. "I don't dance. They look like turkeys hopping on a shared leg."

She snorted with laughter. "They do kind of look that way."

I smiled. "It's alright. I want him happy. He's a good guy, he deserves it."

Layla let out a huge sigh. "What about our deserving, shrinking Violet?" Her boyfriend started to approach, holding a couple of beers.

I scanned the crowd. I suddenly felt a presence that didn't seem to fit in. "Nathan's coming back in a couple of days. I'm sure he'll try to change my mind again."

"Why do you torture yourself?" She lifted my hair off of my shoulders, shaking her head.

"I'm being smart."

"You guys have some sort of pre-destined pact because of your incredibly powerful families, yet somehow you're fighting it, even though he's given in? You're being an idiot." She patted me on my shoulder.

"Something's not right." I kept scanning the crowd. Layla perked up.

"Oh yeah?"

I realized the energy I had picked up on was seeking, probing, looking for... *me.*

"God dammit. It's like I can't do anything anymore without being approached by this dolt."

"Grayson?" Layla asked, eyebrows inching towards her hairline. "Here?"

"Yeah." I scanned the room, trying to figure out where it was coming from. "It's fine, though. He's not here to hurt me."

Layla's boyfriend was impatiently indicating he wanted to dance—it was now some sickening slow song from the 80s. I felt like ripping my hair out. I nodded to Layla that it was okay. I didn't suppose Grayson would try anything stupid in a room full of happy wedding-goers.

As soon as Layla disappeared, I saw Sam and her boyfriend join them. And then, and then I felt warm air tickling the side of my neck. My hair stood on end as I waited for him to talk. I realized I wasn't standing in a spot that allowed me an escape route—my back was against the tent. There were some empty tables around me, but most people were on the dance floor at that point.

Once he was close enough for me to feel his breath on my neck, he asked me to dance.

"I suck at dancing. Just ask your brother," I said surly, turning to my right to face him. He had apparently slid inside the tent at an entrance that was about fifty feet away from where I had been standing.

"I promise, it'll be fine." He smiled that charming smile, and I wanted to assault it right off his face. "You're not threatening me with your walking stick today."

"It's a wedding. I'm feeling friendly."

"Good, so you'll dance."

Damn, I fell into that like an idiot. He wasn't lying—we did somehow fit together well. Like peanut butter and jelly. Bread and butter. Whiskey and sour. Bananas and—"See, there, Violet," he sexily whispered in my ear.

I involuntarily shuddered, acutely aware of where his body was pressed up against mine. I briefly leaned back enough to catch a glimpse of his face, and while I felt irritated by his familiarness with me, I started to feel like he and I were ultimately connected somehow, too, like Nathan and I were. I suspected he had felt it from the first time he had met me, even though I was just picking up on it...or perhaps, admitting it.

This missing box somehow affected all three of us.

Luckily for me, stubbornness is my finest quality, so his charm and our obvious attraction to one another was easy to diffuse and keep at bay. I wish I could have said that for my attraction to his—yeah—I was pretty sure of it now—brother.

"So has my *brother*," he asked sourly, as if he was reading my mind, "finally told you what is in the box that we all seek?" He spun me around and brought me back into his arms, facing him. Jannette's family who had been occupying the closest table to us, got up and headed to the drinks. We were mostly alone, save for a few dancers nearby.

"No, but I'm assuming it will give you both the answers you're seeking. I don't see what difference it makes, it's not going to change anything." He pulled me close and looked down at me.

"Maybe not to you and Nathan, but it will for me."

I pulled away. I realized Layla and Sam were staring at me from across the room, sending out blinding alarms as if their lives depended on it. I nodded I was fine. I heard Elizabeth's laughter in the distance; good, she had no idea what was going on.

"How? You've chosen your path and refuse to get off of it. You're thriving on people's pain and suffering, *only* increasing your own."

He took my hands again, dipping me, and then slowly pulled me back up, gaze traveling from my neck back up to my face. "You're one to talk. I know how you're still denying the company of my brother."

"How do you know all of this shit? Do we have a spy? Or —"

"I'm just that good."

"Legilimency?"

"Child's play."

He smiled and spun me around again, pulling my ear close to his mouth. "You *do* look stunning tonight, you know. Nathan's a fool for having let you go to begin with. I would never keep you in the dark, I'd—"

I pulled back, heart starting to pound. Enough with these games.

He had his arms on my shoulders, directly facing me, and we were no longer dancing in rhythm with the DJ's crappy choices. The people around us began to shift away once they saw that we were no longer a part of the dance floor.

"You've said that before," I hissed.

"Just because the runes have spelled out what's going to happen, it doesn't mean every aspect of the future is chosen. For instance... *Who* the father is."

I was too mesmerized to move, to react—and just then, I felt the feminine energy again, my heart positively racing, time standing still. It's like the energy was circling around the two of us. *Who the father is?* This energy can't be—be a child, could it? "Of course it's a girl," murmured Grayson, but to himself.

So he felt it, too.

The hair on my shoulders literally moved. This energy was playful, and strong. Grayson stepped back from me, looking at me with a pained expression staining his beautiful face. I wasn't quite sure what he had just realized, but I had a bad feeling it somehow concerned me. I could sense the stage of his mind playing out a scenario before him.

Whatever had happened to him in his life had brought him to this moment. And perhaps he finally realized that turning 'good', if you will, was a choice. But as sure as I knew he was seeing his potential future looking different for the first time, I also knew there was no way in *hell* that I was going to be partnering up with him—*or* his damn brother—to turn this feminine energy into a life form.

If that's even what he was getting at.

His eyes hardened as his world came crashing back down for him.

Pity. Yes. I felt pity. If their mother had done something to choose one boy to stay with her over the other... Sorrow, yes, I felt sorrow, especially if it meant Grayson had been tossed aside. If his mother had let one of her sons go—what could be worse than that? I shook my head to myself, trying to piece together this sad tale with the broken information I had at my disposal.

Unfortunately, before I could say anything about what was happening, I could sense Layla, Sam and Jason closing in.

"Ah," said Grayson. "The Cavalry again. Always here to save you. But notice, *never* Nathan. And it's his fault that you're a part of this anyway! He didn't have to mark you for all of this!" He said, seething.

I turned in the direction he was looking, and so I was completely caught off guard when he grabbed me, pulling my back firmly up against his frontside, hissing into my ear. "Tell Nathan that if he doesn't find it by the Solstice, I'm going to take destiny into my own hands." My blood ran cold. This guy was like Jekyll and Hyde. "Take that how you will, Violet." He practically spit out my name.

I stepped out of his embrace and forced him to face me head-on. "I'm not afraid of you, Grayson. I don't think you'll hurt me. Besides, you know I can fight you off." The words fell flat, hollow—I was still trying to catch up to what I had just felt, and what he had just said.

"Can you?" He glared at me, and I could see fire burning in

his eyes; they were no longer that hazel with green flecks. The flecks were flames. "I can tap into things that Nathan wouldn't dare even flirt with. I have access to so much power, there's no *way* you can fight me off."

His mood swings were so hard to keep up with. He suddenly spoke quickly, almost to himself again, "Unless, of course... *Will* you fight me off, Violet?"

The change in wording didn't go unnoticed by me, and as he was moving so rapidly, it took me a beat to realize he had pressed his body against mine again. I blinked up at his face trying to regain composure, stability, anything, but the chemistry was so strong—almost violent—the magnetism could not be denied. He and I were both so caught up in the moment, he lost himself as much as I did. The forcefulness of the kiss quickly subsided to unbelievably tender, and that's about the time my analytical brain came back online.

Finally I was able to curse at him. "What the hell, Grayson!" I pushed him away from me, and he caught my hands on his chest, shakily searching my eyes. His hazel eyes had so many conflicting emotions racing across them, all I was doing was playing catch up. He finally landed and rested on bitter, to which, I was able to respond to that. I asked again, only this time much more quietly, "What the hell, Grayson?"

He dropped my hands and then disappeared into the crowd, as if he were wearing an invisibility cloak, as if he were simply an apparition of my mind.

I grimaced as I turned to my friends, just stunned, the warmth of his lips remaining on my own.

"Things just got more complicated," I managed to say, bringing my shaking hand to my mouth in wonder.

34

"Why the solstice?" asked Nathan for the hundredth time, as he paced in front of my couch. He was back in town and asked if he could stay with me. I didn't tell him no, but I wasn't happy about it. I wished Phang and Barnaby shared my sentiments. Instead, they greeted him each day with unabated happiness. Well, Phang did. Barnaby only liked him when Nathan gave out treats.

"Tollie just texted. I guess Duane took down a crowd at the same time that Victor did. That's a bit odd, isn't it?"

Nathan stopped pacing. It was two o'clock in the afternoon on a Saturday. "Yes, but clearly this Darkness is growing. I just wonder if Grayson is behind it. Or that guy Jason. Or if that guy Jason is using Grayson to stir up crap."

I stretched my legs out before me. "Well, if past history of, uh, *life* is any indication… of course he's being used."

Nathan sighed and walked over to my fridge. "This is so frustrating. I could harangue my mother! I mean, he's probably my *brother*, Violet! My brother!" He took a swig of something that wasn't apple cider, and growled.

"I think I need to meet your mom, Nathan."

He sucked in a huge breath, and held it for what felt like forever. My guess, though, was only about five seconds.

Nathan's pauses were often long, well-calculated and maddening to the observer. I'm pretty sure my hair greyed while I waited for an answer.

"You do. But, he needs to see her, too. If there's any way she can change his mind—"

"Change his mind about what? Me? Whatever's in that box?"

"Prophecy," Nathan muttered. "But even a prophecy is only true if you make it true." He resumed pacing.

Prophecy. Yes. Nathan had finally come clean to me about what was inside this mystery box. It was apparently a prophecy of some sort that his mother had hidden. He didn't elaborate beyond the fact that the prophecy existed, but he had certainly alluded that it included him, Grayson and *me.*

I didn't believe in prophecies. Although some of the other experiences in my life had gone outside a line of demarcation for realism... a prophecy was just too esoteric and outrageous. Insane, if you will.

Nathan's hair had grown quite a bit since the last time I had seen him. "Are you trying to grow your hair out?" I asked, attempting a diversion. He didn't hear me. "Man, I miss the days when Jared was your only problem." I stood up and walked over to the kitchen myself.

That snapped him out of it. "Ugh. Why'd you bring him up? Anytime someone says his name, he appears out of nowhere. I wonder..." He trailed off, looking out the living room window.

"That's it!" I threw my hands up in the air. "I'm going for a run."

I went into my room to start changing, and he followed me as if it were normal for him to do so. While he had slept in my bed before, he had never seen me naked, and he sure as hell wasn't going to see me naked, now.

"Nathan. Get. Out."

"Oh, yeah, sure. I'm coming with you, though." He was still in my room as he started to take his shirt off. I didn't say anything; I was curious to see how far he'd go. He took his jeans off, still mumbling to himself, and took his pants and shirt and lied them neatly on my bed—I suppose on his side of the bed.

I was pretty sure I was experiencing Nathan losing his mind. *Don't react, don't react.*

He turned in my direction, and reached into my drawer to —I'm assuming pull out running clothes?—and stopped mid-reach. He turned *red*, such a deep red I was sure his blood vessels were about to explode all over me.

I felt no shame openly admiring his well-formed body and his ridiculous black socks. Luckily for me, that added to his red face. I just stood there, arms crossed, lightly tapping my foot.

"Nice socks. Is there something you'd like to say, Nathan?"

He regained composure and pushed the drawer back in. "I... I don't live here. My stuff is not in this drawer."

"No, it's not." I bit the inside of my cheek. He stood up, looking back at the clothes on my bed. His color was returning to normal.

He sighed. "This is not my bed."

"Nope."

"You are not... my wife."

"Wiiiiife! Have you bumped your damn head?!"

He smiled crookedly at me. "I'll meet you out there. I'm still coming with you."

***

It had been a good run. I was lying on my floor, chest still heaving, legs propped up on the wall, sweat poring down my face. He was opposite me, legs cock-eyed on my couch, sweat poring down *his* face. "You've gotten faster," he said, turning his sweaty face towards me.

"Or you've gotten slower," I said, grinning at him. I stretched my arms high above my head, seeing about a foot of armpit hair growing out of each pit. *Ugh.*

He looked at me, returning the smile before staring back up at the ceiling. "No, you've definitely gotten faster. I miss running with you," he continued.

I grunted. Whose fault was that? I dropped my arms onto the ground, and our fingers brushed against one another's. Neither of us moved for several minutes, and the only sound was the slowing down of our breathing..

Eventually, I plopped my legs onto the floor and slowly sat up, wiping the rest of the sweat off my face with my t-shirt sleeve. It was pretty dried up at this point, and most definitely salty.

"I guess I'm going to shower," I said awkwardly. I had had a good time with him that day—but dinner was rapidly approaching and I didn't know what to do with him. It wasn't the same as before; before he had been my mentor. Now it was just... just him, just me. And neither of us had anything to do that night.

That morning he had shown up, unannounced, in a rented car. I had blearily let him in the door and made him coffee. He had quickly perked up from the caffeine and we had made small talk before tackling the elephant in the room— Grayson.

From there he'd started to pace. And pace. And pace. And mutter to himself.

Thus the run. I needed to clear his mutterings out of my head. Luckily, although he joined me for the run, he hadn't continued to mutter. Apparently I had gotten faster, so he wasn't able to talk.

Eye roll.

"Okay," he said, just as awkward. "I guess I'll shower after you... Are you... Do you have any plans tonight?" He turned his body to sit up against the couch while I stood up and walked away.

I stopped at the door to the bathroom. "Nope. My plan for the day was to stay in pajamas and read lame romance novels. Walk the dog in said pajamas and scare the neighbors. Order takeout. You know."

"Oh."

He dumbly stared at me, and hesitated before he spoke again. "I'm so sorry, Violet. For everything."

"Hey, now, some of it's not your fault...," I said lightly. "I was meant to be an apprentice, right? That has nothing to do with you."

"Unless it does."

"What does that mean?" I sighed, walking back towards my kitchen, tapping my fingers on my counter. Nathan stood up and carefully spoke as he walked closer to me.

"I knew Mr. Moore's daughter lived down here. I can't say that I wasn't curious about you after all these years. Yes, I was looking for an apprentice because we needed another one. But I was also looking for you. Of course, I realized the odds were that you would end up being the apprentice, but I found it fascinating that you were down here to begin with. You could have been anywhere in the world, but you were here. And you knew my sister. You were easy to track down once I realized you knew Alyssa."

"So you took this job because you knew it was me?"

"Well, I also thought I could visit with my father for awhile." He sat on one of my stools, and looked off towards my bedroom with a faraway look in his eyes.

"How *is* your dad, by the way?"

"Not well. They don't expect him to live too much longer. He's been on hospice for a couple of months."

"Oh, wow—I'm sorry—I had no idea—has your mom—"

"It's okay, Violet," he turned grimly back to me. "It's not like he and I were that close. I only stayed with him a couple of years back in high school. That was a long time ago. I really don't even remember my parents living together. Dad never reached out to me, I always checked in on him. As far as my mother," he looked back out the window, "she feels sadness for him, but that's about it. Besides, she's a little preoccupied with her long lost son at the moment."

"Or nephew."

"I think we all know how this tale goes."

"Yeah, I think you're right." I turned into the bathroom and gently closed the door, thinking about what would make a mother separate her two boys?

***

I had just gotten off of the phone with my own father, and he somehow knew Nathan was in my apartment. He told me to tell him hello. It was the first time he had addressed Nathan by his actual name, and without fear. And it was clear as day—he seemed to be of sound mind.

I walked out of my bedroom and found Nathan asleep on my couch, crammed into a corner with a pillow propped underneath his head, and legs tucked into his side. He was wearing a tank top, and I could see the crude runic language tattooed on his arms. "So in life, is death."

The mantra he lived by, the mantra that was inscribed in our now matching rings. I hadn't known that he had a matching ring when he gave me the one that was back around my neck. I meant to ask him about the powers of them, and if they were connected to any other rings or talismans for that matter.

I wasn't about to wake him up to tell him my dad knew he was there—I figured I'd just tell him later. It wasn't that late, and I wasn't sure what to do. We had already eaten dinner. Should I just go back into my room? Or change the channel on the TV? Would that wake him up?

Phang was cozy on the floor below him, and Barnaby was resting above his head. He opened one eye to watch me as I stood there, frozen, wondering what to do.

And then there was a soft knock on my door. *Dammit!* Who the hell would just stop by without even a cursory text? I furrowed my brow, stupidly opening the door without checking the energy first. I was so preoccupied by Nathan that I was behaving blindly, and inviting danger. I knew better.

"Fuck," I cursed after opening it. Grayson was standing there, looking terse as hell.

"Look, I don't want to be here anymore than you want me here, but I need Nathan to get a message to his mom."

I felt a presence behind me as I opened the door more so Nathan could see him. "Cousin," he said sourly, his hair a mess from having slept on it wet on the couch. He was holding Phang.

"Made yourself at home, haven't you, *brother*? Are you sure she even wants you here?"

"Please drop the testosterone bullshit on my behalf." I walked inside, taking my dog from Nathan's arms. "You may as well come in, Grayson."

"Ah, the lady of the house has invited me in." I could hear the smile in his voice as I placed Phang down on the floor.

Nathan begrudgingly stepped aside. "I thought you'd learned to never open your door without first looking, Vi."

Grayson, in his light jacket, stood just outside of my kitchen as I sat down on a bar stool at my counter. Nathan slid in behind the counter moving past Grayson. To Grayson's questioning eyes, I answered, "I'm notorious for opening the door to unwanted guests."

"Ah."

I looked back and forth between them, noticing their differences. But it was slight. They definitely looked like brothers, and almost could pass for fraternal twins. I couldn't help myself. "You guys didn't think it was strange how much you looked alike growing up?"

Phang had plopped herself down on Grayson's feet. Rather than choosing to answer me, he clenched his jaw, and looked down at Phang as she farted on him. "What in God's name *is* this creature?"

In spite of everything, I started laughing. Loudly. And when he looked back up at me, he had a bit of a smile tossed in there as well. Nathan had managed to make it into my kitchen to my right, and glowered at the laughter Grayson and I were sharing.

"Her name is Phang."

"Fang?" He asked, the word unfamiliar on his lips.

"P-h-a-n-g. Her sister is Mina."

He smiled. "Cute." He stepped closer to me, just shy of touching me, and only then did I realize Nathan knew absolutely zero about the kiss Grayson and I had shared. Before I could even panic about it, though, Nathan slammed down the coffee decanter, causing me to jump.

"It's *real* cute that you two are getting along, but, Violet, don't be so damn naive. This is the same man who threatened you—and me—and everything we believe in—"

"Can't we all just get along?" I groaned in an exasperated voice. It was hard to feel that there was any sort of threatening power anywhere since my dog was farting on my current 'enemy'. I looked beseechingly at Grayson, even though I didn't know him well at all.

It was kind of like how when I had first met Nathan—just an instant connection, for better or for worse. His hazel eyes met mine as he slightly shook his head. "There's too much behind us."

He turned to Nathan and leaned across the counter. "Please tell *Mother* I would like to see her. I know she has the box I seek. It would be best if she would hand it over peacefully. I have seen what happens if she won't, and it's not good for any of us."

"Then forego seeking it to begin with! What if the contents destroy us all? Have you seen *that?*" Nathan gritted his teeth.

"No. I've only seen what happens when she hands it over —or when she doesn't. I've also seen Violet—as a mother of a — "

"Don't utter that nonsense in here!" hissed Nathan. He came from behind the counter to stand face to face with Grayson, hands clenched at his sides in fists. His eyes were the color of deep emerald; his lips were pressed in a thin, red line. His cheeks were reddened with fierce passion, and the power he was showing scared me. I grabbed Phang from the floor and brought her over to the couch where Barnaby was half-hidden under a pile of blankets.

"Violet has a right to know what's inside the box, and what you—and I—are capable of doing. I know you've seen it, too, Nathan, or at least a portion of it," his voice was thick with feeling. "And you and I both know that what is written by runes, *will happen*. But we can only guess at what the path looks like to get there." He paused for a moment, and then taunted, "She might choose *my* way of life over yours."

"I highly doubt that," Nathan scoffed.

"HEY!" I yelled, extremely irritated. "Remember me?! Stop talking about me like I'm not here!" Two sets of similar eyes turned to address me; one a brilliant shade of green, with gold flecks of protectiveness, the other, a dangerous glittering shade of hazel. "I'm a *real* person here, not just a figment of your imaginations! Stop dragging me into this mess that has nothing to do with me!"

Nathan opened his mouth to say something but I interrupted him. "Book the damn flight, Nathan. We're going to your mom's." I pushed past both of them, no longer caring what they said without me being there. They *both* hesitated as I passed, but I felt Grayson's body turn with me as I began to stomp away. Nathan knew better than to push me; Grayson apparently didn't care. He stared in my eyes as I passed him, with an intensity I couldn't read.

I heard them argue for about thirty minutes more after I slammed my door shut, and then it got quiet. I heard Nathan groaning after Grayson must have left, and I heard Barnaby pawing at my door. Nathan opened the door to let him in there, and my cat jumped onto my bed. "Are you up?" asked Nathan in a low voice.

I was half-asleep and uncaring as to what he wanted. I patted the bed to indicate he could sleep in my bed if he wanted to, but I turned my back towards him, instantly falling back into a restless slumber.

I woke up the next day alone, the space in the bed next to me un-rumpled.

35

When I looked down at the island below me as we landed, I was taken in by its beauty. It was breathtaking, and amazing shades of green, lush, lush green. I saw cliffs dumping into the ocean, and slowly roadways came into view. "It's beautiful," I gushed, leaning over Grayson. He stiffened as I touched him.

We were on a small plane coming from the German mainland. Somehow the three of us were sitting in the same row, with me in the middle. The way the plane was set up had windows on either side of us, but Grayson's had the better view.

On the flight from the United States to Germany, I tried to get the boys to share funny tales from growing up, but they were both equally matched in stubbornness and I got nothing from either.

I wasn't even sure how much time they had spent together, considering I couldn't get a straight story about where Grayson had grown up. Nathan had a slight European twist to his American accent, though, and Grayson did not. My best guess was he had grown up in America, somewhere on the East Coast.

Sent there as a young boy? After this prophecy?

I was hoping their mother would shed some light on the situation that neither of her boys were willing to share with me, no matter how much I prodded. I think Nathan was protecting her, and Grayson was probably protecting himself. I'm guessing being abandoned by your mother probably heavily weighed on you.

"Violet," said Nathan cheerfully. "Can't you see that your mere touch to my brother is torturing him?'

I looked up at the very uncomfortable Grayson. "Sorry," I muttered, taking back my station in my seat. I heard Grayson release a breath, and I jabbed Nathan. "You shouldn't be taking pleasure in this."

Nathan purred, petting underneath my chin. "Stop." I removed his hand and prepared for landing by putting my tray back up.

My relationship with Nathan had definitely changed. The urgency to be together with him just wasn't there anymore. The attraction was still there, but with the introduction of Grayson, the overwhelming need to be with him just wasn't as strong.

Of course, it could be because he was staying with me and I saw him every day. I didn't *need* to be with him; I *was* with him.

Preparing for the trip, we all had spent more, sometimes awkward, sometimes almost fun, nights together. I actually found that I had quite a bit in common with Grayson—maybe even more so than with Nathan—but, you know, Grayson was a fan of Darth Vader and all. Sometimes it was hard to believe that we were two opposing ends of the same thing. Whenever I felt too comfortable, though, I would remind myself of the fire I had seen in his eyes at Elizabeth's wedding, the hounds he had sicced on his brother, as well as all of the not-so-veiled threats.

I had no intention of being trapped between the two of

them. I had no intention of being with either one of them, either. I had made myself clear, many times, over the past few days, that I didn't care about any prophecy or vision that they had in the past, present, or future.

We stepped off of the plane, and hailed a cab to Nathan's mother's house. I didn't think Grayson had quite realized where she lived before; I wondered how much her safety was at risk once the three of us arrived. I felt the heat of the necklace pulsing on my neck as we got out of the cab and began to walk up the driveway to this cute little stone cottage. It was situated far enough from the entrance to the drive, that the nearest neighbor was a good acre away.

I found myself gripping both of their hands as we stood outside of the door, waiting for her to open it. Neither of them tried to fight me off; it's like we were all ready to meet our destiny, whatever it was. No fear, and no going back.

The door slowly began to open, and a beautiful, lean woman in her sixties greeted us. Her hair was long, thick, and dark brown, streaked with shiny groupings of white hair. Her skin was dewy, and the white, flowing top draped across her body. She was almost as tall as her boys, with the same green that they both had in their eyes. She was barefoot, and I could tell tears pressed against her eyes as she reached out for us.

She had been waiting for this moment, to be reunited with her boys and the woman who sadly stood between them. She reached out and tried to hug us all at once, and as it didn't work so well, so she hugged me first. I met Nathan's eyes over her shoulder. Then she reached for Nathan, and he gave her a quick kiss on the check. He stepped aside so Grayson, who had his hands in his pockets standing awkwardly off to the side, could be greeted. I could sense Grayson's tremors as she walked over to him.

He cleared his throat to speak, and appeared he was not able to. Alexandra spoke, though, and said, "My son. You are finally home." I reached for Nathan's hand and held tightly, wondering what Grayson's reaction would be. At that moment, Nathan had chosen to hold the door open for me to step inside, but Grayson lifted his head. His eyes were wet as they met mine.

***

We had been at the house for a few days. Alexandra had spent plenty of time with all of us together, as well as each separately. She was a very gracious host. However, the cottage wasn't that big so I was sharing a room with both of her boys. It wasn't entirely ideal, but it did have its moments. Unfortunately for me, they both snored. I thought Phang's snores were loud... Yikes.

I was about to head into the living room to check my computer for an email from Layla about my furbabies (she was on auntie duty), but I stopped in my tracks.

I overheard Alexandra speaking to Grayson, beseechingly asking him to reconsider. "I had to do it... it doesn't have to turn out the way you've seen... You know that... just be strong enough to fight that vision..."

"That's just it, *mother*," he said icily, "I have no strength left. I know you think things would not have worked out well if you'd just kept both of us, but—well—we'll never know."

"What if Violet chooses you? What then?"

"She won't," he said gruffly.

"I see how she looks at you. She has considerably softened towards you, just over the few days you all have been here."

"I want the box. And I want to go home."

"Nathan would be devastated, but he would move on without her." She continued, ignoring his request. "If she chooses you to father the child, then you must change your path. Frankly, you need to change your path anyway. Even if she chooses your brother."

"I am not strong enough to be rejected again," he said,

almost too quietly that I couldn't hear him. "I want the box."

She sighed. "Fine, my son. I will make a trip south here in a couple of days while you all remain here. It is a trip I will make alone. And do not send the lions after me. I know what you did to Nathan."

"That wasn't me," he muttered.

I slipped outside, deep in thought, not even noticing I wasn't alone. Nathan was resting in a hammock between two trees off to my right, and once I realized I was being watched, I walked over to him.

I slid into the hammock with him, snuggling up against his chest as he held me. His mom was right; I was softening towards Grayson, but even more so towards Nathan. "Hey, you," he said softly as I closed my eyes.

"Your mother has chosen to retrieve the box."

"I know. Once she made up her mind, I had a vision."

"And?"

"She's going to bring it back here and present it to us. After that, anything goes, I guess," he sighed.

I rolled onto his stomach, looking down at him. "So everything that happened before..." I paused, trying to find the right words, "It wasn't about the apprentice/trainer relationship *or* my dad, it was about your visions?" I had my hands clasped at my heart, lifting me up so I could see his face.

"*Well*, it was about all of it, but especially your father... I've carried guilt ever since it happened." He slowly breathed out, seeming a little lighter to finally be having this conversation with me. He shaded his eyes and continued, "I didn't expect to fall so hard for you, Violet. I knew the possibility was there, of course, because of the vision, but being with you, in real life, it's just... at certain times, it's been almost too painful to bear." He closed his eyes, sinking into the hammock just a little bit more.

I should have taken his words to heart rather than just brush them aside. I should have really listened to him, really heard what he was saying. Instead, I selfishly ignored them and just lied back down next to him, snuggling against him.

As a friend.

"How long have you suspected Grayson was your brother?"

"After the car accident, I had a vision about you. I was hoping that staying away would keep you safe. Again, I was wrong."

"He sought me out." I wiggled my toes, pulling my hair into a ponytail. "And so where do we go from here?"

"I'm not sure. So many wild cards. I do know, though, that you'll soon be needed back in Atlanta to help Tollie. My future? A little harder to see at the moment."

"Seems super confusing trying to navigate between what may be and what actually is."

"It can be, yes. But I'm well-versed in it now. It doesn't affect me like it used to affect me. Grayson, though, he seems to let his visions run his life."

I slid my hand into his, feeling the warmth from his body pulse next to mine. I closed my eyes, again, deep in thought. I focused on Nathan's even breathing, and wholeheartedly understood that I didn't want to play a role in whatever this prophecy was. I was well-aware of what everyone was alluding to, but I just didn't see how it could ever play out in the real world. Maybe Nathan was right; maybe I was naive. But Grayson had already made his way to be a part of the Darkness, and he had no intention of giving that up.

That made us enemies. And whenever he showed up to try and destroy the light, I would be there to fight against him.

That didn't sound like the potential for love to me.

So that easily left Nathan, but I didn't trust him. Even though I could feel every curve of his body, could feel his breath, and it felt, well, *right. No, no, no, Violet. You don't need either of them. Finish this mess here and get on with your life.*

Just then, Grayson stepped outside. "Either of you want to go for a run?" He called from the doorway. I was happy to be sucked out of my thoughts. I didn't like where they had been headed.

Nathan yelled, "Not me. I'm not as young as I used to be, I'm quite happy relaxing for once." He turned to me, winking, and playful nudging me with his hands. "Go with him. Maybe you can talk him out of his nonsense."

I got the feeling, and not for the first time, that Nathan was giving me many opportunities to get to know Grayson, even though I didn't feel there was any choice to make.

Neither, I tell you! I didn't want *either.*

"I'll go," I called. I squeezed Nathan's hand, locked eyes with him for a beat, and jumped out of the hammock, brushing past Grayson on the stairs. "Give me a few minutes."

He nodded and headed towards the hammock.

Once I was inside, I came across Alexandra. "Hi. I hear you're going to retrieve the box?" I paused outside the simple room I was sharing with the brothers.

"Yes," she said, soulfully. "I wish I didn't have to, but he leaves me no choice."

Curious, I asked, "Do you even know what the prophecy says?"

She sadly shook her head. "After hearing the first part of it, I refused to listen to the rest of it. Once the prophecy was transcribed, I locked it in the box to protect it, hoping this day would not come." She strode towards the front door, looking at her sons. "The position I've been placed in... Violet," she turned to me abruptly, and met me halfway between my doorway and the front door. She took her hands in mine. "I don't envy the position you're in, either. Your heart hasn't yet made up its mind." She reached out to silence me. "Your mind is in denial—it's okay—I know you don't really know Grayson that well. But should you choose Grayson," she looked back outside. "Know that his darkness will never entirely leave him. It will always be a constant struggle for him. His potential for good is great, but, perhaps I made a mistake after all." Her shoulders sagged.

I put my hand on her to comfort her. "Sometimes destiny is more powerful than our free will. I'm sure you didn't make a mistake."

She sighed heavily. "Go change. Grayson waits for you."

36

Running with Grayson was very different than running with Nathan. Nathan and I were always about pushing one another as far as we could go. Grayson seemed to want to cruise more, and take it in. That was fine with me—I wasn't going to push myself, I was really going out of curiosity. I hadn't had much alone time with Grayson, and I just didn't understand how easy it was to get swept into the Darkness.

But maybe I was wrong. Maybe it wasn't easy.

Since he didn't know where he was anymore than I did, every time we came to a new junction, one of us would choose a way to go. We found ourselves at the top of a hill, in what appeared to be town center. There were several people milling around, walking their dogs, and you could see a road in the distance.

I found a water fountain and stopped for a drink, Grayson following me. "Look at that view," I said, catching my breath. "It's beautiful." I glanced at him as he bent down to drink water, and the sun glinted off his hair, creating a redness to it.

He gave me a half-grin as he stood back up. "Me or the water?"

I laughed, feeling awkward. "I meant the water."

"I'm just messing with you, Violet."

We stood there for a beat, looking off into the distance. "Although," he said, with a raised eyebrow and devil-may-care glint in his eye as he looked at me, "*My* current view is more beautiful than your view."

"Ha. Ha. Alright, let's move, just so I can get you to stop talking," I said, giving him a playful shove.

"What?" He asked innocently.

We continued our jog down the other side of the hill, and ended up at an overlook, perched on top of rocks tumbling down into the ocean. I shivered. "Cold?" asked Grayson, the breeze noticeably cooler where we were then than before.

"No," I said. "Just scary."

He brushed up against me, looking down. "That is definitely a hell of a drop." He turned his back to the railing, pressing up against it as he looked towards the town center. "How far do you think we ran?" he asked, nodding his head towards it.

"Maybe two miles. Not too far." I paused. This was my opportunity to talk to him, so I took it. "When is your mom leaving?"

"Tonight."

"Are you going with her?"

"No, she wants to go alone."

"Are you sure you want to do this?"

He slowly exhaled before turning to me. "I have to, Violet. My whole life... I need to know why, I need to know why I'm so different than Nathan," he muttered, spitting out of the corner of his mouth.

I was surprised at his response. "Seriously? You're a grown man. Surely you don't compare yourself to him?"

"It's complicated."

"You sound more like him than you know," I said. These two. "What's so wrong with being Grayson?" I kicked at the earth.

He turned his hazel eyes on mine. "Grayson? Grayson is a tortured soul who was bounced around as a kid." He spit again, his eyes starting to flash a bit.

"So was Nathan."

"Yes, but Nathan had his mother as a constant. I did not. As an adult, I've continued to bounce around. Until I found Jason."

"Why were you in Atlanta?"

"I followed a girl," he sourly laughed. "Needless to say, it didn't work out. I eventually became a firefighter, and that's when I found out Nathan's dad was down there. I went on a medical call, it was Nathan's dad, and Nathan had been staying with him for a few weeks. Nathan and I started to hang out, and that's when I realized what he did for a living, and I began to see what was within me, too."

I was floored to think we'd all, at one point, been coexisting in the same space without knowing it.

He continued, and started to walk back in the direction of the cottage. "Nathan and I started to have major differences. Like when we were kids. And, anyway. It ended on a sour note. His mom... our mom... visited and tried to get us to mend fences, but it didn't help. She left, he left, and I was alone again."

He awkwardly laughed, running his hands through his hair and shaking his head. "Sorry—I don't mean to unload on you—"

"It's fine, Grayson. I asked. I'm nosy, I kind of want to know the people whom I've been destined to know since before I was born. It's bizarre, you know, existing in this world for thirty-five years, not knowing your purpose, stumbling along, and then... Well, I'm still doing that, but at least now I feel at home somewhere while I stumble."

He indicated he wanted to jog again, so I joined him, effortlessly and easily. "At home, huh?" he asked.

"I didn't mean with you two. I meant with the work. Finding out about my parents, my grandparents. You two are just…"

Grayson cleared his throat, changing the subject. "Am I going too slow? Do you want to run faster?"

"No," I laughed. "I like this easier pace."

"Me too."

We ran for a few minutes in silence, side by side when space allowed for it. "Is Jason a firefighter?"

"Yeah."

Ah, I thought. Jason must have taken him under his wing. Jason had to be in his fifties then. "Let me guess. You feel like you owe him because he took you in?"

He shrugged. "What's so wrong with that?"

"Well maybe he's not good for you, that's what is wrong with that."

He groaned. "You can't turn your back on people who have been there for you."

"Is he the one who told you about the prophecy?"

"Sort of. He's been in the know for awhile about all this untapped power, but it wasn't until he met me that he felt propelled to action. He had already done a lot of research and he knew about my family."

"Some random dude in Georgia?"

"Not so random. His family has always supported the Truth."

"Vendetta Veritas," I mused. "So this 'Truth'—that's what we call the Darkness?"

"Yes."

"Grayson, can't you see that—"

He had slowed down abruptly, not knowing whether to go to the right or the left on the path to head back to the cottage. Naturally, I ran into him. My necklace flew out from underneath my shirt and whacked me in the teeth.

"Sorry—I didn't know which way to go—"

He looked down at the necklace and stopped me from putting it back underneath my shirt. We were both panting for breath, now that we had stopped running. He turned the ring over and over again.

"You know what this says?"

"Yeah. I'm not a master by any means but I can read it."

"My mother handcrafted this?"

"Yeah... You don't know about the gift?" He shook his head, wiping sweat onto his sleeve. "Your family is adept at having mastered the runes, and all that it entails. Using the proper ink, magic beyond just written language and messages... Magic in the craft itself."

"I've created things, too. Apparently it came from my mother," he mused.

"Have you made something similar?"

"Yeah, I have a few pieces I've crafted." He softly slid it back under my shirt, and I felt his skin brush mine. I involuntarily shuddered, but he didn't notice. "I think we go left here."

***

Back at the house, Nathan had grown antsy waiting for us. I wasn't sure how long we had been gone, but obviously longer than he had anticipated. We showed up, both spent physically from the exercise, and energetically spent from the conversation we had been having. The sun was still relatively warm and well above the horizon, so I plopped down on the grass.

"You guys were gone so long, I was starting to get worried."

"Don't worry, brother, I'm not going to hurt her. She is not my enemy."

"What does that mean?" I barked from the grass.

"I take it to mean, he's starting to fancy you, Violet. And

perhaps his mentor is losing his hold on him."

"Quiet, Nathan. You, on the other hand, *are* the enemy." He said icily.

"Stop it you guys. You're freaking brothers. You should be thrilled to have one another. I've no siblings at all."

I sat up and saw that they were circling one another like two lions fighting for the same territory. "Up to spar, tomorrow, little brother?"

"I wouldn't think of passing that up if my life depended on it."

Grayson turned back to me, and helped me up. "Thanks, Violet," he said. A strange look crossed his face, but was replaced with sincerity. "I appreciate the talk. More than you will ever know."

"Sure," I said, brushing myself off after he lifted me up. "No problem."

I curiously watched him as he walked inside. I could hear the shower turn on in the house. Nathan slid in to stand next to me.

"Nathan."

"Yeah?"

I paused, and decided to keep it light. "Is there any coconut water here? I'm parched."

37

Alexandra wasn't slated to return until two mornings had passed. It was the first night we three were alone together. We were in the backyard, enjoying a fire from the fire pit, drinking booze and not saying much. I watched the ashes flick up towards the sky, and looked at the trees surrounding the property. "Wouldn't it be wonderful just to stay here and grow old?" I sighed, leaning back in my chair, thinking of the *Forest of Dean*.

"All of us?" inquired Nathan, nodding towards his brother who was poking the fire.

"Yes. All of us." I said defiantly.

He took a swig of the beer, and said, "You have lost your mind."

"Nathan has never much enjoyed my company," Grayson said as he returned to his chair next to the fire, strumming notes on an old guitar that Alexandra had had sitting in her living room.

"On the contrary. I've always enjoyed your company, from even when we were small children and I kicked your ass at Monopoly."

Grayson grinned. "If I recall, I used to kick *your* ass at that silly game."

"Oh, yeah." He guzzled the rest of his beer and let out a small burp. "I've got to stop drinking," he said, looking into his empty beer bottle. "I'll be back," he said, as he headed to the cottage, leaving Grayson and me alone with the crackling fire.

The magic of the fire, and the magic of the island was getting to me. Or maybe I was slightly intoxicated like Nathan. I was all of a sudden very nervous about being alone with Grayson. I had to remind myself that there was no competition, that I was happily single and intended to stay that way.

And then the feminine energy appeared again. She started dancing between Grayson and me, she was so tangible, and so happy.

I started to laugh, standing up, and looked at Grayson. "Do you see her?"

The longing in his face gave him away and the guitar made a ding as it landed on the ground next to his chair. The next thing I knew, he and I were facing one another, and his hands had somehow found themselves in my hair. "Violet," he said, face dipping into my neck, voice muffled by his lips pressing into it. The vibration from the energy was pulling us magnetically together, but Grayson's emotions, his desperation, were pulling us apart. All sorts of conflicting feelings were making their way through my body, and I felt like I was losing control of my faculties as Grayson's face was finally even with mine, having moved up slowly from my collarbone.

I heard the door slam from the cottage. Nathan was back.

"What the—" he asked, and as Grayson and I turned towards him, the dancer sped up towards Nathan, twirling around from his feet to his head. "Whoa!" he exclaimed. "Am I drunk?"

Drunk Nathan was kind of funny—he almost seemed like

a normal guy when he drank too much. Or maybe it was me who was drunk. I had a feeling Grayson was the only sober one. I realized he was still holding me, and as I turned further from him towards Nathan, he narrowed his eyes and asked, "How intoxicated *are* you two?" pulling me back to his body, lifting my face upwards.

The light was still twirling around Nathan and he was laughing in the background. "What is this?"

I poked Grayson. "You're the drunk one."

"That's what I thought." He sighed.

"Nate," he chided as he called to his brother. The light zipped back towards us, and Nathan followed it. Grayson gently pushed me towards him as he got closer. "You both have had too much to drink. You need to get her to bed, as well as yourself. I'll tend the fire. *Alone.*"

I took his tone as a challenge, and was about to accept said challenge, but the light distracted me. It started to slow its dance down, and became more of a throb around the three of us. It was going back and forth between the two of them, circling me in the process. "What *is* this?" Nathan asked again, pretending to be more sober than he was because he was now irritated at his brother's assessment.

"My best guess? Your daughter."

I was lodged between the both of them, watching this magic. Ultimately, the light started to go from throbbing to fading, and it made one last circle around the three of us and was out.

We were left with the embers of the fire, and the silence of the night. "Take her," Grayson said again gruffly, a look of loss on his face. He had been supporting my back, and when he stepped aside, I wavered a bit.

"No. I'm fine. I want to stay out here."

"The lady has spoken." Nathan grinned.

"You're drunk." I poked Nathan that time.

Grayson rolled his eyes and said, "If this place burns down during the time I have to take you two to your room, I hope you feel intense guilt for the duration of your lives." He turned both of us towards the cottage, and I giggled.

I conspiratorially whispered to Nathan, "He's mad at us. He can't be mad at us! We're adultsh."

Nathan smiled and said, "You've developed a lisp."

"Have not."

"Because you two have misbehaved, *I'll* be staying in Mother's room and you two can stay in the other room."

"Awwww. I thought I was getting the big bed." I whined.

Grayson pressed me against the wall in the spare room, and told me to stay put. Nathan sat down on his bed in a heap, the bottom part of a bunk bed, and Grayson took his shoes off and pushed him onto the bed. "Sleep it off, brother. We have sparring to do tomorrow." He tossed a cover over him.

"I'm fine," he yawned, closing his eyes, one foot sticking out of the bed. "'Night, Violet. Feel free to join me aaaaany tiiiiime." He instantly began to snore, as if he hadn't even been aware of speaking moments before.

I was still standing in the spot where I had been told to stay put. I had a huge grin on my face when Grayson approached me. "Stop smiling." He pulled my jacket off, and I kicked my shoes off. My smile broadened.

"Am I making you nervoush?" Nathan choked a bit on his snore, coughed, and resumed slumber.

Grayson pressed his lips together, glanced at his brother and then cornered me on the wall, one hand on either side of my head. "Stop pressing me, Violet. Stop trying to get in... You know how this ends..."

"I don't?" I asked, realizing I was *definitely* more intoxicated than I had thought I was. What the hell was in that beer we'd had? "That could be *our* daughter, you know. You said so yourshelf." I pushed his arms down at his sides, holding his hands down against his legs.

"I heard what your mom said. She's right. I'm shoft... Shoft... Shoftening? Towards you." I put my hands over his heart. "Why, though? You're shuch a jerk."

He had the decency to look away. "Go to sleep, Violet. I've got to get back to the fire." He put me on the daybed and pulled a cover over me, softly kissing my forehead.

My eyes were closed, but I was awake. "I haven't forgotten the other kissh." I felt him pull away and our door closed. I heard another snore emit from Nathan before falling asleep.

***

The next day I woke up to the sound of the door scraping as it closed and sunlight peeking through the window. I had slept like a log. I opened one eye and sure enough, Nathan had just left the room. The room smelled a little bit like beer, dampness and musky body odor—yuck.

I heard the shower going, some male voices talking, and bowls of cereal scraping against the counter. I heard the dishes clang into the sink, one of the toilets flush, and the back door opening and closing. After a few minutes of silence, I began to hear grunting coming from the backyard.

Ugh. Sparring. I had forgotten they were going to spar.

I went to the bathroom and brushed my teeth, pulled my hair back into a ponytail. I went back into the bedroom and pulled on a pair of sweatpants, made sure the musky scent wasn't coming from me, and slid my feet into flip flops. I looked all around the room, and cracked open the window to let some of last night's memories seep out of it.

After that, I went into the kitchen to grab myself some food, and I looked at the clock. It was already eleven! Yikes. We had slept in late, indeed. Every now and then I would hear an oof come from the backyard as I munched on cereal sloshing around in oat milk. My stomach grumbled, suggesting my breakfast choice was perhaps not the best decision in my life. I probably should have had—*KNOCK KNOCK.*

Um... someone was at the door? I was thinking I should probably go get Nathan before answering it—as I always got into trouble opening doors—but he was a little preoccupied at the minute. I glanced out the back window and saw him duck to miss a blow that Grayson had thrown his way. I got a little distracted by their bodies—as I had thought, Grayson was taller and leaner, but Nathan perhaps had more muscle mass.

But frankly, they were both lit. *Ugh.* I had it *bad.*

Knock knock. Oh yeah, the door. I *had* to get out of my damn head.

I opened the door and smiled at the elderly woman on the other side of the glass. Her hair was pulled back into a tight, white bun. She started talking to me in German, and the only word I understood was Alexandra, but I shook my head apologetically and said, "English."

"Ah, English!" the lady said, smiling. "I know English, too. Is Alexandra back from the mountains?" Her accent was thick, but I could understand her English. Certainly better than the German.

"No, not yet."

"And the boys?"

"They're in the back right now... Would you like me to fetch them?"

"They're the ones making the noises, yes?"

"Guilty as charged. Please, come in. Who may I say is calling?" I opened the door for her, and walked her into the sitting room, hoping she was not able to see them through any windows. "I'm Liesel, one of Alexandra's neighbors. She told me her boys were coming for a visit, with their lady-friend. You must be the Violet."

"Yes, hello," I shook the lady's hand. "Let me go get them."

I put the tea kettle on as I hurried out of the kitchen. "Guys!" I yelled to them. At the same time, they both looked at me. Bright green with gold flecks, hazel laced with green flecks. I had grabbed their shirts and ran out to them, instantly noticing cuts and bruises starting to form. I threw their shirts at them, glaring at them.

"What's wrong?" asked Nathan, his lip beginning to scab. He pulled his shirt over his head, and I wiped some of the blood off with a kitchen rag that was placed on my shoulder.

"Your mother's neighbor, Liesel, is here. She said she had known we were going to be in town, and asked if Alexandra was back from the mountains yet."

Grayson was avoiding my eyes, but I caught him by the arm as Nathan began to stride back into the cottage. I folded the rag over itself and wiped it gently across his eyebrow. "Why did you guys feel the need to beat the crap out of one another?" I muttered as he flinched at the touch. "You need some glue on this split. Or stitches. And that cheekbone?" I asked, brushing lightly at it. "It's going to bruise if you don't get arnica on it." I pressed my lips together and tsked.

He chose to ignore me and instead asked, "Who do you think this lady *really* is?"

"I don't know," I said, following him inside. While he went into the room, I took the tea kettle off of the stove and poured it over a tea bag. I brought it into the room for Liesel, and then excused myself to get some arnica for the bruising, and healing ointment for the scrapes.

While the two of them continued to talk to her, gathering whatever information they could, I felt no qualms about rubbing the ointment across their battered faces. I hoped it irritated the hell out of them. Nathan, funnily enough, seemed more annoyed about me doing it than Grayson. He actually looked grateful.

By the time I was done with the primping of the boys, Liesel had left. "Well, what did I miss?" I asked, brushing my hands off of my legs while I sat on the edge of the couch that was housing Grayson. Nathan came back into the room from the front door.

"Interesting," he said.

I slid off the couch arm onto the right side of Grayson. Our knees were touching; he did not move. I leaned forward. "Who was she?"

"Liesel, the nearest neighbor. I've heard my mother mention her, but I've never met her. She seemed extremely interested in you, Violet."

"Me? Why's that?"

He shrugged, and he caught me catching him look at the proximity of me sitting comfortably next to Grayson. He half-smiled in response, before clearing his throat. "So what did you two do after I went to bed?"

Grayson had been leaning back on the couch, legs stretched before him, his one arm casually over my shoulder, resting on the back of the couch. He didn't seem to be aware that he was doing it; but now that Nathan had brought notice to it, I felt Grayson stiffen a bit. I spoke first. "You and I were both pretty drunk, Nathan. What the hell is the alcohol content in that beer? It's not like I drank a ton of them."

Grayson snorted. "It's Danish beer, what do you think?"

"I think I don't know a lot about the Danish other than their pastries." I jabbed him in the ribs. "See what I did there?"

He rolled his eyes, sitting up properly next to me, and crossing his arms against his chest. He had a faint smile on his face, though.

Nathan took a step back, for the first time, and in all of the time I had known him, looking majorly unsure of himself. He cleared his throat before speaking again. "I, uh, I'm gonna go hunt in Mom's medicine cabinet for some anti-inflammatories." He forced a smile as he walked out of the room. I stopped to say something to him, but Grayson held me back.

"Let him go," he said. "He's just upset I gave him a black eye." He leaned back again, arms bent above his head, resting the back of his head in the palms of his hands.

I bit my lip, and then sat back, turning to Grayson. I blew out some air. "From what I can tell, you're the one with the black eye." I moved some of his hair out of his eye, gently touching the swollen part of his face.

"Why would you do this to yourself?" I murmured to myself.

As I leaned in to inspect it more closely, he let out a slight growl. "Stop it, Violet. You're doing it again," he mumbled, and pressed his forehead against mine, trying to push me away. His breath was warm. One of his hands dropped on my lap, and the other one began to wrap around my head.

"Why didn't you let me stay outside with you last night?"

I moved his face upwards with my nose, so we were now more nose to nose rather than forehead to forehead. I found that I was holding my breath, waiting for an answer. He still wouldn't meet my eyes.

I exhaled and wouldn't let him turn away before I took the opportunity to kiss him. He was hesitant at first, but once he fully responded, it turned sickeningly tender. Everything around us slowed down, and the only sound I was aware of was our racing hearts. The only thing I felt was the warmth of his touch. I pulled back and opened my eyes. "Grayson," I whispered. I was completely in his embrace. It was so easy to be with him.

His eyes met mine, full of ache, hurt, and desire. Love was not allowed in this crowded room. My hands found themselves on his chest, pressing into him. "Grayson," I pleaded, desperate to break through the wall.

He shook his head, removing my hands from his chest and then weaving his fingers through mine. He held onto them tightly, lifted them up to his face, kissing them gently before speaking. "I cannot do this."

I responded to him in equal hurt. He was never going to allow me to choose him. It wasn't that his attachment to the Darkness was too great to keep me away from him; it was that his attachment to keep me away was stronger than how easy it was for me to be with him. I searched his eyes, and then removed my hands. "It's not fair for you to make *my* decision. If this has to do with me and which path I choose, then it should be up to me, and me alone. You two should have to deal with whatever repercussions my decision brings."

I started to get angry. I stood up to leave, and he gripped one of my hands and wouldn't let go until I looked at him again. "I would only fail you, Violet. It's not fair to you, or Nathan. Or... The little girl," he said, the ache in his voice thick.

I shook my head. "Dammit, Grayson. Don't you understand?"

He looked hopeless. I walked out.

38

Alexandra had called; she would be back at the cottage the following afternoon. After Liesel's visit earlier on in the day, we had all pretty much kept to ourselves. I was in Hell. I wrote to Layla and looked at the pictures of my furbabies to try and cheer myself up, but nothing was working.

I couldn't, for the life of me, remember what it was like before I had met Nathan. It all seemed like a dream, from the moment I had met him to the moment I was sitting at a table in a cottage on a random island off of Denmark. Surreal didn't even begin to describe the situation.

Was I attracted to the brothers because I was being told that I was supposed to be? Was I being held hostage in this fantasy they had created, and simply unaware of my handcuffs? Was anything even real? Why wasn't I walking away from this house and getting on an airplane back home? It seemed like the stronger my resolve was to stay away from them, the pull back to them was even stronger. I wasn't sure which one of them had more mass, but the gravitational pull was very real.

I really wanted to go home. I really wanted out of this.

For forever. This was insanity.

Grayson was also ready leave. He wanted to leave as soon

as Alexandra brought the box back to the cottage. He planned on catching an early flight to the states, leaving Nathan and me behind. He wanted to get back to Jason with the prophecy, and make their plans from there.

I knew Alexandra would be devastated.

I was afraid Nathan was mad at me—hurt because of whatever it was that was passing between Grayson and me, but also upset because I hadn't been able to turn Grayson around. I felt like they had thought I was the last possibility at saving him.

I had failed.

Nathan was making some sort of cabbage dish for dinner. He seemed fairly happy in the kitchen as he cooked. Grayson had disappeared outside, and I just sat at the table, quietly.

I finally spoke, losing the battle of pretense that I was alone.

"I'm sorry for hurting you."

He didn't answer me for a long while, but finally responded after turning the heat up on the stove. "Violet," he started, "None of this is your fault, and after what I did to you… I just want you to do what's right by you."

"He's not even giving me a chance," I said sadly.

"Oh?" He tried to sound light in response as he walked over to the table.

Had he really thought I was going to be with Grayson? They both knew, or rather, they'd both heard me pitifully state, over and over again, that I wasn't going to be with either of them.

"Let's just wait to see what this prophecy says, what this box holds. I wasn't so drunk last night I didn't notice the dancing energy. The visions... The visions have you as a mother… this is true… but the father hasn't been revealed, or the future of the daughter. And of course... since you don't want to be with me…And Grayson won't let you be with him... I mean… just because we saw you with a child, doesn't necessarily mean she's either of ours, right?"

I could tell he didn't believe a word he said.

I ignored the Grayson comment. "Nathan," I started, unemotional and clear, "Do you even want to be with *me*? I mean... Beyond all this psychic prophecy crap, what are we? Anything? Aren't we just fulfilling this nonsense?" He sat down at the table.

"Violet."

I looked at him pointedly. "What am I supposed to believe? I'm waiting to wake up any moment, before Alyssa was even murdered." I looked away.

"Violet," he said again, intoning in such a commanding, simple utterance of my name that I had no choice but to look back at him. He cocked his head to one side, and looked at me thoughtfully. "Whatever has brought us together... whatever was meant to be or whatever we created... I... I love you, you know. That's real."

His face flushed, and he stood up, pushing the chair back towards the table, busying himself with the cabbage again.

I looked at the back of my hands, deep in thought. "What happens if... if our families 'combine' like this?" I asked.

I hadn't really considered that prospect, about this 'daughter' of mine coming from this powerful energetic line of, hell, I don't know, wizards, right? Real bonafide wizards.

"Let's just see what the prophecy says first." He paused, spoon clanking in the pot as he mixed his foodstuffs. "Can you grab me some kelp powder?" He asked, pointing up above at a cabinet where I presumed the spices were held.

I handed it to him, and he half-smiled as our fingers brushed. "I like playing house with you," he quietly said into the pot.

"Me, too," I said sadly. "I don't not want to be with you, Nathan." I walked away. I just couldn't brush this overall bad feeling in my stomach. I didn't see a white picket fence in my future. All the colors I saw were dark and murky.

***

It was quiet, and around 7 PM. The brothers were cleaning up dinner, listening to music when a brilliant idea struck me. I grabbed the computer and started doing a search. "Have either of you seen a bar or music venue when roaming around town?"

I frantically typed into the computer. I was determined to have a night of fun—one that didn't end up like the previous night, either. After Nathan had told me he loved me I had decided, *again*, that I wasn't going to be with either of them. No freaking way. Not only did I not want to choose one over the other, but the sinking feeling that any child we produced would be in danger—of God knows *how* many things—well, the visions and prophecy could just end there.

Grayson's gift of sight was more intrusive, and his behavior had been slightly strange during dinner. I wondered if he had sensed my decision. I wondered if it worked like that.

I had googled up a spell to bind my decision, found the necessary items, and performed it. Of course, I felt foolish and awkward, but any ritual to make something stick? I was game for it.

Grayson wiped his hands on a towel and lifted me up by the elbows. "Outside. Now." I looked at him like he was crazy.

"Absolutely not!"

"What's going on?" asked Nathan, turning the water off.

"I had a vision about tonight.. So no, I don't think it's a good idea to go out."

My heart started to pound. "Gray... What harm is it going to see some live music for the night, to just pretend we aren't who we are?"

He looked down at me as if I were a child who didn't understand speech at all and said, "Because we *are* who we are, Violet. Don't be so naive."

I wanted to scream. I wished the brothers would stop calling me that word!Nathan came up behind me, and talked over my head to Grayson. "Who is here? I'm putting out feelers and coming up empty."

"Let's just say I don't think Liesel is who she says she is. She's Aunt... Mom's neighbor, and I think she was placed here for a reason."

"Are we any safer at the house than we are out?"

Grayson shifted, "I don't know."

We all had that stubborn streak, and I knew the second mine was stronger than the others, because Grayson tilted my face to search my eyes and gritted through his teeth. "God dammit, Violet."

"Glad you agree."

I sat back down to look for somewhere to go.

They continued to communicate over my head, perhaps telepathically, because they had stopped talking. Nathan let out a huge sigh. "Can we avoid any of this?" he asked out loud.

"We can try."

"Perfect! This place is lovingly referred to as "Hole in the Wall" and they're playing American music tonight. It looks like a complete shit hole. Can't wait."

I glared at them both, looking up from the screen.

"Do we tell her anything?"

"No."

"Wow," I said. "It's nice to know I matter. What good is this sight if I can't help keep bad things at bay? How many? Who? What do they want?" I tapped my fingers on the table.

Nathan wasn't going to budge with what he knew, but I knew Grayson didn't like the unfairness of keeping me out of the loop. "Graaaaayyyyy."

I stood up, grabbed and pushed him over to the counter and stepped on his feet, halfway climbing up him. He looked amused. "You're like an annoying little sister. This must be what we missed out on by having no sister." He looked over my head and Nathan laughed.

"Glad you guys can find laughter in a situation so tense. PERFECT, actually. Which is why we are going out anyway." I paused, waiting for Grayson to look down at me.

His breath had caught a bit—it was alarming to be that close to one another. Nathan cleared his throat. "I can't stop you from telling her what you want her to know." He went back to the dishes.

"We are *all* in danger until I get the box from Alexandra. Once I have the box, the safety issues dissipate. But these other people, whomever they are, want the prophecy as much as I do."

"Why?" I asked climbing onto the counter top next to him. He turned to me.

"That's what makes me so nervous. I don't know. I'm afraid they'll try to use one of us against the others in order to get the box. Which of course, we don't have access to the box until tomorrow anyway. They can be outsmarted, so I think we'll be fine, but…"

"But?"

He turned to face me directly, sliding his arms along either side me, leaning into me. "There're a few scenarios with how this will play out, and the one gets pretty ugly." Shaking his head, he spoke soberly. "I *don't* want anything happening to you, Violet. I don't want a hair on your head out of place." *My* breath caught that time as his eyes locked meaningfully with mine. He dropped his head into my chest; I could feel the top of his head brush against my body. His hands were barely touching my thighs. I kept my arms loosely at my sides, remaining neutral.

Or trying to. Dammit. So much for my resolve. My loose arms began to inch toward Grayson's head and back, but Nathan's washing seemed to turn a little vicious. The disturbance was all Grayson needed to lift his head back up.

His eyes cleared as he looked over at the sink. "Or yours, brother." He slid away from me after that and walked out.

I walked over to Nathan and started to dry the dishes. "Why won't he just stay with us?" I asked into the Nothing, and so we were quiet for a long while.

Eventually Nathan spoke. "Isn't it obvious? He doesn't want to be rejected again. This time, by you. The fear of the anguish from being separated from you is stronger than his desire to actually *be* with you" he waxed poetically. "Unfortunately for me, I already know what that feels like." He paused in between dishes, giving an ironic smile.

Back to the dishes, he continued, "Since we've spent all this time with him, though, I'm seeing he's not actually anyone's puppet. Which, frankly," he grunted, "is a lot better than supporting that whole Darkness concept. There's still hope."

The second part of his statement resonated with me, but the first part did not. "My connection to you is so.. different, though. And I agree with what you said about the puppet-thing." Dry, dry, dry.

"Which may simply be because you met me first. Or because he was given away as a child. Or because a butterfly fluttered its wings in Africa. None of this means, though, that the pull towards *you* isn't the exact same for him, as it for me."

"And so, yet again, I'm rendered useless, merely a product of destiny, of the prophecy, of these visions. My free will doesn't seem to matter much," I said glumly.

The last dish was clean and dry.

"Don't fret about this stuff yet. He hasn't left. We haven't heard the prophecy. Let's go to this place you want to go to, and keep Liesel's people at bay until Mom comes home."

"But in the meantime," said Grayson, who had changed and reentered the room, I'm assuming having caught most of what Nathan and I had said, "We are your bodyguards for the night." He smiled crookedly.

"You know I can fend for myself, Grayson. I'm fully trained. I'm a fucking Jedi."

"You've barely graduated from your silly apprenticeship, Anakin. We're protecting you, and that's that."

I glared at him as I walked to the bedroom to change, Nathan, of course following me. "Dammit. Sorry, Vi—I'll wait."

39

As we stepped outside into the night, my two bodyguards on either side, I found myself laughing out loud about it. It was ridiculous. The boys looked at me, as if they were slightly afraid of me, like I had a contagion that would turn them insane, like me.

Nathan cleared his throat, and spoke, "We can walk, it's less than a mile away. I know the bar you mentioned—I've met the owner before. She's actually English."

Grayson slid his arm through mine as we walked, and spoke quickly. "You need to make sure you stay near us at all times tonight. As long as we are not separated, we will be alright."

I groaned. "I just want to burn off some damn steam. Why can't I burn off some steam?"

"And Violet—make sure you keep Nathan in your line of sight at all times. If you have to hold his hand all night, do it —please."

I raised an eyebrow, but it was mostly dark so I wasn't sure if he could see it or not. This made my stomach flip flop. He had spoken so only I could hear him. What had he seen?

Taking care of myself was no problem, but the thought of one of them being hurt really made my stomach turn.

Especially because of *my* insistency to go to some stupid club.

Nathan had gotten ahead, and waited for us to catch up with him. I slid my hand into his for the rest of the walk. He didn't ask about it, nor did he try to pull away. Grayson walked on Nathan's other side.

We got into the venue, and immediately walked up to the bar. The band was already playing Nirvana when we walked in. I instantly saw a giant mess of a man sitting at the opposite end of the bar. He looked like a bald, obese Arnold Swarzzenegger with chin acne and tanned skin. He glanced up as I sat down, nodded, and looked back at the stage. People immediately crowded him and I couldn't see him anymore.

The bartender spoke to us in German, and seeing as Nathan was the only one who knew German, he ordered a few beers for us. The stage was dead center in the venue, the exit was on the left of the stage, the bar was on the right. Barstools were lined against the bar counter, and a few small, round tables were on the floor in front of the bar, and from there, just floor. The venue was fairly crowded.

The brothers were scanning the people, standing to my right while I sat down on a stool, taking a swig of my beer. It felt good just to be *out*, even under these circumstances. A girl with short pigtails and a nose ring sidled up next to me at the bar and started speaking in lilting German to the bartender. The bartender smiled at her and said, "No worries. I speak English."

The girl ordered her beers and took off back into the crowd. The bartender said something to Nathan in German, and then looked at Grayson and I, and said. "Lots of Americans tonight!"

"Where'd she go?" asked Grayson to Nathan, looking into the crowd to where the girl with the pigtails had disappeared.

"I don't know, but we should keep an eye on her. Their

blocks are up, whomever they are. I don't sense anything out of the ordinary."

American Idiot began to play. Fantastic. I wanted to get closer to the stage, but Grayson grabbed my arm as I tried to go. I shook my head. He nodded towards Nathan, and I sighed. Dammit.

He wanted me to stick with Nathan all night.

"I want to get closer to the band," I yelled at Nathan. "Come with me!" I reached out to him, grabbing his hand and pulling.

"Go ahead," he yelled back. "We'll keep an eye on you from here." He dropped his hand from mine, stepping next to Grayson and giving me a little push towards the stage.

I felt unsure, but by Grayson's shrug, I took the opportunity to escape them for a few minutes. Almost immediately I lost view of them, short of catching glimpses here and there between people. I could head back, frustrated, or give myself at least one song and release some trapped teenage angst out of me. I decided I wasn't going to worry about it, and have some damn fun.

For that one song anyway.

The band began to play some Metallica, and the little pig-tailed girl appeared next to me, devil horns up. "Woooo!" she yelled.

I smiled, my radar instantly piquing, but for the rest of the song, I ignored it. By song two, the girl's energy was still zinging me, and I realized I needed to make a decision. I sent a searching glance for the boys, and I thought I could just make out Grayson's face. Dammit. I had played right into these stupid people's hands.

What should I do? Play along, or just let her know I was onto her game?

The song ended, and the girl shouted at me in the noise. "Hey! You an American?"

Decision made. Play along.

"Yeah!" I shouted back, "How could you tell?"

She smiled, and pointed to my American beer. I laughed. "Where are you from?" I asked, straining to hear her response over the noise.

"East Coast."

"Me, too!"

The band started to play the Violent Femmes. I looked back at the guys one last time, and it was official—they weren't sitting at the bar anymore. *Crap.* The girl indicated I should follow her towards the bar so we could talk while everyone sang about big hands.

"I saw the two guys you were with—also American, yeah?" She didn't even wait until I was sitting.

"Yeah," I said, taking a sip of my beer, half-sitting on a stool.

She tried to behave conspiratorially by giving me a knowing look. "Which one is yours? Or are they both?" She winked. *Oh, God—she winked.*

"Neither. They're my older brothers."

For a second, the girl looked confused, but then she realized that my casual demeanor was actually quite calculated. "Ah," she said, pulling her hair out of the pigtails and popping the nose ring out. "Good—this stupid ring was starting to hurt me." She placed the hair tie and ring on the counter top.

"What do you want?" I asked, taking another sip of my beer. It was pretty much empty, so I ended up finishing it and placing it on the bar, ready for action if need be.

Grayson appeared out of nowhere and looked at me with concern. I did not see Nathan, and I was starting to get nervous. *Dammit. Why had I wandered into the crowd like an idiot? Grayson had warned me.*

The girl glanced up at him as he walked over to join me.

"How nice—your *brother* has rejoined you." She smirked, blatantly ignoring my question.

I looked behind her and saw the same meat head I had seen when we first walked into the building. He cracked his knuckles as he stood next to her. Grayson bent down into my ear, "Do they know we know?" I slightly nodded, and felt my ring flare up with heat.

I met Grayson's eyes with fear as I barely touched the necklace; Nathan was in trouble. He understood me, took me by the arm and said, "Tell your new friend good night."

I stood up with him, eyeballing the distance to the exit. Meatball blocked us. The ring continued to flare, burning my skin. We had to get out of there!

The girl had grabbed my other arm and said, "You're not going anywhere, unless it's with us. This is my good friend, Ted. He's going to escort you outside right now, where you'll be reunited with your *other* brother." She popped her ear piece out.

Grayson had been ready to fight, but when he heard they had Nathan, he tucked his fire back in. I had seen the flames in his eyes again, and it scared me.

The bartender looked up at us as we started to walk away. "Oh, no," she said. "My American friends are already leaving?!"

I looked at her, trying to signal we were in deep shit but she was already helping another person.

We walked outside, me still gripping his arm. Meatball took us behind the venue where I could hear the unmistakable sound of a man getting his ass kicked.

"Nathan!" I screamed when I saw him bent over, spitting out blood.

It was apparent he wasn't going to fight back, and I couldn't, for the life of me, figure out why. There was another Meatball who had just sent him reeling into that position, and

I could feel my automatic PUSH start. I was so angry, and scared, it began to emit from me like a giant force field without my control.

Meatball #1 put up an arm as thick as a tree trunk to block me from moving, and it distracted me enough to control the push. The ring on Nathan's finger and the ring around my neck started to connect, a thin line of light reaching from my neck to his finger. It didn't seem that Grayson even noticed it in the chaos.

Nathan looked up.

Pigtails pointed to Nathan, and then said, "I'm assuming this one's Nathan, and he wasn't very forthcoming with information about the box. Which means YOU are Grayson, the one who seeks the box. And of course," she roughly grabbed me by my hair enough for me to start, "you're Violet, otherwise known as *The Weapon*." I let out a small shriek as she grabbed me.

I looked at Nathan and Grayson with wild eyes. *The Weapon?* I started to sweat. Grayson's fury started to build again, and I could feel heat as if flames were flicking my body coming from him. Meatball #2 seemed to sense something, so he quickly grabbed me from Pigtails and said, in a thick German accent, "We wouldn't want to hurt the girl." Metal flashed in his hands.

Grayson pulled his fury in.

I found myself next to the kneeling Nathan, who still had blood barely coagulating on his cheekbone. Lord knew there wouldn't be enough calendula for that cut.

"Or would we?" Meatball #2 viciously grinned as he shoved me down on the ground. My knee made a hollow cracking sound as it whacked against the concrete, causing me to scream out loudly in pain. Nathan immediately reached over and pulled me into his arms, allowing me to lean on him while I bit my cheek to control my pain response.

I realized I had scraped my palms as I brushed myself off, pretending I had only yelped in surprise and not pain. My jeans had been ripped wide open and you could see the blood on my knee—I was afraid I wouldn't be able to walk, that maybe it had dislocated.

Grayson had rushed forward the second #2 had shoved me down, and Meatball #1 had stopped him by blocking him in the neck. When I regained composure I saw Grayson also on the ground, having air knocked out of him.

We were in deep, deep shit, and it was all my fault. Guilt and terror overwhelmed me, and my natural response of a protective force field couldn't take shape because of it. My stomach began to turn from the pain as I gripped Nathan and held my leg out, trying to straighten my knee.

Pigtails started to parade around us with a sickening smile on her face. "It's very simple. Give us the box, and we'll let you live. If you don't, well, by the looks of it, I'm assuming watching *The Weapon* be tortured may upset you both."

#2 pulled me back up at that moment, keeping Nathan on the ground by pressing him on his back with his foot. The metal gleamed in his hands again as he aimed at my bicep and slashed into my flesh, causing my eyes to see white with pain.

I felt thunder start flowing underneath the street as Nathan yelled, "Grayson, NO!"

The rings had started to connect again; an explosion of light and dark erupted from some sort of meeting of the two in the middle of the alley. Pigtails started to scream as an unseen entity seemed to be burning into her flesh—it was hard to tell what was happening. I could hear the singeing of flesh, smell the cooking skin. It was awful.

The Meatballs both ran to Pigtails, me being thrown down onto the ground again in the process. However, this allowed Grayson, Nathan and I the ability to be reunited.

I was on my stomach, involuntarily vomiting from the intense pain, with Nathan crouching down at one side and Grayson leaning over on the other side to try and lift me up. In the fury of chaos, Nathan once again yelled, "Grayson!" and the burning sound immediately stopped. Pigtails was still screaming though, and Meatball #1 came to his senses and began to advance on us.

At this point, we were all standing next to one another, but without Grayson holding me up, I would have crumbled. "Hold hands!" Nathan shouted a simple order, grabbing my other hand. Our rings created another line of energy, and this time the Darkness was not being called. Nathan started to chant words I didn't recognize, but I found I was having a hard time concentrating. I was fighting the urge to vomit again.

"It's not working!" screamed Grayson, and realizing I was not able to stand on my own, released my hand to place his around my waist to keep me standing. He looked like a wild animal, his hair in thick patches, skewing every which way; his hazel eyes were terrified; his clothes were ripped.

I imagined I looked even worse, hair half-pulled out of its ponytail, vomit and tears staining my pallid face. Clothes… torn to shit. I was having a hard time focusing my thoughts.

I felt Nathan's push, along with the magic of the rings, gather and zoom past the Meatball. He was knocked onto the ground as Nathan's chants grew stronger and louder and took on a shape and consistency of their own.

I lost contact with Nathan, though, because I couldn't control the pain anymore. I doubled over and vomited even more in the confusion. Grayson was struggling, trying to keep me upright as I bent over. He shouted, "Can you walk?"

The sound, the energy, it was tornadic. I lost Nathan's form entirely, grasping at Grayson to not lose my mind. Colors and shapes were bleeding together, sounds and smells uniting. It was sensory overload, and without having Grayson's hazel eyes locked on mine, I would have lost myself entirely and mentally and emotionally disassociated.

"I don't know!" I screamed into the wind, tears rolling down my face, my pain consuming me even more.

And then—and then everything was quiet.

Alexandra had arrived, along with the bartender.

The only sounds were from Pigtails weeping, and weird animal sounds coming from, as it turns out, me. Grayson was holding me up in his arms like a child, and I clutched at his neck with my good arm, burrowing my face into his chest, struggling with pain. He had turned away from the mess behind us, but when I looked back up, I could see everything.

Meatball #1 was unconscious. Meatball #2 was lying on his back, one of his arms lying in a crooked manner. Nathan was on the ground again, looking broken and unconscious.

Grayson advanced towards Alexandra, desperation and horror flowing off of him in waves.

His voiced cracked, "Mom. Help." I leaned back a bit to see his face. His wet eyes met mine and he pressed his mouth at my forehead, shifting his weight a bit as he carried me over to Alexandra.

My vision was becoming blurry, I felt I was losing consciousness. Alexandra lifted her hand up, flicking her wrist and silencing Pigtails, and then a dream-like state overtook me. I did not feel my pain and nausea anymore.

Alexandra's eyes met mine, as she walked over to Nathan, leaning over him. Grayson and I both stiffened, holding our mutual breath. Alexandra's calm was keeping us contained, but if Nathan was dead… I didn't think Grayson would be able to hold me anymore.

She looked up at Grayson and me, "He's alive."

In spite of my pain, I hurled myself back into Grayson's arms, losing myself in relief. His arms tightened around me and he spoke with his mother in terse tones. I couldn't make anything out, because the dreamlike state had begun to take over me again. The last sounds I heard were weeping, but I wasn't sure where it was coming from.

40

There were ambulances, fire trucks and police cars all pulled up to the alley. The bar had been cleaned out, and people were still milling around, trying to figure out what had happened. Liesel was staring out a window of a police car, and the Meatballs were both cuffed on the ground.

Pigtails was in a medic being read her rights as some sort of ointment was being applied to the burn marks on her arms. Nathan was in another medic with his wounds being cleaned with his foot propped up in a pulley. He was now awake. Another medic was tending to me, putting my non-dislocated knee in a brace and telling me I was damn lucky the knife wound I had wasn't worse. I needed stitches, but it hadn't hit any major artery.

I was about to ride with Nathan in his ambulance. They had administered drugs in my system so I wasn't quite feeling such a high amount of pain anymore. If anything, I felt slightly loopy because the drugs were such a heavy dosage. Grayson was more or less fine, a few scrapes and cuts on his arms and face. Alexandra's magic had worn off, but from previous experience of being seriously wounded, I knew we would all probably heal up just fine.

I hoped.

When Alexandra had arrived, her mere presence had been so great that the calm had stopped the fight, even more so than Nathan's force field. Grayson had been focused on me, so at that point he nor I were in the fight.

Apparently Alexandra's intuition went into overdrive while she was retrieving the box. It had been enough to get her to move quicker so she could come home faster than originally planned. When she had gotten back home, Liesel was there and she recognized right away that something was wrong. The bartender, working as some sort of security detail for the Light, had reached out to Alexandra as soon as she realized we were in trouble. Alexandra had put two and two together, gotten the local police force involved by coming up with some nonsense to arrest Liesel, then quickly got to the alley and found us tossed around like windstorm debris.

I couldn't wait to see what cover was created for the whole thing. I knew a major debriefing would be following my amazing escapade to this magical little island off of the coast of Denmark.

As the doors to the medic closed, I saw Grayson's devastated face. As he turned to his mother, she held her hands out to him to cradle him. It looked like a nice moment, at least through my foggy disposition. Nathan caught me watching Grayson, and smiled crookedly at me. "Hey, beautiful."

The medic was busy taking his blood pressure and checking who knows what stats. I held Nathan's hand and felt tears pressing at my eyes. "I'm so sorry. I shouldn't have left you, Grayson told me not to leave you but—," I blubbered as he cut me off.

"Shhh," said Nathan.

"Ouch," I inadvertently replied, seeing how battered my hands were, realizing it was hurting to hold Nathan's hand. Nathan started to speak German to the medic, and I closed my eyes, feeling the bumps in the road.

Once inside the hospital, Nathan got taken into a room. I still needed to be seen, too, but I wasn't as dire as Nathan was with his broken foot and all. That's right—when Meatball had first knocked Nathan to the ground, he had snapped his ankle. The X-rays revealed it was a clean break. How he had managed to stand on that foot during the fight was beyond me.

Must have been magic.

The pills the medics had given me started to wear off before I was seen, and I started to feel like I'd been repeatedly run over by a train. The pain started to overwhelm me again, and luckily, Nathan's German was good enough to finally get me my own room.

The doctor took another look at me knee and reiterated how lucky I was. *"Deutsche Mädchen prügeln sich wie Matrosen. Lächerlich!"* I'd have to ask Nathan to later translate that if I could remember it. The doctor was shaking his head when he said it.

Grayson and Alexandra kept popping back and forth between our rooms, never leaving us alone for very long.

Nathan and I were both released in the very early morning hours of the following day. We were all terribly exhausted, and of course the boys and I were in pain. Alexandra insisted Nathan and I sleep in her bed since we were both the most put out, and her and Grayson shared the other room.

The following day, none of us got up until mid-afternoon. Alexandra had made soup and brought some in to Nathan. I had insisted on getting myself out of bed, even though my brain felt foggy. Alexandra stayed in the room with Nathan while he ate the soup, and I went out into the kitchen with Grayson.

Nathan and I had both been prescribed crutches, but for very different reasons.

Grayson helped me into the kitchen. I popped some pain meds before I started to devour the soup. I hadn't realized how hungry I was—it was about three in the afternoon and I hadn't had anything since dinner the night before. Grayson hadn't said much; he looked exhausted. A five o'clock shadow was showing on his face, his eyes dark with tiredness and something else I couldn't quite place. His hair was askew, it looked like he may have taken a shower at some point and fallen asleep on it wet.

As soon as we had gotten home I passed out; I didn't even remember Nathan making it into bed with me.

Grayson scooted his chair up next to mine and lied his head down between his arms as I ate my soup quietly next to him. He turned his head to mine and watched me. "Stop," I scratched out, sounding raspy like I'd been smoking.

He brushed some hair behind my ear before placing his hands back down on the table. "No." I sighed, pushed the rest of my soup aside and mimicked his position, turning my head to look at him on the table.

"You look awful."

He smiled faintly and quietly said, "You don't."

He hesitated, pushing my stubborn hair back behind my ear again. "I don't think you know, I mean..."

"What?"

"I was there the night of your accident."

"What accident?" I lifted my head back up and furrowed my brow. "What are you talking about?"

He lifted his head and took my hands in his own. "I hadn't met you yet, but I already knew who you were when you got in the accident with your friend. I was working. I've never tried to overpower anyone like they were doing that night—I was so pissed at Jason when I found out he'd known about it."

I took my hands away from him, trying to figure out what

he was talking about. "My accident with Elizabeth? You were there?"

"I can't be a part of this anymore. I can't keep watching this happen to you." I reached out back to him, grasping his elbow, keeping him from turning away from me. He looked like he was ready to run out of the room. "Violet, last night...seeing you like that again—Look, I'm leaving tomorrow."

I didn't even bother trying to hide my emotion. "No." My lower lip wobbled. "No," I said again.

He turned his chair to face mine, gently resting his hands on my knees. "Alexandra has already given me the box. I just need to bring it back home and..."

"And what?" I asked, tears spilling down my face and my voice growing thick. I can't believe I had any tears left in my body. "Did you open it?"

"Not yet," he said, reaching out to wipe my tears. "Don't cry," he mumbled. "Don't make this harder than it already is."

"Just open the damn thing now. I want to know what it says."

His hazel eyes searched mine, and he pulled the box out of his jacket pocket, placing it on the table. It was smaller than I thought it would be. It was beautiful, though; a faded, yellow wood with the blue inscriptions on it, looking almost like a mace, but instead of spikes on top, it was covered in a snowflake.

"That's a bind rune; that makes it more powerful. It looks like Tiwaz and Algiz." I traced my fingers across the indentation. He stuck his fingers inside two holes on either side of the box, uttered some sort of incantation under his breath, and then pulled.

The box opened.

I looked up behind Grayson and saw Alexandra silently

standing in the doorway with her arms crossed across her chest. Her green eyes were focused on the box.

I held my breath.

Grayson pulled out a piece of parchment, and Alexandra came up behind him, taking it from him. As she unrolled it, he picked out of the box a ring that appeared to be identical to mine and Nathan's rings. His eyes asked Alexandra if it was his; she shook her head no. He placed it back into the box and sighed as she began to read the runestaves; you could feel the magic of the words.

I had so many questions about this prophecy, namely, who had made it and why... But I let her read the words without interruption.

Grayson looked expectant for a translation. Alexandra spoke, in her slight accent, "The rough translation is this: The Brothers in youth must be separated to keep The Order or one will perish; The Weapon will bestow upon a brother The Bullet. All will be in peril during these times. Pairing brings forth Peace, or War. Sacrifice leads to Safety. The Bullet must dislodge correctly, or else—"

And that was it.

The prophecy had been cut off.

***

It was late evening and I was in the bedroom with Nathan, sitting next to him in the bed with his leg propped up. My leg was also propped up, as bending it was terrible feeling.

He and I were dissecting the prophecy, while Alexandra was in another room, pleading with Grayson to stay. I was assuming Grayson had realized that he shouldn't share the prophecy with anyone, because otherwise I'd become a target. As long as I was set to reproduce for one of these brothers—and as long as they continued to choose me as "The Weapon"—I was at risk for all sorts of attacks. Case in point—what had transpired the night before.

"I don't understand, though, Nathan. It's not like it literally comes out and says any of these people are us—aren't you guys just trying to fulfill some words that are simply written on this old piece parchment? Aren't we the ones giving it the power?"

"Of course we are, Vi. That doesn't mean it's not true." He stifled a yawn. He didn't seem overly concerned with the prophecy.

Grayson, however, had been proven speechless when he first heard it. It had confirmed his fears—it didn't *have* to be him who was given up when he was a baby—it seemed his mother had just randomly chosen him. I knew he'd never be able to forgive her for that, and because of that, he would always be susceptible to choosing evil over good, even while he thought he was just sticking to this "Vendetta Veritas" nonsense.

"And if Gray shares this with his mentor, or if anyone else finds out, then what?"

"Well. Those possibilities are all bad," he stifled another yawn. "I don't think the government needs to know about this, either." He looked at me, his green eyes watery with tiredness. "We'll talk later about this. I don't want you to be afraid," he said softly. "Plus... I don't want you to feel like you *have* to choose one of us. Like you said... The prophecy's true power lies in our actions."

I groaned and stood up, shuffling to the other side of the bed, head spinning. "I'm going to take a nap too. This is too much."

I sat back on my side of the bed and got situated before turning towards Nathan. His eyes were closed, and his breathing was even. Him being that peaceful was a stark contrast to seeing him sprawled out on the concrete less than twenty-four hours ago. I was exhausted, but I had to speak to him.

"Nathan..." My voice was small.

"Mmmm," he responded.

"I know I've already told you this but... I am so sorry about last night. If anything had happened to you... Seeing you like that... broken and unconscious... I..."

He turned his head and opened his eyes. "Violet," he said slowly. "Grayson and I feel like we failed *you*. Watching you get hurt like that, there are no words to describe... I mean... It ripped out my heart, it ripped out Grayson's *soul*. I know he can channel the Darkness, obviously, but..." he trailed off, and I shivered, thinking about Pigtails' burns and how scary the Dark had been.

But, truth be told, so had the Light. "I think I was as afraid of the Light, to be honest. It was so chaotic when you were chanting, I—"

"You were in a lot of pain then, too, Violet. Don't discredit yourself. If it hadn't have been for Mom arriving when she did, I can only imagine what they would have done to you. It makes me sick."

"Thanks be to Thor for your super-healing power. Without *that*... You've saved my hide more than once."

He studied my face. "How about this? Let's just call a truce. I know how awful you feel about everything, and I know I can't change that feeling for you. Only you can change that for you. And I'm assuming you know how torn out and helpless Gray and I felt, too... So... truce?"

I laughed, rolling onto my back again. "Nathan, you should have been a diplomat." I reached for his hand, and held onto it for dear life. He squeezed back, but soon after I felt his grip loosen.

Luckily for me, I fell asleep almost instantly as well. I hadn't even taken the time to get under the covers, and Nathan's snores? For the first time, I didn't hear them.

Evening gave way to night, and every turn I made felt

incredibly painful, in spite of Nathan's golden touch. He, himself, could barely move at all because of his foot being propped up on pillows. We were a miserable sight, both needing crutches to even use the rest room. Alexandra checked in on us one more time during the night when she heard that we were up talking again.

I hadn't seen Grayson since he'd opened the box.

41

The next day I felt like I had about six inches of sweat and slime on my body; I had to figure out a way to take a shower. It was early; the sun wasn't awake yet. I met Alexandra in the hallway, and she offered to help me in any way that she could. The hot water washed over my body and steam filled the air of the small bathroom. It was heavenly.

Of course, I had to be careful how I moved, because while it was heavenly, it also hurt like hell. I needed to take some more pills. I stepped out of the hallway bathroom feeling like a new person, my hair wrapped up in a towel, and body wrapped up in a borrowed robe. I softly padded down the hallway, quietly moving because I wasn't quite sure who was up or not—the sun had yet to rise all the way.

I needed to get a change of clothes, though, so I slowly creaked open the bedroom door where Grayson was still sleeping in. However, when I opened the door, I found that he was awake. Heat went to my face as well as his when we both realized at the same time that I was scantily clad. He looked away as I hobbled into the room.

"Sorry," I said. "I didn't know you were up."

He was standing at the window, shirtless and in red plaid pajama pants, watching his mother walk away in the rising morning light. While helping me into the shower, she had mentioned she was going to go for a walk to clear her head. I supposed a predawn walk must be amazing this time of year.

He grunted in response, nodding to the coffee on the nightstand. "I've been up for awhile." That's when I noticed his luggage was at the foot of his bed, being packed.

I closed the door behind me and heard it click. I wrapped myself tightly in the robe and stepped closer to him, trapping him between the window and the small desk that had my duffle bag on it. "When are you leaving?" I asked tonelessly.

The light from the rising sun turned his skin golden. He looked like some sort of auburn god of the dawn. Only a chair stood between us as he tugged at the towel off my head, letting my semi-dry hair fall onto my shoulders. "This evening." He murmured, placing the towel on the back of the desk chair. He stepped around the chair, coming up behind me, helping me into it. I stuck my bad leg out straight because it was much too uncomfortable staying bent.

I tapped the desk with my fingers as he squatted at my busted knee, making me feel extremely vulnerable and exposed. There wasn't much fabric protecting my womanly parts. I had my pills sitting next to my duffle bag, and swallowed two with water that were sitting on the desk. I was trying to ignore what he was doing.

Grayson brushed the robe up my leg, exposing the raw, mangled and bruised knee before he swore under his breath. He then moved his gaze up to my arm, and slid the robe off of my shoulder so he could look at the stab wound. He lightly traced his finger along the stitching, and quietly swore again.

He stood up. "How are you feeling?"

"A lot better. Nathan's healing to the rescue again," I sighed. "And how are you?"

It was so quiet, our voices barely above a whisper. The window was cracked, you could hear the birds awakening.

"I still have a slight headache, but most of the scrapes are already gone. You, however…" He trailed off, looking at my wounds again. He squatted, covering my leg back up, but froze when he got to my arm. His hands were resting on the side of the chair, and he was now kneeling.

"Violet… You've got to get out of here, *right now*," he said, eyes turning from concern to desire in a millisecond. "Or I'm not going to be able to…" he continued, tracing my arm wound again, this time along my collar bone, up my neck, stopping at my face.

I closed my eyes and muttered, "Fuck."

"God dammit," he whispered, caressing my jawline, mouth, and then back to my shoulders. I had ceased all intake of air, and held my breath as I felt my eyelids being kissed, my neck, and eventually my mouth.

I had my good arm wrapped around his neck and he cautiously scooped me up, taking painstaking care to not hurt me. In the darkness of dawn, he walked me over to the daybed and then locked the door. He came back to me, propping my leg up on a pillow before untying the robe. His hazel eyes searched my body before meeting my eyes, and with a half-smile, he loudly swallowed. His mouth opened to speak—so many things, and yet, nothing, was said.

I half-turned to him, my right leg slightly behind me on the pillow. He was back on his knees again, and after I made a slight nod, he got onto the bed, pressing his body against mine, his mouth burning my mouth with fire, his hazel eyes alight with green flames.

Afterwards, when the sun had finally risen and his arms were wrapped tightly around me, only then did I feel peace for the first time upon arriving on the island.

***

We faded in and out of sleep for the next couple of hours or so, but we didn't really stir until we heard Alexandra's voice speaking with animals outside of the cottage. I wondered how long she had been home.

While the sun was up, it was overcast outside, so the inside of the room wasn't so bright that it hurt our eyes. I turned my body towards his as best I could, some parts of our bodies touching. He lazily traced my upper lip with his finger before warming my abdomen with his touch. I shuddered.

Neither of us wanted to break the calm spell that we'd created together, but reality was rapidly approaching with every sound Alexandra made outside. Grayson tucked my head under his chin and let out a long breath.

"This doesn't—" he finally started to speak, but I cut him off.

"Gray."

I untucked my head, and forced him to look me in the eye. "I know this doesn't change anything for you, but it changes *everything* for me." I emphasized.

He sadly smiled, still holding me close to him. "It shouldn't, Violet. The prophecy indicates you'll be with my brother fighting the good fight—"

"It *indicates*, that if I'm to bear a child by either of you, my child will be in danger. *Not* to mention, the prophecy was never finished—"

"Or perhaps the rest of it is just missing."

"I—" Damn. Hadn't thought of that.

I sat up, pulling the covers around me. "Frankly I don't give a crap about the prophecy either way. I'm not going to let it run my life; it doesn't have to come true, it only comes true if we make it come true!"

The post-coitus calm was officially gone and I flinched in pain by having bent my knee. Grayson didn't say anything, only rolled out of the bed before finding his pants to put back on. He ran his fingers through his hair, blew out some air, then grabbed a shirt and sweat shorts out of my bag, tossing them to me.

"I'm not going to give Jason the prophecy. Just the box."

"I... What?" I was taken aback.

He kneeled down next to the bed on one knee, taking my hands into his. He looked at me earnestly, and spoke passionately.

"You may not believe in the prophecy, but my visions tell me otherwise. I do not want to be the one who puts you, or your daughter, at risk for harm—I only want to protect you both. You *know* these people will stop at nothing to gain control of you, *or* her. I'm handing the box over as payment of my debts, and then, I'm leaving Atlanta. For good." He stood up as I put my shirt on. "Returning to the northeast, or maybe somewhere else, I don't know. I hope I can find another firefighting job, but if I can't, I'll find something else." His gaze seemed faraway.

I had stood up at this point as he continued to talk, but found I was struggling with the shorts. I was holding onto his arm as he helped me into them.

"But don't you see… I mean… if this is the case... I mean... Why can't we just leave Atlanta together?" I asked dumbly, searching his eyes.

There was a light knock on the door. Grayson had already unlocked it, and so Nathan pushed it open, leaning on his crutches. His voice was gruff and slightly grim—nothing passed by him. He saw the rumpled covers below us, and took in the fact that Grayson was still shirtless, and how I was relying on him to stand at the moment, my hair a semi-curly mess amidst my head.

"Mom has made us breakfast," he said quietly, looking away before walking back down the hallway.

My heart sunk and I felt sick to my stomach. Grayson grabbed a shirt, helped me to the doorway and told me to stay put. He then returned from the hallway bathroom with my crutches, helping put them underneath my armpits.

"*This* is why we can't run away together." I raised my eyebrows in question, feeling raw. "You will always love him more than me," He said simply, kissing me gently on the cheek. "And that's okay, Violet." He turned away, hands in pockets and head down as I hobbled behind him to the kitchen.

42

Grayson had left without much incident, other than two women with broken hearts and one man with anger, hurt and confusion standing in his wake. He caught a taxi to the airport while Nathan had his arm around his mom and me leaning in closely to him on the other side.

Immediately after he left, Alexandra excused herself to her room to be alone, leaving Nathan and I in the sitting room by ourselves. I felt numb.

"I'm sorry he left you." Nathan said quietly, his crutches leaning against mine up against the piano. He was sitting next to me on the couch.

"Did he tell you why he was leaving?"

He shook his head, biting his lip. "Not really, no. He didn't talk to me too much after Mom read the prophecy. He told me he was happy for me, and that he was grateful I hadn't been more injured. He told me to take care of you and Mom." He leaned back on the couch, foot propped up, in its boot, on the coffee table.

It had only been a few days and we were both healing quickly. What a superpower to have!

I didn't instantly respond, looking into the distance for several minutes before speaking. "Grayson told me that he wasn't giving Jason the prophecy, only the box. That he was going to leave Atlanta. He also said that his visions don't lie... And that he was leaving me to be with you because I loved you more than I loved him."

"Oh?" He asked faintly.

Silence.

I squeezed my eyes shut. I painfully stretched my leg out, and turned on my good hip to face him. "Nathan... I... of course I have feelings of love for you. But..." I looked down.

"But you love him, too." He said matter-of-factly.

"How did this happen?" I muttered.

"Fate."

"That's crud."

I looked up at his half-smile. "I'm not mad, Violet. Grayson... Grayson has a good heart, he's just had a hard life."

"We've all had hard lives."

"Well... True... But Grayson's wired differently. He sees the world as a tragedy, he feels so deeply... I just..."

"What?"

He looked sad. "Well. I wanted the girl, right? But in order to get the girl, I lose my brother. If I keep my brother, I lose the girl. I'm not as confident as he is that you would have chosen me over him. Perhaps he is the only reason his vision will come to fruition. Maybe it's supposed to be him..." He laughed. "I mean... if it's either of us..."

I smiled.

Fate. Destiny. Nonsense.

If Grayson had stuck around longer he could see just how much he really *was* like his damn brother. Nathan was such a good guy, though, to put it in those terms without being about *him* and *his* needs and wants. It broke my heart even more with what I was about to say next.

"Before we went to the bar that night... I had already made

a pact with myself that I wouldn't choose either of you. I don't want to be that girl. I may not be able to control my emotions, but I can control my actions."

Nathan closed his eyes and leaned back on the couch. He didn't speak for a long while, and I was half afraid he'd fallen asleep. Finally he said, "I see."

I leaned back next to him, leaning my head on his shoulder. I got the feeling he was hoping he could still save his brother, especially if I wasn't willing to fulfill the prophecy. Of course, maybe he just knew something I didn't know. Stupid vision-having family!

***

A few days later, Nathan and I were back in Atlanta. He still had nowhere to stay, so he came home with me. We were exhausted, and unfortunately had to report to Cox and Perez in a couple of days. Layla was waiting for us when we got there, and promptly told us we looked like hell.

Neither of us were on crutches anymore, but we were both hobbling and of course, Nate still had the boot on his foot.

Phang was overjoyed at seeing us; Barnaby refusing to entertain us with his presence. I figured it would take a few hours before he warmed up to me, and probably a bunch of treats.

***

For awhile, time moved slowly. Hours became days, days became weeks, and of course, weeks became months. I helped Tollie out in the city with flexing our Light muscle to render the Darkness inept. We'd use our power to disperse theirs; those we could rehabilitate would get the debriefing and therapy before returning back to normal life... Just like Sam had.

Grayson's friend Jason had paid an unwanted visit one time when I was alone, another time when Nathan was with me. He was looking for Grayson, wondering why the prophecy had mysteriously disappeared, and of course, we gave him no answers. He repeatedly tried to tell us we were not the enemy, but I kept it all in check by remembering how I had seen Grayson himself channel Darkness to save our asses that night in Germany. Jason could channel that evil, too, and Jason wanted something that Grayson hadn't—power.

I knew I wasn't going to be the one to fulfill the prophecy, and I also knew that whoever the 'Weapon' and 'Bullet' were, were going to spend their lives with targets on their backs. Not just by the bad guys, but the good ol' American government, too. (Nathan had unfortunately told them the entire *Prophecy*.)

My Jason eventually got engaged to the blond; I was happy for him. He always seemed a little wistful around me, and equally confused that Nathan and I hadn't actually panned out, but always respectful of my choices. We remained decent friends.

Elizabeth and her wife eventually moved out of our county and opened up their own yoga studio closer to Atlanta-proper. Sam moved back home; her mother had become ill. She quit her job and opened up a bakery. I rarely saw my ex around town anymore—luckily we didn't run in the same circles. I saw his ex-wife Amanda at yoga classes though; she was always super friendly and happy as a lark, now that she was no longer under the clutches of our ex.

Layla stuck around town, so she and I still hung out. She kept a boyfriend, but he was in the city so she only saw him on weekends. I wasn't sure if it was serious or not—you never could tell with Layla. She was such a free spirit. She talked about moving to London for a few years in the near future, and I supposed she would.

Life became routine, and peacefully, awkwardly quiet. Nathan was still stationed overseas, but when he came back into town, he always stayed with me. We were best friends, nothing romantic, and never any mention of the *Prophecy*. We talked about work, wondered about Grayson, our parents, and normal every day life stuff. Nathan no longer flirted with me, nor I him.

We also didn't date other people, but, at least for me, I didn't feel the need to do so either. I may not have been fulfilled, exactly, but I was certainly in a good place. My life wasn't at risk, I had two good jobs, I was of service to others, I was fed, and at times, found I was happily bored.

The biggest upsets were when our fathers both passed—within weeks of one another. He stayed stateside for a full month, and my tiny one bedroom apartment started to get a little crowded with the four of us. My lease was up at the end of the summer, and he was talking about staying in the United States indefinitely. He didn't necessarily want to stay in Atlanta, but for the time being, he had nowhere to really go, so he thought maybe he'd get a one bedroom in the city.

"Or, we could just get a two bedroom here? I mean, I know this place isn't the portal to much fun, and you have to drive everywhere to get anywhere, but.."

"Your clients, I know."

He was sitting on my couch, petting Barnaby on his lap with Phang at his feet. A true vision of domesticity. I smiled.

"Your mom pissed you want to move back here?"

"Nah. She's used to me coming and going."

"What do you want for dinner?"

"Let's just walk over to that mediterranean place. I'll buy since it's my idea."

"Ha—sold. I won't say no to that." I grinned, and then my phone rang. "Let me take this—it's Nic."

"Tell her I said what's up." He leaned back on the couch, kicking his feet up. It was the weekend, and short of working out, neither of us had anything to do.

I stepped outside onto my balcony, enjoying the warmth of the sunshine. "Hey, Nic, what's going on?"

"We have a development. I don't suppose Nathan is there? I tried to call him but he didn't answer his phone."

"He is, gimme a sec and I'll go back inside."

"Of course he is," and you could hear the smile in her voice. "You two are the most stubborn people I've ever met, I don't understand why you don't just— "

"It's not like that anymore, I told you. We're just really great friends, he's my rock—"

"And he's good looking, and single, and you love him, I know. Why on earth *would* you be an item? My bad."

"It's not like that," I said again.

"Stubborn."

"You betcha." I opened the door, and reached my foot in, jiggling him with my toe to open his eyes. "Nate, it's for you."

He opened his eyes, "Ah, dammit. Just had a vision of Jared."

"Jared?"

He took the phone and I could hear Nicole through it. "Yup, Jared's in town, and he's pissed off about what happened in Germany because he hadn't been contacted about it and it happened months ago."

I stepped back outside, figuring Nathan would tell me all about the conversation at dinner. So much for life being boring and peaceful.

WHAT THE BLEEP?

You may be wondering what all this mumbo jumbo our dear Violet is constantly babbling about! No doubt Google would be most helpful in your research, but here's some information to get you started. And so you know, absolutely NO medical advice is being offered here! Use what ye will on your path. What is shared here is simply riding a wave of all things wonderful—things that Violet thinks are swell. :)

- **Yoga Poses**: www.yogajournal.com/poses *Yoga Journal's* website has all sorts of information regarding yoga. This link will take you directly to the asanas/poses Violet was doing at the beginning of the story. The poses she made mention of were goddess pose with eagle arms; child's pose; corpse pose; and also a vinyasa.

- **Reiki**: www.Reiki.org is a good website concerning the origins of Reiki, what it is, and a slew of other information. Give it a try if you haven't!

- And just for reference, other healing modalities mentioned are: **Emotional Freedom Technique** (EFT) or **tapping; Healing Touch Therapy, Aromatherapy,** and **Reflexology**. *A Course in Miracles*, which is a book that inspires classes and groups across the globe, is also mentioned.

- **Runes**: *Major* creative license has been taken with these books, but runes themselves have been used throughout history! I have some amethyst runes that I play with from time to time. A wonderful resource helping to create this story is <u>The Big Book of Runes and Rune Magic</u> by Edred Thorsson. Two websites I perused are: www.RuneSecrets.com and https://thehistoricallinguistchannel.com/runes/. The following books should delve deeper into these pre-elder futhark runes! (And as far as I know, these don't exist!)

○ **Fluorite** is a common crystal which purportedly helps you protect yourself from psychic attacks.

○ **Calendula** and **arnica** are mainstays in this house which is full of little boy mischief.

And lastly, any time you feel like you need help grounding yourself because you're angry - scared - stressed - whatever - here's a **short little exercise** you can do to regain control of your breath (spirit).

◆ Close your mouth, and breathe normally for a few breaths.

◆ Then slow down your breathing by taking an inhalation in both nostrils for 4, 3, 2, 1 seconds and hold at the top of your breath for 3, 2, 1 seconds.

◆ Slowly exhale out both nostrils for 5, 4, 3, 2, 1 seconds.

◆ You can play with the number of seconds, finding the grouping that works best for you.

◆ You can use alternate nostril breathing as well.

◆ Consciously breathe like this for several breath cycles and you should *immediately* feel more grounded. Ahhhh, breath!

RECIPES

Violet mentions a few witchy concoctions throughout her tale. Feel free to try these recipes, or mix them up as you like!

Citrus and Lavender Spritz

- small spray bottle, preferably dark glass

- equal parts Witch Hazel and distilled water

- citrus (orange, lemon, tangerine) essential oils to your liking

- lavender essential oil to your liking

Start with a few drops of lavender before adding the citrus. Don't let it overpower your senses! You want it subtle. Spray on your yoga mat for a cleanse, or you face to refresh!

Healing Ointment

- a viscous, non-petroleum base, like castor oil (mixed with jojoba, or whatever oil you'd like) or Alba Botanica's un-petroleum jelly

- calendula infused-oil (any base you'd like)

- essential oils like tea tree and/or lavender to your liking

You can make this as-needed. Squirt a handful of the castor oil base in your palm, and add several drops of calendula. Mix it in your palm, and then slowly add a drop or two of the other oils. Know that tea tree oil may cause a warming sensation and/or may dry skin out if it is not mixed well enough in a base.

Always be careful with your mixture amounts! You should test the ointment on a small patch of skin before using your concoction in earnest. **YOU CAN OVER DO IT!** We shall not relive the *Event of Early Aughts* when a certain author used soooo much peppermint oil in a lotion base, she had to immediately jump into the shower to rinse it off. This SHALL NOT BE MENTIONED!!!! ☺

ABOUT THE AUTHOR

allison keli is deliberately in lowercase. She is the author of *Phenix & Fox: Shooting Stars* which is a short, children's book about the Perseid Meteor Shower. She is the Vella author of *The Hauntings of DoG Street: Chownings Tavern*, which follows Melody as she discovers that ghosts have a story to tell.

allison keli is also a blogger, bodyworker, and future podcaster. She currently resides in the eastern U.S. with her wild child of a son, firefighter husband who is *not* torn between good and evil, and her own kitties, Dragon and Pilot. Luckily they aren't as judgmental as Barnaby.

For more information, visit www.allisonkeli.com or scan the QR codes for social media accounts and access to the Vella.

Facebook/Meta

Instagram

Vella

COMING SOON

Not ready to quit Violet and her saga? Her future is uncertain. And by the way, it's a girl. (Duh.) Fingers crossed for a 2023 release of the next novel, tentatively titled *When Violet Ran Away*. Enjoy this early excerpt!

"Grayson?" I asked, holding him as I pulled away.

His eyes started to roll back into his head and he began to make guttural sounds. "Oh my God, what is happening?!" I shrieked, attempting to drag him over to the couch before he hurt himself on the wood of the table. I didn't make it very far, and ended up straddling him on the floor, trying to keep him down. I pushed a coffee table out of the way, then moved back to him, wrapping him as best as I could in a blanket.

"Grayson! Can you hear me? Do I need to call 911? Is this another psychic attack?! Grayson!" I grabbed at his face, trying to get him to see with his eyes again.

I fumbled in my pocket for my phone, and frantically called Nathan. "Where are you? Grayson's seizing or something, I'm trying to pin his arms down and hold his head and —"

I heard a herd of elephants racing up the stairs to the apartment and a key fidgeting at the door knob. Nathan came running in and asked, "How long?"

"Just a few minutes — he's not flapping around anymore like he did at first, he's relatively calm now, but he's not coherent! What do we do? Call 911? I mean, is this psychic or is he having a stroke or are they one and the same or??"

Nathan held a hand up to me, listened to Grayson's breathing and his heart. "He's breathing and his heart rate are elevated but.. He seems okay?" He questioned, looking unsure.

Grayson began to speak after coughing. "Violet.."

"Yes!" I leaned over him, tears pressing at my eyes.

"Nate... Get me up," he mumbled, and we sat him up against the couch. Nathan crouched low in front of Grayson's stretched legs and I sat next to him, holding him, painfully aware of every curve of his body beneath my touch. His eyes were open, but they were heavy. He looked drunk.

"We've got to break your connection with whomever is attacking you, cut the cord. Is it Jared or someone else?"

"Not Jared," he managed to get out. Nathan looked at me with huge questions in his eyes.

"What do we need to help you? A chant? Forcefield? Crystals?"

He looked a little strung out when he replied, shakily drawing in a deep breath, "I don't know."

"But you told Jared about the prophecy and then — ?"

"I just confirmed there was a weapon. I did not mention the child."

"As long as I'm considered the weapon, though, I'm in danger. And if they find out about the child... She's in danger."

We all looked and felt helpless. "I'm so sorry." And

Grayson really did look sorry. "He was already threatening you." He looked into my eyes, asking for forgiveness, hazel on blue.

"It looks like I don't have a choice but to *be* the weapon. Everyone's decided it for me." I sat with my back against the couch, angry, and a little scared. I squeezed my eyes shut, trying to figure out a plan to get us all out of this mess.

Nathan had stood up and had grabbed Grayson some water, and Grayson sipped on the water for a few beats before speaking again. "Yes... and this is a huge problem, your safety. As well as trying to figure out who is invested in this information, and why they're all running scared."

"And the rest of the prophecy," I said, dully.

"But right now we have a more pressing issue. My brother cannot keep having attacks like this. We have to help him."

"But how? We don't even know if it's Jared or someone else — who else have you come in contact with? Did Jason ever find you?"

"Jason's looking for me?" Grayson groaned, almost completely having returned to normal, except for looking extremely tired in the eyes. In fact, he was so normal, so nonchalant now, I wondered if he had completely forgotten about the kissing assault on my face about twenty minutes prior.

"Did you really think you could just abandon everything, Gray?" Nathan sourly asked. "You, more than anyone, should know how things cannot be left alone, no matter how much we try. Suffering comes from denial of the truth.

Destiny always finds a way to grab you — "

"You speak of fulfilling destiny! Rubbish! Why the hell haven't you claimed our dear Violet for yourself then? Why is she still wandering about by herself, thinking there's a way to escape her role?" He hissed with as much fervor as he could muster after the attack. "She still thinks I could be the father. You and I both know this will never be the case. Just end it."

I was silently watching them have this encounter, with my arms crossed.

"She has to find her way on her own. It has to be her decision. *Neither* of us can make that for her."

"A ring was not made for me. One was made for you, her and the child."

"I saw you in the vision."

"Yeah, because I know her, not because I'm the damn father." He was exasperated.

"Guys?" I asked, sighing against the couch.

Four eyes turned to look at me; two a brilliant green with gold flecks, and two a shocking, deep hazel with green flecks.

"I don't feel very good." All of a sudden I felt very faint, and out of touch with reality. There was a great darkness overcoming a portion of my senses, a great disconnect. It was terrifying. I could see Nathan and Grayson staring at me, but I felt unplugged and incredibly empty, like my body didn't matter anymore.

And then there was a connection. A horrible, incredibly strong connection and as it began to reach out to me, I could feel fingers reaching their way at me, tendrils of darkness wrapping around my being. "Grayson?" I asked, trying to be present while it was gripping me. "What is this?" I whispered.

He reached for me, his eyes full of.. sorrow, I think. "It's .. It's trying to get in.." I trailed off, still having the sensation of being in two places at one time, while the Darkness teased at my senses to entirely overcome me.

"Don't let it. You're stronger than me, Vi. Your force field.. Push it out.. Don't let it in…" He seemed so sad, and so surrendering.

Nathan took my other hand, and it was just terribly quiet. He watched me as he held my hand, and I could sense he was trying to pump me full of his light to fight off whatever was happening. It was so still, and dark, and quiet. I looked at them both, one full of soft power, and the other, the other brother totally having just given up.